KISS OF PASSION

Red Hawk walked from the trees onto the path, leading his horse behind him. Kit's heart went to her throat. He was coming nearer now, and the mysterious longing began to build within her. Then he was standing in front of her, his black eyes raking her face and her body.

Kit turned so that he would be forced to walk alongside her. "I had to see you," she said.

"And I, you." His words were low, deliberate, full of meaning.

"I wanted to tell you something," she said.

"Yes," he said, his hand gripping her arm now, and he turned her to face him. "Then you must speak."

But Red Hawk knew that words must await the fulfillment of what was passing between them. He took her in his arms and kissed her. Kit's hands tangled in his long hair, her pulse quickened as his arms tightened around her.

"Come," he whispered into her ear.

Before she could protest, he had lifted her off the ground and cradled her in his arms. In a few swift strides they were in the trees, on a rise, and he knelt, placing her on the soft grass behind a large oak tree. "So," he said, his voice like honey in her ear. "Now you will taste pleasure. . . ."

She was lost to him, and she knew it.

WATCH FOR THESE ZEBRA REGENCIES

LADY STEPHANIE   (0-8217-5341-X, $4.50)
by Jeanne Savery
Lady Stephanie Morris has only one true love: the family estate she has
managed ever since her mother died. But then Lord Anthony Rider
arrives on her estate, claiming he has plans for both the land and the
woman. Stephanie soon realizes she's fallen in love with a man whose
sensual caresses will plunge her into a world of peril and intrigue . . .
a man as dangerous as he is irresistible.

BRIGHTON BEAUTY   (0-8217-5340-1, $4.50)
by Marilyn Clay
Chelsea Grant, pretty and poor, naively takes school friend Alayna
Marchmont's place and spends a month in the country. The devastating
man had sailed from Honduras to claim his promised bride, Miss
Marchmont. An affair of the heart may lead to disaster . . . unless a
resourceful Brighton beauty finds a way to stop a masquerade and keep
a lord's love.

LORD DIABLO'S DEMISE   (0-8217-5338-X, $4.50)
by Meg-Lynn Roberts
The sinfully handsome Lord Harry Glendower was a gambler and the
black sheep of his family. About to be forced into a marriage of con-
venience, the devilish fellow engineered his own demise, never having
dreamed that faking his death would lead him to the heavenly refuge
of spirited heiress Gwyn Morgan, the daughter of a physician.

A PERILOUS ATTRACTION   (0-8217-5339-8, $4.50)
by Dawn Aldridge Poore
Alissa Morgan is stunned when a frantic passenger thrusts her baby into
Alissa's arms and flees, having heard rumors that a notorious highwayman posed a threat to their coach. Handsome stranger Hugh Sebastian
secretly possesses the treasured necklace the highwayman seeks and
volunteers to pose as Alissa's husband to save her reputation. With a
lost baby and missing necklace in their care, the couple embarks on a
journey into peril—and passion.

*Available wherever paperbacks are sold, or order direct from the
Publisher. Send cover price plus 50¢ per copy for mailing and
handling to Penguin USA, P.O. Box 999, c/o Dept. 17109, Ber-
genfield, NJ 07621. Residents of New York and Tennessee must
include sales tax. DO NOT SEND CASH.*

PATRICIA WERNER
CHEROKEE BRIDE

ZEBRA BOOKS
KENSINGTON PUBLISHING CORP.

ZEBRA BOOKS

are published by

Kensington Publishing Corp.
850 Third Avenue
New York, NY 10022

First printing: May, 1992

Printed in the United States of America

10 9 8 7 6 5 4 3 2

Chapter One

Kit Newcomb jostled against her brother, Fletch, as the crowd surged around their open carriage rolling along unpaved Pennsylvania Avenue. Andrew Jackson's landau led the procession, a number of old Revolutionary officers forming his escort to the President's House.

Yelling "Hurrah for Jackson!" and "Jackson Forever!", the crowd gave a shout the likes of which had never before been heard in Washington City. Fletch shook his disheveled red head and laid his tall beaver hat on the seat beside him.

"He is the people's president," Fletch shouted over the noise of the crowd. "It's as if they feel he's rescued the country from some dreadful political danger." In his Southern accented speech he attempted to convey some of the political sagacity of their father.

At the moment Kit was more worried about their carriage colliding with some other vehicle or pedestrian.

5

"Can you get us to the President's House, Caleb?" she shouted to their driver while she held her bonnet as if it might fly off at any moment.

"Don't you worry," answered the black man, turning his head and displaying pearly white teeth. "Caleb'll have you there in no time."

In the throng, hunters from Kentucky, Indian fighters from Tennessee, and rough-looking frontiersmen mingled with the more cultured dwellers of the Eastern seaboard. But Caleb did as he said he would, guiding the pair of iron grays through the melee, eventually coming to the President's House, an elegant white sandstone structure set in a landscaped square. Here the motley crowd was already draining barrels of punch that had been brought out to the lawn, drinking to the health of the new chief of state.

Fletch helped his sister down, and they pushed through the crowd ascending the steps that led from the circular drive to the porticoed entrance. But there was no refuge inside either. Instead of the select group of diplomats they'd hoped to meet, the halls were filled with Negroes, women, and children scrabbling to get into the drawing room and secure more refreshments. Kit clasped her ribboned and veiled bonnet tightly to her head with one hand and clutched the crook of her brother's arm with the other.

"Come on," Fletch said as he dragged her along toward the East Room, which had also been invaded by the noisy mob.

There was a crash of china and glass as the invading crowd circulated among the foreign ministers and citizens, slurping cakes and ices. In an effort to see the president of their choice, some stood in their muddy

6

boots on the crimson satin damask chairs, while the chandeliers above their heads swayed.

Kit discerned President Jackson's white head above most of the others in the East Room. A number of gentlemen, linking arms, formed a barrier around him, where he had retreated for safety against a wall. Finally the windows were thrown open, and some of the crowd found an outlet that way.

"There's Father," Kit said, pointing between the heads of the crowd. "He's one of the men surrounding the President."

Just then the surging crowd pushed Kit toward a group of men in dark frock coats, their heads bowed in an argument. She managed to catch her balance just short of where they stood.

"Further resistance on our part is useless," said a white-haired man with amber skin and brows knotted over dark, piercing eyes. "A removal treaty is the only way out of a desperate situation."

A younger man who resembled the speaker, except for short, black hair and skin a shade lighter, raised a hand. "Now that gold's been discovered in Georgia, our people are powerless against the white man's clamors for it."

"Gentlemen," interjected a white-whiskered man with a heavy Southern accent. "The Cherokees will be treated fairly and will be well paid. Lands have been set aside for the Indian people in the West."

"The lands in the West cannot replace our homelands."

This was spoken forcefully by a tall, bronze-complected man whose straight black hair flowed past rigid shoulders. The white of his shirt front and neck cloth

7

contrasted with his burnished skin. Kit couldn't help but stare at his high cheekbones, long straight nose, snapping dark eyes, and firm lips. Then followed angry words in a strange tongue she didn't understand.

At the same moment, a boot heel came down on her hem, and a sharp elbow jabbed her in the back, shoving her forward. Like lightning, the Indian she had been watching reached out to catch her, his dark eyes still casting daggers.

He noticed the flush of Kit's cheek, the line of green satin bodice that revealed the cleft of white skin where her shawl had slipped apart. Her slim, angular body leaned on his arm for only a moment. Her startled blue eyes asked silent questions, half-parted lips seemed to thank him. The word desirable came unbidden to his mind as he felt himself warm even further in the stuffy room.

Kit gazed back at the Indian in the tailored black frock coat before her. She felt warmth rise in her face as his strong arms righted her, then tried to take a step backward and bumped into Fletch.

Hardly aware of the gathering of arguing men to Kit's left, her brother tugged on her right arm, crushed her billowing satin sleeve against him, and pulled her off balance.

"If we want to meet the President, now's our chance," said Fletch.

She followed her brother through a small opening in the crowd, and finally came face to face with their father.

Jonathan Newcomb was a solid, square-built man of medium height, his ruddy complexion and bushy gray side whiskers setting off bright, expressive eyes that could either beam with joy or shoot sparks of anger. Today he wore a claret frock coat with gilded buttons and matching waistcoat.

"There you are, children," said Jonathan. His hands were clasped behind his back as he rocked forward on his heels. "The President would like to meet you."

President Jackson didn't appear to want to meet anybody. His hair looked even whiter than when Kit had seen him from a distance at the inauguration ceremony on the steps of the Capitol that morning. His gaunt face was extremely pale, and Kit was struck by how he had aged.

Jonathan made the introductions, and she took the President's hand. His handshake was warm and firm, and she saw now the keen expression in his eyes. This last had gained him the admiration and loyalty of his followers.

"So these are the pride and joy of Jonathan Newcomb's heart," said the President.

So here was the most loved, also the most hated, the most admired, and the most feared man in the United States — the last of the Revolutionary heroes.

"Very pleased to meet you, Mr. President," said Kit. Now that she was finally here, she gathered her wits and tried to display her natural Southern charm.

"And our congratulations, sir," chimed in Fletch, taking the hand that Kit had shaken. "I'm sure our family will do all we can to help the new administration."

"I think you children should leave," interrupted Jonathan. "It's been a tiring day for the President."

Kit's gaze again met President Jackson's, their eyes locking in mutual assessment. Then she smiled and turned to go.

Another pair of eyes followed her as she made her exit, and sensing she was being watched, she glanced sideways to see the Indian who stood apart from his party. He was taller than many in the crowd, and his eyes held a look of disdain mixed with curiosity that carried to her across the crowded room.

"Too many people," grumbled Fletch. "Let's get out of here."

Getting out was almost more difficult than getting in, for they had to move against the crowd as they pushed their way out the front door and emerged into the fresh air. The din of celebration rose to a fever pitch as the crowd trampled grass and shrubbery outside while partaking of the hogsheads of punch on the lawn. Kit and her brother stood at the curbstone trying to see where Caleb had taken the carriage.

"Come on," said Fletch. "Caleb most likely expected us to stay longer. Getting a cab in this mess will be impossible. We might as well walk."

They crossed the muddy street, made their way to the next block, passed the bank building, the hotel and other businesses, and finally came to F Street. Leaving the commercial district behind, they came to a square of houses with gardens enclosed by high brick walls. People still stood about in knots, conversing excitedly, but there was far less frantic activity here.

They stopped in front of a three-story, red brick home to scrape the mud off their shoes before climbing the few short steps to the front door, opened by Bella, the Negro housekeeper.

"My, my," said the rotund black woman. "Your aunt Ruby didn't expect you back so soon."

"There was quite a crowd," explained Kit, removing

10

her bonnet, placing it on the hat stand next to a mirror in the hall and shaking out her strawberry curls.

Bella's black eyes sparkled in her ebony face. "Did you get to see the President?"

"Yes, we met him," said Fletch. "Thousands of people stormed the President's House. We were lucky to get near him."

"Well, I'm sure Miss Ruby will want to hear all about it."

They found their aunt upstairs in her private sitting room at a mahogany secretary, inkstand and paper before her. When her niece and nephew came in, she laid down her quill pen.

Ruby Newcomb was a stout middle-aged woman whose face still showed her beauty, her muslin day dress with long, full sleeves and high neck emphasizing the patrician posture that Kit had inherited.

"Hello, Aunt," said Kit, dropping onto the sofa. "We're back."

She longed to take off her shoes as she had the bonnet now hanging in the entry hall. At home in Georgia, she had developed a habit of going barefoot, when she was alone, for which her father had begun to scold her in recent years. One of the reasons he had brought her to Washington City was to make sure she was introduced into proper society, and for that she had to adopt proper manners, a practice that did not always suit her.

Ruby peered at Kit and Fletch over the rims of her spectacles. "So soon?" she inquired.

They took turns relating their adventures, to Ruby's nods and occasionally raised eyebrows. Though not as enthusiastic about Andrew Jackson as some, Ruby nevertheless withheld her critical comments in the

11

spirit of family harmony.

The election had been bitter, and the retiring president, John Quincy Adams, and his aristocratic Federalist friends had refused to participate in the ceremonies. But the simplicity attending the inauguration, the absence of military features, and the omission of an evening reception were not entirely in deference to General Jackson's democratic ideas, but were due to the President's having just suffered the great sorrow of losing his wife Rachel, who had died at their home in Tennessee just before the general had left for Washington City.

For her part, Ruby found Washington entirely gloomy these days, as many of the elegantly furnished houses were being stripped of their splendid furniture and that furniture exposed to public sale. The drawing rooms, where she had so often mixed with gay crowds distinguished by rank, fashion, beauty, and talent, were now being dismantled as political party changes were made in official circles. She gave a melancholy sigh, forgetting to acknowledge Kit's last comment.

Jonathan Newcomb was a Jackson man, and family came before party loyalty, so Ruby had opened her home to Jonathan and his children when he had come to the capital.

"When do you suppose we'll find out if Father is to be named to the Cabinet?" said Fletch, throwing himself down in a French arm chair and stretching his legs before him.

"Now, Fletcher. Not everyone can be in the Cabinet."

"We know that," said Kit. "It's just that it's done Father so much good to have a purpose in life again."

She rose and crossed to the windows that looked out

onto streets on which the crowds spilled away from Pennsylvania Avenue.

Washington was an exciting city. Like her father, Kit wanted to contribute to her country, and not merely by attending the social functions that seemed to be the lot of politicians' wives and daughters. But she had to admit she did miss Georgia. Wytheridge was not large like the plantations of the flatlands above Savannah. But the modest plantation with its two-story frame home that nestled at the foot of the mountains, surrounded by live oak and tall pines was deep in her heart.

What she had said about her father was true. Some of the life had gone out of him when Kit's mother had died — six years ago when Kit was thirteen — but politics had revived the fire in Jonathan Newcomb.

"We'll certainly hear all the news at the Rutherfords' ball," said Ruby.

Kit brought her wandering thoughts back to the present.

"Perhaps by then we'll know about Father," said Fletch, springing up.

He had had enough drawing-room conversation and had to be about his business. A gnawing feeling in his stomach reminded him that they hadn't gotten close to the refreshments at the President's House.

"What time is tea?" he said.

Kit listened to the carriages rolling incessantly past outside as she examined herself in her green silk gown, humming a tune and tapping her foot. The effect flattered Kit's statuesque form, bright hair, sparkling blue eyes, and fair complexion.

13

Ruby's maid, Samantha, had coiled Kit's tresses in a smart chignon.

"Umm, you'll do."

She whirled to see her brother grinning at her from where he leaned against the doorjamb, arms crossed as he examined her dress critically.

"Fletch, you startled me."

"So I see. You were lost in a world of fantasy from the look you were giving that mirror."

Her cheeks darkened at her brother's teasing, but she had to admit he looked dashing in his high white neckstock, dark blue double-breasted cutaway, and the close-fitting trousers ending at his half-boots. The cutaway's color complemented blue eyes that danced, the same color as Kit's; and his short hair, several shades brighter than hers, was only slightly less disheveled than usual.

"Well," he said, holding her dark green cloak. "Shall we?"

Jonathan waited downstairs with Ruby, also looking elegant in a gown of deep purple, shot silk.

"Can these be my children?" said Jonathan, as the two young people descended the stairs.

Tonight he, too, wore a dark blue cutaway, with matching trousers and silver brocade waistcoat.

"Come now Fletch," Jonathan said. "We shall have to prove very able escorts this evening or else all the eligible bachelors in Washington will attempt to sweep these lovely ladies off their feet."

"Pshaw, Jonathan," said Ruby. "Save your flattering tongue for better uses. Though I do agree with you that our Kit looks lovely. I knew that green would do her well."

14

Fletch bowed, placed his high top hat on his head, and followed the others out to the waiting carriage. He had no intention of escorting his sister farther than the door of the Rutherfords'. She would not have need of him after that.

Half of Washington thronged to the ball that Friday evening. Torches lined the street in front of the big double house, and it seemed as if a hundred carriages all tried to disembark their passengers at the same time.

At one end of the second-floor ballroom, a small platform had been erected for the black musicians, and an open door led to an adjoining room, in which a table was laden with refreshments. Pillars were festooned with laurel, wintergreen, and roses. Long slender tapers flickered in the crystal chandeliers above, so many it seemed the room was lit by hundreds of candles.

Kit was admiring the ladies in their ball gowns and the gentlemen, some in military uniform, when a young lady with flashing eyes swooped down on her.

"Oh, Kit, there you are."

Merilee Fitzsimmons wore a dress of white crape trimmed with satin and pearls, her dark ringlets dressed with orange blossoms. Kit rained smiles on her friend.

"You look wonderful, Merilee."

"And so do you. My Lord, that is a beautiful color on you. Turn around."

The skirt of Kit's green silk gown was coquettishly short, as her aunt, who had supervised the fittings, had assured her was quite fashionable, allowing for the freer display of silk stockings and slippers fastened with ribbons that crossed over the instep and ankle.

As she twirled for Merilee's inspection, a young man

of moderate height, with thick brown hair and squarish jaw, approached them.

"So it is," said Breckenridge Grover. "A color made for the prettiest young lady in the room. That is," he said with a cough, "one of the two prettiest young ladies."

"Oh, go on, Breck," said Merilee, for she had already caught Fletch's eye.

It was precisely eight o'clock, and Mr. and Mrs. Rutherford, now at the center of the floor, opened the evening's dancing with a stately minuet. The couple executed the steps skillfully, arms curved, toes pointed out, rising onto the ball of the foot, closing with the left and following with a graceful *plié*. Introducing grace steps now and then, they moved sideways to their left in a half-circle that brought them face to face in the center.

When the master of ceremonies announced the quadrille, Breck touched Kit's arm. "I hope you'll do me the honor," he drawled, leaning closer.

She nodded absently, her eyes still scanning the crowd to see who was here. Breck led her to their place in a square of four couples, Fletch and Merilee among them. Then they all moved to the music for the first figure.

Each time they joined hands, Breck let his thumb caress Kit's wrist. The music lifted her spirits, and the colorful movements of the gaily attired guests made her smile; but Breck's glances and the pressure he applied to her hand began to annoy her.

They advanced toward the couple opposite and retired backward, then crossed and changed places, Kit's free movements earning her many admiring glances.

They moved through the remaining figures of the dance, the room around them glittering with candle-light and jewels.

When the dance was over, Breck mopped his brow with a handkerchief, then reached for Kit's hand, thrusting his jaw forward.

"It's a bit warm in here," he said. "Let's step outside for some air."

"Well, I don't know."

She fluttered her ivory fan, but she knew they would cool off if they rested a few minutes.

"If it's Merilee or your brother you're lookin' for, don't waste another thought on them." He gave a know-ing smirk, as if to say he knew what those two were up to.

Kit shrugged. "Very well."

Downstairs, Kit and Breck passed the card room, where several lively games of whist were in progress. She fetched her cloak, then they proceeded to the ter-race at the back of the house. Outside, a bright moon shone on sculptured gardens. Breck wasted no time in putting his reason for their excursion before her.

"I have somethin' to say to you, Kit," he announced as his arm encircled her waist.

She tried to step aside, but he held her where she was, his face hovering near hers.

"My darlin' Kit, you know you are very beautiful. Every one of the gentlemen in there was admirin' the way you look."

"Why, thank you, Breckenridge."

Her smile was set in place, and her eyes still bright from the dancing, but she began to feel uneasy at his words. She resented his imprisoning arms.

"It's more than that," he continued. "I want to express my feelin's for you in the hopes that they are returned if only in half-measure."

"I don't know what you're talking about, Breck," she said.

Since she'd been in Washington, Breck had often acted as her escort, but it was nothing more than that. If she had given him any attention, it was no more than she had given any of the young men she'd met through her brother.

"Surely you do, Kit. After the time I've spent in your company, you must see what my intentions are in regard to yourself."

"I don't know what your intentions are, Breck, but please don't say any more."

"But I must. I know we're young, Kit, but I'm sure my father will approve of my plans. I want your hand in marriage. There can be no other for me."

He bent to kiss her, but she turned her head so that his wet lips landed on her jaw. Still he held her arms with his large hands.

Decorum gave way to irritation. "Don't be foolish, Breckenridge. You're not finished with college, and you have your law degree to get. I can't think of marriage yet."

She had inched backward, but he followed, so that she was lodged against a hard brick wall that bit into her back.

"Give me one sweet kiss, my lovely Kit. Then you'll see what I mean."

"I don't want—" But he trapped her mouth with his own in a rough wet kiss. His arms pinning hers to her sides, he pressed himself against her, making her feel

18

she would choke.

Finally he released her mouth and she gasped. "Let me go, Breckenridge."

But his ardent advances were not to be denied. As the passion pounded in his ears, he could no longer hear her protests. He mumbled amorous phrases, his hand straying to her breast, but Kit twisted suddenly, wrestling out of his embrace after jabbing a sharp elbow in his stomach.

"Agh!" He bent double.

Once free, she fled down the steps and into the garden.

"What . . . !" He broke off his expostulation.

Seeking solitude in order to catch her breath, Kit hid behind a bush, out of the light cast by the torches that lined the walk. She heard Breck curse. Then his footsteps crossed the terrace in her direction.

She waited behind the bushes, panting from embarrassment. She silently willed Breck to give up on finding her in the dark. Finally she thought she heard him return inside. She expelled a breath of air and stepped around the bushes to the walk. Then she gasped.

Standing half in, half out of the shadow cast by the torch above was the Indian she had seen at the President's House. He was dressed in black frock coat and white cambric cravat, his firm lips drawn in a pensive line. Kit's heart beat wildly in surprise, and her eyes widened. Making no sound, he had been standing so still that she had assumed no one was there.

The Indian had been lost in thought, but now he focused on the tall girl as she appeared, seemingly from nowhere. He stared at this vision, at moonlit, flaming hair, fair skin, blushing cheeks, eyes the color of a sum-

19

mer sky, glistening, long white throat where her cloak opened, and angular shoulders. Her hand held her skirt, which exposed well-shaped ankles.

He heard her shoes scrape the flagstone walk and he saw her tremble. The color of her hair reminded him of the rich red earth of his homelands. His eyes were drawn to the bosom that rose and fell beneath her gown, and he knew she was just as human as he.

"Good evening," he said in a rich, fluid voice.

They stared at each other for a moment, the directness of his gaze causing her skin to prickle and her already labored breathing to come in quick, shallow breaths. Was it a trace of amusement she saw in his black eyes—or merely her embarrassment reflected there?

"My name is Red Hawk," he said. "What is yours?"

She cleared her throat and let go of her skirt. "My name is Kathryn." She paused, then said, "But people call me Kit."

As Red Hawk tried her name on his tongue, the planes of his face relaxed a trace. Though he hated Southern whites, her husky drawl was not unpleasing to his ears.

He watched her for a moment, then said, "I am Cherokee."

He stood straighter as he said it, and she was suddenly aware of the muscular shoulders and arms that the fitted frock coat could not hide.

"Oh. Yes." She swallowed, trying to bring her voice into a normal range. "You must be part of the delegation."

He grunted. "We are here to oppose a treaty that would cede more of our lands in Georgia."

20

She nodded. She knew of it only too well, for her father was an advisor on the subject to Georgia's governor.

"I've heard of it," she said.

He shook his head thoughtfully, his long hair falling over his shoulders as he took a pace to the side.

"I long for these negotiations to end, so I can return to my woodland mountains, lands that are sacred to my people." He hesitated. "But you would know nothing of that."

Though Red Hawk was a full-blooded Cherokee, raised in the Cherokee tradition, he was educated in the white man's language, and had learned the skills of negotiation, except that he had difficulty keeping his emotions under control. Like the other Cherokee leaders in his deputation, he had been selected because he was shrewd and was dedicated to fighting for the rights of his people, though Chief John Ross had to caution him often about his quick temper. For Red Hawk seemed especially heir to his ancestors' warlike disposition.

His impatience had made him leave the party inside, to which he had been invited with other members of the delegation. He was not at home at such a gathering. The rooms were stifling, the people too interested in themselves, and the music strange to his ears.

Kit did not know what to make of the tall, brooding Indian. From the resentment in his words and the angry spark in his eye, she sensed a savage primitivism beneath the formal dress of an Indian diplomat. The coat and trousers did little to mask the man's contempt for these surroundings. And his masculine presence was unnerving.

21

Red Hawk narrowed his gaze, as if he could look past her eyes to her very thoughts. Kit was not used to being stared at so directly. She had often heard her father berate all Indians as being worthless, ignorant savages without souls. That accusation echoed in her mind now in strange contrast to the virile dark man before her.

"Who . . . who are the other members of your delegation?"

She made a gesture meant to indicate those she had seen him with at the President's reception.

"We are with Chief John Ross," he began.

She had read of the well-loved Cherokee chief. Only one-eighth Cherokee, and primarily of Scottish descent, he was nonetheless revered as a leader of the tribe, and she could hear the respect and warmth in Red Hawk's voice as he spoke his chief's name.

But then his expression darkened as he continued. "Also here are Major Ridge and his half-blood son John."

She realized at once that Major Ridge must have been the white-haired full blood she had seen at the reception, the younger man with him, his son. But she could think of nothing more to say to this tall, introspective member of the Cherokee delegation, and she felt awkward standing there.

She sought her voice, but no pleasantry seemed appropriate.

"My . . . friends will be waiting for me," she stammered.

Red Hawk moved aside, watching her brush past. He had developed a great disdain for all whites and their hypocritical ways. White women were no less to be faulted than their husbands and fathers who spoke of equality and justice for all and then flogged their slaves and drove the Indian people from their forest homes.

Red Hawk's people were children of the soil, bound to the land for generations and protected by solemn treaties on which the white man trampled at will. Yet he felt the quickening of his flesh as he watched the red-haired maiden go, and his curiosity roused him from his solemn, warlike thoughts.

Chapter Two

"Kit." Merilee broke away from a group when she saw Kit return to the ballroom. "What happened? I saw Breck. . . ." Seeing Kit's flushed face, Merilee stumbled over her words.

Kit shook her head. "It's all right." Indeed she had quite forgotten about Breck.

Merilee glanced stealthily over her shoulder to make sure they were alone; then she lowered her voice.

"You must tell me what happened."

Kit was not about to tell her friend that the brightness in her eyes and the tinges on her cheeks were not caused by their friend Breckenridge. But there was no more time for discussion. Her brother approached.

"Ah, whispering in a corner. Just like two women," Fletch said, flashing his smile for the benefit of the young woman he had set his heart on.

Merilee tilted her head coquettishly. "What are you accusing us of now? Will you have no mercy on two friends who have not spent two minutes together this evening?"

"No mercy at all. I am in want of a partner for the

contradanse." He tried to assume a mournful look that would make Merilee take pity on him.

She batted dark lashes at him. "Well, in that case."

Merilee gave Kit a woeful look, her curiosity being nearly as great as her desire to dance with Fletch. But the latter won out, and Kit was left mercifully alone.

Having no wish to dance again, she seized a glass of punch from a passing waiter and gulped it down as she watched the couples on the floor form two columns facing the top of the room. She glanced toward the doors to the terrace, but she daren't go out there again.

Her father was standing by the wall with a group of men discussing politics. Seeing him break away, she hurried over.

"Father," she said, catching him just as he was heading for the refreshment room. "I . . . I'd like to leave."

"What, so early?" He peered closely at his daughter. "Are you feeling well?"

"Yes. No. That is, I have a headache. The music just seems to make it throb. I think I ought to go home."

Jonathan frowned. Something was amiss. His daughter was not given to sick headaches. Neither had he ever seen her wish to leave a party early. But he shrugged.

"I'll see you home and then return. I promised Rutherford a game of whist."

"I'm sorry, Father. I could go in the carriage by myself."

"Nonsense, nonsense, my girl. I'll just get our things."

Kit made her way downstairs to wait for her father. All about her, guests chattered about the inauguration and the changes in Washington City.

25

Jonathan descended the staircase, hat, cane, and Kit's wrap in hand. She felt a pair of eyes on her back and turned to see Red Hawk standing with the same group of men she had seen him with at the President's House.

The dark-haired gentleman with thick dark brows and blue eyes must be Chief John Ross.

Then her father took her elbow and hustled her outside, where they found Caleb waiting with their carriage.

"Father," Kit said, unable to keep silent. "Did you notice the men standing in the foyer as we were leaving?"

Jonathan's thick gray brows drew down. "What would you be wanting to know about them?"

She shrugged. "I saw them at the President's reception."

"Those Cherokees are trying to stall negotiations for a removal treaty. They've been refusing to move to the Western lands that've been set aside for them in Indian Territory. Luckily there's dissension in their ranks. And now that Jackson's in office, the Cherokees won't stand a chance."

Jackson was known far and wide as an Indian fighter, and had been lauded for bringing the Indian people to heel in Tennessee.

"It won't be long before decent white folks'll be able to settle in the fertile valleys of South Carolina and the western part of our state," Jonathan continued as the carriage bounced along the rough street. "We'll soon be rid of the Indians there."

"And where will they go?" Kit asked, remembering the defiance in Red Hawk's gaze under the torch light.

"Doesn't really matter where they go, long as they

26

move out of Georgia. We can't allow Indians to stand in the way of progress. Bloody reprisals occurred in the past whenever we negotiated for more of their lands, but Jackson'll bring them to heel like he did the Creeks."

Jonathan shook his head. "The tribes fought each other until we came along to teach 'em to live together. Maybe they've learned their lesson."

Kit said no more as they jostled along in the darkness. When they reached her aunt's house, she bid her father good night, wishing him a good game of whist.

As soon as Samantha had helped Kit out of her dress, she donned her dressing gown and sat in front of the mirror. She dismissed the shy black girl and then released her hair from its pins. Her curls fell to her shoulders, and she took the brush to her tresses, wincing as she pulled with long, hard strokes, staring at herself in the mirror.

For a moment, the image of the tall Indian came to her as if he were standing behind her, his hands poised over her hair, ready to arrange it over her shoulders. Then the image was gone.

She laid the brush down slowly, stood, and moved toward the fourposter that stood in the middle of the room. She wasn't sleepy yet, but she slipped between the covers and lay back, letting the wick in the pewter lamp beside her burn down. What had Red Hawk said about longing to return to his homelands in Georgia?

In the dark, she stared at the underside of the canopy for a long time, listening to the bellows of the cows and the grunts of the pigs that roamed the streets at night, the sounds blending with the barking of dogs and the creaking of the carriages still rolling past. Though un-

27

like the country sounds of home, she found comfort in this chorus in the city at night, and soon the images provoked by it in her mind turned to uneasy dreams.

When Kit went down in the morning, all talk was about what Jackson would do now that he was in office. She took a plate and helped herself from the steaming dishes on the mahogany sideboard as the others talked.

"He'll name the Cabinet members within the week," Jonathan said, as he polished off a plate of ham and eggs, along with one of Bella's freshly baked biscuits.

"Now, Jonathan, I've warned you not to get your hopes so high," said Ruby. "Not everyone can be in the Cabinet."

"No," said Fletch, swallowing the last of a biscuit and reaching for another. "But President Jackson will make other appointments this week as well, won't he? And we can't help but hope you'll be among the chosen."

Jonathan cleared his throat. "I hope the President sees his way to give me a modest appointment. He is not a man to forget those who have campaigned for him."

He had been one of Jackson's close advisors, and knew the loyalty of the frontier hero. He could not believe he would be forgotten. On the stump during the campaign, Jonathan Newcomb had found out to his own satisfaction that in simple language and without apparent oratorical effort, he could breathe his own spirit into whoever listened and sway them with the power of his reasoning. And now he held his politics as dear as some held religion.

"Then would we remain in Washington?" asked

28

Fletch, unable to keep the eagerness out of his voice. He used the sugar tongs to drop another lump of sugar into his coffee.

"That remains to be seen," said Jonathan. "If I stay here, I'll need someone to run the farm, now it's planting time. I was counting on you, Fletch." He eyed his son over the rim of his coffee cup.

Fletcher's reluctance to return to Wytheridge was apparent from the grimace he made at the prospect. "I'd rather remain here for a while, Father. Perhaps I could learn something about government."

Jonathan burped, wiped his mouth, and tossed his napkin onto his plate. "We'll see, we'll see," he said. "I make no promises."

"First we have to see how things turn out here," Ruby reminded them. She signaled Bella to clear the plates, then turned the conversation to everyone's agenda for the day.

The men excused themselves, but Ruby remained with Kit over another cup of coffee.

"I might see if Merilee will accompany me on a drive," Kit said slowly. "That is, if we're not expecting anyone."

"That's quite all right, my dear," said Ruby, her thoughts already on the letter she was about to compose. "In weather so fine, someone's likely to call, but there's no need for you to be here."

There was never a respite from the endless visits and return visits demanded by Washington society. Though no one ever saw Ruby's chains, she was a slave to society's demands. She was hopeful that she would have at least one or two days this week when no one rang the bell so she could get some domestic chores done.

"We won't be gone long," Kit said, rising from her chair.

"Have a nice time, dear."

"Thank you."

Ruby sighed, watching Kit go. She envied Kit's being able to do as she pleased, but she wanted her niece to take advantage of that freedom while she had it.

Kit found Caleb in the carriage house adjoining the alley at the back of the house and told him she wanted to drive out; then she went upstairs to get ready. She dressed in a tarlatan walking-out dress with jacket bodice and a poke bonnet with a lavender ribbon that she tied under her chin.

She was glad she was getting out of the house. A cool breeze came up from the river, but the sun promised to warm the day. In truth, the forced idleness of the last weeks had made Kit restless. At Wytheridge, there was always work to be done. For though the Newcombs had a score or more of slaves, it was still a big task to run a plantation, even a modest one like Wytheridge. And since her mother had died, Kit had taken on managing the house, a responsibility she had never minded as long as, at the end of the day, she could take long walks with Shep — he was part sheepdog — or ride one of the mares.

But here, away from home, her every need was taken care of, and her aunt seemed to think Kit's main occupation should be making social visits and keeping an eye out for a prospective husband. In fact, Ruby had introduced her niece to several young and not so young widowers, seeing nothing wrong in a girl Kit's age marrying someone older if he was well established.

Still, the Fitzsimmons house was nearby, and it was

30

not hard to persuade Merilee to accompany her on a drive. Indeed Merilee looked appealing in a pea-green and white striped costume, her broad-brimmed bonnet ornamented with flowers and ribbons that hung to her waist.

Kit instructed Caleb to turn up Pennsylvania Avenue, drive past the Capitol, and then down to the Potomac.

Along Pennsylvania Avenue's mile and a half, the principal part of the city had built up, and there were numerous shops and businesses. In the residential areas, houses were sparsely situated, giving a feeling of space to the new city. Broad avenues were laid out but not yet paved, and several immense public buildings demonstrated the grandeur to which the city aspired. The ungraded, unpaved streets followed the roll of the land, and the parks remained unfenced.

"Now, Kit," said Merilee, "you promised to tell me what happened between you and Breck last night."

"Did I?" Kit said, watching the scenery. "I don't remember."

"Well, I'm not sure about your promise, but you do know I can't live without finding out." Dark eyes twinkled with curiosity.

Kit turned and gave her friend a wry look. "He seems to have mistaken my interest in him, considering it something more than friendship."

"Well, he's not a bad catch. He's from a good family and he's going to read law." Merilee arranged the folds of her skirt as she spoke.

"I hadn't thought of marrying yet."

A mischievous light came into Merilee's eyes as she said, "Well, you have to marry someone."

31

"Why?" The question sprang from Kit's lips spontaneously, causing Merilee to raise her dark brows.

"Because, dear Kit, there's nothing else for you to do. If you don't want Breck, you'd better make yourself available to one of the other suitors the city offers. From what your brother said, your chances here are far better than at Wytheridge. Your family already knows all the other landowners around. And Fletch says there's no one suitable there."

"Oh, did he really?" Kit wondered what else her know-it-all brother had said on the subject. But she shrugged. "I suppose. But Father needs me right now."

Merilee opened her mouth to say something and then closed it again, but not before Kit noticed her friend's look of confusion. She was not blind to Merilee's interest in her brother, and didn't mean to say anything to dampen Merilee's enthusiasm on the subject of marriage if that was what she wanted. Though it was a bit hard to fathom someone actually wanting to *marry* Fletcher.

"I hope Fletch does have enough sense to marry you," she said, tossing her head. "I wouldn't mind having you for a sister-in-law."

"Truly, Kit?" Merilee leaned forward. "I mean, do you really approve?"

Kit gazed out the side of the open carriage, but it was not the street she saw. "North Georgians have cleared the land they need right up to the Chestatee River. They build homes and work the land. Many of the women I've met here wouldn't have the stamina for that kind of life. Wives work hard, even with slaves. We're not wealthy like the landowners on the plains to the south. North Georgia women work hard."

She didn't have the heart to add and have babies and die young, but that, too, was true for many of the women in the sparse population that had staked claims up to the Chestatee and Chattahoochee rivers. The rivers that formed the borders of the Cherokee holdings.

She turned back to Merilee. "But there are rewards. The misty mountains, the brilliant sunsets. Oh, Merilee, you should see it, walk in the woods, and listen to the hoot owls at night. Whoever Fletch marries will have to learn to love that land."

They fell silent as the carriage took them along the shore of the Potomac, its glistening waters wrapping themselves around the city. Steamboats plied the river between Washington City and Alexandria on the other side. The Potomac Bridge, a mile in length, stretched across the river to their left, the drawspan at the far end raised for a tall-masted vessel to pass through. Ships from Europe were moored to the docks of Alexandria, while merchantmen from the West Indies glided by, laden with goods for the port of Georgetown, a little distance to the northwest.

Caleb stopped so the girls could get out and stroll along the parkway that had been laid out atop the embankment. Kit removed her bonnet, wanting to feel the breeze lifting her curls. She was just beginning to gain control over her wandering thoughts and focus them on other passers-by when she noticed a horseman dressed in bright colors coming toward them at a lope. The rider was bent low over the horse's neck, and with a start, Kit saw the long black hair that flowed behind the rider.

There was something frightening and yet exciting about the Indian's appearance, and Kit's breathing

33

quickened at sight of him, as Merilee shaded her eyes with her hand to see what her friend was staring at.

"He's an Indian," exclaimed Merilee.

Kit jerked her head around. "Yes. I saw him last night."

"Where, at the Rutherfords'? I didn't see any Indians."

"Then you just didn't notice them. He was with the Cherokee delegation that's here to talk to the President."

Merilee raised her eyebrows. "How do you know so much?"

"I don't know very much. I only overheard people talking." She saw no reason to mention that she had actually spoken to Red Hawk.

The girls continued their walk, turning their backs on horse and rider, but Kit remained uncomfortably aware that Red Hawk could not be far away.

Merilee chattered on, and Kit listened with half an ear. But even Merilee soon became aware that her friend was more silent than usual and that their pace had slowed. At the sound of a horse's hooves on the ground behind her, Kit knew that a rider approached. She did not have to turn around to guess who it was.

She turned slowly as Red Hawk reined in his horse and looked at her from his seat on a magnificent roan mare. She stared at the man before her dressed in bright green, fringed hunting shirt, a blue neckerchief tied around his forehead and soft leather boots on his feet. The arrogance in his expression she had seen before. Kit was determined not to reveal her response to the sight of his strong shoulders and to his long, muscular legs straddling the horse.

He shifted his weight in the saddle, and her own body responded to the movement. The image of him she had conjured the past night came unbidden. Her mouth felt dry as she glanced at his full, straight lips and then looked away. She swallowed, trying to concentrate on the horse instead.

An experienced horsewoman, Kit recognized the good breeding of the animal he rode. She removed her glove and reached up to let the horse get her scent, then she rubbed its neck.

Red Hawk gazed with pleasure at the woman before him. She is lithe and strong, he thought to himself. For he was not fooled by the fashionable clothing that covered her. He was glad she had removed her bonnet, for he preferred to see the sun on her face, her hair coming unbound. He allowed himself the pleasure of thinking about his own fingers loosening that hair of such rich color and arraying it about her naked shoulders.

Desire flooded him, but he did not show it, for it would not seem proper, especially with the other woman present. He controlled his emotions and prevented the words in his heart from forming on his lips, but he acknowledged them within himself. His features relaxed a trace.

"The horse is beautiful. Is she yours?" Kit asked, not looking up.

"No, she is not." His voice was deep and musical. "We used the white man's way of travel and came to Washington City on the riverboat. We did not bring our horses."

Kit dared tilt her head to look up at him. "I see. But you must enjoy riding her."

He leaned forward to touch the horse's neck with his

fine long fingers and strong hands. "She is a good horse, but she has not been used well. She needs to have her head, to run with the wind."

His overt maleness made Kit drop her eyes again. Still, she was aware of his breathing, of the sinews in his arms, and she risked another glance at the straight, coal black hair, the proud thrust of his chin, the purposeful set of his shoulders.

"Do you ride here often?" The words came out of Kit's mouth of their own volition.

"When I get away from the meetings I must attend."

She saw the lines that tightened in his face as he spoke about his duties. Finally, she withdrew her hand and stepped back, expecting him to ride on. But he remained, gazing at her as the horse shifted its weight from one foot to the other and tossed its head.

Then Red Hawk slowly turned his mount, dug his heels into the roan's sides and rode off, letting her have her head, just as he had said he would. Kit watched them fly along the patch at the edge of the sparkling water.

She turned, her face flushed, but she was hard put to rein in her thumping heart.

"The mare reminds me of one of ours at Wytheridge. Good lines, though our Stormy is only fourteen hands high and a trotter."

But the words came out stilted, and Merilee wasn't fooled. "You didn't say you actually spoke to the Indian last night. Who is he?"

"His name is Red Hawk. He was in the garden after I . . . after I ran away from Breck."

There was a long pause. "Oh."

"It's not so odd really, there are plenty of Indians in

36

Washington." Kit set her angular shoulders straight as if she were not to be contradicted.

Merilee nodded slowly. "Yes, I've seen some of them. They stay at the Indian Queen Hotel on Philadelphia Avenue."

The hotel next to the stage and steamboat office often provided lodgings for Indian chiefs and their delegations when they came to see the President.

Merilee went on. "But most of them are dressed up in feathers with painted faces and they put on exhibitions or sit in headdresses for their portraits."

"Well, the Cherokees are more civilized." Kit could hear the defensiveness in her own voice, and she wished the blood would stop rushing through her veins, making her feel lightheaded.

Merilee gazed speculatively at her friend for a moment, but Kit looked straight ahead as they walked back to where Caleb waited with the carriage.

"I wonder if we'll see him again," Merilee mused.

Kit turned her head and gazed in the direction the Indian had taken. The grassy banks were crowned with trees, and wild grape vines climbed from tree to tree. In the shade grew magnolia, wild rose, and honeysuckle. But Red Hawk was nowhere to be seen. He had blended into the fertile nature scene.

"I don't know," she said softly.

He was not a man such as any other she knew. He was not even one of her kind. But there was something about his bearing, the fierce pride behind the civilized facade that thrilled her. The Indian was strange and exciting. He mirrored something of the wildness of her own heart.

She looked again at the shining river and the graceful

37

outline of the Virginia hills beyond. She had yet to explore the opportunities of Washington City, but if her father did not get a post in the new government, they would be returning to Georgia. If she returned to Wytheridge, she would most likely not see Red Hawk again.

Chapter Three

Kit and Merilee returned to Ruby's house to find a visitor. When Kit entered the drawing room she at first did not recognize the dark-faced man with high, broad forehead, prominent nose, and deep black eyes. He had been leaning back comfortably on the navy blue upholstered sofa with gold stars spangled across its seat, his arm stretched along the back. But he rose, his eyes fixing on Kit's as she stood at the edge of the room.

Ruby smiled. "My niece, Kathryn Newcomb," she said from her seat on the damask loveseat. "May I present Senator Daniel Webster."

Of course. Her father had often spoken of the well-known New Englander, and she moved toward him with enthusiasm, then stopped in shyness as he bowed before her with great dignity.

"A pleasure to meet you," he said. His smile was gentle, his voice ringing. She had read in the newspapers that it was often compared to a clarion. She nodded in return.

Then his eyes met hers again, and she saw in their

black depths the mark of sorrow, remembering that he had lost his beloved wife a year ago.

"I am very pleased to meet you, Senator," said Kit. "My aunt has told me so much about you."

"Indeed your aunt has been a dear friend for a great many years. She was a friend to Grace also."

"Yes, I am sorry for your loss," said Kit.

She knew from Ruby that the married couple had been exceptionally congenial and though Kit had only met Webster, she felt sympathy for the pain he must have sustained.

She introduced Merilee, and they all took seats. The senator drew them into the conversation. Webster had supported John Quincy Adams in the recent election, though some said reluctantly so, and having been a member of the losing party did not seem to have dampened his spirits politically in the least.

As he spoke of the upcoming debate in Congress over a tariff on foreign goods entering the country, Kit was impressed with his flawless logic, melodic voice, and graceful gestures. She could well imagine that he was considered one of the great orators of their time and expressed a desire to hear him debate in public.

At that he gave her a wry smile. "No doubt there will be such an occasion."

"And what are your plans now, Daniel?" interrupted Ruby. "Now that you are no longer in the position of supporting an administration you did not like."

His eyes took on a sparkle at her frankness. "It is true I had my differences with John Quincy Adams, even if it was my duty to support him in the last election," he said. "But now that I am a member of the opposition party I will have more time to try cases before the Supreme Court. I am even considering returning to my law practice in Boston. Alas my debts have piled up so as a civil servant that it is tempting to return to private practice. I have no dearth of clients."

"But what would Congress do without you?" said Ruby. "Indeed, the President will need you on the floor of the Senate to see that all the important issues get a fair debate."

"Hmph," he murmured. "I'm no follower of Andrew Jackson, but on one issue we see eye to eye. The preservation of the Union. This issue of states' rights is a thorn in all our sides."

"I understand that some states claim the right to nullify a federal law passed by Congress."

His eyes flashed as he replied. "It all hinges on whether people understand that the Constitution does not stem from the states but from the people. It is made for the people, by the people — and is answerable to the people. The people have declared this Constitution to be the supreme law of the land. It is created for one purpose, to unify the states under a greater authority. A state cannot nullify a law passed by Congress."

His speech made Kit sit up straight and listen, for she knew that her father, a Southerner, was a great advocate of states' rights.

Webster softened his tone and turned his dark eyes on Kit. "But I must not get carried away with such boring political talk in your charming company."

Kit blinked. "Why, it's not boring at all," she said. "I would like to hear more of your opinions on the matter."

Just then a rumble of thunder was heard. Merilee rose from her seat and called Kit to the window to watch the clouds lower over the city. The wind rose and gusted violently, sweeping pedestrians down the street at a quickened pace.

The outer door slammed and Fletch came in, his collar turned up.

"Just made it," he said. "Looks like a downpour."

"My nephew, Fletcher Newcomb," Ruby said. "Fletcher, this is my dear friend, Senator Daniel Webster."

Fletcher stepped forward and shook the senator's hand. "An honor, sir, I've read many of your speeches."

"Ah, yes," replied Webster, humor lighting his dark eyes. "What a job that is, to wait for printer's proofs to see if one's been set right."

Ruby ordered the shutters closed, the curtains drawn, and the fire in the parlor rekindled. Bella brought in the lights. Then guests took seats around the fireside and the lively conversation resumed.

Daniel Webster began to make protestations about imposing on Ruby's hospitality too long, but Ruby would hear none of it.

"You will stay for some music," she insisted. "We cannot let the talents of these young people go to waste. I have it on the best authority that Merilee plays the harp. If Kit will accompany on the piano and her brother on the flute, we will have a concert."

Webster's eyes lit with interest. "Well, in that case," he said.

"Only if you sing," said Fletch to his aunt, while he fetched his flute.

Ruby gestured with a jeweled hand. "We shall see about that."

Seeing that the company would not release her, Kit rose to open the piano. Fletch set candles upon it, then placed the harp near the piano as Webster settled himself on the navy and gold sofa to listen.

Just then the outer door opened and closed once again, and Jonathan entered. Webster rose and the two shook hands.

"I fear I have interrupted," said Jonathan, seeing the young people going over sheet music at the music stand.

"Why, Jonathan, you've arrived in time for the concert," said Ruby.

"Ah," said Jonathan. "I'm afraid my committees allow me little leisure. I must keep my hat, for I cannot stay."

"Committees," said Ruby. "Even Mr. Webster has found time away from the floor of the Senate to help us entertain ourselves."

"Ah, but perhaps he has more cause," said Jonathan, eyeing his daughter.

Webster did not reply but reseated himself. Jonathan made excuses about fetching some papers from the study and left the room.

The three at the piano agreed on a piece, and Kit began the introduction. Webster listened with obvious delight, tapping a finger on his knee and moving his large head back and forth in time to the music. After the first piece, Ruby declined the invitation to sing, but demurred to Kit. Fletch chose an Irish song, and the trio executed the tune skillfully, Kit's voice lilting above the others. When the song was finished, Webster put his hands together in approving applause.

"There is in the soul a sympathy with sounds," he said. "And yours were so heavenly I was transported to Elysium. I will not ask for a continuation, lest I become spellbound and not get away tonight."

"Perhaps the senator will join us for supper one evening and we may all hear more music at leisure," said Ruby.

"Of course," said Kit, catching the cajoling undertone in Ruby's voice.

She glanced at the senator, who appeared to be in his late forties. He was a widower, but twice Kit's age. She had to repress a laugh, knowing that Ruby was probably already thinking up ways to keep the eligible and famous senator under her roof long enough for him to become acquainted with Kit.

But Kit felt no such response to the senator. He had a certain magnetism, it was true, but it was the magnetism that sways crowds, persuades judges, and forces bills into laws. She was interested in his mind, not in the intimacy of a potential spouse.

The conversation drifted into trivialities until Ruby rang for tea. By the time Webster rose to leave, Kit felt extremely informed on the issues of the day, especially the niggling debate about states' rights versus federal laws that applied to the states.

Again Daniel had thundered, "It is high time that the people of the United States know what the Constitution is, and by the blessing of heaven, they will learn what I take it to be."

By the end of the afternoon, Kit decided that Daniel Webster was a man to have on one's side in any cause.

After promising to call 'round again soon, he took his leave. He held Kit's hand in his own large, warm one, and she saw that the music had moved him.

"I hope for the pleasure of your company again soon, my dear," he said in his mellifluous voice.

44

"I find my mind stimulated by your conversation," replied Kit honestly.

Her reply was ingenuous, but she saw her aunt watching them curiously. Then Ruby saw the senator to the door.

"There would go my heart if I had one to give," said Ruby when she returned to the drawing room. "But fortunately the eligible senator will be looking to younger hearts than mine. The good widower is in need of a fair wife to complement his position. I believe you pleased him, Kathryn."

Kit pulled at the corner of her mouth in an expression of confusion. She had enjoyed Senator Webster's conversation, for she hungered for intellectual stimulation. But she was surprised to think that it might have seemed she had thrown herself at him for other reasons.

"I did not mean anything by it," she said.

Fletch laughed at his sister's discomposure as he began to put the flute away. "I will see Merilee home," he said.

Merilee blushed her acceptance.

Kit envied the carefree happiness that abounded in her brother and Merilee, and as she tidied up the music, Ruby's remark gave her something to think on. It was true that Senator Webster might be an interesting man to be married to. Surely the wife of a politician would have ample opportunity to question her husband about the weighty decisions being debated each day on the Senate floor.

She admired Senator Webster and felt a certain rapport with him. But surely in marriage the mind and the heart must agree. And what her family, who she knew had her best interests at heart, did not know, was that at the moment, Kit's heart was not hers to give.

The next day a message came summoning Jonathan to the President's House. Kit, Ruby, and Fletcher waited anxiously for his return. By the rigid set to his features when he got down from the carriage, all three watching from the windows concluded that he had not been selected to the Cabinet.

They were correct. Jonathan Newcomb had, however, been asked to take a post as one of the President's personal advisors.

"I need you to help me keep a pulse on the nation," Jackson had said as Jonathan had stood before him in the oval room. "I know no man who can mingle better with the people, tell me what the common man is thinking, and guard against the evils that can easily plague our country."

It was not the post Jonathan had longed for, but he would be close to the President and would have a hand in guiding the land even if he had no official vote in the government. He accepted the President's confidence and made the announcement to his family. Ruby immediately began to plan a reception to which she would invite dignitaries of government and members of society.

Bella's husband, a tall, straight black man with a gray head who served as Ruby's butler, stood stiffly in his black suit, ready to open the door for those invited to the evening affair and direct them to an upper room where they could take off their wraps.

In a new gown of lavender brocaded satin covered with tulle and ivory lace, Kit stood with her brother, her aunt, and her father in the drawing room to receive guests as they came down. She smiled and shook hands with politicians and diplomats in their full evening dress, their dark coats set off by brightly colored waistcoats of satin, velvet, or brocade, starched cravats, and frilled shirt fronts. The military gentlemen were in complete regimentals, and the ladies were adorned in frilly evening gowns and matching slippers.

Merilee passed through the line with her mother, and after casting a backward glance at Fletch, made her way to the dining room, which had been cleared for dancing. Kit saw Breckenridge, with his family, come down the stairs and wondered if he would try to find a way to avoid her. He did glance around the room, but he was trapped between the foyer and the receiving line and so took his place stiffly behind his father.

He shook hands cordially with Fletch and formally greeted Ruby and Jonathan. His back was so straight when he stepped in front of Kit, he might have had a rod stuffed down it. He looked above her head, took her hand briefly, and then hastened to the dining room. Kit managed to maintain a fixed expression while slowly exhaling the breath she had been holding. At least he wasn't going to make a scene over her refusal of his proposal the other evening.

She soon forgot about Breckenridge, however as she began to greet other dignitaries, many of whom she had never met before. Chief Justice John Marshall entered in his long-skirted black coat, badly-fitting waistcoat, knee breeches, and voluminous white cambric cravat. Though more than seventy now, she had heard that he relished the whist table and was quite adept with the billiard cue.

Henry Clay, a tall, thin, homely Kentuckian with gray eyes and an easy smile, came through the receiving line and then Vice President John C. Calhoun, his long hair brushed straight back from a high forehead, his gray-yellow eyes looking stern.

Daniel Webster appeared in a blue dress-coat with bright buttons, a buff waistcoat, and a high, white cravat. He greeted the family pleasantly, then grasped Kit's hand warmly. His voice boomed over the din of the company.

"Ah, I hope I may have the pleasure of another stimulating conversation with you later this evening, that is if you are not kept busy dancing with the young swains of the city."

She smiled at the older man, honored by his friendship.

"I most certainly do not intend to spend the entire evening dancing," she said. "Conversation is much more appealing to my taste."

He bowed and then passed on to mingle with the other guests. Clay and Calhoun bowed to him stiffly, and she sensed the political rivalry between the two Southerners and the outspoken Northerner, Webster.

Aided by the pianist, two violinists were tuning their instruments as Kit and her family made their way to the dining room to start the dancing. Fletch went directly to Merilee to lead her onto the dance floor, but Kit glanced around, seeking a partner with whom to begin dancing. Out of the corner of her eye she saw Breckenridge and panicked, hastily searched for a different partner. Seeing Webster smiling at her from the

48

side, she walked over to him and extended her hand.

He bowed slowly and followed her out to join her father and Ruby, now with their respective partners, and Fletch and Merilee to lead off the dancing.

They began with a contradanse, speaking little, but executing their steps to the music. Webster danced gracefully, holding his broad chest and shoulders erect. His dark face wore a pleasant expression, but Kit could still see, deep in the black eyes, the melancholy seriousness that bespoke a lingering emptiness over the loss of his wife.

Through the din of the evening, Kit heard many people congratulate her father on his new post, congratulations which he accepted graciously. If any outside the family knew he had hoped for something else, they did not show it. Of course the talk all evening was political, and as she mingled with the crowd, Kit took note of what was being said. For being in the presence of so many politicians was feeding her curiosity about the workings of the country more than any newspaper or circular ever could. Here was gathered the greatest talent in the nation — the men who actually had a hand in running the government. What they thought and what they did could change the course of history.

As she was nibbling a piece of cheese, she caught a glimpse of Fletch and Merilee standing close together and whispering to each other. Then she saw Merilee glance up at Fletch with a knowing smile, and the two of them slipped out the door that led to the hallway, undoubtedly seeking a room that offered some privacy.

Their actions brought unbidden to her mind the Indian Kit had spoken to, and she felt a fluttering in her chest. She set down her plate of food. Feeling suddenly stifled, she decided to leave the room for a breath of air.

Her father was in the corner, in deep discussion with the lanky Henry Clay. Daniel Webster stood near them, his face grim. Evidently he did not like what Clay was saying.

Having had enough politics for one evening, Kit stepped into the hallway, where a few guests mingled, some climbing the stairs to seek the wraps that Bella had put in one of the bedrooms. Kit proceeded toward her own room, and as she passed Fletcher's room, she thought she heard a moan.

She did not mean to eavesdrop, but she slowed her step long enough to hear rustlings through the door that was not quite closed. Then she distinctly heard Merilee's voice quavering breathlessly.

"Fletch," she said on a breath. "We shouldn't."

His protestations were lost in sounds of movement and hands upon silk, and Kit felt her face redden as she realized she was listening to a stolen moment of intimacy. She hurried on to her own room, where she shut the door behind her, her own breathing quickened.

Knowing what was going on in Fletcher's room only served to stimulate her own imaginings in a way that surprised her. For did she not also long for someone that would fill a void, comfort her, hold her?

Holding her hands to her face, she knew very well what she wanted. She wanted to see Red Hawk.

Hardly thinking about her actions, she fetched a long cloak and threw it over her shoulders. If anyone asked where she was going, she could always say that the house was so crowded she needed some fresh air. No one could fault her for that, not that she had any particular plan in mind.

She put on cloth-topped boots, fearing that strolling outside in her slippers would ruin them, for there had been enough snow during the month to leave the streets sticky and muddy. Then she made her way downstairs, passed the gossiping guests, and went out the front door and down the stoop. Standing on the sidewalk, she took in deep breaths of night air.

Outside it was no quieter than within. Animals roamed the streets, some bawling, and carriages rolled by. But the sky above and the distances between the houses around the square offered more breathing space.

A short walk would not hurt. It was early yet, and though she was unchaperoned, there were people about. Indeed, in many ways Washington City seemed never to go to bed. There were always callers on their way home from visits, laborers going to and from work, congressmen rushing to the printer to read proofs of a speech made in Congress that day, so that Kit felt little different than if she were going for a walk during the middle of the afternoon.

If she ever saw Red Hawk again, she reasoned, she would ask him more about his people's plight in Georgia. She did not understand the issue very well and wished to know more. That decision served as partial justification for wanting to see him, and it offered her security in the knowledge that she would have something to talk about if they did meet.

Her footsteps took her toward President's Square again, and she walked along, gazing at the white sandstone house, with its many rooms lit now and carriages dropping off and picking up callers.

She was curious about President Jackson, the more

so after having met him. His military feats were widely celebrated, and she wondered if he would force his measures through Congress with the same determination he had shown to the British at New Orleans or in chasing the Spanish into Florida.

She walked on past the brick building that housed the Departments of War and Navy and returned to the business district along Pennsylvania Avenue, realizing that she had gone farther than she'd intended. Walking helped cool her senses, and she knew she must return to the party before anyone started asking about her. She had told Bella she was going to get some air, but her family would think it strange if she remained absent from their guests very long.

She quickened her pace, glad for the cloth-topped boots when she had to cross the street. There was still much activity in the business district, and she moved along toward 7th Street. She had passed the Stage and Steamboat Office and was on the sidewalk in front of the four-story Indian Queen Hotel before she knew it. Seeing several Indians in a variety of dress emerge from the hotel, followed by a group of white men, made her realize where she was.

She glanced up, wondering which of the rooms might be Red Hawk's. But of course she would never inquire inside. It was happenstance that she had passed by the hotel, and she must hurry on. She hesitated for only a moment, looking into the lighted downstairs rooms, allowing, for only a moment, her imagination to wander.

In one of the second-floor drawing rooms, Red Hawk sat, staring moodily into the blazing fire in the fireplace. John Ross was deep in discussion with Major Ridge and the younger John Ridge. Red Hawk did not trust the two Ridges and feared that the chief would be influenced by their willingness to give in to the white man's demands. He suspected they had been bribed, but with no proof, he could not make such an accusation. He only hoped that John Ross's wisdom and experience would enable him to stand firm for their people.

Troubled by the discussion, Red Hawk rose and walked to the windows, folding his hands behind him and looking out. He glanced at the street below, watching the coming and going of the busy crowd. It was too dark to see far. And even though the new city's widely spaced buildings offered views of the rolling hills and pleasant vistas, Red Hawk found the place too crowded for his taste. He longed for his own village of New Echota, the capital of the Cherokee Nation.

And even now that was no longer safe. The Cherokee land in the state of Georgia was being threatened by the white man who wanted it for the gold that had been discovered there. Red Hawk often wished he had been born in another time when his people had led a simpler life, had roamed the Southern hills, feasting off the land. But fate had thrown the Cherokee into early contact with the white man, from whom they had learned the ways of civilization. That had done them little good, Red Hawk thought.

His eye was drawn to a woman standing near the entrance to the hotel, gazing at the windows. He noticed her because passersby were having to move around her. She was a stationary point in the melee of the street below. Then she turned her face toward the floor where the drawing room was situated, and his breathing halted for a moment. It was the woman he had seen by the river, the one he had met that night in the garden.

He did not stop to question what she was doing here, but turned to his colleagues and told them he would be back in a little while.

John Ross barely paused in his persuasive argument directed at Major Ridge, but just waved a hand as Red Hawk quietly crossed the room and passed through the door.

Downstairs, Red Hawk hastened through the lobby and out onto the steps. She was still there, her eyes looking over the building, a trace of curiosity in them. Red Hawk felt his own pulse quicken.

Not wanting to startle her, he stood near the stone railing until her eyes moved toward him. Then she saw him and her lips parted in surprise. She looked for a moment as if she might flee, but his eyes held her and he moved down the steps and onto the sidewalk toward where she stood.

Her lips trembled, and she pulled the hood of her cloak up over her head as if trying to protect herself.

"Good evening," he said when he had come within a few feet of her. He paused.

Her eyes were wide, her cheeks flushed with embarrassment, but she managed to stammer, "Good evening."

Then her gaze dipped below his as if she were prepared for an accusation, but Red Hawk stepped nearer and softened his voice as he spoke.

"I saw you from the drawing-room window," he said. "I was tired of my colleagues' conversation and looked for an excuse to come out of doors."

She glanced up briefly and then down again. Was it hope he saw in her eyes?

"I see," she said, then realizing she must offer her own explanation, she added, "My father is having a party. But the room was crowded. I needed to take a walk."

She glanced helplessly at her surroundings. "I'm afraid I came farther than I meant to. I should be getting back."

But Red Hawk was not prepared to let her go so easily. Already he was beginning to feel that this woman had something to do with his life. He had not met anyone in Washington City that attracted him so. And since fate had brought them together three times, it must mean she was part of his destiny. He did not question it, he only followed his leanings.

"Then I shall walk with you," he said.

She started to protest, but shut her mouth as if knowing that to be futile. She had brought this on herself, and she knew it. She had been curious about the Indian since the night they had met, and now he had caught her gazing like a strumpet at his hotel. She pulled the hood closer over her face, hoping no one she knew would see them. This was not acceptable behavior for a young lady in the city, and she would be chastised for it. This unnatural fascination with a stranger, a man not of her race or station, went against all she had been taught.

But a moment passed, and she did not tell him to leave. As she turned and walked slowly in the direction from which she had come, Red Hawk fell into step with her. When they reached the curbstone, he took her elbow to guide her across the rutted street.

Thinking they were better off away from the main thoroughfare, she turned back toward the residential squares. Here, at least, they might not be seen. As they strolled along the sidewalks where houses were set back in yards, they left the lights of the business district behind. There were no street lamps here, and Kit realized suddenly how much darker it was.

She trembled, but Red Hawk walked close to her, not touching her but conveying his presence in a way that was both fascinating and frightening.

"Do you walk about the city often?" he asked, breaking the silence.

"Not at night." Her answer was sudden, an attempt to defend herself.

"During the day, then?" he went on, unperturbed by her nervousness.

"I . . ." She didn't know how to answer that. "Of course, sometimes."

"Ah." His answer conveyed pleasure and an unhidden suggestion of the desire to walk with her again.

They neared the square where Ruby's house was situated. Kit slowed down, not wanting Red Hawk to accompany her there and already worried about getting back into the ball without anyone noticing her absence. Perhaps the servants' entrance would be unlocked.

Red Hawk perceived her hesitation and matched his pace to her until they were standing still, half-turned toward each other near a protective elm tree at the edge of the walk. A carriage approached, and Kit turned her face away in the event the passenger was some acquaintance. As she did so, Red Hawk instinctively reached for her and guided her under the low branches of the tree.

His own responses to this woman were unmistakable. She was like an intricately patterned blossom he wanted to explore. He did not know where it would lead, but he was ready with mind and body to pursue knowledge of her. He must approach her carefully though, as one would approach a doe in the woods, for one sudden or threatening move would send her skittering off.

Kit attempted a glance at his face, but when she did her throat went dry. In the shadows, she saw the sensual line of his lips, the firm planes of his cheeks. And she felt as well as saw the intense gaze of his dark eyes.

"I must go in," she said on a breath, even as she moved an inch closer to him. Already his nearness was creating havoc within her. Her body felt hot and cold at the same time. An aching sensation drew her toward him, and she longed for his hand, now touching her arm lightly, to press against her side.

She actually began to shake, and Red Hawk, responding to her trembling, placed his other hand on her waist and drew her closer. He did not pull her close enough for further contact. Nor did he lower his head toward hers, but held her between his hands, steadying her, breathing in her scent.

Kit's heart threatened to rise up in her throat, and she raised her face an inch, feeling his warm breath on her forehead. Rational thoughts fled as the longing for this man increased. She didn't understand how she could feel this way, why she had never felt this way before, even though she had read many stories of romance. The sensations she felt while standing near him were momentously different from anything she had previously experienced. She could not tear herself away though a voice in her mind pleaded with her to do so.

A moment longer, she told the voice. A moment's temptation, then I will go.

The instant was long enough for Red Hawk. He sensed the battle within her, and in the moment she lifted her face toward him, he knew he had won. She desired him.

Chapter Four

Red Hawk knew nothing more would occur that evening, but he had to make sure of her. Chance had brought them together three times. The fates meant for him to take matters into his own hands henceforth.

"I will ride by the river tomorrow," he said in a low voice.

She knew what he meant. Still, she could not bring herself to agree outright to see him. It was too bold. But he pressed her.

"Will you come?"

"I . . ." She should say no. She should return to the party, to the protection of her own people. But in a moment she remembered how stifled she had felt among them.

"Yes, no. That is, I cannot come to the river."

She hesitated, moving backward a pace, drawing rein on her feelings. Perhaps it would not be too dangerous to ride in broad daylight with him. It was not only the man himself that drew her, but curiosity about his people. Her mind was always hungry to understand the great issues of the day, for she sensed that the young nation was making history and that she was somehow a part of these changes. She had many questions to ask Red Hawk about the Cherokees and their plight in Georgia. Yet that, too, was dangerous. For it meant questioning the statements her father had made. She wanted to learn the truth for herself. If states had rights, surely Indian people did, unless they were truly a lesser race, like the black slaves, who, her father had taught her, were slowly having their veil of ignorance raised by white masters.

She swallowed. She must decide quickly. "I will ride to Rock Creek. There is a marker that delineates the edge of the city between here and Georgetown. It is on the turnpike. I will ride there."

Then she turned and fled down the sidewalk, her cloak billowing behind her, the hood falling away, her red tresses mingling with the night.

When she reached the alley beside the house, Kit stopped running and walked along, waiting for her heartbeat to slow. None of the servants were about, and she saw that she could go in a side servants' entrance without being seen.

She hurried to the door and opened it. Then she stood in the dark in the narrow hallway after she had closed the door behind her. Standing for a moment, she let her eyes adjust to the darkness. Then she removed her cloak, folding it over her arm. She pressed her hands to her cheeks, which were cool from the night air and no doubt red from exertion and her own state of excitement.

Passing a maid on the landing, she made her way up the backstairs, but she neither spoke nor looked at the girl. On the third floor, she walked quietly down the hallway, coming at last to her own room. At the other end of the hall, guests were emerging from her aunt's sitting room, bearing wraps. Kit ducked into her own bedroom quickly.

A candle flickered in its holder on her walnut dressing table, yet left the room in soft dimness. Kit hung her cloak on a peg on the side of the clothes press so that no one would suspect she had been out. Then she sat down in front of the ornamented, gilt-framed mirror to repair her appearance.

Her hair had come loose, so she used combs and brushes to neaten the curls, then repinned the coils on the back of her head. When at last her face had returned to its natural color, she felt she was ready to descend to the party. Only the brightness of her eyes gave her away, but perhaps the guests and her family would attribute that to the excitement of the evening. She was about to rise when there was a knock on the door.

"Come in," she said.

It was Samantha, come to inquire about her.

"Miss Ruby asked me to look in on you," said the maid, a troubled expression on her round face. "She thought maybe you took ill."

"No," said Kit. "I'm fine. I was just coming down. I went out for a bit of air, became chilled and then came up here to refresh myself."

She gave Samantha what she hoped was a reassuring smile. "Tell my aunt that I will rejoin the guests now."

The door closed, and Kit closed her eyes for a moment, breathing deeply. When she was ready, she stepped into the hallway, walked slowly past the rooms. At Fletcher's door, she listened briefly. But there were no more sounds. Evidently he and Merilee, for she was sure they had been together in his room, had returned to the guests. Thinking of their tryst made Kit's face flush again, for wasn't she guilty of something similar, only much worse?

By the time she had descended to the crowded rooms below, she had decided that no one would be able to detect her secret. She mingled with the guests, chatting with acquaintances.

Her father passed her and smiled benevolently at her, betraying no curiosity about her whereabouts, for which she breathed a sigh of relief.

She wasn't hungry, but neither did she feel like dancing, so she went to the refreshment room and took a bit of cheese on a plate and a glass of punch. Seeking a seat in some unobtrusive spot, she turned to find Daniel Webster breaking off a conversation with an attractive matron. He spied her and beamed a smile at her.

"Ah, my young hostess. Pray sit with me and partake of your refreshments so that I may have the excuse of resting my legs. I have been standing this last hour."

"Have you not been dancing?" she asked, trying to sound cordial.

"Your Southern gentlemen never think they are too old for dancing," replied the senator. "We who are descended from the Puritans think it a kind of madness to dance after the blush of youth has passed."

She nodded assent, and he took a plate and joined her at a pair of velvet upholstered chairs with a small round corner table between. She relaxed in the privacy of the corner, feeling at ease with Webster's manner.

"Are you enjoying the party, Senator?" she asked.

"It is a distraction, I will admit. Still, I find that even in the drawing room I am easily riled to argument by my noteworthy colleagues who bring to mind issues upon which there is still much disagreement."

He shook his thick head of black hair and sighed. "I fear there is still much work to be done before this country grows into the great nation it perceives itself to be."

Kit suddenly had an idea. Here was a knowledgeable man who might be able to answer some of the questions that rattled around in her head. She had to choose her words carefully lest Webster suspect the reasons for them. So she took refuge in the fact that she was from Georgia.

"I have been wondering about something, Senator Webster," she began. "I believe you can explain the matter to me."

"And what is it now that concerns your lovely head? Still filling it with government problems?"

She gave him a half-smile. "Perhaps. I have been thinking about the matter of the Cherokees in my home state of Georgia. I know only a little of the Cherokees' history."

"Ah, the Cherokees," he said.

"I am of the impression, or at least my father

63

would have me believe, that in ancient days they fought other tribes. And were they not allies of the English during the Revolutionary War?"

"That is true," said Webster. "The former warlords of the Appalachian Highlands have turned into shrewd diplomats in the last quarter-century. Since President Washington had the Cherokees educated and Christianized, they have learned to fight with the white man's own weapons, smooth diplomacy."

She thought of the impeccably attired delegation Red Hawk was with and the heated discussion she had overheard at the President's reception. She turned back to Webster.

"My father has spoken of bloody reprisals every time our government negotiates for more of their land."

Webster raised a dark brow.

"It is not just that negotiations are carried on for more of their land. It is the fact that treaties are often broken, and the Cherokees feel their lands are confiscated anew." He nodded thoughtfully. "I will admit it is a problem. Many in our government mean well and pay fairly for Indian lands. The treasury has paid tens of millions of dollars on lands purchased from Indians, far more than any other nation has paid to a conquered people for lands won or negotiated for. It is inevitable that our civilization will expand, but difficult to do so around those who also claim the same land for their homes. But since I have not dealt much with your Indian question directly, there may be some injustices I have not had the opportunity to examine."

"I see."

She knotted her brows. If the government was playing fair, why did Red Hawk seem so disturbed over the fate of his people, so grim over the prospect of negotiations?

Webster set his plate aside and leaned back in his chair, glad to have a new conversation to sink his teeth into.

"Of course in this case I believe that the Cherokees' argument is not with the United States Government, but with the state of Georgia. After the Cherokee concessions of 1819, the federal government promised that no more land would be required from them. But the state of Georgia has demanded that the United States government enforce the Georgia Compact of 1802, which the Jefferson administration made."

Webster's lawyer's mind remembered all the details even though it was not his state that was involved.

"When Georgia ceded its Crown-granted territory lying westward to the Mississippi to the federal government, the United States government promised to remove all Indians from the state as soon as that could peaceably be achieved upon reasonable terms."

"You mean that the federal government promised the Cherokees in 1819 that they wouldn't have to give up any more land, but it had already promised Georgia in this Compact of 1802 that it would remove the Indians from the state?"

"That is correct. An obvious conflict of interest. Your governor, Gilmer, has threatened several times to take Georgia out of the Union and into war with the United States unless the Indians are bought off and forced to move."

"But what if the Indians don't want to give up their lands?" she said it a bit too quickly and took a sip from her nearly empty glass to hide her interest.

Webster caught some of her passion, but did not question it. He was impressed with the bright mind of the girl, thinking it healthy for women to discuss politics. And it was comforting to him to be able to discuss such issues with the fairer sex now that he was a lonely widower.

"It is all a matter of negotiations. Lands have been set aside west of the Mississippi for the Cherokees. Indeed, some have already moved there."

She frowned again. "Is there enough land for them all?"

Webster eyed her closely. "I do not know, having not seen the deeds myself nor counted the Cherokee population. But tell me, is there a personal interest involved here? Is your family's plantation near the present Cherokee lands?"

"No, well perhaps near. I did not know much about this situation when I was there."

Her face burned, and she feared she had said too much. Webster would be able to read her thoughts. She tried to demur and attempted a smile, which came across more as a look of pleading.

Webster was gentleman enough not to press the girl. She was young and life held drama for her. Looking at her, he was reminded of his daughter Julia, and he wished the two could meet.

Kit glanced around. "I suppose I must see to the rest of the guests. But thank you for taking the time to explain the matter to me. It is difficult to understand such weighty issues."

66

"Indeed," he said, a trace of amusement curving his mouth. "Would that there were more Southerners who were interested enough to examine both sides of a question that involved their own state's rights. It is a pity such a mind as yours cannot be trained for Congress itself."

She knew that he was teasing her, but she didn't mind. Anything to lead him away from the truth. She lifted her chin and returned the twinkling humor.

"Since my father has received a post in government I feel it is my duty to educate myself so that I may speak to those with whom our family will inevitably come in contact."

"Do you plan to remain in Washington and act as your father's hostess?"

"Um, I don't know." She swallowed, then sought a way out of what she had said. "My brother may be married at our home soon. I would, of course, have to return to Wytheridge to prepare for the wedding. After that time, I shall go where I'll be needed most."

He took her hand and patted it. "You must do what you deem is best of course. For my own sake, I hope you continue to brighten the drawing rooms of Washington."

She smiled as they rose together. "Thank you, Senator."

"The pleasure is mine, my dear."

No sooner had she left Senator Webster than she came face to face with Breckenridge Grover. They stared at each other in surprise for a moment, neither able to think of anything appropriate to say.

Kit realized that since she was one of the hostesses

of the party, she could not simply snub him. Although she had nearly forgotten his behavior on the night of the inauguration, she remembered it now. The misunderstanding between them was embarrassing, but she had not thought of how to speak to him if she met him in public.

In a moment Breck got himself under control. The lines around his mouth were stiff, but he gave her a little nod of the head.

"This is a very nice entertainment, Kathryn," he said. "I have offered my congratulations to your father on his post."

"Thank you." She returned the courtesy. "We are very pleased for him."

Perhaps it would not be so difficult to put the unfortunate incident behind them. After all, they did belong to the same circle of friends. For the peace of their social group, they need not mention what had happened, she reasoned. And of course there was no danger that such a thing would ever occur again. She had made herself clear on Breck's proposal. From the two glasses of punch in his hands, she judged that he was already looking in other quarters for feminine companionship.

Breck glanced over her shoulder to the side of the room, and Kit was about to pass by him when he spoke again in a lowered voice.

"I wanted to speak to you," he said, an anxious expression passing over his face briefly. "Now perhaps is not a good time, but I believe it will clear the air between us if we have a few words."

She gave him a nod. "Of course." Apparently he, too, wished to put their relationship back on a friendly footing, if only for the sake of Merilee and Fletcher, their respective best friends.

He seemed relieved. "Good. I am otherwise engaged at present. Perhaps you will join our small group which is attendin' the theater tomorrow night. It is a rare opportunity to see John Philip Kemble and Sarah Siddons. I have heard that the performance of *Macbeth* shows both of their dramatic talents to great advantage."

Though Kit was still greatly distracted, the idea of going to the theater appealed to her. Sitting in a dark theater box, watching the great tragedians might help relax her and take her mind off of herself.

"Yes," she said slowly. "That would be very nice. Who else will be attending?"

"Your brother and Merilee. Also my cousin William, up from New York, and perhaps his sister."

In a group that size, Kit felt she would not be drawn upon too much for conversation. It would be a pleasant evening.

"Yes, of course. Thank you. I would love to join you."

The satisfaction he felt was evident in his eyes. His mouth relaxed, and he puffed up his chest slightly.

"Very good then. Curtain is at seven o'clock. We shall dine afterwards."

She nodded and stepped aside so that he might pass, taking the punch to whoever must be waiting for it.

Following her conversation with Breck, Kit circulated among the guests until eleven o'clock, by which time most people were leaving. Webster, Clay, and Calhoun were among the last to go.

Kit was yawning when Bella marched through the house ordering the additional servants hired for the evening to clean up this and that. It was a relief to climb the stairs, to let Samantha help her out of the new gown and brush her hair. It was only when the maid was putting the gown away that Kit saw the telltale splotch of mud on the scallops that edged the hem. She was about to tell Samantha to have it cleaned off, then she hesitated. She did not want anyone to gossip about how she might have gotten mud on her gown when she had supposedly ventured no farther than the yard during the party. She would find a way to get it off herself.

Kit had been able to shut from her mind what had occurred when she had been alone with Red Hawk, but after Samantha had left her and she had blown out the candle beside her bed, the full weight of her conversation with him came back to her.

She lay on the feather bed and pulled the coverlet up under her chin. Images of the evening faded into the back of her consciousness, leaving only the face of the Indian as it hovered near hers.

She shut her eyes and swallowed. The enormity of what she had done seized her, and confusion washed over her. It was wrong to be alone with such a man, much less feel what she had felt. She must control such feelings.

She tossed in the bed, unable to sleep, trying to think of familiar things in order to bring herself back from her recklessness. She had told Red Hawk she would ride by Rock Creek tomorrow, but of course that was out of the question. She must forget him and return to a normal routine.

70

She was going to the theater tomorrow night. She would spend the day looking forward to it. Even now, as she gave up on sleep and opened her eyes to the dark room, she tried to concentrate on what she would wear. But thoughts of her gowns simply spun in her head like the kaleidoscopes with which the children played. In spite of her determination her mind came back again and again to Red Hawk's gentle touch on her arms, to his breath feathering her forehead, to the powerful masculinity she had sensed in his limbs. These were forbidden fantasies, but powerful, and as she became drowsy, sensations lulled her until she floated in dreamy pleasure.

In the morning Kit rose and sat at her dressing table longer than usual. When Samantha came to lay out her clothes, Kit was still indecisive as to what to wear. She had looked at the riding habit several times and had tried to turn her attention to a muslin day dress instead. But when Samantha opened the clothes press to lay out clothing, it was the riding habit Kit pointed to.

Chiding herself all the while for the aberration that was making her dress to go out so early, she nevertheless put on tricot drawers, riding boots, white ruched shirt, masculine-style neckcloth, and the mauve riding habit with its extremely full skirt and tightly fitting jacket with velvet collar. With the full leg-of-mutton sleeves, the masculine top hat, and dark gauze veil, she realized as she looked at herself in the mirror, that she appeared quite fashionable.

An image of her usual modest attire at home in

Georgia passed through her mind, and she shook her head in amusement. These fine clothes had all been purchased on their arrival in Washington City, when Jonathan Newcomb felt that the appearance of his family would have something to do with his attaining the place in government he desired. As if it would matter to President Andrew Jackson what Jonathan's family wore. From what she had heard of the man's backwoods past, she could not imagine that it would, and besides, he had only glimpsed Fletcher and herself for a few moments before giving their father his assignment.

But Kit was not averse to pretty things. It was just that unless someone else helped her pick them out, she was at a loss as to city clothes. At home, she had altered many of her mother's gowns for dressy affairs, which were few and far between, and in any case, there fashion did not matter very much. Georgia landowners were still struggling for a day-to-day living, except for the few wealthy ones in the southern part of the state, who had an army of slaves to do the work for them. At Wytheridge, Kit was sure that she worked as hard as the slaves did.

She set the silk top hat and veil aside and went down to breakfast. Fletch looked up from brushing crumbs off his shirt front.

"Going out?" he asked.

"Yes," she replied.

Then inspiration came. Aunt Ruby would not think it proper for her to go out unaccompanied. But if she could lure Fletch into joining her and then suggest he fetch Merilee, she ought to have no trouble leaving them alone for a while.

"I had hoped you would come with me," said Kit. "We could ask Merilee to join us."

The suggestion brought a secretive smile to his face. "As long as Father doesn't need me. I've been helping him catch up on some of his correspondence."

Kit did not press. She took a plate from the sideboard and helped herself to eggs and potatoes from the steamy serving dishes. Then she sat down across from her brother.

"Of course," she said.

She gave him a look that conveyed her knowledge of his wish to be with Merilee, then looked at her plate, leaving it to his imagination to follow the rest of her plans.

Fletcher wasted no time in changing into double-breasted riding jacket with long tails, top hat, and muffler tied loosely around his neck. Ruby's groom, Hiram, saddled two riding horses and helped Kit into a sidesaddle.

The day was again sunny, and the spring weather did much to lift Kit's spirits, helping her to assure herself that she had done the right thing.

They dismounted at Merilee's and waited in the drawing room for her to change. Kit found herself quite impatient. She itched to pace the room, but dared not, for Fletch lounged on a sofa reading a circular.

Finally Merilee came down, elegantly attired in a riding habit of burgundy and velvet. Her horse had been saddled while she was dressing, so at long last they were on their way.

They had started riding through the streets toward

the Potomac, but at the point where they must turn, Kit spoke up.

"I fancy going to Georgetown," she said. "I have not been there but twice since we arrived in the city."

Then, seeing the surprised look on Fletch's face, she added, "They say Rock Creek is very lovely and idyllic. Much of it is still in its natural state, since Washington City only goes to its eastern edge. Would it not be fun to . . . to look at the shops in Georgetown and then ride by the creek after luncheon?"

Fletch was quick to catch on. He glanced at Merilee, and Kit thought she saw him moisten his lips. If it weren't for Fletch's own eagerness, he might more readily have noticed the nervousness with which Kit made her suggestion.

"What do you think, Merilee?" he said as if the idea greatly appealed to him. "It is a fine day for an outing."

Merilee smiled at her intended. "I am sure the shops have many interesting things to look at. And as to the creek, I have never seen it."

"Good," said Fletch, as if it had been his idea in the first place. "Then that is where we will go."

Chapter Five

Kit allowed herself a trace of amusement. She was still unsure of her own plan, but watching Fletch around Merilee was like looking at a peacock, fluffing out its feathers in order to attract the female.

A good turnpike had been built between Washington City and the older settlement of Georgetown, and they passed many travelers on the road. As they approached the hills of Georgetown, Kit's nervousness grew. She knew she should abandon her idea of seeing Red Hawk, while on the other hand she knew that if she were to see him, she would need to get Fletcher and Merilee to go off alone together. It was not until they had reached the busy town and were riding through the traffic going to and from the canal that inspiration struck.

As they headed toward the shops on the main thoroughfare, Kit turned to her brother.

"I thought I would browse for a present for Aunt Ruby," she said. "And I might like to buy something to take back to Ossie Lee." She referred to their housekeeper at Wytheridge. Though a servant, the woman was practically part of the family, having been their mother's nanny before she came to Wytheridge.

"Perhaps you and Merilee would prefer to spend some time alone," said Kit so that only Fletcher could hear.

She saw the color that tinged his cheekbones and knew he struggled as to whether or not this would be proper.

"Father wouldn't like you to be unchaperoned," he said stiffly.

Kit was certain he was dying for her to break down that argument. The temptation of taking Merilee off alone would be too great for Fletch to worry about decorum.

She shrugged casually. "I will surely be all right in the shops. And I will sit in that inn over there and have a cup of tea and something to eat if I get tired. Why don't we meet there in two hours?"

Two hours would be time enough for Fletch and Merilee to find some isolated spot and plan their future together. Fletch seemed to reach the same conclusion.

"Are you sure you will be all right?" he asked, taking off his top hat and shaking his crop of red hair.

She smiled. "Perfectly. I think I'll just ride to the end of the street and decide where to shop first. There's a livery stable behind this street. I can leave the horse there."

Adventure and an attempt at decorum warred for a moment in Fletch's face before the former won.

Then he grinned at Merilee who had ridden up beside him.

"All right. We will meet you at the inn two hours from now."

He explained the plan to Merilee; then they turned their horses to follow the road back along the canal, which provided many interesting sights.

Kit paid attention to the way they went, not wanting to double back on them. Her heart pounding, she urged her horse forward at a slow walk, passing her eyes over the shop fronts and shingles indicating the businesses of the town. But she paid little attention to what she saw.

When she reached the end of the street, she urged her horse along more quickly, circling through the backstreets of the town. She still told herself that she might not see Red Hawk. They had not set a time. He might be tied up with the delegation. Nevertheless, she felt a sense of excitement as she crossed the bridge over Rock Creek, passed the stone that marked the boundary between Georgetown and Washington City, and turned the horse from the main byway and trotted onto the softer soil of a narrow path beside the creek.

The rock-girt stream flowed between high, wooded banks rising above Georgetown. On these a park had been cleared and partially landscaped. She followed the winding creek, gazing at the green clearings, occasionally spying grapevines on the banks, ripe with fruit.

The countryside refreshed Kit in any case and she realized how shackled she had felt in Washington. She was interested in government, but there was too much love of nature and green hilly woodlands in her to allow her to remain satisfied for long in the staid drawing rooms of the capital. Being in the park reminded her of the way she felt at Wytheridge when she rode out alone into the lush green woodlands.

Then she saw him. His horse was drinking from the cool water in the creek, and there was no mistaking the flowing black hair, hunting shirt, buckskin leggings, and high, fringed deerskin boots.

Though the danger still lurked in her heart, she watched intently as Red Hawk turned his head and observed her approach. His features remained fixed, and she drew rein at first, feeling hesitant. But her horse bobbed its head and whinnied, sensing the other horse and not understanding why they were stopping. She gave her mount its head and moved forward, straightening her back. If she were going to speak to Red Hawk it would not do to show embarrassment. She summoned pride to match his own.

When she was near enough she could see the pleasure in his dark eyes, the gentleness of his sensual mouth. Then he pulled his horse's head back from the water.

He met her on the path, and for a moment neither spoke, but Red Hawk turned his mount to ride beside her as if in perfect understanding and harmony.

Tongue-tied though Kit felt, she must say something, she told herself, so she stole a sideways glance at him and spoke.

"You did not have trouble getting away from your meetings today?" she asked.

He drew down the corners of his mouth as if he hated to be reminded of the reason he was in the city.

"The meetings go on. I can do nothing to change your president's mind. John Ross is better than I at negotiations. I have heard him present his arguments, but I fear his words fall on deaf ears. For myself, I feel our work is done here. My place is with my people."

She nodded. They rode for a bit, ducking to avoid several branches. Finally she formed the questions that had been in her mind.

"I would like to know more about your people. I knew nothing of them at home except that they lived in the mountains."

He gave a half-grunt. "For many generations our people were not a problem to the white man's state of Georgia because cotton could not be grown in our hills. Now they've found gold on our lands, and they sneak across the rivers at night to steal soil so that they may pan it for gold the next day."

She frowned, remembering what Daniel Webster had told her. "So I understand."

She still felt lost and ignorant. She had come to Washington City to learn about the workings of this great nation, but here she was, riding beside a descendant of one of the native peoples of this land, and she didn't know enough about his people to even try to speak.

Fortunately Red Hawk now seemed disposed to talk without prompting.

"Time after time the white man has broken his word to the Indian people. My forefathers would say

79

our lands were given us eons ago by Asga-Ya-Galun-lati and are therefore considered sacred. But our lands have shrunk from the many thousands of square miles we once occupied to half that. Most of them lie in your white state of Georgia."

He tossed his proud head. "All your people care about is the gold. They do not know how the Indian gains strength from the earth. This strength cannot be measured in white man's dollars."

Kit swallowed. How could she tell him that her own father was one of the men who wanted the Indians removed from Georgia in the name of progress?

"Have not many of your people already left for lands in the West?" she asked.

Red Hawk gave her an angry look and then spit on the ground.

"If we move westward, what is to stop the white man from coming along someday and wanting that land too? Will they move us westward until there is nowhere to go but into the ocean? No. Honor is everything. The Cherokee long ago gave up the life of the hunter for the settled life of the farmer. We learned from the white man's schools, took up the white man's plough, his religion; wrote down our own laws as your people do. All this we did to gain your government's respect. But in vain do we do these things. The white man has made us live in his fashion; therefore, he must allow us to live beside him. I will return and keep the gold-hungry white man out of Cherokee lands."

They had stopped the horses, and Kit watched emotion fire his eyes, determination ripple through him. Her own heart strained at her ribs, but she had no reply for him. The Indians were a strange people. She still did not quite understand how she had come to meet this one, yet she could not draw herself away.

She stared at Red Hawk until his face seemed to soften. The militant expression gradually faded as he drew himself back from some distant scene and gradually became aware of their peaceful surroundings. The skin, stretched taut over the planes of his face, began to relax. He threw a leg over his horse's neck and dismounted. Then he ducked under his horse's head and reached for Kit's bridle, waiting for her to dismount.

Again warring factions rippled through her. Her white Georgia blood fought with her desire to know more about the man before her. She could turn her back on him and ride away, returning to the life that was cut out for the daughter of a Georgia landholder. No, she could not. Red Hawk's eyes were too deep. His challenge was too great.

She removed her foot from the stirrup and, as he held his arms to catch her, slid downward. Once she had her footing, he released his hold on her waist. Then he untied a blanket he had rolled behind his saddle and carried it over his arm as he led the way along the footpath. She could tell by the way he walked beside her that he was not forcing her to stay. It was not his will that kept her there. She had to realize it was her own choice.

She glanced around them. Red Hawk had chosen to stop in a small clearing shielded from the rest of the park by a thick cover of woods. The creek beside them ran swiftly with the melted snows from the hills above them. Tiny buds strained to push outward on the twigs of the sturdy elms.

Confusion still raged within her. She sensed the intimacy that washed over them, as if they were both children of the nature that surrounded them. She was drawn to Red Hawk. Whether it be aberration or the curiosity born of her desire to stretch beyond the limits of her own life, she could not tell. She had come to Washington to explore the heartbeat of the nation. In Washington City, black man, white and red rubbed shoulders in their cry for equality, even though it was obvious that some might be more equal than others.

Was that what she wanted to know from the strange man walking beside her? His words on injustice to his people? But she was even more aware of the excitement she felt at being near this man. Perhaps that was due to the enigma of him. There was something wild and arrogant in his bearing, yet his speech was articulate. His passion was not the passion of a savage. It was laced with logic. His emotion was not based on greed but concern for his people. His compassion touched her.

Red Hawk found a patch of dry grass halfway between the creek and the rail fence that delineated the edge of the park and spread the blanket. He sat down on it cross-legged and gestured that she should join him there in the sun.

She, too, sat down on the blanket. It felt good to stretch her legs out before her, and she bent a little, stretching her back. Then she sat up straight and tucked one leg under her. She did not know how to

82

begin a casual conversation, so she reverted to the political one that had brought them together.

"Is it likely that your people will get to keep their homelands, or will they have to relinquish part of them?" she asked tentatively.

Red Hawk's face clouded, and he thrust his chin forward as he reached out to pick up a reed from the ground.

"I will fight to keep them," he said. "I will die if necessary."

Her heart clutched at the image of brave Indians being killed, and she wished there might be some compromise. Perhaps they could share part of their lands in Georgia—enough to pacify the gold hunters. She suggested as much to Red Hawk. But he shook his head in scorn.

"My brothers are fools to believe the white man's lies. It is not only land the white man wants because of the gold in the ground in Georgia, it is the Cherokees' integrity he wants to destroy."

Red Hawk had little respect for most white men, seeing them as two-faced hypocrites who had religion on Sunday, but killed, cheated, and lied to their own brothers on other days.

"We offered to share our lands once long ago. We welcomed your people then, hoping to learn from them. But time and again we have been cheated. We have signed treaties, each time giving up more land, and now we will not give up any more.

"We are a proud conquered people," he went on in a lower voice. "Though the white man has degraded us. The white man has called the Indian soulless, even though the missionaries have forced your religion on us. But the old ways are better."

Kit sat in silence for a time. If he hated white people so, why was she here? To be a whipping boy for his resentment at how her people had treated his? She wanted to learn from him, but the stream of venom that poured forth from him was not likely to teach her anything except the bitter hatred that existed between their two races. She felt herself draw inward as she sat stiffly, not looking to him.

Red Hawk sensed her withdrawal and watched her out of the corner of his eye. He did not know why he was telling her so much. It was not to speak of the old arguments that he had brought her here. But it took him some moments to cool his anger so he could observe the soft beauty that attracted him to her. She had a directness, an honesty that was yet unspoiled. Her questions had riled him, but he knew she would not learn if he continued to rave. No, she deserved the chance to be told the facts in a more gentle way.

But why teach a white woman of the ways and thoughts of his people? He himself had said the white race was evil and hypocritical. But even as he'd said it, he knew there were exceptions. There were white missionaries such as Samuel Worcester in his own village of New Echota. Worcester had refused to take an oath to support the constitution of the state of Georgia, and he encouraged the Cherokee to stay on their lands. There were a few white men who cared.

Red Hawk attempted to quell his anger while he looked at the bright flower beside him. He could not explain why he wanted to reach for her in the same way he might want to pick a blossom whose scent and beauty he longed to hold near. Perhaps it was because she was the salve he needed to make him forget his troubles. For there were times he wished to sate his senses in a woman's flesh.

He thought briefly of Standing Doe, a woman of his nation who loved him. He had sampled her soft flesh, had satisfied his body with her, but he knew now he did not want her. Standing Doe's soul was poisoned, and it threatened Red Hawk's spirit. For a woman was more than flesh and soft bosom. She was solace in time of need, a staff to support a warrior. The image of Standing Doe reaching out for him faded as the sight of the woman next to him replaced it. He reached for Kit's hand slowly, the way he might extend a hand to a shy deer that would run away if one moved too fast. His strong hand closed around her cool one, and he held it.

Kit's heart jumped into her throat. She was powerless against the charm working on her. In his touch was the sensation of strength she longed to taste. She knew her body's responses to his nearness were wrong. Some would call it sinful, but the temptation was too great. Destiny had cast her to him on that night she had run from Breckenridge, a man of her own kind—a man she found revolting.

And now she longed to see into the soul of the red man who held her hand. She dared not raise her eyes, but she hungered for his gaze on her face, his soft breath on her cheek.

Her heart beat quickly as she sought for words. Perhaps she could still the racing of her pulse if she talked to him. If she heard him speak, perhaps that would satisfy her terrible need to appease the flesh.

"I . . . I would like to hear more . . . about your ways," she said, dimly remembering him speak of them. "What are these old ways that you mentioned?"

Red Hawk was pleased by her question. He saw the struggle in her soul and determined to move slowly. His own loins throbbed with desire, but it was a desire that communed with the nature around them, with the life of the universe of which he and she were a part.

He picked up a small stone that lay in the grass and held it in the palm of his hand.

"The white man thought the Indians worshipped the stone," he began. Then he moved his head from left to right. "The Indians do not worship the stone. We use the stone to remind us of the oneness of all creatures of the universe and of the spiritual energy that flows through all things."

He looked toward Kit's face. "The wisdom of life is learned from the greatest teacher, Mother Earth. The Indians seek harmony of man with the universe in the way of the rainbow, the waterfall, and the sunrise in which ugliness is impossible."

She turned her face to meet his, her words a mere whisper as she watched his lips.

"Your words are beautiful," she said.

He raised his fingers to touch her cheek, his eyes burning into her face.

"As you are beautiful. A child of nature."

Her lips trembled as she knew what was about to happen. But her spirit rose. This time with Red

Hawk would be her secret. She would tell no one because no one else would understand. This was something she had to know for herself. Her spirit would not rest until she knew the mystery of this man's touch. Her heart longed for it, and she knew it would not be denied.

He sat near her, finding it harder and harder to keep his hands from straying. His eyes longed to penetrate the material of her dress, and at last he let one hand move to the back of her hair, seeking the cool flesh of her neck beneath the spring of red curls. She did not resist as he gently pulled her toward him, so that their lips met in softness.

Kit leaned toward him, and when his tongue opened her lips and touched hers, the fire leapt up in him. But he moved slowly, savoring the new taste and feel of her. He used discipline to prevent the energy he felt from running away too quickly.

Pleasure flowed through Kit as she returned his kiss. Her hand tentatively reached for his shoulder and glided around his neck. She felt his energy infuse her, and her heart sang at his nearness. She did not understand it, but she felt as if they were meant to be together. His slow sureness gained her trust. Her soul fused with his, and she shut her eyes to the world around them so that there was nothing in her consciousness but the two of them.

Red Hawk reveled in the pliant form in his arms. His fingers explored her waist, her back. When he could wait no longer, he placed both hands on her shoulders and looked down at her bosom, seeing her ragged breathing.

In spite of his resolve, his fingers found their way to

the bodice of her jacket, and as he gazed at the curve of her bosom, he managed to unfasten the cloth buttons. He opened the jacket and sought the fastenings of the white shirt beneath. Kit herself unwound the neckcloth. Then slowly he pushed aside blouse and jacket until her shoulders were exposed. The lacings of her corset beckoned to his fingers, and as she did not move, he gently pulled the ties until the corset sprang apart at the top, allowing him to feast his eyes on her round breasts.

Kit could not move, spellbound by his movements, his touch. The sensuality was overpowering and whetted her appetite for more, causing sensations in her she had never even imagined. She supposed what she was doing was wrong, but the purity of him, the sun warming her flesh, these could not be so wrong. And the soaring place where he took her heart was not wrong. Red Hawk's touch was gentle. She closed her eyes, letting him work his magic on her delicate skin, the fire of his touch racing from the tips of her breasts to the spring within her and throughout all her limbs.

But Red Hawk knew he had done enough, seen enough. He must control his desire to taste more of her. He would bind her to him slowly, make her his own. To move too quickly would be to drive his white flower away. This was enough pleasure to dwell on for now. More pleasure than he had ever experienced, for her white complexion was like the freshness of dawn, her skin fine and delicate, her red hair like the fire that burned his fingers, and her clear blue eyes like a sparkling lake.

Red Hawk prided himself on his self-control,

which made erotic pleasure, when it came, all the sweeter.

He closed the material over her breasts, laying his hand over them once more, then he pulled her against him, devouring her mouth in a kiss. Her arms wrapped around him, and he held her, his tongue probing, then his lips caressing her cheek, her forehead, her ear as her ragged breathing gradually began to slow.

Kit was lost in the whirlwind of emotions for some time, but only as Red Hawk cradled her did her mind and body gradually begin to return to earth. She took several deep breaths, looked down at her disheveled costume and pulled the cloth together.

Then suddenly she became aware of how long a time they had spent together. She sprang away so suddenly it startled Red Hawk.

"My brother," she said by way of explanation as she fumbled with her buttons. "I promised to meet him in two hours' time."

Red Hawk looked at the sun above them, judging how long they had been in the clearing. He smiled in amusement as she arranged her clothing, reaching for the white cloth to wind it about her neck.

They stood, and Kit replaced her hat as Red Hawk folded the blanket. Then he held her hand and led her back to the horses.

Now she felt too embarrassed to look at him. Her head throbbed as she realized what they had done. Surely he would think less of her for having been so foolish. The enormity of her lapse was so great that she refused to consider it further. She concentrated on getting back to Fletch. That was enough to worry about at the moment.

Kit rode ahead of Red Hawk, her face burning, her hair trailing out from beneath the hat. She did not speak, but watched the trail until they came to the bridge over Rock Creek and passed onto the main road.

Red Hawk sensed her embarrassment and he understood. The white woman was prey to the strict rulings of her own society. She had the seeds of nature within her, but she had been taught to reject them for so long that as she approached her own kind again, her fears would overcome her senses. But he did not think she would keep from him for long. He pulled his horse in beside hers, not looking at her as he spoke.

"I will return to the city by way of the hills. My horse needs exercise. You will return to the town and your brother."

She lowered her head, glancing at him only from the side. Then she gave a little nod and urged her horse forward.

She did not look behind her to see how long Red Hawk sat astride his horse, watching her. But she sensed that he finally did turn. She rode slowly into Georgetown, keeping to the quiet residential streets for a time. Surely her face and her thoughts would give her away. She was glad for the veil attached to the hat she wore. She could say that she was keeping it over her face to protect her skin from the sun.

She neared the business district where housewives were returning from market with baskets of produce. Workmen wheeled barrows of bricks to a new building site, and pigs roaming the streets squealed as a team of horses drawing a heavy wagon forced them to stop foraging in the middle of the road.

Kit found the livery stable and dismounted on a block. Then she led her horse in. A stableman set down a pitchfork and looked up.

"Good afternoon, miss," he said. "Leaving your horse?"

"Only for a little while. I am to meet my brother at the inn."

The man came forward and took the reins from her. "I'll give your mount some food and water and rub her down for you."

She nodded as he named the fee, and then repeated that she would not be long. The stableman decided the horse must have been ridden some distance; if it had not, she would merely have tied her mount in front of the inn while she took her refreshment.

Kit did not tell the man her real reason for wanting the horse rubbed down — that it must look to her brother as if she had spent the whole morning in town with her mount in the stable.

She hurried around the corner and down the street. Then she forced herself into a slow walk. She stopped in front of a shop and stared in the window, hardly aware of the goods inside. If Fletch or Merilee saw her, they must think that she had gotten involved in shopping and had forgotten the time. Then, seeing a tall clock by the door of the shop she stood before, she noted it was just noon. She was not late.

Breathing deeply in relief, she turned from the shop and waited for some of the carriages and riders to pass before stepping into the street. Walking where there was the least mud, she negotiated the thoroughfare and stepped onto the sidewalk on the other side. She glanced around slowly, but still saw no sign of Fletch or Merilee and so went on to the inn.

It was an old one, having been established for travelers going from the port of Georgetown to points along the turnpike to Baltimore. Kit stepped into the beamed entryway, adjusting her eyes to the dim light inside. A gentleman and lady were settling up with the landlord as Kit glanced toward the refreshment room to her left.

"May I help you, miss?" The landlord moved away from his desk and gave her a polite nod.

"I am to meet my brother and his . . . fiancée here."

The jovial landlord smiled. "If your brother is blessed with an even brighter color of hair than yourself, and if his lady casts him dark, mysterious looks, then I believe you are in luck. The pair took refreshment some time ago and are relaxing in one of the corners there."

"Oh," she said. "I hope I have not kept them waiting."

The landlord raised a bushy eyebrow and gave Kit a sly grin. "If I am any judge of such matters, I do not think they have minded the wait."

Kit blushed at the implication and then entered the room that served as tavern, dining room, and waiting room for travelers and weary shoppers alike.

A buxom girl served ale to two men who were bent in deep discussion. Beyond them, a heavyset woman sat snoring on the windowseat, her head to the side and her eyes closed, packages stacked by her side.

Kit heard Merilee's giggle and then a smart slap of palm against cheek. A grunt followed, and the rustle of clothing. These sounds led her to the high-backed chairs in the corner. She stopped a few feet from them and cleared her throat.

Merilee popped up, her dark eyes wide, a blush on her cheek. Fletch stuck his head around the chair more slowly.

"Kit," said Merilee. "There you are."

"I, uh, hope I haven't kept you waiting," she said, removing her hat.

She did not fear for the heat in her own cheeks in this light, and she realized that if anything might save her from her brother's and Merilee's speculations on her own activities it would be their preoccupation with their own affair.

"Why, no," Merilee said, still sounding a little breathless. "The landlord recommended we try a spiced drink and then left us alone to talk."

Fletch stood, brushing his wrinkled coat. "Did you have a nice time?" he asked his sister.

She swallowed, but managed a bright smile and nodded. "I found the shops fascinating, but alas, I could not choose what to buy. I am afraid I shall have to come again, now that I know what they offer, so that I might pick out the right gifts before our return to Wytheridge."

At the mention of Wytheridge something passed between Fletch and Merilee. His face seemed to flush, and he took Merilee's hand.

"Sit down, Kathryn," he said. "Merilee and I have something to tell you."

Kit repressed her amusement at his use of her formal name. When Fletch tried to act like a man in charge she always wanted to laugh. He had some of the mannerisms of her father, but in him they came off so boyish that she always saw through his attempts at maturity and respectability. Nevertheless, she moved around them and sat in a worn leather seat opposite them, understanding that what they were about to say should be received with the formality it deserved.

Merilee and Fletch sat down, both looking grave. Then Fletch cleared his throat.

"I have asked Miss Fitzsimmons for her hand in marriage."

Kit smiled. Had she expected anything else?

"And she has accepted," he went on.

Kit beamed at them. "Why that's wonderful."

She rose and hugged Merilee, whose tears she felt on her cheek.

"I'm so glad," she said, holding the bride-to-be away from her. "Father will be happy, I am sure."

"Do you think so?" asked Merilee, momentary concern as to how she would be accepted crossing her face.

Kit winked at her brother, who tried not to let his own elation overpower the dignity he was trying to put on the occasion.

"Of course," she said.

Then she felt a momentary twinge in her heart. How lucky were these two to have their love blessed by all that was familiar to them. It made her own secret actions with the defiant Red Hawk that much more shameful, something she must banish from her mind.

But she tried to keep her expression one of joy.

"When will the wedding be?"

Merilee glowed, looking at Fletch and taking his hand again.

"It will be at Wytheridge. Merilee wishes to be married in her new home," he stated proudly.

"How wonderful," Kit said. Again she felt the tightness of envy in her chest. How proper for such a marriage. How fortunate that the two of them had come together so felicitously.

"Our house will be blessed with your presence, Merilee," she said, sounding rather formal herself.

But Merilee was too full of her own excitement to notice that Kit was somewhat reserved.

"I shall try to make myself a useful . . . wife," she said, swallowing and clasping Kit's hands. "But I shall need you there to tell me what to do. I mean it is your home."

Kit saw that Merilee was trying to reassure her that she would in no way usurp Kit's position, but at the moment, that was the least of Kit's concerns. Merilee rambled on.

"I mean you must live there for as long as you want to, until you marry I imagine."

Until I marry, thought Kit in confusion. And when will that be? And to whom? Surely not to an Indian who has gazed this very day intimately upon my breasts?

She flushed in shame and hoped that the radiant couple took her embarrassment to be that of youthful confusion for their happy state.

She hugged Merilee again and then Fletch, who returned her embrace with surprise, for she rarely displayed tender emotions to him so openly. But the gestures gave Kit time to compose herself.

Finally she sat back again. "Then I will return to Wytheridge as soon as possible to prepare for the wedding."

She had already told their father that she wished to return home, and she realized that she had been right to do so. It would be an escape from the Indian who would forevermore haunt Washington City for her. She would not be able to see a street corner or a stately building, not even the gleaming Potomac, without being reminded of where they had met.

She had risked something to meet Red Hawk today, to taste with daring what it was like to be with such a man. But even as she had done it, she had known that it would remain a secret and could not happen again. For if it did, she would be lost.

"Yes," she said, reinforcing her decision. "It will be good to go home."

Chapter Six

Kit had nearly forgotten that she had promised to go to the theater that evening, but Fletch reminded her.

"We shall celebrate this very night," he said to the two girls. "We shall have champagne before the theater."

"Oh, wonderful," said Merilee.

"Oh yes," said Kit, coming to her senses. "We had best get home then directly after lunch, or we shall never be ready."

"Yes, lunch," said Merilee. "We saw a dining room in that little hotel we passed down by the wharf. Let's eat there."

"A capital idea," said Fletch. He had brought ready cash for just such an eventuality, and he did not consider the tavern they were in fit enough for an engagement celebration. He took each lady on his arm and led them out of the inn.

They repaired to the hotel dining room that Fletch and Merilee had spied and found the noon repast refreshing. Then they returned to fetch their horses from the livery stable and rode back along the turnpike to Washington.

Once Kit felt a prickling at the back of her neck and turned to look at the hills behind them. She saw a spot of color flash between the trees in the woods and thought that perhaps Red Hawk was watching their progress. The deep trembling began within her again, and she had to force her mind away from the dangerous thoughts that had led her into his arms. She should feel ashamed, but she was aware of the thrill the memory brought her. She shut her eyes and bit her lips. She must forget. Perhaps the evening at the theater would help her to put it from her mind.

She opened her eyes again, remembering with a dip in spirit that Breckenridge Grover would be with their group. She tried not to hold a grudge against Breckenridge, but she could not help but compare the way his rough grasp had made her feel to the excitement of Red Hawk's light touch.

She glanced at Merilee who was riding happily by Fletch's side. Surely Merilee could not have experienced any such thing with Fletcher. Kit could see that they had eyes only for each other, but she just could not imagine how her cocky brother could arouse anything close to passion in anyone.

Kit succeeded better than she had expected in occupying her mind with dressing and letting Samantha do up her hair high on her head. She added a black shawl to the lavender dress she had worn for the party, and when Fletch knocked on her door to tell her that the party awaited them downstairs, she thought he looked quite the dandy in ruffled shirt, high neck-stock, black evening dress and green satin waistcoat.

He came into her room and examined her appearance, his mind already elsewhere. In fact, from his manner he seemed a little nervous.

"Are you ready, sister?"

"I am." She took note of his distracted look. "Will you make the announcement, then?"

His eyes widened as if she had looked into his mind.

"Yes, I must."

"Come now, Fletch," she scoffed. "This afternoon you were only too thrilled to have persuaded Merilee to marry you. Why this sudden agitation?"

He cleared his throat and tried to act as if nothing were the matter. "I suppose I can stand a bit of teasing from my peers."

Then, more seriously, he said, "It is rather a responsibility when you think of it. In a few years I will have a family saddled to me."

She exhaled in exasperation. "Well, what would you rather do? Go to endless parties as a bachelor until you are too old for any eligible women to look at you? Fletch, stop worrying. Merilee will be quite happy at Wytheridge once she gets used to it."

She hoped that was true. She had tried to warn Merilee that Wytheridge was not a wealthy Southern plantation with hundreds of slaves to wait on her every whim. She had made it clear that Fletch's wife

99

would be required to work as well as manage the servants they did have. Nonetheless, if Merilee loved Fletch enough, Kit supposed she would not mind.

She swallowed, such thoughts bringing that unwanted twinge to her heart. Then she tried to tease her brother out of his mood, and by the time they descended the stairs together, he seemed more his jovial self.

Breck was in the downstairs drawing room entertaining another young couple with some story, but he broke off when Fletch and Kit appeared.

"There he is, the man of the hour. Your secret is out, old man. You cannot keep such news to yourself for long. May I be the first to offer congratulations."

He pumped his friend's hand, and Fletch looked relieved that he did not tease him. Then Fletch introduced the other couple, Breck's cousin, William, and his sister, Jane, to Kit. They all wanted to hear about the plans for the wedding, so Kit was not called upon to speak.

When they were ready to don their wraps, Breck held Kit's, a gesture she accepted politely. He met her gaze briefly, but did no more than offer his hand once they were outside and getting into the carriage. Kit sought refuge in the formal outing. The others' chatter saved her from too much introspection, yet allowed her not to have to think of clever conversation.

It was a short distance to the theater that had been built several years ago so that Washington's society could partake of the entertainers that traveled throughout the country, some with small companies of actors to help them create their spectacles.

As Caleb pulled the carriage to the bottom of the steps and a footman opened the door for them to get out, Kit saw that this evening's program was indeed popular. Already, gentlemen and ladies were climbing the wide steps to the mezzanine that led to the boxes, and crowds were jostling in at the side doors for seats in the pit.

Once inside, an usher showed them to their box. After a brief discussion of who would sit where, Kit found herself in the front row of the box between William and Breck. Then William and his sister traded places, for which Kit was thankful, thinking that a little visit with the newcomer might keep her from any awkward moments with Breck.

She pointed out members of the government she recognized, and Jane expressed her excitement to be in the capital city.

Their box was the fourth one back from the stage, offering them an excellent view. Jane commented that she had been to the Park Theater in New York several times, but that this one was every bit as well ornamented and seemed to be arranged so that none of the seats had an obstructed view.

When the conversation lagged, Kit caught Breck's glance. He cleared his throat but said nothing, straightening a cuff and looking over the crowd.

Kit was thankful when the gas lights at last dimmed, and the curtain-raiser act began. She found that she was paying less attention to the music and dance on the stage than she was to her own predicament. The house was not completely dark, and she could still observe the audience, seeing it for the first time as if with new eyes. She thought of the group of friends she was with and reminded herself that this was her culture; these were her people. She wondered if the members of all the other theater parties in the house were complacent about their lives, thinking nothing more than that they were enjoying an evening out.

Of course the politicians would probably not put aside their work entirely, no matter how distracting the play. But for them, such an evening provided relief from the constant cares of running the government or jockeying for a better position. She wondered suddenly if President Jackson ever came to the theater. Not now, perhaps, while he was still in mourning for his late wife, but when he became more used to the routine of office and was able to socialize again he probably would.

She did not know why her thoughts turned to President Jackson. She remembered that Red Hawk had said he did not expect the President to side with the Cherokees. Of course Jackson was known as a great Indian fighter.

Indian fighter. The phrase was a common one, denoting men who took the lead in conquering the great wilderness that was now a part of the United States.

She shut her eyes. If she had never met Red Hawk, she might never have given any thought to the Indians' situation. If she had stayed home in Georgia, she would have heard rumblings over states' rights and might have been aware of the negotiations with the Indians over the lands that had the gold, but something was happening to her now that she did not know how to face.

She had come to Washington City, excited at the prospect that because of her father's close involvement with General Jackson she herself might learn at close hand something about the running of the government. To what use she could put that knowledge she did not exactly know. Women did not have any say in government, but a woman could help her father or her husband think out the ideas he presented to other politicians and could in some small way help him reach decisions.

Sitting in the dimly lit theater, Kit knew that she must put distance between her experience with Red Hawk and her own life. He had said his people had been unfairly treated. Perhaps she could find out why. Perhaps she could get her father, who had influence with the Georgia legislature, to do something about it.

But the moment she allowed the hopeful thought to express itself, the reality of her father's views on Indians asserted itself. She had heard him comment often enough that the white man was taking over the country so that he could teach the lesser races. The white man's advance meant progress; Jonathan Newcomb did not consider a man of any other color an individual who might have feelings . . . or passions of his own.

Breck moved restlessly in his seat at her side, and Kit glanced up. The curtain raiser was over and the scenery was being changed for the main fare. She glanced at the playbill on her lap.

"Did you enjoy the act?"

Breck's question was so sudden it startled Kit.

"Oh, of course."

Breck leaned closer to her, a skeptical eyebrow raised.

"I could swear from the frown on your face that you disliked it. Either that or you were thinking of something else entirely."

Her face warmed, and she fiddled with her gloves. When she answered him, her voice came out rather strained and high pitched.

"It is distracting, is it not, to simply sit and let whatever thoughts come to one's mind float in and out."

He gave an unconvincing chuckle. "Perhaps."

Members of the audience wandered up and down the aisle before again finding their seats for the tragedy that was about to begin. Once again the house lights dimmed, and Kit determined to maintain an expression less revealing.

The audience applauded the appearance of John Philip Kemble, who was clad in a costume meant to suggest some period of antiquity, though not specifically. For some time Kit's attention was held by the great actor's dignity. His style of acting was measured, commanding, and powerful, and in spite of her earlier preoccupations, she was drawn into the play.

But it was Sarah Siddons' emotional rendering of Lady Macbeth that moved her most. When the actress moved across the stage in a nightdress, horrible guilt driving her to rub her hands in an effort to blot out the blood that haunted her sleep, Kit raised a hand to her chest, her own guilt mirrored.

Then, at once self-conscious about the gesture, she lowered her gaze and slid her hand to her lap, hoping neither Breckenridge nor Jane had noticed, and if they had, that they had assumed it was because Kit was moved by great acting.

At the end of the performance Kit applauded with sincere emotion, wishing the illusion could last a little longer. She heard the others in hushed discussion around her; then, as the unwanted sense of reality gradually intruded on her, she realized they were all rising to leave before the after pieces.

"Are we leaving so soon?" Kit said to no one in particular.

Breck gave her an odd stare, then picked up a corner of her shawl, which had slid off her shoulder.

"The play is over, or hadn't you noticed? Let us leave before we have to compare the performances of two great artists with the froth of song and dance that is sure to follow."

She moved with them as they left the box. In the lobby, a crowd milled, and she was swept along with its flow until they reached the doors and made their way down the steps. Fletch went ahead to fetch the carriage while the rest of them chatted about the play. Kit didn't feel like indulging in small talk. To her, Sarah Siddons' emotion had been a personal thing. The woman's drive and feeling, her convincing characterization of the evil Lady Macbeth, were too close to Kit's own turbulent feelings for her to be free to lightly dissect the tragedy.

The party returned to Ruby's house, where supper was laid out. Kit tried to put a cheerful face on for the sake of Merilee and Fletcher. After all, this was a celebration. Why then could she not take part in the merriment? She was happy for Merilee and her brother, feeling that a wife was just the thing the occasionally ornery Fletch needed. And Merilee had a level head, whereas her brother could be emotional and stubborn. Perhaps together they would strike a balance.

Of course, deep down she knew why she was haunted by melancholy. There was no such happiness for her in this group. She had refused Breck's advances, and during the conversation she had had with William, she had found Breck's cousin dull and narrow-minded. Her attempt to act as if nothing was wrong did not fool everyone however. Breck approached her when they had finished supper and moved to the drawing room.

"You've been awfully quiet, Kathryn," he said.

She managed a feeble smile. "I'm tired, that's all. But I did enjoy the theater. I was quite moved by the performance."

"Indeed. It was very fine actin'."

She nodded. Breck sat by her for a moment, but it was apparent that they did not have anything to say to each other. The last thing she felt like at the moment was chitchat. She was about to make her excuses and go upstairs when she heard the front door open and close. When her father pushed open the drawing-room doors, she remembered that he had been to dinner at the President's House this evening.

"Ah, Father," said Fletch, going over to greet him. "How was your evening with the President?"

The rest of the group gathered around him as he came in to join them. Kit could tell by the satisfied look in his eyes that the evening must have gone well. She couldn't help but be glad for him. He had worked so hard at campaigning for General Jackson, and she knew he hoped to have a hand in the new government.

"Very well," said Jonathan, sitting on the navy sofa and leaning back. He patted his middle. "The food was excellent."

Fletcher groaned. "That is not what we mean, Father?"

"Oh?" Jonathan teased his son. "Oh, you mean how did the meeting with the President go?"

"Of course."

"Yes," said Breckenridge. "Did you discuss matters of state?"

Jonathan stroked his chin. "As a matter of fact we did. President Jackson must value my advice after all, for he has asked me to head up a special advisory committee which will deal with the matter of states' rights."

"Excellent," said Fletcher.

"Congratulations, Father," said Kit.

"Indeed," said Jonathan. "President Jackson feels very strongly about a strong central government, but he is willing to listen to special concerns of states such as Georgia."

Those in the merry group began to chatter all at once, but through their random comments, Kit heard Fletcher ask their father when he and the President would meet again.

Jonathan winked at his son, then drew out a square envelope and opened it. The invitation was engraved and signed by the President, with the date and time filled in. The family was invited to a reception at the President's House. Merilee, as Fletcher's fiancée, was also invited so that President Jackson could offer the young couple his congratulations.

Merilee gasped and her hands went to her cheeks. "Oh my. Then I shall meet the President."

Fletcher sat up straighter. "Yes. We met him, of course, on the day of the inauguration."

Kit shook her head. You could hardly call the melee in which they had found themselves on that day, a proper meeting, but she let Fletch impress his bride-to-be with his supposed acquaintance with the President.

"I don't know what I shall wear," Merilee was murmuring, but no one was paying any attention to her.

"As to further business with President Jackson," continued Jonathan. "I am to call on him tomorrow morning. He desires my opinion on the matter of enforcing the Georgia compact. He is anxious to bring negotiations with the Cherokees to a successful conclusion."

Kit's heart jumped to her throat. "What would

that mean?" she asked. "A successful conclusion, that is?"

"Why, removal, of course. The Cherokees must be completely removed from the state."

Much later, when Kit had finally succeeded in saying good night to all the guests and could finally be alone after Samantha helped her out of her clothes, she sat at her dressing table, her hair falling about her shoulders, her head in her hands. Slowly, she looked up at her face in the mirror.

Thoughts of the confusing day plagued her, but there was one decision she must make. She could not rid herself of thoughts of Red Hawk. Perverse as it was, he had had a profound effect on her. Not that anything could come of it, but he had in some way touched her mind and her body, if not her heart and soul. She was a different person since she had met him. What that meant for her future, or for her place in the world, she did not yet know. But she knew she must see him one more time.

She must tell him that they could not meet again. She must explain that what she had done with him had been wrong. It had in no way been his fault. She had allowed it. But she must explain that what had happened between them must never happen again.

At the same time she wanted him to know that she was interested in what he had told her about his people, and that she planned to continue to learn about the Indian peoples. Perhaps she would find some way, even if it was small and insignificant, to help them.

She knew that there were people who worked directly with the Indians—missionaries and Indian agents. And while it was unlikely that such a role would fit her, these were things that merited exploration. At any rate, she wanted Red Hawk to be aware of how she felt—and to realize that knowing him had made a difference in her life.

Most of all, perhaps, she wanted him to know that though she was Jonathan Newcomb's daughter, she did not agree that all Indians must be removed from Georgia. Surely a compromise could be reached. She would encourage Red Hawk to be patient with the negotiations and tell him that even if he considered himself too impatient to talk to President Jackson, perhaps Chief John Ross would succeed. She did not want Red Hawk's delegation to give up or to leave Washington City without being heard.

Satisfied that she had at last decided what she wanted to say when she next saw Red Hawk, she drew back the covers and got into bed. It was so late, and her eyes were so heavy, that she did not have difficulty falling asleep.

In the morning, she again went down to breakfast in her riding habit. Ruby was at the table and looked up with a pleasant smile as she replaced her cup in its saucer.

"Going riding again today, dear?"

Kit smiled politely and sat in the chair that Fletch pulled out for her. She looked up at him, surprised by his sudden attack of good manners.

110

"Yes, Aunt," she said. "I saw some things I wanted to buy in Georgetown yesterday, but I could not decide on them. I mentioned to Fletcher and Merilee that I wanted to go back and make my purchases."

"Then you must take the carriage."

"I . . . uh, prefer going on horseback. I enjoy the exercise."

"Then I suppose your brother must accompany you."

"Oh, I wouldn't want to impose on Fletcher's time. Surely, dear brother, you have your own business to attend to."

Kit poured herself a cup of tea, then buttered a biscuit. Fletch grumbled something which she didn't hear. She continued to press the point, determined to ride to Georgetown alone.

"After all," she said, "I know the way now. And it is a well-traveled turnpike. Surely no one is worried that I might be attacked by a highwayman."

Ruby looked on, wryly amused by her headstrong niece. Both of Jonathan's children had his will. It was unfortunate that their poor mother had died so young, before she could instill some of the feminine virtues in them, such as patience. Not that Ruby faulted the children overmuch, she was just aware of traits that might lead them into difficulty if they were not tempered.

"Well, I don't mind the ride," said Fletch, tossing his napkin onto the table. "I'll turn to fat if I sit in the house all day. And when we get there I can sit in the inn and refresh myself while my sister shops."

From the cheerful look he gave her, she suspected

111

that the day would not pass without his spending time with Merilee again. And this suited Kit's plans very well.

Fletch dressed for riding while Kit asked Ruby's groom to saddle the horses. When they mounted up and rode onto the street, Kit looked slyly at her brother.

"I suppose you would like to see if Merilee will join us."

"Of course."

They followed the same routine as the day before, and soon the three were on the road to Georgetown. As they passed riders, wagons, and coaches, Kit began to debate the wisdom of her decision to come out. With every milepost they passed, her apprehension became stronger.

What was she doing here? Remembering her resolve of the night before, should she simply not ride out to see Red Hawk again? Surely if she did not appear, he would understand the message.

She was so distracted by her thoughts the foolishness on her mission that she nearly forgot her excuse for coming.

"Perhaps I should visit the shops with Kit," said Merilee to Fletcher. "She might need my help. And besides, I have no idea what the shops in Georgetown offer."

"Oh no," said Kit quickly. "I mean, that won't be necessary. I know you two would like to spend some time together away from the company of others, that is."

Merilee glanced at Fletch shyly. "Well, perhaps we

112

do have some things to discuss. Plans and what not."

"That's really quite understandable," said Kit. "I'm sure I'll be unpleasant company in any case," she went on. "I shall want to look at everything and consider carefully if I should buy it. Fletch has never had any patience with my shopping when we've gone to town or looked in a catalog."

That much was true. Wytheridge was self-sufficient only to a point, and there were always trips into Clarkesville or Dahlonega to buy merchandise at the general store or to order equipment and hardware that they needed from a catalog. Fletch had never displayed any patience with such details and had left the buying to Kit and their father, who made the decisions about what tools and supplies they needed.

At the edge of Georgetown, the traffic increased. From the road, they could see the many ships being loaded and unloaded in their slips. The steamboats that plied the river reminded Kit that she would be aboard one of them and on her way home very soon. As soon as arrangements for the wedding were settled, she imagined she would be leaving, taking one of Ruby's servants with her, of course. For she doubted her father would allow her to travel alone. If Ruby couldn't spare a servant, then Jonathan would probably have to buy another for Kit to take to the farm.

The three young people dropped their horses off at the livery stable; then Fletch and Merilee left Kit. She watched her brother take Merilee's hand as the pair crossed the road, saw Merilee laugh at him when they reached the other side, saw him squeeze

113

her waist, bringing his face close to hers. A pang of despair went through Kit. Not from jealousy for their happiness, for in spite of her natural rivalry with her hard-headed brother, she only wished for his happiness. But because their happiness was so easily had—it fit so well with everything they knew.

She stifled the dizziness she felt and turned to head down the sidewalk. She was racing past the shops when she realized that she had to purchase something. So she stepped into the nearest shop. Once in the door, the odor told her she was in a spice and herb shop. That was perfect. She could buy some herbs for Ossie Lee, for medicinal remedies and cleaning aids were always needed at Wytheridge. And she would take something to their cook to make their meals more interesting. She would also find some exotic spice for Ruby to show appreciation for her hospitality.

It did not take long. She told the storekeeper what she needed and let him make suggestions. She paid with the specie her father had given her for the shopping trip.

"Would you mind if I left these packages here?" she asked the proprietor. "I have some other errands, and I'd like to pick them up later."

"No problem at all, miss," said the bushy-haired storekeeper. "I'll just wrap these up and keep them behind the counter for you."

She thanked him and left. Once back on the sidewalk, she debated what to do next. Rock Creek was not far. She need not get the horse out of the stable, which would arouse suspicion in any case.

She decided to walk.

At the edge of the business district, she turned into a quaint street that was not far from the footbridge. Upon leaving the noise of commerce behind, she should have found the peaceful setting of the houses in the lanes reassuring.

Instead, her heart began to feel constricted. She rehearsed in her mind what she had planned to say to Red Hawk and found she could remember little of it. She walked farther toward the footbridge that led from the quiet lane into the park and across the creek. She glanced over her shoulder to make sure no one saw her, but she had left the pedestrians behind in the lanes.

Once across the creek, she hurried along the path until it curved a little into the trees. Then she slowed down. What she was doing was foolish. She did not know that Red Hawk would ride here today. She almost hoped he wouldn't. Then she could return for her packages, meet her brother at the inn, and put this madness behind her. Surely with time she would forget her strange encounter with the Indian. She was about to turn and go back along the path when she heard the soft thud of a horse hoof behind her. She started and turned, then bit her lip.

Red Hawk walked from the trees onto the path, leading his horse behind him. He paused when he saw her, some distance away; then he turned to quiet his horse.

Kit's heart went to her throat. She glanced at the path beyond, as if considering simply fleeing down it, but her feet remained rooted to the spot. He was

115

coming nearer now, and she could see the pleased light in his eye. She tried to hang onto her thoughts, struggled to prepare herself for the meeting, but with every step he took, she felt her resolve slipping.

She had spoken with him because she had been interested in learning something about the Cherokees, hadn't she? What then did the virile movement of his limbs, the black hair flowing over his muscular shoulders, the gaze that even from this distance burned through her clothing have to do with the cultures of a people?

All she knew was that as he stepped nearer, that same mysterious longing began to build within her. That same madness seized her, the madness that she knew, in some small part of her mind, she must put a stop to.

They did not speak, but she felt the flush of her cheeks as he turned his horse loose to graze nearby. Then he was standing in front of her, his black eyes raking over her face and her body as they both remembered what had occurred between them.

Kit turned so that he would be forced to walk along beside her. "I had to see you," she said.

"And I, you." His words were low, deliberate, full of meaning.

She drew a breath and tried to explain herself. She must tell him who her father was and explain what her intentions were.

"I wanted to tell you something," she said.

"Yes." His hand gripped her arm now, and he turned her to face him. "Then you must speak."

But seeing the object of his desire made Red

Hawk put words aside. He understood something of her troubled heart. There were many kinds of troubles, and remedies for some. He would hear her words, but they must await the fulfillment of what was passing between them. Red Hawk followed his instincts far more than he waited upon words, and from the quivering of her limbs, he knew that she needed the outpouring he felt.

He took her in his arms and kissed her, and as the kiss went on and on, Kit swooned against his strong frame. Her hands tangled in his long hair, her pulse quickened as his arms tightened around her, and she gasped as he pressed against her, his body making evident what he desired. She was lost to him and she knew it. Not that this could go on forever. She would escape to Wytheridge, where she would put her own life back together. Perhaps she would never marry, for who would want to marry a woman who had been in the embrace of an Indian? If anyone ever found out.

But right now that did not matter. The sensations he created in her were not to be denied. Surely no other white woman she knew had ever experienced the magic of such a man's embrace, the wildness of a man who has lived close to nature in spite of all his Christian education in her people's schools. In spite of the fact that he could put on the clothing of a diplomat from his nation, adopt the white man's mode of government and negotiation, she sensed in Red Hawk his primitive blood, the blood of his ancestors, and found him to be a being who knew things about the earth that she had not learned. And she hungered for all that he offered.

Confusion mingled with the thrill of desire and need as he pulled her to her knees. She went willingly, as his kiss and embrace became more urgent.

When he had caressed her before, he had held back, had worked slowly, lighting her spirit with desire, bringing their souls into harmony so that each could recognize the other, so that she could return his feelings. But now she had tasted of him, and he knew she wanted more. Her small gasps of pleasure, the kneading of her fingers against his muscles spoke more than her words ever would. But they must move into cover. For though they had seen no one, this was a public place, and their coming together demanded privacy.

"Come," he whispered into her ear.

Before she knew what had happened, he had lifted her off the ground and cradled her in his arms. In a few swift strides, they were in the trees, on a rise, and he knelt, settling her in the soft grass behind the large trunk of an oak.

She blinked up at him, trying to rise, to speak, but he held his finger to his lips as his eyes pinned her to the ground, and his hands softly brushed over her breasts. Then he lay over her, his body covering hers as his soft kisses assaulted her ears and neck while his hips and thighs pressed his hardness against her.

Kit moaned, afraid of what was happening, but wanting it too. What had happened to her protests? Why could she not tell him to stop? But the thought that she could not be with him because he was not

118

of her kind died as she kissed him back fervently. She yearned to explore further what he was making her feel. The newness of these sensations tingled throughout her body, and she could not stop herself.

Red Hawk was ready, and his hand sought the smooth thighs under her skirts. He willed himself to move slowly, for even though his need throbbed in him now, he knew her inexperience and did not want to be cruel.

She did not know it, but if she had told him to stop, had made some gesture of refusal, he would have desisted. But Kit was seized with the madness of desire. All thought banished as she lay under him, drinking in his power and his maleness. Her body responded to his, rose to serve his need, meeting it with her own.

And so Red Hawk did not stop in his lovemaking, but let his senses and his instincts lead him. He raised her skirts to caress her. His hands found the smooth skin of his desire. Then in a swift motion, he lowered his trousers so that she might feel his hard flesh against her. He pressed into her thighs, giving her time to get used to the new feeling. Then he guided her hands to his buttocks, which she grasped, sending even more pleasure through him.

Kit lay, her lips parted in ecstasy as he worked his magic on the lower part of her body. Her breasts tingled as he pulled her jacket and her shirt open to take each nipple in his mouth. Surely such ecstasy was like nothing else on earth. Red Hawk had sent her to another place, and she knew without doubt that what he was doing, no other man could ever do, would ever do. What was happening between them was some heaven-sent miracle, the union of two unlike beings who shared twin souls and who had been destined to find each other that night upon the garden walk.

Red Hawk entered her and held her against him gently as she cried out in pain. He cupped his hand around her buttocks, kissing her neck and ears. Then slowly he began to move inside her. She clasped her legs about him, standing the pain for the pleasure her senses still brought her.

Red Hawk gave a silent prayer of thanks for the joy he felt as he approached the pinnacle of pleasure and satisfaction. His thoughts were shattered with the bursting of energy that bound her heart to his. His whole being shuddered, his soul flew upward, his eyes were blinded.

Seconds passed and Kit held her breath, her soul soaring upward with his, her senses shattered with something from another life, another time. She knew she would never be the same again.

Slowly, as slowly as night turns to day, their breathing evened, their minds returned to earth so that they again became aware of the twitterings of the birds in the trees above them, felt the wind that whispered in the leaves beside them.

Kit still held Red Hawk against her, but gradually became aware of things around her, of his weight on her. He rolled to her side, pulled up his trousers, and lowered her skirt. Then he pulled her against him and laid his cheek against hers, his arms curved around her back.

When her breathing returned to normal, she let her head fall back to the ground. She felt suddenly shy again and did not know what to say. But Red Hawk gazed directly at her. When she risked a glance at him, she saw the corners of his mouth curve in pleasure, saw the light in his dark eyes.

"So," he said, his voice like honey in her ear, "now you have tasted pleasure. I am the first man to bring this pleasure to you."

She flushed in embarrassment. "Yes."

He did not say the only man to bring her this pleasure, for though they had joined their bodies, he sensed that she was not ready to bind herself to him. There were barriers between them yet. What fate meant for them, he did not yet know. That they would be together, he was certain, but how he had not yet discerned. Still, he would use what medicine he could to bring her to him. For in his heart, Red Hawk was sure.

Chapter Seven

Kit struggled for words. She sat up, busied herself by brushing off leaves that clung to her and straightening her clothing. Suddenly aware of time, she still had to tell Red Hawk what she had come to tell him and then return to the inn looking as if nothing had happened. She could not actually think of what she had done with Red Hawk, not yet. She would find a way to do that later.

She stood up, and he rose with her. For a moment she wanted to say nothing. She wanted only to lean against him in the quiet woods, listen to the gurgling of the creek. But already the outside world began to impinge on her.

"Red Hawk," she said, her voice hoarse.

And he smiled, bending to brush his lips against those that had spoken his name. But she pressed against his shoulders gently.

He understood that she wished to speak, and he raised his head, watching her, ready to listen.

She looked at the proud, virile Indian who was

unashamed of what they had done. She blinked once and moistened her lips.

"I must leave Washington City," she said.

"Leave?"

She nodded. "Yes. I must go back to Wytheridge, back to my people. My brother is getting married there."

"You must tend to duties there, prepare for the ceremony."

He did not sound at all disappointed or surprised that she was going to leave, and she hastened to explain further.

"Of course, but it's more than that. I must . . ." But the words caught in her throat. "I must . . ."

He lifted her chin, his eyes glowing into hers. "You must return to your people."

"Yes," she said.

He sensed her struggle. He had been right in knowing that she could not bind herself to him while in her present state of mind. He would not rush her. All he would do was show her the way he loved.

"I, too, return to my people in our nation in two days' time."

He lowered his lips to hers again gently, stilling her words, stilling even her thoughts. She returned his kiss, no longer able to protest, realizing the futility of trying to explain anything at all. For a moment she gave way to the sense that fate was leading her she knew not where. Yet she was powerless to resist.

And then in the next instant she realized that what she must do would have to be demonstrated in action. She had lain with Red Hawk, but she must return to Wytheridge. She would not see him there, for she would be surrounded by her own kind, protected from him by the river that divided white and Cherokee lands. But she could not bring herself to say it. She could not deny this moment that their hearts beat as one.

With no more words, they turned and moved through the trees, coming out onto the path. Red Hawk whistled to his horse, which trotted over to them. They walked slowly along the path, savoring the long afternoon with the web it had spun around them. They had gone farther than Kit realized and had come to the footbridge. Another couple was crossing it. The gentleman tipped his hat to Kit, but the woman stared openly at Red Hawk.

Kit meant to leave Red Hawk at this point, but he followed her over the footbridge. She was about to turn and say goodbye when the sound of galloping hooves came from the road to her left and made her turn. She gasped. Fletch was thundering down on them, his face a mask of anger and horror, and he pulled on the reins so hard his mount whinnied and reared, kicking its front hooves before lowering them again.

Fletch was off the horse's back and upon Kit before she could take two steps backward.

"What do you think you are doing here?" he bellowed, his fingers biting into her arm.

He had raised the crop as if to strike her, and she turned her face to the side to avoid the blow.

"Nothing. Let me go, Fletcher," she said.

But he grasped her shoulder and shook her.

"Look at me," he said. "Who is this . . . this Indian?" Disgust came from his mouth like venom.

But Kit clenched her jaw, refusing to speak until he let her go.

Her brother glared at Red Hawk, who had moved up to stand erect a few feet behind Kit, the anger in his dark face a match for Fletch's own.

"Stop it," Kit said through gritted teeth. "I don't know what you're thinking, but this is Red Hawk. He is in Washington City with the Cherokee delegation to the President."

Fletch glanced at Red Hawk once in dismissal, then looked back at Kit.

"I don't care what his name is, but I want to know what you are doing with him. I saw you come over the footbridge."

Kit stood straighter. She was no longer afraid that Fletch would actually use the riding crop on her, but she knew she must prevent any violence between her brother and Red Hawk.

"I met him at the Rutherfords'. The delegation was there with Chief John Ross and Major Ridge. If you had looked around you instead of sneaking off with Merilee all evening, you might have noticed."

She hoped the bitterness in her voice might shake Fletch out of his rage. But he only glared at her.

"You have lost your mind. Why were you alone with this man? Who has seen you? What on earth will you tell Father?"

Red Hawk had regained his composure, seeing the rage in Fletcher as that of an angry boy unable to control his emotions. The red-haired lad was no warrior. He was unformed. Red Hawk would not be intimidated by his kind. He folded his arms in front of him, assumed a straight, defiant posture, and waited until he was called upon to speak or to defend Kit in some way.

"We were . . . talking," Kit said, struggling to sound calm. She needed to diffuse her brother's anger with reason if she could.

"I wanted to know something of his people. You might have followed the debates over his people's lands if you had shown any interest in the political pages of the newspapers."

"I have no interest in his people," said Fletch, his rage settling to a simmer. "They are none of my business, just as they are none of yours."

"Oh, no?" Kit said defiantly. "Well, I can see you don't have the makings of a statesman or you would realize that Cherokee lands are practically next door to our acreage in Georgia, and there are great issues at stake if we are to live peaceably side by side with the Cherokees."

Fletch smirked at the tall, silent Indian standing in the road.

"I am not sure if we will live peaceably, but whether we do or not, you have no business talking to him."

He reached out to take her by the arm, but Red Hawk finally moved. In a single, graceful movement, he swept Fletch's arm aside and placed himself between Kit and her brother.

"Who is this man who comes to take you away?"

126

he said, his glance one he might have used to inspect a crawling insect.

His haughty expression told Kit that he was not going to be humiliated, nor would he hear his people insulted by this ignorant young white man.

Kit sighed. "He is my brother. I apologize for his hasty behavior."

Fletch's eyes bulged as he took in the fact that she was apologizing to the heathen standing between them, but Red Hawk's look kept him from speaking. Red Hawk remained in control.

"He has slandered your honor."

Fletch narrowed his eyes at hearing this sophisticated statement come from the Indian, but he did not move.

Kit laid a hand on Red Hawk's arm. "Please," she said, her tone of voice imploring. "It is all right. I will go home with him."

Then she looked directly at Fletch. "He will mention this incident to no one."

Anger made Fletch shake, but as he opened his mouth to reply, Kit hurried on.

"What is the harm in my speaking to a member of an important Indian delegation compared to the sin he has committed with his intended this very hour?"

She was guessing, but the haste with which her brother clamped his mouth shut and the redness of his face betrayed him. Of course, with so much time alone together, he and Merilee had not been able to keep themselves from each other. They were as much victim to the freedom of this Eastern seaboard port and the opportunity of being away from prying eyes as she had been.

Kit and Fletcher faced each other, the challenge crackling between them. Red Hawk watched them, and then smiled as his angry white dove faced down the brother with the angry eyes.

Finally Fletch took a deep breath and retreated a step.

"We'd best go," he said, not looking at Red Hawk again.

She turned to say something to Red Hawk, but he raised his hand in a gesture of silence and sprang up on his horse. Kit swallowed hard, anger and embarrassment battling for supremacy within her.

Fletch turned his back and began to walk off. Kit glanced once at Red Hawk, who turned his horse; then she followed her brother.

Red Hawk did not look back. He knew he would see her no more in the seaboard cities. Negotiations with President Jackson were stalled, so Red Hawk's place was with his people. He had already gotten Chief John Ross's permission to return to New Echota by steamboat and horseback. In perhaps a week, he would be there.

He needed to give the message to his people that there was only one way to save the Cherokee Nation from Indian removal and that was unity. In the past, Indian nations had not been able to stand against the white government because of disunity within the tribes.

Such disunity threatened now, and it was up to Red Hawk and the rest of Ross's circle of followers to instill in the people a determination to stand together and not listen to those within the tribe who favored a removal treaty, such as Major Ridge and his son.

But he knew he would see Kathryn Newcomb again. The feelings in his heart would not be ignored. Her home was in the state of Georgia. Fate would bring them together in the mountains of his homelands.

Since Kit did not have her horse, Fletch did not mount up. They walked for a while before he spoke, and she could see he was still angry, trying to decide what to say.

"Don't you care anything for your reputation?" he finally asked. "After all, our father works in the new government. You shouldn't be seen alone with . . . with heathen savages."

She bristled. "He isn't a heathen. The Cherokees have been Christianized. And he's no savage. You heard him speak. He's quite noble. I just thought I could learn something from him about his people."

"Alone? In the woods? You must be mad. He might have taken advantage of you. I have heard that Indians have a taste for white females. What you did was dangerous. Father will have my hide. I was charged with chaperoning you."

She did not look at him, hoping he would not notice her flush. "I can take care of myself. He is a gentleman. He would never force himself on someone like me."

That, at least, was true. She had invited Red

129

Hawk's attention. He had not ravished her against her will.

"I can't imagine what you thought you could gain from such a conversation."

"For heaven's sake, Fletch. They are a conquered people. It might help if those they negotiate with try to understand them," she said.

"We conquered them just as they conquered the natives who lived on their lands before them. Such is the way of the world. And besides, for your information, in case this Red Hawk did not tell you, our government does not simply steal Indian lands. We purchase it. They have probably gotten more money for their lands than any other so-called conquered people in the course of history. You see, I am not completely ignorant of such matters."

She pressed her lips together. What he said echoed what Daniel Webster had told her.

"That might be true. But what if they don't want to sell their lands?"

"What if they don't?" Fletch sounded exasperated. "Can't you leave it to the government to deal with them?"

She said nothing, but walked along in silence. They were approaching the business district, yet she could not leave the conversation without one more comment.

"I know that gold has been discovered on Cherokee lands. Red Hawk says that the white Georgians are simply moving in with no right and digging for it. Some even sneak across the river at night to steal gold."

Fletch shrugged. "I wouldn't know."

He turned and frowned at Kit. "Stay out if it, sis. For your own sake."

His temper had cooled now, and she could see that behind his angry flare-up had been honest concern for her. She swallowed. She appreciated his caring for her, but she felt he was wrong to jump to such hasty conclusions about the Cherokees in Georgia. Nevertheless she sighed and shook her head.

"I didn't mean to do anything to make you angry, or to embarrass anybody," she said.

Fletch lowered his head. When he raised it, he touched her shoulder, gently now.

"Just don't do something like this again, all right? I would hate to have to explain to Father. And someone might see you. If you must meet Indians, do it at public receptions or at some of their public exhibitions, which I understand can be quite entertaining. The dancing and all."

She knew he was trying to compromise, but it didn't work. She frowned. "That's not the same."

"Kit, Kit. What am I going to do with you?"

She opened her eyes in surprise. "Why, nothing. You certainly don't have to say anything to Father. As far as anyone knows, the three of us have been together for most of the afternoon, haven't we?"

He met her look of challenge sheepishly, then glanced guiltily at the inn where he had left Merilee. How his sister could have guessed that he and his fiancée had gone off to a room for a while, he did not know. But that was different. They were engaged to be married. He frowned at his Kit.

131

"All right. We'll consider the matter closed. Now, you'd best get your horse."

They spoke little on the ride home. Merilee rode along in a sort of wide-eyed silence, and Kit was lost in thought.

She couldn't blame Fletch. Some of what he had said was true. She had not meant what had happened to have occurred. She closed her eyes, the dull pain between her legs reminding her of the perverse pleasure she had experienced.

At all costs she must tell no one. She remembered the fear and danger that went hand in hand with the pleasure. She forced herself to concentrate on the ride, and for some minutes stared numbly at the scenery around her. It was as if she needed to reach out and touch the horses and riders that passed by in order to remind herself that this was the world she lived in.

A tacit agreement was reached between Kit and Fletch: he would not mention her secret provided she did not mention his. Obviously he and Merilee had indulged in their own pleasures, and she had hit on the truth. Fletch must wonder what she knew, and how.

It was possible that she had gone to the inn before meeting Red Hawk and had seen them together in some dark corner or perhaps had caught them entering one of the bedrooms. She wasn't going to disabuse Fletch of such a notion.

In spite of her fervent desire that Fletch and Merilee might understand her, she did not mean to cause a scandal. She sighed audibly. Perhaps when she returned to Wytheridge, her restless soul would find an outlet in riding among the pines in the company of Shep. She would, at least, have a chance to think about what had happened. She dared not admit that she might see Red Hawk again. She figured the most she could do would be to find out more about the situation of the Cherokees within the state of Georgia. She did not know what she could do about that, but now that she had learned of it, her mind would not let go of it.

The reception at the President's House was the first evening party the President had had. It was small and personal, for he was still mourning the loss of his wife. But, as Jonathan explained to his family, President Jackson felt that the memory of his late wife would allow for some small entertainments, due to his many obligations toward those who had helped put him in office. Jonathan Newcomb had been one such strong supporter and so was included as one of the guests of honor. The party served a dual purpose in that the President could honor Jonathan's son upon his engagement.

Ruby's household was in a dither as the family prepared for the evening. Ruby had at first refused to attend, claiming that her politics were too opposed to those of the present administration for her to be able to set foot in the President's house. But Jonathan persuaded her, saying that other Whigs would be there. Daniel Webster had been invited, among others. Ruby liked the senator from Massachusetts, so she finally agreed to go.

She had artfully made over a burgundy satin gown of her own for her niece so that Jonathan would not have too much expense just before Fletch's wedding. She herself wore a dignified gown of black silk trimmed with silver lace, and she had hand-tailored new white brocade waistcoats for Jonathan and Fletch.

Kit tried to work up some interest in attending the reception, but she was so distracted that she had difficulty concentrating on the evening ahead. Since the ride to Rock Creek, she had walked about the city in a sort of confused haze. Life here had not changed. Commerce was carried on. Workmen laid bricks for new buildings. Vendors hawked their wares in the market, and slaves were auctioned off. But Kit felt a stranger to it all.

She had gazed at the Indian Queen Hotel once from a distance, but had not dared go near it. She thought she remembered Red Hawk saying he was going to return to his people, and she wondered just where they were. She knew that the Cherokee capital of New Echota was within the state of Georgia. Was that where he had gone?

She tried to still her unsettled thoughts, but she found it difficult to concentrate for more than a few minutes on the things around her. She longed more and more to go home. But her father had the President's ear now, and she must go to the reception to show good will. In the back of her mind the thought formed that she might be able to ask the President what he intended to do about the Cherokees, but she dismissed it. It would be brash to raise such an issue at this time, especially since she did not know the President well.

But then, she mused as she examined the coif in which Samantha had arranged her hair, if she did not raise such a question with the President at this event, then when?

Caleb and the young groom, Hiram, were in dress livery, and at seven o'clock, Jonathan handed first Ruby, then Kit into the landau. The evenings were beginning to get lighter now, and there would be no need for the side lanterns to be lit until they drove home. The top and sides were folded back so that they could enjoy the balmy evening as they drove the short distance to fetch Merilee before riding on to the reception.

Ruby and Kit sat beside each other so that there would be room for Merilee across from them between Jonathan and Fletch. That way the women's skirts would not get crushed.

They pulled up in front of Merilee's house, and Fletch went to fetch her. She looked radiant in a new gown of yellow satin adorned with yellow bows and cloth roses. Kit could see that Merilee was exhilarated by the thought of an evening with the President.

But everyone's good spirits grated on Kit. She turned and looked at the houses and people they passed, hating the gnawing disturbance within her. Her knuckles were white from clutching the side of the carriage, and she feared she was losing her mind.

They passed a Negro church, within which freed slaves were raising their voices in a hymn of praise. Kit did not resent the outing. She had enjoyed Washington City so far. Why then this sense of dissatisfaction? She tried to put on a smile and listen to Merilee's banter.

"Don't worry," Fletch was saying to his fiancée. "We won't speak to the President for very long. He will have a great many guests to attend to."

"And," added Jonathan, "he does not care for late evenings. He is greatly overworked and tires easily I'm afraid."

There certainly were a great many guests, as was evidenced by the carriages pulling into the circular drive and letting people off at the steps to the south entrance which faced the garden, with a view of the Capitol beyond.

The party alighted, and as Caleb drove away, they ascended one of the two flights of steps leading from the ground to the level of the principal story. In spite of herself, Kit began to look about her with interest. She had seen so little the day of the inauguration, and they had come and gone by the north entrance then.

They came up to the semicircular colonnade of six columns, and then passed through the doors, held open for them by servants. Inside, they admired the tasteful but luxurious decor. The walls in this part of the house were covered with light blue wallpaper with gilt borders and were finished with handsome stucco cornices.

They were directed into the oval room, where Kit

and Fletch had met the President before. Now, however, Kit could see the marble chimney piece and tables, the crimson silk of the draperies at the windows and the covering of the chairs, the French-wove carpet with the coat of arms of the United States in the center. Two large mirrors and a cut-glass chandelier gave the room an appearance of elegance, and all evidence of the disastrous reception after the inauguration had been removed.

No sooner had they entered the room than Kit spied Daniel Webster, his large, dark head bowed in argument with the tall, homely Henry Clay. Webster turned their way, and broke off his conversation to come over and greet them. He bowed over Ruby's hand first, charming her with his compliments.

"How good to see you, madam. Ah, how elegant you look this evening. It refreshes the eye."

"Oh, go on, Daniel," said Ruby. "You do flatter. You look as if work has not been keeping you entirely from enjoying yourself," she returned.

He smiled, including Kit, who stood next to Ruby, in his glance. "One must mix and mingle with people. And besides, even upon a social occasion as this one, I get a chance to practice my arguments."

Ruby chuckled. "I have heard it said by more than one acquaintance of mine that when they heard you speak in the Senate, they had to scratch their heads to recall where they had heard the same words before. Oftentimes it was on a walk in a garden during a conversation with you."

Webster took her teasing gracefully. "It pays to try

137

out one's ideas before one makes a fool of oneself in public, even if it is wearing on one's friends."

Then he turned to Kit and her father. But with a brief nod and shaking of hands, Jonathan hurried off to speak to someone, leaving Kit with the senator. She smiled sincerely. At least here was someone she liked and she felt she could talk to.

"Well, are you looking forward to seeing the President this evening?" asked Webster.

Her expression did not quite cover her reservation. "It is an honor to have been invited."

Then she gave a small grimace, feeling she could be honest with the senator at her side. "I only wish I could discuss what is really on my mind with him, but I fear that would not be welcome in such a setting."

Webster raised his dark eyebrows. "What could one so charming have to ask the President that he might not wish to hear?"

She looked at him for a moment, wondering if he even remembering talking to her about the Cherokees as they had sat in her aunt's dining room.

She tilted her head slightly. "I am most curious as to what he will do now that our state of Georgia is evidently putting pressure on him to help remove the Cherokees. I just wondered where the matter stood."

"Well, I see that your mind is still on that matter. But perhaps you are right. This may not be the time or place to ask."

She looked straight at the intelligent, dark-headed senator. "Then when might I ask such a question?"

The intensity of her response took Webster by surprise, and he blinked. But before he could answer, Fletch tugged on her sleeve.

"Come," her brother said. "If the honorable senator will spare you, there are refreshments in the other room." He looked respectfully at Webster, who smiled and gestured that they should proceed.

"Please," said Webster. "I would not keep you from the other guests." Then he gave Kit a half-smile. "And please do let me know how your conversation with the President turns out."

Fletch led her to an adjoining room, where cake was being served on a long table. This room was papered in lemon yellow with a rich cloth border. Four mantels of black marble with Italian style black and gold fronts and handsome grates were surmounted with mirrors framed in bronze and gilt. On each mantel sat a pair of candelabras and a pair of French vases painted with gilt and flowers. The carpet was of fine Brussels fawn, blue and yellow with a red border. The effect was dazzling, and for a moment Kit stood and stared.

Then Fletch poked her in the arm and nudged her forward, toward the cake being handed out by liveried servants.

"I think the senator from Massachusetts has taken a fancy to you."

It took Kit a moment to comprehend what he meant. But then she opened her mouth in surprise. "Why, he is Father's age. Don't be ridiculous. I enjoy talking to him because he has a brilliant mind. Have you never read any of his speeches?"

139

Fletch ducked the question of whether or not he had read the published speeches.

"He is a great orator with a distinguished career. Surely you know he is a widower."

She shook her head in impatience. "Of course I have heard that. I believe he still grieves for his wife. I only try to bring him a little cheer."

Fletch leaned closer to speak into her ear. "If I were you, sister dear, I would look at such a man as a potential suitor. If my guess is correct, he will not grieve for long."

Kit felt insulted by her brother's suggestive tone. She respected Daniel Webster and was impressed by his accomplishments in Congress. Nothing more.

Merilee joined them, her eyes glittering, her smiles at Fletch admiring. Jonathan came to fetch them and introduced them to several other statesmen. Finally, it was time to speak to the President, who was receiving his guests in yet another room on the west side of the oval room. A servant approached and bowed.

"The President will see you now." He gestured across the oval room.

The party moved in a dignified manner, Jonathan with Ruby on his right arm and Kit on his left, Fletch behind with Merilee. They approached President Jackson who was flanked by his hostess, Emily Donelson, the wife of the President's nephew and private secretary. Mrs. Donelson smiled graciously as Jonathan presented Ruby.

Jackson took Ruby's hand and bowed. "A pleasure," he said. "I am aware, madam, that your politi-

140

cal sentiments lie with the retiring party. I am glad you have accepted my invitation this evening."

In spite of herself, Ruby was impressed by the man's manners. She had been led to believe that he was a rough backwoodsman, but his grace and charm surprised her.

"And my daughter," said Jonathan, standing a little to the side as Ruby moved on to shake hands with Mrs. Donelson. "You will remember that you met my children the day of the inauguration."

Jackson smiled at Kit as he bowed over her hand. When she raised her eyes she could see the lines of fatigue and age in his face. She also sensed the charisma and leadership that had won a place for him in the hearts of the American people. She curtsied politely.

"Welcome to my house," he said to Kit. "I am glad you are having the opportunity to visit it on a quieter evening than previously."

She smiled at his humor in spite of herself. He looked past her to Fletch, who stood, his back as stiff as a board, with Merilee, who looked as if she might faint if she weren't holding on to Fletch's arm.

"And this is the young Mr. Newcomb and his wife-to-be."

"Good evening, Mr. President," said Fletch, his voice nearly cracking. "It is an honor to be here this evening."

"My pleasure," said Jackson, waving an arm as if wanting to put everyone at ease. "Especially as I have the occasion to congratulate you and your lovely fiancée on your coming marriage."

"Thank you," said Fletch. "I do not believe you have yet met my fiancée. May I present Miss Merilee Fitzsimmons."

"How do you do, sir?" Merilee had a voice after all, even if it sounded pinched.

Jackson took her hand and bowed over it. After introductions were completed, the young couple drifted away, but Kit stayed near her father, not thinking it proper to walk away from the President unattended.

However, Jackson seemed disposed to talk to Jonathan, and so Kit found herself listening to the two men. The President, in fact, included her in the conversation.

"Jonathan tells me you have a head for politics," Jackson said to her, his tired eyes glimmering with amusement.

Kit blushed. "I try to take an interest in what is going on in the country, if that is what you mean. But I am sure I do not have a full grasp of the matters discussed in Congress."

"Ah, and modest too," said the President. "I must say, your father has been a great help as an advisor to me of late. Especially on this matter of getting the Indians out of Georgia, your home state."

Kit's throat turned dry, but she maintained a level gaze. "And why do you want to get them out, sir?"

Her father frowned at her, but she ignored him. Jackson raised his bushy white brows.

"Why there is pressure for my government to honor the agreements made with the state of Georgia to remove them. But perhaps you are not aware

142

of this, having been here in Washington City," he said politely.

Kit frowned, and out of the corner of her eye noticed that Fletch and Merilee had drifted back toward the little group. Jonathan moved nearer to Kit.

"Mr. President," said Jonathan. "I fear I have been so busy of late that I have not kept my own family informed of the affairs in our native state."

Kit knew it was now or never. Part of her longed to flee, to retreat into expected feminine behavior and be subservient to her male escort. But a sudden memory jarred her. Dark eyes that had pierced her conscience, a beating heart not unlike those of her own people. And she knew she had to go ahead.

"If you don't mind my asking, Mr. President," said Kit, who had not moved from her spot in front of Jackson. "What about the agreements your government has made with the Indians?"

President Jackson raised his head an inch, and Kit heard her father's sharp intake of breath.

"Sister," said Fletch, grasping her arm, "why don't you join us for some punch?"

She did not mistake the threating tone in his voice, but she was not about to let the others drag her away. She had asked an honest question, and it deserved an answer. Evidently Jackson was prepared to give one. He smiled in a patronizing manner.

"The Cherokees will be just as well off in the West, my dear. Their Eastern lands will be paid for. We are in negotiations presently."

Kit stood her ground in spite of the fact that she knew her father might disown her afterward.

"But there may be bloodshed," she continued. "Some of the Cherokees will fight for their lands." She only hoped he didn't ask her how she knew that.

Jackson warmed to the subject. "Surely you realize, my dear, that there was much Indian bloodshed before the white man's law put order into this country. And besides that, the white government can put these new resources of gold to better use. Our country needs to progress."

Anger flared in Kit that surprised even her, but a part of her feared that male politicians must be better informed in these matters. It was on the tip of her tongue to say that moving women and children to a strange new territory in the West was not progress for the Indians, but she could not quite bring herself to argue with the President further. Her emotions fought with the suspicion that she might have more to learn about the situation before she discussed it with anyone.

Jackson continued to patronize her. "If you weren't your father's daughter, I would suspect you were an Indian lover." Then he attempted a chuckle, which did little to lighten the mood.

"Perhaps such a lovely young lady is mistaken to fill her head with these government problems. Thanks to your father, Jonathan here, I am being kept well informed as to the Cherokee situation in Georgia."

Kit had no reply and dared not open her mouth again. She allowed her brother to lead her away, but she felt the stunned disapproval behind her as her father and Ruby no doubt struggled to smooth over

144

the situation.

Merilee awaited them, her mouth open in curious surprise, the cake on her plate uneaten. But Fletch was in a fit. Before he let go of Kit's arm, he squeezed it, hurting her.

"How dare you talk back to President Jackson that way? Did that Indian you met leave you mad? Are you going to disgrace the entire family? Surely you realize what an honor it is to be invited here. You could have ruined Father's career."

But Kit turned to Fletch and shook her arm loose. "I doubt I can do that. Father must make his own decisions, whether they are right or wrong."

The party circulated among the guests until Ruby signaled that it was time to leave. Kit spoke to Senator Webster once more to bid him good night and then followed her family out. They all climbed into the carriage, but the ride home was strained.

Chapter Eight

Red Hawk stood in the whites' President's office in a rigid pose, his hands clasped behind his back. He had not accepted a chair as had Major Ridge and John Ridge. John Ross had at first sat, but now paced back and forth in front of Jackson's large desk, pleading his case. As Red Hawk watched the old man who governed the white people, however, he could see that his chief's arguments were not reaching the white man's leader. For the man did not have ears to hear.

Beside and a little behind President Jackson stood his trusted advisor, Jonathan Newcomb. As a resident of the state of Georgia, and a man who had been active in the state legislature, Jackson believed that Newcomb could offer valuable advice in the present situation.

Jonathan stood stiffly, looking straight ahead. He refused eye contact with any of the Indians, feeling that the Scots-Cherokee John Ross was a man much misled.

John Ross walked purposefully as he described the

picture of the white man's gold rush in Georgia. His broad gestures and his passionate expression argued well the case for his people.

"Surely you have not forgotten our help against the Creeks at the Battle of Horseshoe Bend," said Ross, stopping in front of the President's desk and leveling his blue eyes at the man behind it.

"I have not forgotten," said Jackson tiredly. He frowned in concentration and drummed his long fingers on his desk.

Ross continued. "It is true that our people have never understood the white man's desire for gold. We are happy and prosperous on our lands. But now rough, cruel gold miners are overrunning them, stealing from Cherokee gardens and killing Cherokee cattle and hogs. Men who try to protect their families and their possessions are beaten by these miners."

Jackson raised a hand. "I have done what the last treaty calls for. I have ordered troops into Georgia to protect your people and your lands."

"But not enough," pleaded John Ross. "The handful of soldiers there can do no more to control the robbery and murder than our own Cherokee marshals. We are helpless against the numbers." Ross raised a hand and clasped his fingers into a fist. "You cannot understand unless you see the desperate situation we are in."

Jackson rose and walked to the window to gaze for a moment over the gardens below. Jonathan followed him and leaned over to whisper a few words in his ear.

"I have done what I can," repeated Jackson, not turning around. "I have no more troops to send. May I remind you there is another way."

Major Ridge cleared his throat. "If I may interrupt Chief Ross, I might agree with the President. I say that our people want no more blood on their hands. Surely an . . . er . . . accommodation can be reached."

John Ridge leaned forward, his mumbles those of agreement.

Red Hawk stiffened. He had come to despise the two Ridges. He could not understand how two of his own people could be swayed by the white man's arguments, but it had become clear to him that Major Ridge and John Ridge were traitorous. Perhaps someone had bribed them, for they were all too willing to negotiate a new treaty and send the rest of their people to the lands in Indian Territory to the west. Red Hawk clenched his jaw as his ears were forced to hear the Ridges speak.

Major Ridge gestured to John Ross in an appeal to reason.

"Can you not see, Chief, that we will never be able to stop the white men who want our gold? Why not sell it to them for a price now rather than lose some of our people in a bloody fight? Many of our people would favor such a treaty."

Red Hawk could withhold himself no longer. "That is not so." He took a step forward and looked accusingly at Major Ridge. "You have not the vote of the council behind you. You have no right to say these words."

Major Ridge frowned at Red Hawk, and John Ross intervened.

"True, Red Hawk, he does not speak for the people but for a few only. Please, gentlemen, we are not here to speak of negotiations but to remind our friend the President of the laws that protect our people. This gold the white man cares so much for will surely be found in other parts of your great country," he said to Jackson. "Can you not help us to defend our lands? We have so little left that is ours."

His plea ended on a humble note, and there was a brief silence.

But Red Hawk's heartbeat was loud against his ribs. He did not trust the white leader or the red-faced man who whispered in his ear. This Newcomb was no example of manhood. His florid face, paunch, and sallow eyes were evidence of unhealthy pursuits. It was men like this that Red Hawk's people hated with a deep resentment.

Jackson sighed and resumed his seat in the leather chair behind the desk. "You must take the matter to the state of Georgia. It is the governor who must keep these Georgians off of your lands. If," he addressed Major Ridge, "your people conclude that it would be in their interest to write a new treaty, my government will be prepared to negotiate."

Major Ridge sat a little straighter; then a caustic look from John Ross made him lower his gaze in a thoughtful frown.

The afternoon sun crept across the smooth wood floor and onto the thick circular rug that covered the center of the room. We've been here too long, thought Red Hawk, and to no avail. He refused to look at Jackson again.

Red Hawk had fought at Horseshoe Bend. If he had known how this frontier general was going to turn his back on the Cherokees who had helped him against the fierce Creeks, he would have killed him when he'd had the chance. This man chosen to lead the white usurpers had fought many Indian peoples, and evidently to him they were all the same. He had no love for any of them.

Red Hawk could feel the bitterness travel through his body, carried on the blood that gave him life. With every beat of his heart hatred spurted toward his brain.

Chief John Ross ran out of words and stood erect, concluding the meeting. He shook his dark head sadly.

"Perhaps the generals at the head of the troops you have sent to us will return word of our true circumstances. It is my hope that then you will listen to our pleas for protection of our rights." He paused. "There are always the courts. We will not hesitate to hire the best lawyers to press our claims there."

The tips of President Jackson's fingers reached to the edge of his desk, but neither man said any more. The interview was over.

Chief Ross gave a stiff bow, turned on his heel, and walked toward the door. The Ridges rose together to follow him, but Red Hawk did not miss the glance Major Ridge exchanged with President Jackson. It promised doom to their people.

* * *

150

Ruby lent Kit Samantha for the trip to Wytheridge. The extra pair of hands would be useful on the farm with spring planting to be done and preparations for the wedding to be made. Kit was glad to be going home at last. Following the incident with President Jackson, the entire family treated her as if she had a contagious disease or as if she had lost her wits.

She herself did not know what had made her speak out the evening she had stood before the President. She had chastised herself a hundred times. As she and Samantha packed the two wooden trunks, the leather hat cases, and the carpet bags, Kit found herself impatient to be off. Ruby's house and all of Washington society seemed suddenly stifling. She had not the head for politics she'd thought she possessed. Her father did not need her. Thinking that she could play some part in his life in the new administration had been a foolish girlish dream. She belonged on the Georgia plantation.

Perhaps hard work, getting her hands in the soil and supervising the servants, would make her forget her dalliance with the Indian. At present the experience was still in her conscience. If she stopped her chores for long enough, she would find herself staring in a mirror at a young woman who had changed. Does everyone else see the change? she wondered.

But she must shut away thoughts of the Indian's hands on her skin. She dared not close her eyes or she would see his face, his sensual lips. So she kept her eyes open and delved into housework, sewing, cutting out patterns for Ruby, trying out a new recipe. Anything to have done with her memory of Red Hawk.

Finally they were ready. Caleb delivered the luggage to the dock. Kit wore a dress of muslin topped by a short jacket for traveling. The days were warming Washington City, and as they traveled south it would get warmer. But they had lap robes for the cool nights in the coaches, for they were traveling partway by steamer and then by stage.

Ruby knocked on Kit's door and, at Kit's answer, came into the room. She looked sadly at her niece, and then her bosom rose and fell on a sigh.

"I shall miss you, child," she said. She pressed her lips together and batted her eyelids. Kit rose and went to her, holding out her hands, which Ruby grasped. In her niece, the older woman saw the bloom of youth. She both envied Kit and feared for her. She shook her head, thinking that after all she really did prefer her settled, mature years with all the entrapments of life's maze behind her.

"I shall miss you too, Aunt," said Kit. It was heartfelt, for though she knew she must go, Ruby had been very kind to them all.

Ruby squeezed her hands. "I worry about you on that plantation all alone, my dear. I don't see why Jonathan can't give it up and move to Washington City permanently." Then she held up a hand. "I know, I know. Politics is not a secure thing. And he is a farmer at heart. He knows the value of land. It's our future. I wouldn't be surprised if he tires of his job in the administration within a year. Then he'll be back digging in his fields again."

Kit nodded in agreement. Her father was full of himself at present. Being so close to the President had lit a fire under his entire family. But Ruby was a realist. She had seen administrations come and go, and she knew her brother.

Kit patted her hand. "Well, don't worry about me. You've given me a dependable maid, and we have lots of help at home."

She found, for the first time in days, that she could actually smile. "That is, they are good help when one of us is there to see that they are doing their jobs. With everyone gone and work in the hands of our foreman, Lucius, no telling what's happened."

Ruby chuckled sympathetically. But she still looked deep into Kit's eyes. "I still worry about you my dear. I know you are at a vulnerable age. What was it made you speak to President Jackson so the other night?"

Kit flushed and looked away. "I'm sorry if I embarrassed you. I didn't mean to. It's just that I have been hearing things . . . about what's going on in Georgia. It doesn't sound fair, that's all. I just wondered if the President was going to do anything about it."

Ruby raised her brows. "I see. Well, I am not fond of General Jackson, and I don't know what's going on in Georgia. Oh, Jonathan speaks of this gold business. But surely the parties negotiating will come to some accommodation. The gold is on Indian lands, isn't it?"

Kit nodded, not wanting to look at Ruby again. But she was forced to. "Yes, it is."

"I see." Ruby observed her, but said no more. Then she suddenly roused herself. "But why are we standing here like a couple of gossips. You'll have to be leaving within the hour. The docks are always so crowded, it's best to get to the steamer in plenty of time."

"Yes, Aunt. And thank you again."

The two embraced and Ruby went to summon Caleb. Samantha closed the carpet bags they would carry with them, and Kit made sure everything was ready. Then Fletch burst into the room.

"Well, all ready? We must be going. Father will meet us on the boat. He'll be coming directly from ·the Capitol."

They went down to the carriage, and Ruby saw them off. Samantha sat stiffly in her traveling cloak across from Kit and Fletch, her black eyes huge as she looked at the street. She had never been out of Washington City before and was partly frightened because of stories she'd heard about slaves being beaten on Southern plantations and partly excited about seeing another part of the country.

She tried to tell herself she wouldn't be beaten. This family had always treated her nice. But there'd be a foreman at the new place. And she knew a lot of black foremen beat their black sisters and brothers in an effort to impress their masters.

Oh, Lord, she prayed silently. Deliver me not into a place of suffering and degradation and I will be the soul of Christian kindness to all my sisters and brothers and the white folks You have seen fit to put over me.

At the docks, Fletch guided his sister through the melee to the ramp. Caleb would see to the luggage, and Samantha, carrying two of the carpet bags, followed close behind, so close she nearly stepped on Kit's heels because she was afraid someone would come between them and she would be lost forever.

But Fletch managed to guide them up the ramp, show the tickets, and explain that he was just getting his sister settled and would return to shore.

"Sailing time in three-quarters of an hour," said the officer collecting the tickets.

They found the small cabin in which they would be traveling, and after leaving Samantha with their things, Kit followed Fletch through the lounges.

"Well," her brother said rather pompously, "this ship looks well enough fitted out."

The lounge was luxurious. Several handsome-looking glasses in ornate gilt frames were hung in it, and the dark mahogany woodwork had been waxed to a shiny finish.

"We'll only be on two nights." Then the stage would rattle and bump them over the hills toward home.

"Yes, yes. Be sure and sit at the captain's table at dinner. Father made sure he has your name."

"Of course, Fletch." She was impatient with his patronizing tone. "I'll be fine."

He cleared his throat, rising up on his toes and then settling back on his heels the way their father often did.

"In only a month I'll be bringing Merilee."

"Don't worry, Fletch. Everything will be fine until then."

Their father had wanted the couple to have a longer engagement, but Fletch pointed out that with Jonathan in Washington City, he could hardly be spared the entire planting season. And Merilee would be a help as well.

Not that Fletch was anxious for his bride to ruin her fine hands with housework, but he knew the realities. They were not wealthy Southern plantation owners like the cotton-growers farther south.

The steamship whistle tooted, piercing the air with a frightening warning. Kit turned her cheek so that Fletch could kiss her goodbye.

"Take care of yourself, my dear," he said.

She smiled and shook her head. Since when had he begun to call her "my dear."

"Goodbye. I'll have everything ready when you and Merilee arrive."

Fletch stepped back. Then his pseudosophistication dropped for a moment and his eyes widened slightly. He swallowed.

"Do you think she'll really like it there?" he asked.

She could see that he needed reassurance. He was trying to be so adult now that he was about to marry. But beneath the bravado was the same impetuous, uncertain hellion she had grown up with.

"I'm sure she will."

The whistle sounded again, and she shoved him toward the gangplank.

"Go on. I'll see you in a month."

Fletch made his way to the dock, and Kit leaned on the rail to wave to him. Then he turned back to find Caleb and the landau.

She watched her brother move through the crowd. He was becoming a lot like their father, and she wasn't sure she liked that. She had always loved her father, loved their home. But now new feelings stirred inside her, and she was seeing everything with different eyes. She wasn't sure she liked the change in herself any more than she liked the change in Fletch.

She took a deep breath of moist air and lifted her gaze to look over the spreading city. Far to the left the hills rose above Georgetown, and as she gazed at their green, hidden folds, her heart swelled once again. Then she put her hand to her hot cheek in shame. She must not think of the hills of Georgetown or of what had happened there.

It was night in New Echota, capital of the Cherokee Nation. Red Hawk entered the log cabin of his friend, the medicine man Waiting Bear.

As were many of the other cabins in the village, Waiting Bear's was divided into two rooms with a loft above the second room. In that room stood a bed constructed from white oak. A curtain of sewn hides partitioned off a lean-to pantry.

Tonight a fire burned in a small pit in the center of the main room. The smoke rose and drifted out to the clear black night through a round hole in the roof. Red Hawk did not sit on the benches at the sides of the room. Instead, he joined his friend on the floor in front of the fire.

They sat in silence and watched the flames. Waiting Bear knew his friend was troubled, but he also knew Red Hawk would speak of it when he was ready. For had not Waiting Bear counseled many such lovelorn. At last Red Hawk spoke, his strong features glistening in the firelight from a light sheen of sweat. His eyes looked far beyond the room, seeing for many miles, but when he spoke his voice was gentle, his lips not quite hiding a smile of pleasure.

"I have met a white woman," he said.

Waiting Bear grunted and picked up a stick to poke the fire. He put the stick down.

"And she has stolen your heart."

A small movement of Red Hawk's head signified that Waiting Bear was correct.

Waiting Bear nodded. "But that is not all. You are displeased with yourself for wanting her."

Red Hawk nodded definitely. He did not look at his friend.

"But you desire this woman?" Waiting Bear asked.

"I do," Red Hawk confessed. "But she is not of our kind. She is the daughter of one of the white men. The white men are bringing evil down upon the Cherokees. My visit to Washington City confirmed my belief that there are few good white men."

Waiting Bear nodded thoughtfully. "Our people are well aware of your feelings," he said. "You have much bitterness in your heart."

"Our people are beset by white intruders. There is much reason for bitterness. The whites' President

158

will not help us. His troops are helpless against the white hordes wanting to steal the gold from our ground."

Waiting Bear sat in silence for a time. Then he said, "What you say is true, but you came to me because you wish to love. You must overcome the bitterness in your heart before you can love any woman. Red Hawk's heart is a warrior's heart. Such a heart is easily blackened by too much hatred."

Red Hawk lifted his eyes toward the dark shadows at the edges of the room. He narrowed his gaze as he looked into the future.

"I believe our people are entering a dark time," he said solemnly. "The peace we had hoped to gain by following the white man's ways will be lost. In the coming years there will come soldiers with muskets. I see a time when there is no New Echota, no nation, no hope. The graves of our dead will be like teardrops on a long sandy trail. Then there will be only courage."

A blanket of dread settled over Waiting Bear. After a moment he spoke again.

"What you say is ominous."

Red Hawk nodded. Then he brought his gaze back to the fire. "Nevertheless, we must fight. We must defend our hidden valleys. We must not let disunity be the ruin of our people."

For a long time there was nothing more to say. The fire burned lower, and Waiting Bear put more wood on it. Finally Red Hawk spoke again.

"My disappointment at what our nation has suffered already at the hands of the white man has marred my soul," said Red Hawk. "Such thoughts have left me little room for beauty."

"That is not good," said Waiting Bear. "The woman. She is beauty in your eyes."

Red Hawk lifted his chin. "Yes."

Waiting Bear grunted again. "I will help you. With the white woman, the object of your heart's desire, and in finding peace within your soul. For you cannot have the first without the second."

"I accept your help," said Red Hawk.

Waiting Bear sat straighter. "I can give you a love incantation, a ritual no woman can resist. But you must be warned. The lovesickness that results from the use of such magic causes the woman to be repelled by her familiar surroundings and drives her to seek surcease in the arms of her enchanter.

"But it is white magic, good magic," chuckled the medicine man. "I use white magic to crush evil and bring happiness. Waiting Bear will help Red Hawk cure the bitterness in his heart and find beauty again."

Then Waiting Bear reached for a pipe made of hickory with eagle feathers tied to its stem. He filled the bowl with tobacco, lit it, and then handed the pipe to Red Hawk. Red Hawk sucked on the pipe, inhaled the smoke, and then poured it from his lungs. Waiting Bear began his teaching.

After an hour he had taught Red Hawk the love chants for attracting, for creating loneliness and longing, and for retaining affection. Finally Red Hawk unfolded his legs, stood, and took his leave. He bid Waiting Bear good night and then opened the door to the night.

Outside, he stood in the crisp air, breathing in its sweetness. He turned toward the east and whispered one of the love charms into the night.

"Your soul and mine will ever be inside of each other. Your flesh and mine will become one for as long as time endures."

Then he walked over the soft ground to his own cabin to lie down and sleep.

Kit tossed and turned in the narrow bed of her small cabin and then rose early, just as the steamer was coming into Cape Charles. She watched the crew maneuver the ship into port. As the gangplank was lowered, a crowd of poorly clothed, unkempt slaves stared from the dock.

Some of these had a lazy, reckless look as they sauntered along. How different they seemed from the slaves on Wytheridge. Though the servants on Wytheridge worked hard, they were neither mistreated nor overworked. Their lives were regulated, and everything was taken care of for them. And they kept themselves clean.

Kit turned from the railing. At a glance she decided this place was uninspiring. She paced the deck as passengers disembarked. Since there was nothing to look at, she decided to return to her cabin and try to read the book she had brought along.

She allowed Samantha to go on deck to watch the loading and unloading of the steamer, but soon she felt restless in the tiny cabin and threw down the

161

book. She could not concentrate on the story for more than a few pages at a time.

Kit went on deck again and made a complete tour from bow to stern. A new restlessness had settled on her, and she did not know how she would tolerate the remaining part of the journey. It would not be long to Portsmouth, where they would change for the stage. Perhaps that, at least, would provide some variety.

But she knew what she longed for. At journey's end, she would be home. There she could throw herself into the familiar routine of work. She did not mind the labor that went into building a plantation into something they could be proud of. Their father had erected a fine house. A place to which Fletch could bring Merilee. Not that it was as grand as the homes in Washington City, but it was their own.

She tried to think thoughts that would soothe her, and yet underlying all her plans, her relief at being away from the strange turn her life had taken in Washington City, was a sense of longing—an unease that sent her pacing around the deck time and again.

With relief, she went to make sure Samantha had their belongings ready for the landing at Portsmouth. As before, Negroes gathered around the gangplank and watched in wide-eyed fascination while the passengers disembarked and were transferred to waiting stagecoaches.

Kit waited with Samantha while the trunks were strapped onto the rack behind and valises and packages were consigned to the boot beneath the driver's seat. Bandboxes were put on top. Then ladies and an elderly gentleman were ushered into one of the coaches. Samantha took her place with the other Negroes and the young men on top of the stage.

The sight of the guard, armed with blunderbuss, sitting beside the driver's seat, made Kit silently pray for a safe trip. While she had never been on a coach stopped by highwaymen, such waylayings were not unheard of.

The female passengers and the elderly male were packed onto the three rows of seats within the coach by a man with a booming voice and arms he waved about while seating the travelers according to their destinations.

When one of the ladies—by her accent Kit judged her to be English—complained of having to ride with so many in one coach, with even more hanging on above, the man in charge answered smartly.

"A tight fit'll prevent you from bein' tossed about like a few potatoes in a wheel barrow. Ye' wouldn't want a loose ride over a rough road else yer heads and yer limbs bounce about and cause ye a concussion."

Kit settled in between a modestly dressed dark-haired woman a little older than herself and a sallow-faced matron with rickety teeth and an infant on her lap. As soon as they had got themselves arranged so that their knees were not jabbing those of the passenger across from them and their elbows were not in each other's waists, the driver cracked his whip and the team was off.

"Lord I dread this rough road," the matron to

163

Kit's left said. "This babe'll squall from here to Wilmington."

Her fear was realized as the coach at first pitched and lurched along and the baby cried. All the other women, including one who had a skinny young child with her, offered advice. Eventually the ride became smoother, affording them the chance to converse and look out of the carriage windows. And eventually the baby slept.

"Going far?" asked the pleasant-looking woman with dark hair pulled back under a straw hat.

Kit smiled at her neighbor. "To my home in the Georgia hills. I've been away since the presidential elections in November."

"Oh?" said the woman. "Where is your home?"

"I'll get off at Dahlonega at the stage stop. Our plantation is nearer Clarkesville, but the stage doesn't go there."

The woman gave a knowing nod. "Very near the Chattahoochee."

Kit showed surpris. "How did you know?"

"I live with my husband in New Echota."

Kit gave a gasp. "But New Echota is . . ."

The woman smiled. "I know. In the Cherokee Nation. My husband is a missionary. But please forgive my rudeness. My name is Harriet Worcester. My husband is the Reverend Samuel Worcester. He has worked among the Indians for several years."

Kit still could not hide her surprise. "Then you actually live there?"

Harriet gave a warm laugh, and her brown eyes twinkled. "Yes, I do. It is quite civilized. But many

164

outsiders do not know that if they have not seen for themselves. We have a comfortable home, and the Cherokees accept us."

"Oh." Kit struggled for polite words. "I'm sorry. I didn't mean to . . . to . . ."

"It's all right." Harriet nodded in understanding as if she'd had similar conversations many times before.

Kit looked down at her hands. "I did meet a Cherokee delegate actually, in Washington City."

"Ah, yes." Harriet's voice turned more solemn, and her expression became more serious. "You must have come across the delegation that went to plead with President Jackson for help against the white intruders."

Then she looked at Kit. "If you have not been in Georgia in six months, I'm afraid you will find it quite changed."

Kit stiffened. She could not help the discomfort she felt at being cast into the presence of someone intimately connected with the Cherokees. She was returning home in search of respite from the turbulent emotions that had beset her since she had met Red Hawk. She did not want to think about the Cherokees or their political problems just yet. She wanted to be left in peace until she could put the matter into perspective, but she knew politeness demanded she make conversation with the woman who rode with her.

"I understand gold has been discovered in the mountains there," Kit said.

"Yes. It is quite sad."

In spite of her desire not to be a part of the situation in Georgia, Kit responded to the concern in the other woman's voice. She knew it was her own confusion that prevented her from not wanting to enter into a discussion about the strife in her home state, but it seemed she would be forced to learn something of the situation.

Indians had been conquered in many wars. She had simply never considered that there might be anything wrong with that. But then, she had never met an Indian personally before. Like many of her kind, she had never considered that the Indians were being ill treated. There had never been any reason to question the political pressures that had pushed the Indians aside in order to develop Georgia lands—the very land she lived on.

She squirmed in her seat, hoping the passengers assumed she was simply trying to be more comfortable on the bumpy ride. Then she pressed her hands against her skirt and swallowed, trying to rid her throat of its dryness.

"My father has told me something of the negotiations," Kit began. "He is an advisor to President Jackson."

Harriet turned to observe her more closely. "I see."

Kit wanted to explain, but did not want to reveal too many of her own unresolved questions.

"Cannot the matter be solved in some way?" she asked Harriet. "I understand the Cherokees will be well paid for their lands. If they do not want the gold—"

Harriet cut her off. This time she did not hide her feelings behind the polite demeanor of a missionary's wife.

"And force them off their lands? The gold is theirs, whether they want it or not. They do not want to be moved again. But perhaps you do not realize how much of their vast holdings have already been given up to the federal government."

Harriet took a breath and attempted to stem her anger. "Perhaps they did not need as much territory as they once claimed. When the first settlers came, perhaps they believed there would be room for all. But now the state of Georgia wants to force the Indians out altogether. Either that or annihilate them. The Indians are powerless against the hordes overrunning their lands now that this gold rush has begun. You will see for yourself."

Kit's heart had begun to beat faster. "But how will I see? My home is far from the Cherokee Nation." She knew the phrase was meaningless. It was not her home that was in question.

"You ride the stage to Dahlonega, do you not?"

Kit nodded.

"You will see then," said Harriet. "It begins there."

Chapter Nine

The stage crossed a stone bridge and wound along the road, which offered little in the way of scenery. Nothing seemed to move in the forest solitude outside, and the gloomy vegetation hid the sun, giving the effect that it was dark early. They passed no dwellings, but came at last to the stopping place for the night. There was no town, only a rude inn in a small clearing.

The coach rumbled to a stop, and the host from the inn, a man in rustic clothing, stood outside while the passengers unbent their limbs.

"We leave at four o'clock in the morning," called the driver as he came around the coach to supervise the unhitching of the team. "Them that's late'll be left."

And with no further word of instruction, the driver left the passengers in the hands of the innkeeper. Kit followed the other women upstairs, where they divided themselves into small groups to share rooms. The small beds were crude, but the rooms were clean. Kit and Harriet fell in with the sallow matron from the coach and her unhappy child. The woman told them her name was Dora Mae Johnson. Samantha found them and poked her head into the room.

"Would there be anything you're needin'?" she asked Kit, blinking her wide black eyes.

"If you could find us some towels, we could wash up," Kit said. When she turned back into the room, she saw Harriet looking in the direction in which Samantha had disappeared.

"I didn't know you traveled with a slave," said Harriet.

Kit blinked. "She doesn't actually belong to me," she said. "She is my aunt's servant in Washington City. But my father would not let me travel alone, so Aunt Ruby lent her to me."

"I see," said Harriet.

She spared her new acquaintance a lecture on slavery, for she had perceived a vulnerability in the girl from Georgia and she scarcely knew her. If there was one thing Harriet had learned from her husband it was that lectures only brewed resentment unless the hearer was willing to listen.

The women did their best to clean themselves with only a bowl and a pewter pitcher of water. Samantha succeeded in locating only one towel for the room, which the women shared. But with a little water splashed on her face, Kit felt somewhat revived and she joined the others at the common dining table for a meal of hot bread and chicken. The landlord's wife, a portly woman with drab clothing and greasy hair, sat at the head of the table and poured tea with the most dignified of manners.

When the meal was finished, the male members of the traveling party withdrew to one end of the large room, and a large screen was pulled across to separate them from the women. Harriet touched Kit's arm.

"The beds upstairs may not look inviting, but the fireplace in our room looks like it might be capable of holding a cheerful fire."

Kit warmed to the other woman's companionship and followed her up the creaky wooden stairs to find that an imp of a black girl had laid several pine logs across the andirons and was now coaxing the kindling. When she saw Kit and Harriet, she threw in the last piece of kindling and rose to slip past them.

Harriet stopped her by placing her hands on the girl's skinny shoulders.

"Thank you for the fire, my girl."

The little girl opened her mouth and stared for a moment at Harriet. Then she slipped out of her grasp and fled down the hall.

Harriet shook her head, her eyes betraying her concern for the child. There were many such children in this part of the country, she knew. And most were in greater need of food in their stomachs than the word of the gospel, something even her husband was aware of.

Soon the fireplace blazed with warmth, and Kit and Harriet drew up low wooden chairs with reclining backs and wide, sturdy arms. They made themselves comfortable, and Kit began to appreciate the fact that they were sitting still instead of bouncing around in the coach. The tension she had carried with her since they had left Washington City began to recede as the fire crackled before them.

Harriet, too, was calmed by the sight of the roaring fire, whose warmth was not unneeded in the room.

For though it was spring, the hilly country remained cold at night.

"Tell me of your family," Harriet began.

They would no doubt retire early, but she sensed in Kit a need to talk, and nothing made sleep easier than a long chat, especially when one needed to unburden oneself.

The comfort of the fire, the privacy of the room, and the compassion Kit sensed in the other woman had an unexpected effect on Kit. As she was about to speak, she felt near to tears. No words would come. Instead, a sob caught in her throat.

"I'm sorry," she managed to get out, grief stabbing at her chest. "I don't know what's wrong with me." Her last words came out in a little squeak, and she felt ashamed, for she wasn't much given to tears.

Harriet watched her. "It's all right. You need not be ashamed. If you feel like talking about it, I'm glad to listen. Sometimes it helps to express ourselves to one another, no matter how disoriented we think we may sound."

Kit sobbed foolishly, then shook her head, wiping her eyes with the back of her hand and trying to smile.

"I'm not sure I can explain."

"Ah," said Harriet, turning her gaze to the fire. "I think I understand." She spoke softly. "Judging by your age I would guess that what troubles you may have something to do with your heart, though I do not mean to pry."

Again a wracking sob threatened, but this time Kit took a deep breath and determined to gain the upper hand. It was silly to break down like this in front of a

171

complete stranger. Surely the hard journey had weakened her resistance. What she needed was rest, but sitting with the woman she would most likely not see again tempted her to confess. For sometimes it was easier to unburden oneself to a stranger because when the stranger passed from one's life, the confession did too.

"Yes, I suppose," said Kit. "I did meet a man in Washington City. I . . . I did things I shouldn't have. I can't explain it. It was the most . . ." she pressed her lips together, the grief welling up again along with a deep unexplainable feeling of loss.

"I can't excuse what he did to me—what I did. But it was . . . it was the most wonderful thing." Her eyes brimmed with tears again, and she wiped them away impatiently. "Do you know what I mean? That something can be both bad and good at the same time?"

Harriet smiled compassionately. "Of course. It is often that way with love." She sighed. "Unfortunately our passions do not always wait for the blessings of our families and the formalities of the wedding ceremony."

She waited a moment for Kit to get control of herself. "Do you wish to marry this man?" she asked.

Kit's face reddened, and her eyes widened as she stared into the flames. "It would be impossible. No. I could never marry him."

Harriet had seen many barriers prevent people from being married. "I see. An impossible match. Is he married already?"

Kit blinked. Actually she had not even considered that. She shook her head helplessly. "I don't think so."

Harriet raised her brows. "Did you not ask?"

She tried to make it a gentle question, but her surprise was real. The girl seemed innocent; perhaps she had been so swept off her feet she had assumed there was no such barrier and had been given a hard fall when the man had not asked her to marry him.

But Kit merely shook her head. "We knew each other only briefly, I'm afraid."

Then she looked directly at Harriet. She felt more in control of herself now. Perhaps the outburst had helped. But she was not about to speak of Red Hawk to this woman.

"Thank you for listening," she said awkwardly. "I do feel better." She glanced toward the bed. "I believe I can sleep now."

Dora Mae came in with her baby and after nursing it, lay down on the bed nearest the far wall with all her clothes on, the baby tucked in her arm. Harriet and Kit undressed and got in between the sheets on their small beds, and Samantha curled up on a straw pallet by the fire.

In spite of her words about being able to sleep, Kit tossed and turned in her bed, thoughts pounding at her from every direction. It seemed she had barely dropped off to sleep when a loud knock on the door roused them. Though it was still dark, it was time to dress and go.

"Hurry," said Harriet once they were all awake, "or else we'll miss getting anything in our stomachs before the coach leaves."

Samantha lit candles for them to see by, and in no time they were downstairs. The portly landlady filled bowls with some kind of gruel—no one asked what it was—and her young black servants handed them around.

Then Kit and Samantha gathered up the carpet bags they had brought with them, and Kit tumbled sleepily into the coach again, finding her place between Dora Mae and Harriet. The whip cracked, and the team got off to a trot.

Though the ride was bumpy, Kit could not keep her eyes open; she drowsed to the sound of the coach wheels and the moist smell of the morning air.

In the afternoon they stopped for a meal, and most of the women's conversation turned to children and child-rearing. When it became known that Harriet had two children of her own, the other passengers wanted to know if she had left them with her husband.

"Yes," said Harriet, sipping more of the black liquid that passed for coffee at this particular establishment. "But he is too busy with his translating work to care for them as a mother would. My good neighbor Mary Red Tail has accepted the main responsibility."

Harriet smiled. "Of course in New Echota, the children have many mothers who adore looking after them."

A stuffy woman from Charleston named Mrs. Hodge sniffed. "I can't believe you let your brood run wild with a bunch of Indians."

But Harriet was not put off. "What better way for children to grow up than in a small village where they can play outdoors and learn many of the crafts at which the Cherokees are so skilled?"

"Waste of time to my way of thinking," said Mrs. Hodge who had not been so vocal until she'd learned that Harriet's husband was a missionary among the Cherokees. "How do you know those Indians even understand the Bible?"

Harriet remained the soul of patience. "They are taught English at school, and my husband is translating the Bible and many hymns into Cherokee."

Suddenly, all the women who had been reserved and reticent until then plunged into the argument. Kit found herself warming to the subject, taking Harriet's side. While she herself knew relatively little about the Cherokees in New Echota, she was angered at the narrow-minded viewpoint most of these Southern woman seemed to have.

"You can't Christianize savages," said Mrs. Hodge. "My husband says so."

"They are not savages," said Kit, thumping her coffee cup down on the torn tablecloth.

For a moment the others all turned to look at her. Only Harriet's eyes were cast down.

Kit cleared her throat. "The Cherokees have been educated to use our methods and our diplomacy. Many of them attend our schools in the East."

"Well then, you must have met some of them," said Mrs. Hodge. "Where did you say your home is?"

"I didn't meet them at home," Kit went on, thrusting her chin forward an inch. "It so happens my father has met with the Indian delegation in Washington City. I have seen some of them at receptions. They are civilized, educated men."

She tried to say it with a calm demeanor, but she prayed the conversation would turn away from her before the blood rushed into her face. She turned to ask one of the servant girls for more coffee.

The grumbling continued, but the conversations broke down as each person chattered with her neighbor. Harriet raised her eyes to Kit's. She did not smile, but a look of understanding passed between them.

From then on when Kit found herself alone with Harriet, usually at night before they went to bed, the two women talked of their lives, sharing their friendship. While Kit never expanded on exactly who it was she had met from the Cherokee delegation, she felt at ease telling Harriet about her family, their plantation, her life growing up on it, her father's political involvement, and the many other confidences that friends share.

In return she listened with interest as Harriet described her life in the Cherokee capital, and was pleased when Harriet wrote out some words in Cherokee for her. Harriet said that the Cherokee language was complex, and that many had thought it could not be written down. But a man named Sequoyah had dreamt of making a "talking leaf" like the white man had. It took him twelve years to produce his syllabary of eighty-five symbols. His alphabet had been approved by the Cherokee chiefs in 1821, and now a newspaper was being printed in Cherokee.

For Kit, Harriet became an extension of Red Hawk, teaching her things she had begun to wish to learn when she'd met him. Learning about the Cherokees whiled away the long hours in the coach and the time spent in tiny, rude taverns and way stations along their route until, finally, they crossed the Tallulah

River and were in the mountains of Georgia.

Kit's senses came alive as she neared home. Sometimes they had to get out of the coach and walk up the inclines when the road twisted around mountain passes. But she loved the fresh, foggy air and gazed rapturously at the sun lighting the thick green forests that covered the mountains like plush carpet. As the men worked together to dislodge a wheel that had got caught by a boulder, Kit wandered down to a stream and cupped her hands to gather clear, cold water to drink.

In the joy of being back in her beloved mountains, she forgot the concerns that had beset her. She had been certain she would be revived by coming home, and she had been right. That night as the sun set over one of the verdant hills, Kit began to make plans for what she would do when she reached Wytheridge.

The spring plowing would be in progress. Lucius, their black foreman, would have the hands working in the fields. Even the wives and children would be helping. Kit would put Samantha under the housekeeper's care. Ossie Lee Tatum would take the girl under her wing for work in the house and kitchen.

And Kit herself would have to catch up on all the family chores that had been left undone these many months they'd been away. The thought of planning for Fletch's wedding was overwhelming. She had already begun lists of what she must do and had consulted with Ruby in Washington, for her aunt had had experience with weddings. Kit was grateful to be able to put the preparations of food and of the house into Ossie Lee's capable black hands. The trustworthy housekeeper would know what to do once Kit told her how many people would attend and the number of days they would stay.

Kit herself would have to see to a great deal of sewing. The wedded couple must have newly embroidered linens. The curtains in the house must look their best. Merilee would take care of her own trousseau, and Fletch would be able to order clothes in Washington City, but Kit had to have something to wear.

The amount of sewing ahead worried her. She had acquired the skill from her mother, and a good thing too, for the mending and making of new things never seemed to cease. Perhaps she would be able to enlist the help of Lucius's wife, Vashti.

Once, in exasperation over the sewing that needed to be done, Kit had gathered together all the female help on the place and had taught them all how to turn hems, embroider, and quilt. Vashti had shown the most talent for the fine, detailed work which required such nimble fingers.

So engrossed in her thoughts was Kit that she hardly noticed when darkness settled between the clefts in the hills and the sky turned pewter. But she felt the coach slow to the driver's "Whoa!"

Travel-weary, the passengers disembarked and clattered into the yard of another inn. Harriet held Dora Mae's baby while the tired mother pulled out her carpet bag, and then they all stumbled into the large log-built inn.

"We'll reach Dahlonega tomorrow," Harriet said when she joined Kit.

"I know," Kit replied. "I'll have to send word to Wytheridge for someone to fetch me—unless I'm lucky enough to run into one of our neighbors in town buying supplies."

"Then you may have time to see what I mean about the miners who are overrunning the area," said Harriet, a trace of brittleness in her voice.

As the new arrivals were being shown to their rooms, Kit became aware of the laughter and the fiddle music drifting toward them from the large downstairs room. Then one of the young men in the party discovered that dancing was going on and let out a whoop.

He crossed the board floor of the entry hall and opened the door opposite. The thump of feet stepping to the lone fiddle spilled out. Several of the younger people forgot all about getting their places for the night and rushed to join in the merrymaking.

Kit smiled. Though she remained beside Harriet, the fiddle was music to her ears and again confirmed that she was home. For the Georgia mountaineers were exceedingly fond of music-making.

In spite of the usual inconveniences of staying at an inn, Kit slept well, and the women were up before light, standing in the yard before boarding. Kit breathed in the fresh air of the pine, oak, and hemlock forest. When they finally got settled, the coach lurched forward and began its twisting route over the highlands once again.

The road took a hairpin curve, and before them a finger of golden light pierced the gray dawn, streaming from between the clouds across the unfolding valley below.

They made steady progress, stopping twice to walk up inclines where there was danger of the coach getting stuck in ruts formed by a recent rain. Kit walked beside Harriet, but they spoke little, each consumed by her own thoughts. The camaraderie that had grown between them on the journey was strained by the knowledge that they were going separate ways. Kit was going home to the hard work of a north Georgia plantation, Harriet to her missionary life among the Cherokees.

When Kit looked at the sturdy and purposeful, yet graceful and warm, woman beside her, she couldn't help but want such a friendship to continue. Kit was trying to forget the Cherokees, but part of what drew her to Harriet was her connection with them. Harriet might even be acquainted with Red Hawk.

Kit dared not ask, yet the idea would not leave her all day. Perhaps Harriet knew Red Hawk well, knew his desires and his plans. The more Kit let her mind dwell on that possibility, the more obsessed she became with breaking down and asking, and yet she kept her silence. For one thing, there was little privacy for such a conversation, and with every turn in the road, they neared Dahlonega.

Even before they reached the small town tucked away in the blue and purple rolling hills, Kit noticed the increase of traffic on the road. The coach had had to slow for they had passed several wagons laden with equipment and men who dangled their legs off the side.

Kit grew curious. As the coach finally rumbled toward the little knoll sloping to the east, she leaned forward, trying to see out the window as they entered the busy town. When the coach pulled up in front of the Cane Creek tavern, she stared at the crowded yard. But it wasn't until she got down that she could see what Harriet meant. Dahlonega used to be a quiet mountain town, but no more.

Now men in high laced boots walked about the streets or leaned on the posts of newly built pine-board buildings that had been quickly thrown together. A mist shrouded the scene, but still, the clop of horses on the road, the loud braying of mules and the shouts of women scurrying about and attempting to get their children inside mingled with the rattle of harnesses and the squish of boots slopping through the mud.

Kit simply stood in the yard, letting the heavy mist seep into her. Where had they all come from? Harriet saw her look of dismay and raised her eyebrows.

"You see what I mean?"

Kit shook her head. "All of this is because of gold? It wasn't like this when we left last November."

"In November the cry of gold had not reached the farthest corners of the country."

Then surprisingly, out of the crowd emerged a tall, gangling black man walking barefooted through the mud, holding a beat-up hat in his hands. He bent sideways, thrusting his face toward them. Then the black face broke into a smile.

"That be Miz Kathryn?"

Kit blinked at the familiar face appearing like a spirit conjured out of the mist. She gave a shriek of delight and hurried forward.

"Brutus," she cried, running toward him, red mud splattering on the hem of her dress. "I hoped for such a miracle. I'm home. How good to see you."

She could have kissed the man, so relieved was she to see one of her own household in the tavern yard. But she skidded to a stop before him. He still grinned, but he straightened up, holding his hat respectfully in front of him.

"We knew you was to come home 'bout now," he said. "Miz Ossie tell me to look in the tavern yard if there was a coach come in."

"Oh yes, yes. How clever of her. We've just arrived. Did you come on foot, or did you bring a wagon?"

He wrinkled his thick brow. "I come on hossback, but I'll ride home again and tell Miz Ossie and bring the spring wagon fer your things."

"Oh, thank you, Brutus. I'll wait inside the tavern."

Brutus bowed his head in acknowledgment, but before he left, he looked up again in concern.

"If you don't mind my sayin'," he said hesitantly, "the tavern's got to be a rough place these days. Will you be all right there?"

Kit turned to glance at the tavern. Numerous men were entering and leaving it. When the door opened, she heard the uproar from inside. The Cane Creek Tavern was run by a widow whose husband had moved the family to the little settlement some years ago. The man had died when a mad dog had bit him.

The place used to cater to both men and women, but the rough-looking men pouring out of the tavern were not the mountaineers and farmers she knew. Then she caught sight of Harriet, who was gathering her belongings and helping to load them onto the back of a wagon.

It was then that she noticed the driver of the wagon

182

was Indian. The buckskin-clad man lifted a small trunk onto the wagon and turned, his dark eyes and strong Cherokee features making Kit draw in a breath. But she knew Brutus was waiting for her to say something. She turned back to him.

"I'll be all right. You go for the wagon, Brutus. I'll leave my things at the tavern and then I'll walk across to the Watkins' store. I'll watch for you."

"Yes'm," Brutus said and turned, bending his tall body into the mist.

Kit lifted her cape to avoid some of the mud and crossed to say goodbye to Harriet. The Indian had finished loading her things and was waiting for her to climb up on the wagon seat. Harriet waited for Kit.

"I wanted to say goodbye," said Kit.

She avoided looking at the Indian, whose black hair flowing over his shoulders reminded her all too well of Red Hawk's. The man climbed into the driver's seat and held the reins, looking straight ahead.

"My thoughts will be with you," said Harriet, kissing Kit on the cheek.

Kit returned the affectionate hug. "And mine with you."

The two women looked somberly at each other.

"Until we meet again," said Harriet; then she turned, placed her foot on the step, and pulled herself up onto the wagon seat. She turned and held up a hand in a farewell gesture as the Indian clucked to the horses and the wagon moved away.

Kit stood back, watching them go. The Indian looked neither to the right nor left as the wagon found a place in the busy street and rolled between the many white miners who had converged on the town.

The coachman had unloaded Kit's trunks and placed them on the board sidewalk in front of the tavern. The other passengers who had gotten down to stretch their legs were now back in their seats, and the driver climbed up to his. Dahlonega had not been a rest stop, and the coach had to make good time to get to its final destination for the night.

As the stage pulled away, Kit was again confronted with the change which had taken place in Dahlonega. She stood on the board walk to avoid being trampled by wagon wheels or having her bonnet nibbled by mules and horses. But she did not wish to wait out in the wet, so she looked for an opportunity to cross the street.

The porch opposite was covered and would offer some shelter, but just as she got to it, she was stopped by the sound of her name. She looked up to see Jared Patton, a son of one of the wealthier farmers, whose lands lay a few miles from the Newcombs'.

"Kit Newcomb," Jared said again as he reined in a bay gelding.

His smile glowed from a handsome face, his cheeks pink from the chill, and his blond hair flowed past the shoulders of his broadcloth coat. Kit had gone to school with Jared from the time they were both able to walk the three miles to the schoolhouse that lay equidistant between their places. Jared had finished school, but Kit had quit to take care of the house when her mother had died.

"Hello, Jared."

His smile of delight remained fixed on her as he dismounted and tied his reins to the hitching post. Then he planted his high-top boots on the little porch

184

on which Kit had sought refuge.

"It's been months," he said. "Where have you been?"

"Washington City. We left at election time."

"Lucky city. Our loss, but now you've returned."

"Oh, Jared, go on," she chided. Nevertheless, it was good to see a familiar face.

She was inured to Jared's flattery, knowing it meant nothing. For years, Jared Patton had chased girls around the school, and, it was rumored, he had gotten more than one of his father's servants pregnant.

For Jared's part, he had always been attracted to a pretty skirt. His father knew his son wanted to dally with female flesh, and desiring that Jared maintain a good reputation in the community, he had given him a free hand with the servant girls, for that was what slaves were for.

But now, Jared's blue eyes held Kit's rapturously. He took her arm and guided her closer to the weather-boarded building to get out of the way of passersby.

"Kathryn, you know I am always glad to see you. It is you who never give me the chance to shower you with the attention a woman like yourself deserves."

His speech made her laugh. "I'll wager, Jared, that you have not given me one thought in these past months. Only seeing me now reminds you of the taunts you have undoubtedly missed."

He grinned with her. It was true that in school, she had not let him chase her, nor had she come near enough for a kiss. But she had not been above besting him when the opportunity arose. He relished the challenge she presented nearly as much as he relished catching a pretty girl.

"But now you've come back. Are you alone?"

"Brutus found me when the stage let off passengers. He's gone for the wagon."

"Well, I'm glad for that. For I know you would not deign to ride behind me on my horse."

She met his teasing stare with a grin. "No, I would not."

"Come, though. You will at least let me buy you a cup of hot cider to talk over all the news."

"What news?" she asked.

He gestured with the sweep of an arm toward the activity going on in Dahlonega.

"Why, the gold of course. It's going to make us all rich."

Chapter Ten

"But I thought the gold was on Indian lands," said Kit as they stared at the flood of miners on Main Street.

Jared laughed. "That's true. Ben Parks stumbled over a good-sized piece of quartz in the forest south of his homestead. When he picked up the quartz that rolled along the ground, that's when he saw it. Gold."

"But doesn't it belong to the Cherokees?" said Kit stubbornly.

Jared shrugged. "They don't want it. They don't use gold for money. They don't mine it. What good is it to them?"

Kit said nothing more. She did not really want to have anything to drink with Jared in the noisy tavern. But it was damp out, and it made sense to seek some shelter. She would not have minded saying hello to the Watkins family, who ran the general store. But until she went home, she didn't know what she needed to buy, and the store looked busy too, so Stella Watkins might not have time to visit.

Reluctantly she allowed Jared to grasp her elbow,

and when there was a break in the traffic, they dashed across the street. Inside the tavern, a group of men were gathered around the long table that ran down the center, and the widow Sarah Jorgenson was serving ale. Jared and Kit sought a place by the fireplace, and Jared ordered them two mugs of cider.

"It's good to see you, Kit," said the harried widow. Then she went to fetch the ale.

"So tell me about Washington City," said Jared, stretching out his long legs and propping his booted feet on a stool. Though it was April, the chilly mountain air made the fire welcome.

"Did your father get a post in the government?"

"He did," said Kit, warming her hands on the mug Sarah brought and taking a sip of the pungent cider. "But he'll be home for Fletcher's wedding next month."

"Well, so old Fletcher is getting himself hitched. Who's the lady?"

"Her name is Merilee Fitzsimmons. Her family are friends of my aunt."

"Ah, that's right. You had connections in high society when you went there."

His tone was slightly mocking, but that did not bother Kit. She had known Jared a very long time and was aware of all of his flaws. Still, he was a friend, and he had grown up in similar circumstances to hers. Talking to Jared was her first taste of home after these many months. It ought to make her feel relaxed, but the changes in Dahlonega made her uncomfortable.

A shout went up from the men at the long table, and then one of the men reached into his pocket and pulled out a small drawstring bag. He poured several nuggets onto the table and pushed them across it to the man who had won the bet.

The others pointed and halloed, and the winner, a skinny man with long whiskers growing down the sides of his face, picked up the nuggets and grinned, exposing his broken, yellow teeth as he put his winnings into a vest pocket.

Kit realized that being in Washington had changed her in a number of ways. As she looked at the hewn beams of the old tavern, the whittling on the arms of the chairs, where the idle knives of drinking men had carved out whimsical designs, she realized that being back here might not be what she had expected. The thought was not a comforting one.

"And did you meet the President?" Jared went on. "Does he really speak with the voice of the people?"

Kit blinked. She did not know how to answer that. "Which people?" she finally said.

When they finished their cider and left the tavern, they found Brutus waiting with the wagon. He had fetched Kit's trunks and placed them in it.

"So you're going to manage Wytheridge by yourself," said Jared as she prepared to climb up to the wagon seat.

"Until Fletch arrives," she said. "I'm lucky we have such capable help."

Jared grinned. "You tell Ossie Lee I'll be by for some of her biscuits and honey."

"I'll tell her."

When she was settled on the seat beside Brutus, Kit smiled down at Jared. She realized that having him stop by once in a while would be better than having no company at all.

"You come by any time, Jared."

He looked up at her questioningly, then stepped back and smiled. He clicked his heels together and raised a hand in a mock salute. She waved as Brutus clucked to the horses, and the wagon rolled away.

On the way out of town Kit's attention was drawn to several more new pine-board buildings hastily thrown up and she noticed several men panning gold in the creek at the edge of town. Then the wagon left Dahlonega behind, and Brutus urged the horses into a trot on the curving road that followed a line of trees.

"How have things been at Wytheridge, Brutus? Have the fields been plowed?"

"The field's been plowed, and ole Lucius's just waitin' for the right moon to plant the corn."

Kit gave a wry smile. Many farmers in this part of the country believed that when planted at the wrong time of the moon, the corn grew a big stalk and a little ear. Planted at the right time, it produced a good yield on little stalks.

She wondered suddenly if the Cherokees believed the same thing. Then she pressed her lips together and reminded herself that she had not come all the way back to Georgia to be thinking about the Cherokees at every turn.

As they wound deeper into the country, Kit looked forward to getting home. There would certainly be enough work there for her to lose herself in it. She took a deep breath of moist air and drew energy from the lush forest and the red clay beneath the wagon wheels.

During the hour's ride to Wytheridge, she got Brutus to tell her news of the farm. She was surprised to learn that so much had gotten done during the winter in spite of the fact that the Newcombs were away.

She hadn't expected too much, knowing that the help would probably not work so hard when their masters were not around to oversee them. But then, Ossie Lee considered herself in charge of them all, and her great size and loud voice gave her the authority to keep them in line. And her loyalty was unquestionable. Having Ossie Lee there was one reason the family could pick up and leave for so long a time.

The forest thinned, and they came to a cleared field belonging to one of the smaller farms that bordered Wytheridge. Kit leaned forward and then saw the neighbor family digging in the rows. George Potter leaned on his plowstock, wiping his forehead with a big red handkerchief. The family all looked up at the sound of a wagon rumbling past, and Kit waved a hand. The children jumped up from the dirt and waved back, and George, after a look, waved his big handkerchief.

After the next stand of oaks Kit knew they were driving beside Wytheridge land. She saw that on both sides of the road the fields had indeed been made ready for planting, with the exception of one far field which would lie fallow for a year in order to renew the earth.

Beyond the fields, fenced off on the rise toward the hills the Durham cattle grazed. Then the wagon turned a bend, and the plantation came into view.

The two-story frame house rose two stories, red brick chimneys at either side at the end of an avenue of cedars, with corn fields on one side and a large vegetable garden on the other. Set apart from the main house were the outbuildings, consisting of barn, poultry house, corn crib, smokehouse, storage shed, wagon shed, saddlery, servants' quarters, and tool shed, all built of the same whitewashed heart pine. Off by itself the springhouse stood near a grove of trees. Behind the red-roofed house, a gazebo stood near the stream, and across the stream uncleared forest climbed the mountain.

Jonathan Newcomb's grandfather had crossed the mountains from North Carolina and hacked this modest plantation out of the wilderness. The old man had fought the British, and when the war for independence was over, he had settled in the mountains, preferring the highlands to the cotton-growing flatlands farther south.

As they left the road and pulled along the drive, chickens and hogs fled out of their path. A gold and white creature, part sheepdog barked and bounded around the side of the house, and the large turbaned black woman sweeping the clay drive directly in front of the wide porch steps stopped her work and raised a hand to shield her eyes.

Kit was nearly out of the wagon before Brutus could rein in the horses. Shep leapt up, whining and licking her face and hands.

"Oh, Shep," Kit cried, grasping the dancing, leaping dog. "I missed you, boy."

Then she ran toward Ossie Lee Tatum, the woman who more than anything symbolized home for her, for Ossie Lee had been with the family since before Kit was born.

The woman grasped her in a bear hug. "Land sakes child you're a sight for sore eyes."

4 BESTSELLING HISTORICAL ROMANCES BY YOUR FAVORITE AUTHORS CAN BE YOURS, FREE!

Kensington Choice, our newest book club now brings you historical romances by your favorite bestselling authors including Janelle Taylor, Shannon Drake, Rosanne Bittner, Jo Beverley, and Georgina Gentry, just to name a few! Each book is filled with passion, adventure and the excitement of bygone times!

To introduce you to this great new club which is part of Zebra Home Subscription Service, we'd like to send you your first 4 bestselling historical romances, absolutely free! And once you get these 4 free books to savor at home, we'll rush you the next 4 brand-new books at the lowest prices available, as soon as they are published.

The way the club works is that after your initial FREE shipment, you will get our 4 newest bestselling historical romances delivered to your doorstep each month at the preferred subscriber's rate of only $4.20 per book, a savings of up to $7.16 per month (since these titles sell in bookstores for $4.99-$5.99)! All books are sent on a 10-day free examination basis and there is no minimum number of books to buy. (A postage and handling charge of $1.50 is added to each shipment.) Plus as a regular subscriber, you'll receive our FREE monthly newsletter, *Zebra/Pinnacle Romance News*, which features author profiles, contests, subscriber benefits, book previews and more!

So start today by returning the FREE BOOK CERTIFICATE provided. We'll send you 4 FREE BOOKS with no further obligation: A FREE gift offering you hours of reading pleasure with no obligation...how can you lose?

*We have 4 FREE BOOKS for you
as your introduction to
KENSINGTON CHOICE!
To get your FREE BOOKS, worth
up to $23.96, mail the card below.*

FREE BOOK CERTIFICATE

Yes! Please send me 4 Kensington Choice (the best of Zebra and Pinnacle Books) Historical Romances without cost or obligation (worth up to $23.96). As a Kensington Choice subscriber, I will then receive 4 brand-new romances to preview each month for 10 days FREE. I can return any books I decide not to keep and owe nothing. The publisher's prices for Kensington Choice romances range from $4.99-$5.99, but as a preferred subscriber I will get these books for only $4.20 per book or $16.80 for all four titles. There is no minimum number of books to buy and I may cancel my subscription at any time. A $1.50 postage and handling charge is added to each shipment. No matter what I decide to do, my first 4 books are mine to keep, absolutely FREE!

DP01K7

Name _____

Address _____ Apt. _____

City _____ State _____ Zip _____

Telephone ( ) _____

Signature _____

(If under 18, parent or guardian must sign)

Subscription subject to acceptance. Terms and prices subject to change.

4 FREE
Historical Romances
*are waiting
for you to
claim them!*

---◆◇◆---

(worth up to
$23.96)

---◆◇◆---

*See details
inside....*

KENSINGTON CHOICE
Zebra Home Subscription Service, Inc.
120 Brighton Road
P.O.Box 5214
Clifton, NJ 07015-5214

IΙₗₗₗₗₗₗₗₗΙΙΙₗₗₗₗₗₗₗΙΙₗΙₗΙₗΙₗΙₗΙₗₗₗΙΙₗΙₗΙₗΙₗₗₗΙΙₗΙₗₗΙΙₗₗₗΙ

"I'm glad to see you too, Ossie Lee. Brutus tells me you've taken care of everything marvelously."

"Well now. What did you expect? I couldn't have the likes of you comin' back here and the yard not swept nor the cows milked. 'Course I had to poke those lazy men with my broom handle a few times to get them up and doin'."

Ossie Lee grinned, her white teeth shining in her black face.

Brutus had climbed down from the wagon and begun unloading the trunks. The other hands had slowly crossed the fields when they'd seen Kit and were now gathering at the fence to solemnly greet her. She straightened and then walked down the drive to meet them. It was natural to assume the role of owner in the absence of her father or her brother, and she knew that the hands would respect her orders as much as if they were coming from either of the Newcomb men.

The young children did not wait on ceremony like the older folk, but slipped through the split rails and ran toward her. Just shy of where she walked toward them, they tumbled to a stop, gawking up at her, but saying nothing.

"Hello," she said to the youngsters and then went on to the fence, where two strong black men, the foreman Lucius and Oscar, the next in command, waited with their wives. The rest of the hands stood with their hats in their hands behind the two leaders.

"Welcome home, Miss Kit," said Lucius, the softer spoken of the two. He unconsciously put a hand on his wife Vashti's shoulder.

"Thank you, Lucius," she said. "I'm glad to be back."

She gazed at the plowed red earth behind them and farther up the slope at the grazing cows.

"I see you've been taking care of things here."

The men shrugged and nodded shyly.

Kit could see from their worn clothing that she would need to cut out new material for them. She had tried to teach the women to cut out material for clothing, but for some reason none of them except Vashti could do it well.

"We be fixin' to plant when the moon's right," said Oscar, leaning on the fence rail.

She smiled wryly. "I'll consult the almanac as soon as I've settled in. I imagine we'll need to plant soon."

"Moon's got to be right," said Oscar.

"Yes," said Kit. "I know."

After a bit more small talk, she sent the hands back into the fields and returned to the house. She introduced Samantha to Ossie Lee, and though the girl seemed intimidated by the older woman, Kit hoped the two would get on together.

"Samantha helped my aunt," she explained to Ossie Lee. "But Ruby thought we would need some extra help with Fletcher's wedding so soon."

"Land sakes, is that boy getting married after all? What poor girl is going to tie herself to him? Or is she the kind of woman that'll train him to mind his manners?"

Kit laughed. "She loves him, and I believe the feeling is mutual. I think it will be a good match. But they expect to come here in the next month. We have a lot to do to get the place ready."

"Well, I guess we do," said Ossie Lee, inflating her big chest, obviously pleased at yet another chance to show off her housekeeping abilities.

Kit chatted with Ossie Lee as they climbed the steps to the wide porch that stretched across the front of the house. Samantha followed shyly, and Shep pushed his way in before her. Just before she entered the house, Kit turned to view the place she loved so well. As she did so, she noticed that Oscar had stopped work and was staring at them. She turned and saw the object of his gaze. Samantha was looking toward the fields as well, and must have caught Oscar's interest.

Well, Kit said to herself as she went back into the house. Oscar's wife had died last year, leaving him with two young children who were growing up with Lucius's young ones. If Samantha interested him, Kit would not put a stop to the match. But she would make sure Ruby agreed to let Samantha stay here. Kit did not believe in separating married servants.

Brutus dragged the trunks up to Kit's room. After unpacking some of her clothing, she got out of her traveling clothes.

"Sit, Shep," she told the dog.

He obeyed, but thumped his tail loudly on the braid rug as he watched her. She asked Ossie Lee to fill a tub with hot water in the kitchen so that she could bathe. Having been ten days in a coach and some less than spotless inns, she felt filthy.

She donned a wrapper, found clean towels, and went downstairs, Shep at her heels. She followed a passage to a side door which opened onto a walk that led around the side of the house and across the herb garden to the separate kitchen.

"Stay here, boy," she told the dog.

He was allowed in the house, but Ossie Lee put her foot down when it came to having the dog in the kitchen. She had once told Shep he'd be butchered and eaten if he set his foot in there.

In the kitchen, Ossie Lee was already showing Samantha where things were kept, and the girl was following her every gesture with rounded eyes.

The hearth was broad enough to take in logs of wood six feet long. It was four feet deep and had a crane for swinging large pots on and off. A bread oven sat in the hearth. Pots and pans hung from hooks on the wall, and various cooking implements lay on the wooden work table in the center of the room and on the counters at the sides under the windows overlooking the herb garden and the fields beyond.

Brutus swung the huge cast-iron pot in which water had been heating from the hearth and emptied it into the large wooden tub.

"Thank you, Brutus," said Kit as he left the women.

Kit tested the water with her fingers and finding it to be the right temperature, she undressed and slipped in. Ossie Lee handed her a scrub brush and soap, and Kit bent her knees and slid down into the tub until the water covered her up to her shoulders.

She unwound her hair and let it soak behind her.

"Ah," she sighed. "That feels good."

The housekeeper took a seat on a wooden chair and settled herself in for a visit after setting Samantha about the task of churning butter outside in the shade.

196

"And what about you, miss," said Ossie Lee. "Did you meet any young gentlemen suitors in Washington City?"

Kit blushed, but stared at the soap in her hands as she answered, "I met no one suitable."

Ossie Lee slapped her knee and gave a chuckle of amusement. "But you met some young men. You can't fool old Ossie Lee. That red hair of yours and that lily white skin can't fail to make some dashing young man turn his head."

Kit's discomfort increased, and she handed the black woman the scrub brush as an excuse to avoid her knowing gaze.

"Would you please scrub my back, Ossie Lee? I haven't had a proper bath in weeks."

The older woman obliged, pulling her chair behind the tub, and as Kit held her hair on top of her head, Ossie Lee raked the rough sponge up and down Kit's back in strong strokes.

"So your brother's to be married at last. But what are we going to do with you? Last I heard that Jared Patton was still footloose and fancy free."

Kit gave a short grunt. "I ran into Jared in town. Ossie Lee, you know he is the last man I would marry. He's nothing but a flirt and a rake."

"Many a young man's that way at his age. Just take the right woman to settle him down."

Kit shook her head. "Don't be ridiculous. Just because he wraps you around his little finger doesn't mean he'd make a good husband. And by the way, he told me he was looking forward to some of your biscuits and honey."

The black woman chortled as she grasped Kit's hair

and gently shook it loose from Kit's hold. Then she pushed her mistress down in the tub so that Kit's hair could get a good soaking. Kit doused her locks and then sat up a little so that Ossie Lee could run fingers through the tangles and massage her scalp.

" 'Fact last time Jared was here he asked about you," Ossie Lee went on. "If'n you ask me he had that lonely look about him."

"Jared was here?"

"He spent many an hour in this kitchen. You'd think he don't get enough to eat at home."

The idea of Jared Patton sitting by the hearth with Ossie Lee was a curious one. Of course, Kit knew that Jared was always fond of good cooking.

"He probably came here to fill himself—you had no one else to cook for—and then left to go whoring among his father's servants or to spend the evenings at the tavern."

"Told me many a tale about the goings-on other side of the Chattahoochee," Ossie Lee said.

Kit tensed. "What goings-on?"

"Ain't you heard? Gold's been found over there, and the white men is movin' the red men aside to get it."

Kit tried to relax the muscles in the shoulders that Ossie Lee was massaging.

"I had heard something of it," she said.

"Come to no good, that will," said Ossie Lee. "You'd think gold was the potion of happiness instead of the root of all evil. Blood's already been shed over it."

"Blood shed?" Kit felt her heart sink, and she fought the image of a defiant Red Hawk that penetrated her mind's eye.

"They say the Indians're standin' and fightin' rather than lettin' their land be taken away. Some ways the red man's no luckier than the black man in this world. Those of color jest have to wait to get to heaven afore peace and happiness is agonna come to 'em."

Kit reached for a towel. "I'm sorry to hear it. Some of the Cherokee leaders were in Washington to see the President."

Ossie Lee rubbed Kit's back with the fluffy towel. Then Kit took it and finished drying herself as Ossie Lee held the wrapper out for her.

"Seems the sins of this world follow us everywhere," said Ossie Lee, shaking her head. "The white man needs to learn that his greed'll end him up in hell. But none of 'em listen."

It was one of the contradictions of life in the South that Kit had learned long ago to live with: black slaves who were well cared for loved their masters devotedly, while at the same time regretting the state of the white man's soul.

Kit took her leave, anxious to end the discussion about the Cherokee Nation. She had run away from Washington to escape the overwhelming and confusing experience she had had. Only now did she fully realize that it was with her right here in her own back yard. She had always thought of the other side of the Chattahoochee as being another world. Never before had the Cherokee Nation seemed so near to her home.

That night, after a hot, tasty dinner prepared by Ossie Lee, Kit tucked herself into her feather bed. But as she gazed out her window at the sliver of moon, she felt a strange yearning and melancholy.

When Shep came to put his nose on her bed, she petted his silky hair. He whined and licked her face, offering her comfort.

She scratched his ears and kissed the top of his head. But even the dog's furry warmth could not bring her the peace she had felt in this room in times past.

The next morning Kit spread a bolt of cotton cloth out on the dining-room table, and she was showing Samantha how to cut out a pattern when a rider came up the drive. As boots sounded on the front steps, she glanced through the windows. She recognized the horse, and she heard Ossie Lee open the door and exclaim a greeting. Then Jared's voice drifted along the hall, along with laughter and the smack of palm against soft flesh.

"Lord 'a mercy, Jared Patton. You ought to know better than to try to get away with that in this house."

Kit shook her head. She knew Jared was not above smacking servants on the behind, and it confirmed her certainty that he had not matured in the least.

Ossie Lee appeared in the dining-room door.

"Mr. Patton here to see you, Miss Kit."

But Jared appeared beside her.

"Oh, stop with the formality, Ossie Lee. I can announce myself. Can't you see the mistress of the house is working. Far be it from me to stop her. I would, if you could spare it, however, appreciate something wet for my throat. My horse needed stretching, and I let him gallop almost all the way from my place."

"Hello, Jared," said Kit. "Ossie Lee, bring the

pitcher of lemonade." She knew he would prefer port, but she thought to make him suffer.

Jared grinned and bowed in mock gallantry to the housekeeper as she clucked her tongue, tossed her turbaned head, and left to do as she was bid.

Samantha did not even look up at Jared, but sat down on the edge of a chair and bent her head further toward her work. Jared let his eyes drift over the pretty, slim black girl. He lifted his blond eyebrows curiously, but brought his gaze to Kit.

"And how are you finding things at home?" he inquired, taking a seat on an upholstered side chair.

"Fine," she answered, picking up the scissors and resuming her work. She was not about to stop what she was doing to entertain him, nor did he expect it.

"I've consulted the almanac, and we are going to plant tomorrow," Kit said.

"We?"

"Yes. We don't have enough hands to sow all the fields at once. With Father and Fletch gone, I plan to help."

"Well, just be sure and clean all the dirt from underneath your fingernails before the dance Saturday evening."

"What dance?"

"Ah, I knew you wouldn't have had a chance to hear of it. The Mileses' have invited everyone."

Kit knew that "everyone" meant the landowners in the community. The Mileses' place was in the next valley at the foot of the knoll where the schoolhouse stood. Often, the gentry gathered to dance, eat the dishes the women created in competition with each other, and socialize. It would be pleasant to go and see the neighbors again.

"That will be very nice. Thank you for telling me," she said.

"You'll need an escort since your menfolk aren't here. I don't suppose you'd let me squire you."

She gave him a mocking glance. "No, I wouldn't. I'll have Brutus drive me."

"And deprive him of the party his own people will undoubtedly have? Come now, I did not know you were such a cruel mistress."

She stood and expelled a breath of air. "Then I'll drive myself. Nothing can happen to me between here and the Mileses'."

A shadow of doubt crossed his normally mocking face. But instead of answering with a calculated quip, Jared frowned and rubbed his forehead. His look of concern sent a tingle of anxiety crawling up her spine. She said nothing, however, but returned to cutting along the line she had drawn on the back side of the cloth laid out on the pad protecting the table.

When her scissors clipped the last thread at the far end, she glanced down and realized that she had unconsciously offered Jared a sumptuous view of her bosom. She quickly stood straight and cast a glance at him. But to her surprise, his eyes were not on her. Instead, he was glaring straight ahead, drumming his fingers on the side table. Kit placed the scissors on the table and sat down slowly.

Her mouth felt dry, and she wanted to ask him what he was thinking, but just then Ossie Lee swayed into the room with a tray, which she placed at Jared's elbow.

"Thank you, Ossie Lee," he said. And he lifted the

pewter pitcher and poured himself a glass. Raising it to his lips, he gulped the liquid down. Then he expelled a breath and wiped his mouth on his sleeve.

Finally he looked at Kit's face. "Believe me when I tell you it's not my own ulterior motive that makes me warn you, but you would be wise not to go out alone at night that far from here."

She turned to Samantha. "Go see if Ossie Lee has work for you. I believe we'll stop the cutting for now, Samantha."

The girl darted out of the room, and Kit returned her attention to Jared.

"What do you mean by that?"

"The Cherokees may go on the warpath. Federal troops have been sent to keep order. There may be bloodshed."

Kit's throat went dry. She stared out the windows across the room and tried to moisten her lips with her tongue.

"You saw what was happening in Dahlonega," Jared continued. "The miners are overrunning Cherokee land before the state can reach agreements to buy it. Legislation has been passed confiscating large sections of the Indians' lands, but some of the Cherokee agitators have been trying to influence the tribe to stay and fight rather than emigrate west. The rabble-rousers are being arrested."

Her eyes flew to his. "Who?"

The word was out of her mouth before she stopped to think.

Jared frowned and poured more lemonade. "I don't know the names. I've heard Chief John Ross is a reasonable man. More than half Scot, I believe. But no doubt some of the hotheaded full-bloods will put on war paint and do the war dances as in former times."

Kit rose slowly, unable to stop her racing heart.

"I . . . I think I need to go outside for some air," she mumbled, and she made her way from the room.

She pushed open the front door and stepped down to the verandah. Shep rose from where he had been curled up under a chair and came to rub against her skirt. She let her fingers drift into the fur at the back of his neck as she stared out over the yard and the fields, and beyond to the trees that separated this valley from the hills and the mountains.

The door squeaked behind her, and Jared came out to join her.

"You all right?" he asked. "Don't you want to sit down?"

Shep whined, his nose straining in the direction in which Kit was staring. The pull she felt in the direction of the trouble was overwhelming, and she fought to control her emotions.

Jared moved to face her. Then he put a hand on her shoulder, shaking it gently.

"For heaven's sake, Kit. What's wrong. You look as if you'd seen a ghost. Did what I said about the Indians frighten you? I didn't mean it to."

She shook her head, knowing Jared would never understand what was wrong.

"It's awful," she said. "Why can't they leave them alone?"

"What?" said Jared, at first not understanding what she meant. But then he shook his head. "The Indians will have to leave. It's inevitable. They don't want the gold anyway. They might as well let those have it who know what to do with it."

Anger rose in Kit as she stared at the prejudiced, hypocritical, loose-moraled man she knew so well. Her hatred for what he represented was so strong that she felt the urge to slap him.

The fact that Ossie Lee could not see through him filled her with resentment as well. In the past Kit had deigned to pass the time conversing with Jared and the other men in the community like him. Now the urge to throw him off her place was so strong she could hardly control herself.

Jared looked at the emotions visible on her face and brought his head up in surprise. He did not know what had gotten into her, but he could see that she was angry. In spite of himself, he took a step back.

Just then Ossie Lee came to the door behind them. "I'm fixin' to make lunch. Is Jared going to stay to eat?" she asked.

"No," Kit said sharply, gripping Shep's collar. "He's leaving."

Then she released the dog and ran down the stairs and around the side of the house, the movement helping release the pent-up energy inside her. She kept running all the way to the little gazebo that stood next to the gurgling stream at the edge of the property.

Shep bounded along behind her, barking. When she reached the gazebo, she slowed, but she did not stop. Instead, she went on to the stream, knelt down at the edge and cupped her hands in the water, while Shep leapt into it.

Then she splashed water on her hot face, her hard breathing mingling with the sobs that struggled for release.

Chapter Eleven

Kit did not return to the house until after Jared had left. When she did it was only to tell Ossie Lee that she was going to ride into Dahlonega.

Ossie Lee protested that if she wanted to go to town she should have Brutus drive her in the buggy.

Kit shook her head. "No need for that. This is something I must see to myself."

"You haven't even eaten your lunch," grumbled Ossie Lee. "Young Jared wouldn't eat without you, so I'm left with two plates of boiled guinea fowl, my best sweet potatoes, and hominy. What am I to do with it, feed it to the hogs? Land sakes, girl. If you're going to ride to town, you'll need something in your stomach."

"All right, Ossie Lee, I'll eat."

She took the plate into the house and ate at a corner of the dining-room table. The tasty food stuck in her throat, but she forced it down. When she was done, she returned the plate to the kitchen and went outside to find Brutus, who was shoeing the dapple gray mare.

"I'll be driving the trap into town, Brutus. Which of the horses shall I take to pull it?"

He straightened some. "I'll catch Hannabel. She's as gentle as she alus was and she's in need of some exercise."

"Yes, if you would catch her for me I'd be obliged. And please harness her to the trap."

She felt better for having decided to go to the gold fields and see for herself. What she would do there she had no idea. The fact that it might be dangerous or that she might be in the way was no deterrent. At last her unsettled emotions had an outlet.

She ignored the curious, hooded looks she got from Ossie Lee and Samantha as she stormed into the house and up to her room in search of suitable clothing for the trip.

When she was dressed in jacket, skirt, and high, laced boots, she returned downstairs and went out to the yard, where the blood bay mare with black mane, tail, and legs, was already in the harness. She nodded an acknowledgment to Brutus, who looked up again from his shoeing as she seated herself in the carriage.

Shep bounded up, ready to follow.

"No, Shep," she commanded. "Stay."

The dog sat on his haunches, but whined and flicked his ears back and forth.

Feeling pity for Shep because he could not understand, she nevertheless said, "I'll be gone some time. You must stay here and guard the farm."

The dog had been trained to understand the word "guard."

"That's right," she said as Hannabel pawed the ground, "Stay and guard."

Shep lifted first one paw and then the other, but remained seated, his expression alert.

"Good dog," she said again. "Guard the farm."

Then she touched the whip to Hannabel's haunches and the sorrel trotted down the drive.

The field hands watched her go. Only Oscar, seeing his mistress leave, glanced toward the house, wondering if Samantha might come out. He had worked harder and faster since the mistress had brought the pretty black girl here, hoping he would have some time when work was done to talk to her. Her shy, dark glances from the back porch, where she had been struggling with the churn, had quickened blood that had grown sluggish with the prospect of the long days of sowing fields ahead.

As the trap rumbled over the road to Dahlonega. Kit came upon a turkey drover herding his fowls before him, and she had to slow considerably. She chafed in impatience until the slow-moving Tennessean got his flock to one side so that she could drive the trap through. Luckily Hannabel was used to all manner of barnyard fowls and did not shy at the large, noisy birds.

Even before she reached Dahlonega Kit sensed the impending confrontation. A man emerged from one of the poorer farmhouses just outside town, entered his barn, came out with a pitchfork, and climbed into the back of a waiting wagon. He shouted something Kit could not understand and then clapped the reins across his ill-matched team and took to the road ahead of her.

The town itself was full of men shouting and running from building to building. Kit did not know exactly what was happening, but she sensed the danger. So did the horses tied to hitching posts. They whinnied and pranced excitedly. Hannabel began to shy, and Kit spoke aloud to quiet her. Then Harvey Watkins, the owner of the general store, stepped off his porch and waved his hat at Kit.

She reined in her excited horse.

"What're you doin' here?" Harvey called. "You pick an odd time to return to these parts."

"I returned the other day," she said to him as he dodged a rider and grasped her horse's harness, holding Hannabel steady.

"You'd best go back home," Harvey said. "There's goin' to be trouble."

Kit strained to see through the dust at the other end of town.

"What's happening?" she asked.

"The Indians are taking a stand out at Sander's Bend."

She frowned. "Sander's Bend is in Cherokee territory, isn't it?"

He shook his head and spat his chewing tobacco into the road. "Not for long. Least not if the governor gets his way. White miners been digging in those fields. Indian never did anything with 'em. Why should they care now?"

Kit straightened, resisting the impulse to lean over

and remove Harvey's hand from her harness.

"Thank you for warning me," she said, as civilly as she could. "I'll be careful."

She snapped the whip over her horse's head, and Hannabel leapt forward. Harvey had to jump aside to keep from being run over by the wheels of the trap.

It took all of Kit's skill as a driver to negotiate the trap through the street, which was now full of white men of every description. Some were mounted, some carried rifles. Others had slung shovels, hoes, and other pointed tools over their shoulders. All were moving out of town, and Kit was caught up in the flow.

She was finally able to pass those on foot and began to gain on the mounted riders. That they were headed for the Chattahoochee, there was no doubt, and though some of the men cast her curious looks, she leaned forward and kept a tight grip on her reins.

Anxiety gripped her, and while she knew that she ought to fear for her own safety in such a motley, riotous crowd, she was more frightened about the bloodshed that was about to take place. It was foolish to think that she could stop it. But she could not sit at home and wait while men were killed.

Red Hawk, where are you? she whispered to herself. Would he be among his people? She did not even know if he had left Washington.

The horses around her started running, and if she had not held tight to the reins Hannabel would have run with them. Shouts went up around Kit, and as she approached a clearing that rose gently up an incline she saw men leap from their horses. With curses and oaths they poked the Indians who rose from their digging with hoes and shovels.

Kit managed to turn Hannabel out of the way; then she wrapped the reins around the whipstock and jumped out. Her hair blew across her face as she ran toward the confrontation. She stumbled over a mound of red dirt and fell. Sprawled on the ground, she thought the breath had been knocked out of her.

A man stopped and pulled at her arm.

"Get outa here, girlie," the bearded mountain man told her as he pinched her arm, pulling her to her feet. "Ye'll git hurt."

Then he was off before she could murmur her thanks. She stumbled forward in time to see the whites, formed more or less into a line, poking their weapons and tools at a group of Indians who had retreated into a circle, their backs together for mutual protection. The Indians were dressed in hunting shirts and buckskins, and she searched for the one face she knew she would not mistake among them.

Then Red Hawk pushed his way through the group and stood, his red chest bared against spades, hoes, shovels, pitchforks, picks, pointed sticks, and rifles. He thrust his chest and chin forward, spread his feet apart, and placed his hands on his hips.

The white men massed in front of him shoved their implements toward him. Some nicked him, but none was jabbed forcefully enough to move him.

A cry caught in Kit's throat, and tears stung her eyes as she clasped her hands over her mouth.

Just then she heard the rumble of hooves behind her, and she turned to see a company of federal troops galloping along the road, their gold braid flashing in the sun. The captain shouted orders and the troops broke rank and surrounded both groups, whites and Indians. Out came ramrods as the soldiers drove balls into musket barrels.

Another order was shouted, and the soldiers trained their rifles on whites and Indians alike. The white rioters grumbled, but most lowered their weapons. Some turned and fled. The troops made no attempt to stop them. Kit stared through moist lashes at the stalwart Cherokees who stood, looking straight ahead, their shovels and hoes pointed into the ground in front of them.

"Stand where you are," said the blond, red-faced captain who now rode to the center of the chaos. "No one moves. It's all over."

Many of the white men lowered their implements and leaned on them, waiting to see what would happen. Others jeered. The soldiers had not lowered their rifles, and the air was still charged with hate. An angry word could start a massacre, Kit realized. In an instant the courageous, angry man Kit knew so intimately could fall to the ground, his blood spilling across the yellowed grasses.

Please, no, she silently prayed.

Some of the leaders of the riot moved forward, yelling explanations to the captain who ordered them to lay down their weapons.

For another moment all was chaos as the captain shouted for his men to fire on any man who raised a weapon.

Kit saw Red Hawk's fists clench, but they remained on his hips, a hairsbreadth away from the long knife sheathed at his side. His black eyes flashed murder.

When the soldiers had the unruly crowd under control, the captain turned his horse toward the Indians who stood as if carved out of marble.

"That one," the captain barked, pointing to Red Hawk. "Take him and the other troublemakers."

Kit gasped and moved forward. Red Hawk had made no trouble. She had seen it with her own eyes. The Indians were only digging in their fields. It was the white intruders who had antagonized them. She had to tell someone.

Two soldiers got off their horses and approached Red Hawk, his fierce gaze seemed to make them hesitate.

"Hurry up," ordered the captain. He directed two more soldiers to dismount. "Take those two as well."

He pointed to two men who stood near Red Hawk, hands wrapped around their hoes, ready to fight with the only weapons at hand if necessary.

The soldiers moved behind the Indians and forced their hands to their backs, then handcuffed them. Kit stood paralyzed, wanting to run forward, and yet somehow knowing that such an action would be useless.

One of the soldiers rode up to where she stood.

"Get back, miss. This ain't no place for a lady."

She brushed the tears from her face and stared up at him.

"Why are the Indians being taken in?" she asked.

"Don't ask me," said the surly young soldier. "We jes' follow orders."

"But this is their land," she said, reaching for the man's reins. "You have to listen to them."

"What're you, an Indian lover?" The soldier used the butt of his rifle to knock her hands away.

She gasped and fell back.

Across the field the Indians had been lined up and a company of guards surrounded them.

"March," ordered a barrel-chested lieutenant, and he leaned over and shoved his rifle into the back of the Indian at the rear of the line.

Red Hawk turned and spoke in Cherokee to the men following him. They straightened, and when he stepped out, they followed proudly.

In spite of the danger, Kit rushed forward as the soldiers approached. She could say nothing, do nothing, but her heart twisted inside her at the injustice of what she was witnessing and in her anguish over Red Hawk's safety.

He gazed straight ahead, and she doubted he would even see her. Her mouth was too dry for her to speak, but she was certain he would not hear her if she did. All she could do was watch with dread as he approached.

His shoulders were thrown back, and she could see blood running from the cuts inflicted by the tools and weapons with which he'd been prodded. But he marched defiantly, as if feeling no pain, his coal

214

black hair flowing down his shoulders. He was almost even with her when his eyes flicked her way.

She opened her lips, tightened her clenched fists. He did not slow his pace, but as he focused on her face, she saw the skin tighten across his cheeks, saw his jaw clench, saw the hatred in his eyes.

Kit was paralyzed by his look of rage, and her breath came in ragged gasps. There was no mistaking the malevolence in his eyes. He was blaming her.

Pain wracked her chest as she was pierced by his gaze. And then he looked forward again.

Kit could do nothing but wait until the soldiers passed. Then, slowly, the motley crowd that had gathered broke up, with a few soldiers waiting until the last of it had left the field.

Kit turned to glance at the few Indians remaining. These men still stood with their tools, watching their brothers being marched away for something they did not do. Kit wanted to speak to them, but what could she say? She did not know any Cherokee, and she did not know if any of these Indians spoke English like the Cherokees in the Washington delegation.

When the Indians finally turned to each other and conversed, some of their strange words floated to her on the wind. She watched their gestures and saw the anger in their faces. But as the remaining soldiers waited, the Indians broke up their discussion and left the field, walking toward the river and their homes.

Kit had thought the federal troops were supposed

215

to protect the Indians against the Georgians intruding on their lands. But what she had seen bore little witness to that fact. Finally, her shoulders sagging, she walked back to the trap, took up the reins, and turned Hannabel's head toward town.

Light had faded from the hills, and the shadows seemed to leap out from the side of the road. When she reached Dahlonega, lanterns had been lit, and while here and then pockets of bystanders talked excitedly, the crisis had abated for the moment.

The soldiers had kicked up dust as they'd ridden through town, and Kit blinked her eyes against the particles still suspended in the air. Most of the soldiers were now making their way from the livery stable toward the tavern. Kit drove through town and pulled the trap around a corner where there was less congestion.

"Whoa, there, girl," she said, and when she'd reined the horse to a stop, she weakly wrapped the reins around the whipstock and leaned back in her seat, drained. It was dark now, and she took deep breaths.

In the house across the road, a curtain moved at a window. Then the door opened and a short, plump woman pulled a shawl over her shoulders and scurried out into the yard.

"Kit Newcomb," she called. She crossed the road and Kit sat forward, still feeling dazed.

When the woman came up to the carriage, Kit's overwhelmed brain registered who it was.

"Oh Mary," she said. "I didn't recognize you at first."

"What are you doing here at this time of day? You ought to get inside. There's trouble brewing. Indians put in the jail and more fighting expected. Why are you so far from home?"

Kit swallowed, unsure of how to answer these questions.

"I was there. I saw the soldiers threaten the Indians," she said through dry lips.

"My lands, girl. You oughtn't to've been caught out there."

The excited little woman finally seemed to notice that Kit was alone.

"Don't you have a hand drivin' you? You can't have come to town alone at a time like this."

"I did come alone," said Kit.

"Well, good heavens. You can't drive back alone. The roads won't be safe. You bring your trap around back. We'll put you up for the night. I'll have one of my help take word you're spending the night so's your family won't worry."

Kit did not bother to explain that her family was not at home either. But she would appreciate it if Mary did send word to Ossie Lee so the poor woman wouldn't wonder what had happened to her.

"Thank you," Kit said, picking up the reins again.

Mary walked before her, leading Hannabel by the bridle through the gate, along a short drive, and into a weather-beaten stable. The two women unharnessed the horse, and Kit fed her from a bin of fodder and gave her something to drink. Henry Jones, Mary's husband, came round with currycomb and brush to rub the horse down.

"Thank you," Kit said to the man, feeling suddenly very exhausted.

She went into the house in a daze, sitting at the kitchen table mechanically and accepting the bowl of stew that Mary put in front of her. The woman chattered on excitedly about the gold and the Indians. But Kit felt as if she floated above it all in some sort of detached manner, and the sounds coming from Mary's mouth were foreign meaningless noises much like a chicken would make while fluttering around the yard.

After eating, Kit followed Mary upstairs to an attic room where a narrow bed had been made up under the roof beams. A small window faced onto the street in front of the house. It was open for fresh air, and every now and then Kit could hear men shout or a wagon rumble by.

After bathing herself with the towel that had been left beside the porcelain pitcher and bowl, Kit got out of her dusty clothes and put on the nightdress Mary had loaned her. Then she climbed into the narrow bed and snuffed out the candle that sat by her bed. But she did not sleep.

Instead she lay staring at the hewn beams above her, listening to the occasional street noises. Red Hawk's face was imprinted on her mind. The hatred on it, the rigid lines, sparked turbulent emotions in her heart. She felt as if he held her personally responsible for what had happened to the Cherokees, as irrational as that notion might seem.

Why could she not forget him? If she wanted to help the Cherokees, why hadn't she stayed in Washington and let influential men like Daniel Webster plead their cause, asking President Jackson to send more federal troops to protect them. The small company that had appeared in the field was a mockery, taking the word of the white men that the Indians had caused the trouble, which was far from the truth.

Were the soldiers blind? Could they not see the evidence of a gold rush on Indian lands where the white men were not wanted? And why should she care anyway? Why was a white Georgia farm girl suddenly so concerned about justice for a people not her own?

Still as she lay first on one side and then the other, Red Hawk's piercing eyes would not let her rest. The memory of his hands on her fair skin and the sensation of his lips on hers came poignantly back. Then anger made her throw aside the bed covers and put her bare feet on the hooked rug beside her bed. How dare he claim her like that? How dare he cast his Indian spell on her in the hills of Georgetown? Time and distance had made no difference.

She rose and walked to the window, pushing it farther open in order to breathe cool air. When she leaned out, she could see light from the windows of the tavern and from the lanterns on the wagons of farmers heading home.

Now Red Hawk thought she was one of the white traitors. Perhaps he had learned who her father was. She regretted more than ever not staying in Washington long enough to explain that circumstance to him. But she had been under the mistaken notion

219

that she could just walk away from him and it would be over. She would retreat to her own plantation and immerse herself in her life again.

"Ha!" She voiced the expletive aloud. What a fool she had been.

She inhaled a deep breath of air and let it out, then went over and sat on the springy stuffed mattress. She would have to go see Red Hawk. Tomorrow morning she would visit the jail. She had to talk to him — try to straighten out some of the misunderstanding between them. If he would listen. . . .

That decided, Kit lay back on the bed. She spent the dark hours planning what she would say to the defiant Cherokee whose blood was filled with war cries of old, but who also knew the gentleness of love. For she could not live letting him think she had betrayed him.

Chapter Twelve

Kit said nothing of her plans to Mary at breakfast the following morning. After thanking her for her hospitality, she left the house and went to the barn, where Henry had harnessed Hannabel to the trap. She thanked him and led the blood bay mare into the road. She did not want to leave the horse with the neighborly Joneses, for she did not know her plans. If she walked to town, Mary would inevitably ask her what she had done, and she didn't want to have to answer to anyone.

In the early morning most of the town still slept. Smoke curling from chimneys was the only sign that ambitious housewives had begun the day's chores. From behind a log cabin came the rhythmic chop of an axe on firewood. Kit drove the trap through the street and then stopped in front of the little weather-boarded structure that served as courthouse.

The squat stone structure that served as jail sat apart from the rest of the buildings, at the other end of the town square. Its unpainted wooden door was shut. Sunlight had not yet found the menacing bars

221

on the sides of the building, and there was no jailer about.

Looking at the forboding structure, Kit began to lose courage. Surely she could not simply walk in and talk to Red Hawk. There would be no privacy, for other prisoners were imprisoned as well. And the jailer might not even let her see him.

But as she stood by Hannabel, stroking her nose, Kit realized the truth. There was no place left to run to.

Kit heard the jingle of keys even before she saw the sleepy-looking man sway around the corner. He paused before a sagging bench in front of the jail and swirled a tin cup of some kind of liquid, then took a drink. After swallowing deeply, he heaved his bulk onto the bench and slowly leaned back, rubbing his eyes.

Kit left her horse and trap at the edge of the square and walked up the worn path toward where the man sat. When he saw her, he frowned and stared at her as if she were some sort of apparition.

"Good morning," Kit said hesitantly.

"Don't know what's good about it," grumbled the jail keeper.

Kit had no appropriate comment. Instead, she straightened her spine and cleared her throat. She tried not to show that her hands were sweating and that she would much rather turn and flee than do what she intended. But she feared for Red Hawk at the hands of these men, and she was ashamed that her own father had a hand in this.

"I'd like to see one of the prisoners," she said in as strong a voice as she could muster.

"Ain't no prisoners, 'cept the Cherokees."

Her irritation at the man's attitude fired her resolve.

"It's one of them I wish to speak to."

The man looked up then, his bloodshot eyes widening as he stared into her face.

"Now listen, young lady, I know who your father is. If you don't turn around and march right home, I'll send word as to where you are. I doubt Jonathan Newcomb would approve of his daughter calling on these Indians."

Kit clenched her jaw and snapped back at the indolent man.

"If you refuse to admit me to the prisoners' presence, I will see that you don't have a job after this."

She could not tell if he believed her, but she could see the indecision in his eyes. Finally, he said, "You sure you want to do this?"

She nodded stiffly and stood with her feet planted in the path, indicating that she was not about to leave the premises until the jailer granted her wish.

Slowly, the man set his tin cup on the bench, reached for the bunch of keys, and sorted through them one by one. Kit's impatience and her nervousness about seeing Red Hawk tangled in her stomach, threatening her ability to do what she had planned.

The man pulled himself to his feet and took the few steps to the wooden door. The keys rattled as he inserted a large one into the lock. The squeak when he turned it grated on Kit's nerves.

"Come on, then," he said gruffly over his shoulder, and he swung the door open behind him, disappearing into the dark interior.

223

Kit tried to swallow the lump in her throat and followed. She crossed the threshold onto the dirt floor. There was no waiting room. Only two rows of cells on either side of the long, narrow corridor. Those to her immediate right and left were empty, and the jailer lumbered slowly ahead of her.

In the next cell, two men lay stretched on pallets on the floor. In spite of the small shaft of sunlight that spilled in from a barred window, the cell was so dark in the corners that she could not discern whether the prisoners were Cherokee or white. Finally the jailer banged on the bars of the cell at the end of the long, dirt corridor.

"Got a visitor," he said, then spat into the dirt by the cell door.

Kit waited until the jailer stepped back and moved past her, shaking his head and muttering under his breath. Then she cautiously approached the cell.

Her eyes had begun to adjust, and she saw that in this last cell men sat on the edges of two cots, speaking in low voices. She stood next to the iron bars unable to speak.

Red Hawk sat on the end of the cot nearest the bars. He was still naked from the waist up. The men stopped talking, and Red Hawk turned his head. He did not move for a few seconds, and the shame Kit felt made her wish she had not come. But then he rose slowly and approached.

Scabs had formed over the cuts and scratches on his chest, and she winced looking at them. He came nearer, grasped the cell bars, and looked down at her with cold, angry eyes. His features were hard, and the muscles in his face worked as they stared at each other. She read the accusation in his eyes.

Then his upper lip curled in disgust, he spat out her father's name and slowly turned his back on her and crossed his arms.

The other Indians in the cell turned away from Red Hawk as if they saw and heard nothing. They spoke together in low tones, allowing Red Hawk privacy with the woman.

Kit stepped forward, gripping the iron bars.

"Red Hawk, listen to me. You must let me explain."

But he stood resolute on the other side of the iron cage that separated them.

"I wanted to tell you about my father. I had planned to only . . ." Emotion choked off her words, which sounded feeble even to her. She tried again.

"Red Hawk, you've got to believe me. I did not know about any of this before we met. I know what my father is doing is wrong. I should have stayed in Washington and tried to change his mind. Instead I came here. I . . . I thought I could turn my back on all of this, but I found I could not."

Tears streamed down her face, and humiliation sluiced through her.

"Please forgive me," she finally whispered, her forehead falling against the bars her hand grasped.

Still Red Hawk did not move. He presented only his strong bronze back to her resentfully as she stood there sobbing, trying to collect her thoughts, trying to think of something to say that would convince him. But she knew she had done nothing but make a fool of herself. She turned away, gulping down another sob. She should never have come to try to ease Red Hawk's pain. All she had done was make it worse.

225

When they had ridden together by Rock Creek, she had thought nothing of the words he'd spoken, and she certainly had repeated none of them to her father. But she had withheld from him who she was, and now he clearly thought she had been deceitful.

She pushed away from the bars and fled down the corridor, opening the squeaking door and running into the sunlight. Outside she kept running, brushing the tears from her cheeks until she came to a wide, old elm tree and stopped to lean on it. Then she sank to the ground, leaning one shoulder against the elm's rough bark.

At the edge of the town square and away from the prying eyes of the citizens of the town, she momentarily succumbed to anger and humiliation mixed with grief. What had she accomplished? Nothing. Red Hawk did not have ears to listen. It had been a mistake to come.

The image of his shoulders and back burned into her mind. Red Hawk misunderstood her intentions. Her concern for him was futile. There was nothing she could do to relieve a situation that seemed to be out of her hands. She must find a way to forget Red Hawk, as impossible as that had been up until now. But surely in time, she told herself, her ragged breathing beginning to ease, she would forget.

She and Red Hawk were not of the same people, and it would have been better if she'd never met him. He was not only an Indian, but he was a bitter man as well, capable of unleashing a fury that she was not prepared to withstand. Resentment built in her of the vulnerability he had awakened in her.

She had experienced grief before when her mother

had died. She still thought fondly of her, but the years had numbed the pain, and she had gotten on with life. There were always new horizons, people to fill one's life with love.

Love. The thought brought a new wave of pain to her heart. Where would she ever find love? Not with the Jared Pattons of this state, nor with the dilettantes like Breckenridge Grover in Washington City. It seemed most of the young men her age were either pompous bores or Southern renegades. And even if she found a decent man in time, who would want a woman used at the hands of an Indian?

Kit leaned against the elm, seeking strength from its sturdiness. The town around her was rumbling with industry now, but she closed her eyes as the sun found her face and tried to still her thoughts. She had not slept well last night, and now the familiar sounds of casks rolling down the street, horses clopping along in the dirt, and a blacksmith's hammer striking an anvil lulled her into a doze.

The next thing she knew, she was being shaken awake. With a start, she stared into Jared's amused face.

"Taken to sleeping on the village green like some vagabond?" Jared laughed, squatting on his heels before her.

Kit shook her head and reached for the bonnet that lay at her side.

"I was just resting, that's all. You startled me."

Jared sat back on the ground and wrapped his arms around his knees. His blue eyes took in her disheveled state.

"After yesterday's excitement I would think you'd be

well away from here."

Evidently he had not heard that she had been in the thick of it, and she did not enlighten him.

Instead she asked, "What do you think will happen now?"

Jared shrugged, picked up a reed that lay on the ground, and stuck it between his teeth.

"Our worthy governor's coming here today. Maybe he can talk some sense into the Indians."

Kit sat up straighter. "Governor Gilmer?"

Jared nodded. "That's right. My guess is he'll order the Georgia militia in to keep order so the miners can look for gold."

Color flared in Kit's cheeks. "On Indian land?"

"Does it matter? It'll be ours soon enough."

"Are you looking for gold as well?" Kit asked bitterly.

He tossed the reed aside. "No. I know better than to cast my luck with something so chancy. Sure a handful of men will make millions, but most will leave here broken and poorer than when they started. I intend to make my money off the gold rush in a different way."

"How?"

"By furnishing the hordes of men with the staples they need to keep alive. We've ordered production on our plantation increased by thirty percent. There'll be money in our pockets for sure when the bigger mining operations get running."

Kit paid less attention to Jared's bragging about his money-making scheme than she did to what he had said about the governor. Thanks to her father, she knew Governor Gilmer. She would try to see him

228

when he arrived. Perhaps he would listen to her, and she could tell him what had actually happened at Sander's Bend.

Kit scrambled to her feet. "What time is the governor due?"

Jared unwrapped his limbs and pushed himself up as well. "I heard tell he's due at the hotel at noon." He eyed Kit with amusement. "You thinking of paying him a call?"

She brushed the grass from her skirt. "I just might do that."

Jared followed her across the square to where Hannabel was munching grass at the side of the road.

"Well, well now," he said. "I didn't know you were on a first-name basis with our eminent governor."

She looked at Jared just as she took the reins and put her foot on the rim of the trap floor. "We've been introduced."

Jared took her elbow and assisted her up to the seat. Then he gave a mock gallant bow.

"In that case, I will delay you no longer, Miss Newcomb."

She had no more time for Jared's mocking foolishness. Her mind already spun ahead. She nodded once to Jared and then took the reins in her left hand and the whip in the other. Soon she had the trap turned around and was rumbling along through town.

Noon. There was just time to drive home, change into respectable attire, and return to call on the governor—if he would see her. No doubt he was already set on his mission, but she must get his attention.

She flicked the whip over Hannabel's head and loosened the reins in her left hand. She must hurry.

The horse's quick trot stirred up dust behind the trap as it wove through town. Once on the road, Kit set the mare at an even pace in order to get home quickly without tiring her too much. Kit concentrated on driving, for the trap was light and she had to avoid ruts in the road left from heavy wagons which had passed through after heavy rains.

The miles passed, and this time Kit had no eyes for the fields or the herd of Durham cattle grazing on the side of the hill.

Mare and trap raced up the drive and halted by the stables. Then Kit hopped out and called to Brutus, who was pumping water into a trough.

"Brutus, I need a fresh horse. I'll be returning to Dahlonega in less than an hour. Will you take care of Hannabel?"

Then without waiting for a reply, she fled to the house and went in by the back entrance. She ran through the rooms, stopping only when she spied Samantha polishing the brass andirons in the drawing room.

"Samantha," Kit said breathlessly, "please find Ossie Lee and tell her I'm changing clothes and returning to Dahlonega. I'm going to see the governor."

Samantha's dark eyes widened, but she silently put down her cloth and polish and went off to find Ossie Lee.

Upstairs, Kit flung open the armoire and fingered various dresses before settling on a blue and silver off-the-shoulder gown. As she began to undo the dress she wore, she heard Ossie Lee knock on her door.

"Come in," she called, and when the servant entered, Kit turned her back to her.

"I just can't reach the hooks and eye in the middle of my back, Ossie Lee. Can you please help me?"

"What's all this fuss about, child? You breezed up that drive like a cyclone itself. Now Samantha tells me you're off to see the governor. But she say he's in Dahlonega. What's he doin' there?"

"There's trouble in town," said Kit as Ossie Lee helped her out of her dress.

She went to the wash stand and began to sponge herself down as she talked.

"I saw a confrontation between the Cherokees and the men intent on robbing the gold out of their ground. The governor's coming to order in the Georgia militia. I want to tell him what actually happened."

Ossie Lee stood with her feet wide apart and her hands on her hips. "And what business is it of yours?"

Kit picked up a brush and started pulling tangles out of her hair, but Ossie Lee took it from her and, grasping Kit's shoulder, steered her to the bench in front of the dresser. Then the black woman began to pull at Kit's hair from behind.

"Just that it's not fair," said Kit to Ossie Lee's questions.

"Hmph," said Ossie Lee. "What's fair got to do with it? You know there ain't nothing fair on this earth. We got to get to heaven for that."

Kit sighed and then winced as Ossie Lee pulled a little too hard on her scalp.

"I don't believe it should be that way. We should work for all the fairness that's possible in this country."

Ossie Lee just grunted again, but she finished dressing Kit's hair and then helped her into the evening dress. Kit threw a pelisse over her arm and then called out directions as she led the way downstairs.

"Don't wait up for me. I don't know what time I'll get back."

"Where will you take your noon meal?" demanded Ossie Lee.

Kit waved a hand. "I don't know. In town. There's not time."

And before Ossie Lee could protest further, Kit raced out of the house. Brutus had a sorrel gelding harnessed to the trap and was checking all the fastenings when Kit arrived at the stables.

"Oh, thank you, Brutus."

As she took the reins from him and got into the trap, the hands in the field looked up from where they sat roasting pork for their noonday meal over a small fire. They had seen the mistress drive up at a rapid rate, and now she sped past them again without so much as looking up. Only Oscar nodded slowly to himself. The mistress had not returned last night, and he had succeeded in getting Samantha to sit outside his cabin with him. Maybe the mistress had more business that would keep her away for another evening. Of course, that did not mean that Ossie Lee would not find something for the girl to do in the kitchen even if an evening meal did not have to be prepared for one of the family.

The little sorrel that had replaced Hannabel in the harness sped along the road. Still, Kit was careful not to push the horse too hard, and she watched ahead for ruts or boulders that might cause an upset.

Reaching town before noon, Kit drove around to

the livery stable and made arrangements to leave the horse, for she didn't know how long she would have to wait for the governor. Once back on the main street she saw that he had arrived. His red and gold coach with top-hatted coachman and groom was just pulling away from the hotel.

A company of Georgia militia in uniform filled the street. At the command "At ease," the soldiers dismounted. Some led their horses toward the livery stable. Others tied them to the hitching posts and headed into the tavern. A small guard was posted at the door to the hotel.

Kit marched boldly passed the soldiers and into the hotel. It was not hard to discern which way the governor had gone. Two guards were posted outside closed double doors Kit knew led to a formal parlor. Evidently that was where Governor Gilmer was setting up his headquarters. She approached the friendliest-looking militiaman, a muscular blond lad who looked little older than herself. He stood at attention, his blue eyes fixed straight ahead.

"Excuse me," she said.

He blinked and lowered his eyes to hers.

"I would like to see the governor."

Her request seemed to surprise him. He glanced at the other guard, a dark-headed older man whose gaze made Kit's skin crawl.

"Wait here," said the blond soldier.

He slid open the double doors and went through them, closing them behind him. In a moment the doors opened. A tall, dark-haired captain appeared behind the guard. He stepped out to where Kit was waiting and frowned.

"May I ask your business, miss?" said the captain.

"I would like to see the governor. He's acquainted with my father, who has served in the Georgia legislature."

She handed him a card she had taken the time to write her name on while still at home. The card carried the Newcomb monogram.

The captain turned the card over. "I see. I am sure the governor will want to receive you later on this evening. At the moment he has urgent business that cannot wait. If you will tell me where you are staying I will see that he gets your card."

She shook her head, impatience building. "This is not a social call. I am aware of his business here, and it's that I wish to speak to him about. I was at Sander's Bend when the Cherokees were arrested. I'm a witness, and I wish to tell Governor Gilmer exactly what happened. Surely that will have bearing on what he does here."

The captain looked doubtful, but he finally acquiesced.

"If you'll remain here, I'll give him your message."

And he walked toward the double doors, which the young blond soldier hastened to open. Kit tried to peer through, but the soldier closed the doors again before she could catch a glimpse of the governor.

She paced before the double doors. When nothing happened after several minutes, she finally sat down on a sofa, resting her chin in her hands while she tapped her foot. Soldiers, citizens, and rough-looking miners mingled in the hotel lobby. Kit could not help overhearing much of the conversation.

". . . prohibit further meetings of the Cherokee

234

legislative council . . ."

". . . make their lands a county . . ."

". . . stake claims now so when the Cherokees are gone the claims'll be ours . . ."

The conversations around her only served to further agitate her. She got up and wore a path on the carpet, strolling through the lobby and back. But even though soldiers and other officials were allowed in and out of the headquarters room, Kit was not admitted. Finally she approached the blond soldier again.

"Could you please inquire within as to whether or not the governor has seen my card. I assure you it is most important."

The boy stuttered and mumbled a reply, but seeing that Kit would not be put off he finally went in. When he returned, Kit jumped up from the sofa. The soldier stood at attention before her.

"Governor Gilmer would be pleased if you would dine with him this evening at eight o'clock here at the hotel."

"This evening will be too late," Kit said and she started around the soldier, heading for the doors.

However, the sly looking dark-headed soldier stepped between Kit and the doors, and she felt the boy's grasp on her arm from behind. The lecherous-looking soldier grinned at her, showing yellow teeth.

"You heard the lieutenant," he said, leering at her. "The governor cannot be disturbed."

Kit let a breath escape between her lips. Dining with the governor seemed to be the only concession she was going to get. She might as well accept it. At least then he would be seated with her over the dinner table and would be forced to listen.

235

"Very well," she finally said. "Eight o'clock. Please tell him I accept."

And she turned and crossed the lobby to the desk. She might as well ask for a room. She did not intend to make the trip to the plantation and back again on this day. It was too far, and she needed to be fresh for the evening appointment. She could not go see Red Hawk again, so there was nothing else to do.

She accepted the key from the clerk behind the desk, then climbed the narrow carpeted stairs to the third floor. Once in the room, she undressed and refreshed herself with a towel and the ewer full of water on the dry sink. Then she lay down on the fourposter bed to rest.

She had not slept well the past night, and with nothing to do but wait, Kit closed her eyes to doze. A warm afternoon breeze floated over her, coming from the window that faced away from the main street and so brought less noise. Images buzzed in her head, keeping her from falling into a restful sleep, but in the late afternoon, sleep did claim her.

She was surprised at how long she had slept, but reasoned that she must have needed it. Feeling sluggish, she stumbled to the sink to splash water on her face. The cool shadows of early evening stretched across the room, and she lit an oil lamp in order to see better. Then she began her preparations for meeting the governor.

She heard shouts from the street below, but in her still-sleepy mind, they meant little more than the shouts of the last few days. When the acrid smell of

236

smoke assailed her nostrils, however, she turned around. Gray wisps were seeping under the door to her room.

Fully awake now, she heard running and shouting in the hallway. Fire! The warning penetrated her brain. She rushed to the door of her room and then jumped back for the door handle was too hot to touch.

"Help!" she called, pounding on the door. But either no one heard her or there was too much smoke for anyone to come to her rescue.

She lunged across the room and stepped into her dress, not wanting to leave the hotel in her underclothing. But she did not wait to fasten the back. Instead, she dragged the quilt from the bed and threw it around her shoulders. Then, using the quilt as a pad, she managed to turn the doorknob.

A blast of heat assailed her when she opened the door and panic filled her at seeing tongues of fire lick their way up the hall. She couldn't even see the stairs. There would be no escape that way.

Her heart in her throat, she pushed the door shut and fled to the window. She gasped at the sight that met her eyes. Dressed in bright hunting shirts with war paint on their faces, Cherokee warriors rode through the streets, brandishing torches and setting the town ablaze. One fiercely painted warrior rode beneath Kit's window and tossed his brand to the porch roof, causing her to step back in fright. Other Indians threw blazing brands onto houses and stores, and already flames were leaping from roof to roof as the sun set behind the hills beyond Dahlonega, lending a red backdrop to a town going up in flames.

She had to get out, but how? More and more

smoke billowed underneath her door, forcing her to take refuge on her small balcony. And yet the flames were flicking ever closer to her. She would have to try to jump to the street, risking a fall. But surely broken limbs were better than being consumed by fire.

Tears and smoke nearly blinded her, but the heat at her back pressed her forward. She stood for a moment, leaning over the balcony, then she raised her skirt to more easily negotiate the railing, lifted one leg, and hoisted herself over onto the sloping porch roof. The whole town seemed to be on fire around her.

Suddenly she saw Red Hawk riding through the circling, whooping Cherokees. He had spied her and was racing to her as she slipped and slid toward the edge of the roof.

Chapter Thirteen

His face was not painted, and he wore the same broadcloth trousers he had had on in the jail. A plain white, yoked shirt covered his scratched chest. He drew rein beneath her.

Seeing Red Hawk only frightened her more, but his eyes were not angry, and he gestured that she should lower herself to him. She swallowed in fear, for the fire was swiftly blowing across the very roof where she sat, her feet dangling over. There was no choice.

Gunfire exploded around them as the citizens began shooting at the Indians. She turned on her stomach and lowered herself over. Then in a perilous moment she slid downward until only her hands clutched the splintery wood. But she felt Red Hawk's grasp on her ankles and giving a scream, she let go.

He was prepared to receive her weight and caught her in his arms. She grasped his shoulders tightly as strong arms clutched her to him. Then slowly he lowered her to the ground so she could mount more securely on the back of his horse. She quickly stepped onto an overturned crate, then scrambled on behind him, pulling herself upward by holding onto Red Hawk's arm.

The frightened horse was shying from the flames, and no sooner was she mounted than Red Hawk pressed his heels into its sides and headed her away from the burning building. They turned away from the confusion in the town and rode out a lane into the countryside.

Kit wrapped her arms around Red Hawk's firm waist and squeezed her legs around the horse's powerful body as they raced along beside a field, leaving shouts, gunfire, and smoke behind. The sun had lowered behind the hills, and shadows claimed the woods that rose to their left.

Red Hawk left the road behind and headed along a small path that wound among the trees. He slowed to ford a small stream, then guided the horse between the trees and through underbrush that had been cleared just enough to allow horse or man to pass.

Kit hung on, her chest aching from smoke and exertion. She paid no attention to the direction they took as she gulped deep breaths of evening air, trusting in Red Hawk and the mare.

A creek tumbled nearby, and tall, straight hemlock and birch rose beside them as the horse worked its way upward into the hills. As Kit's heartbeat slowed, she began to realize where she was. She had escaped the burning town, but now she was no safer. She almost let go of Red Hawk and slipped to the ground in the leafy darkness as a new fear pierced her heart. She was his prisoner.

He was angry with her, and for all she knew had abducted her so that he could punish her. And she had come willingly! Panic filled her, and she did not know what frightened her more, the revenge he might inflict on her once they reached some lonely camp or the eerie hooting of owls in a wood with which she was unfamiliar.

She tried to think. She had been in the woods alone at night behind the plantation. But there she had landmarks, even in the dark. If she got lost all she had to do was walk downhill until she came to the fields or the stream that fed the land.

But west of Dahlonega was strange territory, and she had no doubt that soon they would cross the Chattahoochee and she would be in the Cherokee Nation. She cursed herself for not finding some shelter in town once Red Hawk had helped her from the burning roof.

The Cherokees must have been riled to resort to such extreme measures. Their war paint and the burning brands were a far cry from the dignified diplomacy they had pursued in Washington City. But Red Hawk had said they would fight for their lands. She tried to remind herself that these were civilized Indians. Surely she would not be scalped. Still, fear nagged at her and she half swooned against Red Hawk's back.

He did not stop or speak for some time as they made their way through rolling hills. The tumble of a waterfall seemed to come nearer and then faded away. Eventually the land cleared and they rode through grassy meadows in the moonlight. She wanted to ask him where they were going, but the words stuck in her throat. She had let him carry her too far from the country she knew to ever find her way back. And she was unprepared to do battle with a bear or mountain lion that might make its way down from the higher ridges she could see silhouetted against the moonlight.

Red Hawk turned the horse toward a stand of trees in a hollow that led downward to a gurgling stream. To her surprise, he stopped and dismounted. Then he held up his arms to help her down.

Her heart fluttering wildly in her chest, she commanded her legs to give up their viselike grip on the horse and slid off into Red Hawk's arms. When she had her footing, he released her and led the horse to the water to drink.

Fighting the urge to flee, Kit looked about her. They were in a protected spot. Leaves of covering maple spread above them, shielding the stars she had seen in the black sky out in the open.

When Red Hawk judged the horse had had enough, he led it away to where it could munch on grass and leaves. Then he approached her. She stood still, afraid to move. He held out a hand to her.

"Are you thirsty?" he asked.

They were the first words he had spoken to her since she had seen him in the jail, and a rush of emotion filled her. She nodded. He grasped her hand and led her to the water. Then he knelt, cupping the cold water in his hands. He drank himself, then he wetted his hands again and stood.

He raised his hands to her face and bathed it with the cool drops from the stream. Kit closed her eyes. The water and the soft touch of his hands soothed her burning skin. The sensation was so welcome that she wanted more. But then he made her kneel and take water in her own hands to drink.

She hadn't realized how thirsty she was. But when the cool moistness found her parched throat she cupped her hands for more. Finally she let water run down her chin and throat. Then Red Hawk took her hands and raised her to stand by him.

She could not meet his eyes, but she felt his gaze on her. Embarrassment filled her, and she suddenly became aware that the dress she had thrown on was torn. She had not fastened it in back, and it had slid down one shoulder. She reached up to straighten it, but he took her hand in his, stopping her. She did not resist him. Whatever he would do, she would be powerless to stop him.

"Your father is a Cherokee hater," he finally said.

His stern, angry voice pierced her heart. She wanted to explain. She wanted to tell him . . . But her words would sound futile. She gave a slight nod.

Red Hawk dropped her hand and grasped her shoulders, giving her a little shake.

"You did not tell me. Why did you not speak of this?"

"I planned to," she said, thrusting her chin up at him. "I wanted to, but I did not think you would understand. What my father is and what I think are not the same. You must believe me. He did not know I was seeing you."

Red Hawk pushed her from him in disgust. "A daughter obeys her father. Such is the way of women."

Tears of exasperation and anger threatened, but she managed to stand her ground.

"I did not obey my father when I came to the jail. I came because I was concerned for your well-being. I did not come to taunt you."

She turned her back, not wanting to have to meet his accusing eyes. No matter what happened, he would not trust her.

Red Hawk gazed at her milky white back, visible where her dress parted revealing the torn, singed camisole. His own suspicion was threatened by the yearning he still felt for this woman. And like a hunter, did he not also rise to the challenge of obtaining the unobtainable? Of taming the daughter of the enemy?

He was still suspicious, but his anger at the unlistening white men and his desire for this woman he believed was his by fate warred within him. Cherokee women were subservient to their men, but he saw that this white woman was not cut of the same cloth. Did that not challenge him all the more?

Kit's humiliation and anger smoldered. When he did not move toward her or speak, she turned to face him again.

"Have you brought me here to punish me for some imagined wrong?"

Red Hawk gave a small grunt and turned halfway from her.

"The ways of justice have not worked. As of old, the war hatchet has been sent to all the Cherokee towns. Our warriors are blackening their faces, streaking them with vermillion. We will annihilate the white enemy, the intruders who will not let us dig in our own fields."

His words sent fear through her heart. Tribal revenge would only lead to more killing. The thought sickened her.

"It must stop," she said, more to herself than to

him. She clenched her fists and shook her head in despair.

Red Hawk narrowed his eyes as he watched her. "When my red brothers broke open the jail, I saw that our people would punish those who had worked against us."

She lifted her chin. "Then why did you rescue me from the burning building? You could have left me in the flames."

She saw the twitch of his lip. "If you had deceived us, no hands would be lain on you in revenge but my own."

She flinched, angry at his words. Knowing she had done nothing to deceive him, she thought that perhaps her father and the rest of those concerned for her welfare were right. If savage instincts were going to lead to her being punished when she had done nothing to deserve that, then Red Hawk was no better than her father thought all Indians were.

The two stared at each other in stubborn anger. Red Hawk saw that perhaps she was telling the truth about her intentions regarding his safety. But she had not been honest with him in Washington. She had not told him her father's name, or that the man would be present when the Cherokee delegation met with the white President, urging the traitorous Andrew Jackson to act against the interests of the Cherokee people.

But he still battled within himself. He did not pretend to understand the way the white woman's mind worked. And he was aware of something else now. His body, heated from the excitement of fighting and their flight through the hills, responded to hers. When he had bathed her face with cool water from the stream, his fingers had tingled. As she now drew her gown up around her shoulders and hugged herself, his heart beat louder.

Her eyes met his, challengingly. She did not crawl piteously before him, but held her head high. Now his fingers wanted to wind themselves in her coppery tresses. He desired her.

In two steps he was near her. Perhaps he should take her here. Perhaps her heart told her the same thing. If she deserved any punishment for being untruthful with him when they met, for stirring his emotions, it was that she owed herself to him. He reached out slowly to touch her face.

Her chin quivered at his touch, but she did not withdraw. His movements were not those of someone about to harm her. Rather, she stared at him as he brought his face nearer hers so that she felt his breath on her lips. He opened his mouth to draw breath, and she did not shrink back. Rather, the thrill of his nearness rippled through her.

Was this not what she had longed for since she had left him? Was this not what had made her nights fitful? She had struggled with her feelings during this exasperating time, but as his strong arms pulled her closer to him, her beating heart and all her racing senses told her that this was what she had waited for.

Then his mouth was upon hers, his hands pushed the gown down from her shoulders, his arms trapped her body against his, and her arms snaked around him, her hands resting against the rippling muscles of his back. Desire flooded them as all the emotions that had plagued them found outlet in this drinking in of sensations.

Her mouth opened as his tongue entwined with hers. Thought fled as his hands found the opening of her dress at the back and peeled it off her shoulders and arms until she stood shrouded only in her camisole and the cocoon of his arms. He held her still, the prisoner of his deep kiss.

Then he lifted his head and cradled her against him for a moment. His hands slid along her arms, and he quickly turned from her and went to his horse. He untied the rolled blankets on its back and spread them on the ground. He had brought her to this protected place because he knew they must spend the night here. He could not take her to his village tonight. If he returned with her to his own people, he did not know if she would be safe. Though his people did not usually harm women and children, the rage they felt was strong. His people might shed blood.

He could not risk a fire, for if they were caught by the Georgia Guard, he had no doubt as to what the soldiers would do to him. And was too late to ride farther. His horse needed rest, and this place provided as good a cover as any. He knelt on the bed he had prepared and held out a hand to her.

Kit shivered in the breeze, saw the beckoning hand, the soft blanket on which he invited her to lie. She knew she should refuse him. But she had waited too long, had come too far. She walked toward him as his eyes smoldered into hers.

Then she was on her knees, her arms reaching around his neck, her fingers entwined in thick, dark hair as his mouth took hers again. His hands were like embers on her skin, caressing her limbs, then seeking her breasts. He pressed her to him as they sought each other hungrily. Then he leaned onto the blankct, bringing her downward beside him.

He threw one leg over hers, trapping her beneath him so that he could savor her cool flesh. Clothing was pushed aside, and she reached eagerly for his naked, hard-muscled limbs. Dizziness consumed her as he covered her with a blanket of pleasure that made the earth seem to spin around them. Their love sparked, then flamed as Red Hawk moved urgently against her while still tasting of her sweetness and exploring creamy, moonlit flesh.

Never had she felt such joyous surrender, drinking in lips, black hair that fell across her breasts, hips that moved against hers. She felt she was one with him as their spirits rose out of their bodies to commune with the night. For the budding trees, the restive birds, the clouds that drew across the moon like silvery curtains were part of their celebration.

Gone was the pain that had accompanied her initiation into this rite of love when they had lain among the grasses of the eastern hills. Now her own moist flesh opened with eagerness to his throbbing pulse. In feverish excitement their lovemaking mounted to explode in shattering ecstasy. Only the solid earth under them kept them from flying upward into the stars.

Kit dug her fingers into his back, pressing him closer as their heartbeats pounded following the release of passion. Still they clung to each other as the feverish pulse subsided. Soon a breeze cooled the perspiration that had dampened their skins, and Red Hawk moved to lie beside her, cradling her against his chest.

As their heat cooled, and the night's chill crept over the ground, Red Hawk pulled the blanket around them, wrapping them in a nest of love. His cheek lay against her hair, and he gazed at the knowing owl that hooted above them and at the moon that peered from behind the drifting clouds. He knew that his love chants had worked. She would never desire any other man.

His hand rested beneath her breast. His horse grazed nearby. The night would be safe.

In the morning, they refreshed themselves at the stream. Kit dressed in the ruined gown, fastening it as best she could. Then they mounted. Red Hawk struck a course that circled the hills, keeping well within cover. Often he would stop and listen, his keen senses watchful for the white Georgia Guards. They were still in Cherokee territory, but that no longer mattered, for the greedy whites had infiltrated it. Even the Cherokee religious sites would not be left untouched if they stood on ground coveted by the white traitors.

Late in the day they crossed the last river that separated the wilderness from the farms clustered around Dahlonega. Closer than this, he dared not go.

"I must leave you at the edge of the woods," he said when at last he dismounted. "There is a trail that will take you where you want to go."

Kit slid down and stood in the shade of a maple tree as sunlight dappled Red Hawk's face. She saw the invitation in his eyes, but she knew she could not go with him. A sob caught in her throat. She did not know how she could return home and act as if nothing had happened. Neither could she throw away her life and all that she knew to flee with an Indian she hardly knew, even after she had given herself to him.

If she did such a thing, her family would disown her. And if she became an Indian's woman, what would happen when he grew tired of her? Kit had heard many horrible stories of the ways Indians treated their women. The Cherokees were civilized, and the stories might have been exaggerated, but still, Indians were a strange people to her.

No, it would be better to return home and see if she could influence her father to see the Cherokees as people and not just obstacles in the way of progress. For though she did not know all the Indian ways, she did know that they were fighting for their right to that which they loved most — their land.

She lowered her head as Red Hawk waited until she gained control over her feelings. Then she raised her head to him.

"I will tell my people I was dazed in the fire, that I escaped the burning hotel but that the horse I took ran away with me."

He nodded, seeing the wisdom of her story. He did not believe she would betray him. And she knew nothing. He had spoken only of the Cherokees' vow of revenge, but the white usurpers would know of that soon enough. For a moment, he wavered. If she returned to her people she might not be safe. But it was not the right time to ask her to come with him. He drew in a breath, expanding his chest. They must be strong.

She reached up to touch his face, and he grasped

her hand, bringing it to his lips. Then, with tears in her eyes, she turned from him and struck out on the trail he had indicated.

Perhaps she would never be with Red Hawk again, Kit realized as she walked toward town, her hair tangled, dirt on her face. But she would never forget him. She would carry him in her heart, and she would do everything she could for his people.

She followed the path from the woods through a meadow. Finally she came to cultivated fields and then to a road that led into town. After she had walked about a mile, one of the black servants from the Patton plantation pulled up alongside her. He was driving a wagon load of bushels of peaches.

"Be that Miz Newcomb?" said the man, grinning at her from the driver's seat. "You look like you been to hell and back."

"Hello, Amos," she said in relief. "I feel like I've been to hell and back. I was caught in the fire in town. The horse I escaped on ran away with me and threw me some distance from town in the woods. I spent the night with some settlers," she said vaguely.

"If you're afoot, then you're welcome to ride to town with me."

"I would appreciate it. Thank you."

She climbed onto the seat beside him, grateful for the ride and grateful that she had run into someone who would not question her too closely.

Once in town, Amos delivered the fruit to the Watkins' merchandise store, then offered to drive Kit home. She accepted since there was no one from Wytheridge in town. She wondered if a search party had been sent out for her, or worse, if Ossie Lee thought she had perished in the flames.

The day was warm, and ashes blew across the street from the ruins of buildings. The fire had been put out before it totally destroyed the town, but the Cherokees had succeeded in doing a good deal of damage.

While Amos unloaded the goods, Kit spoke to the Watkinses, who were angry over their loss.

"Governor's called in the Georgia Guard to control the savages," said Harvey. "Time the Cherokees were removed from the state for good."

"But this wouldn't have happened if white miners hadn't trespassed on their lands," said Kit.

Harvey only glared at her. "Whose side are you on?"

"I'm on the side of justice," Kit said resolutely. "Surely this can all be resolved if everyone will only listen."

Stella picked up her broom and continued sweeping charred splinters toward a dust pan. "You know as well as we do the time for talk is past.

Kit left Stella and Harvey and went to find Amos, who was ready to drive her home. In her heart she knew Stella Watkins was right. A leaden feeling told her this was one of the times when the forces of history took their course and there was no stopping them. Would that mean that the Cherokees would have to leave Georgia for the Western lands that had been set aside for them?

Perhaps that would be for the best, after all. And Red Hawk would go with them.

Chapter Fourteen

Standing Doe watched Red Hawk ride into New Echota. She stood beside her cabin, where she had been scraping the hair off a hide. The slim girl with a smooth bronze complexion and black hair that shone in the sun straightened from her task as she watched Red Hawk. She wore a yoked blouse and long cotton prairie skirt of red and yellow. A cloth band around her forehead held her hair in place.

Long had she wanted Red Hawk for a husband. Every woman in the village admired his stern, commanding presence. He drew rein in the square in front of the printing house, and several men gathered around him to speak with him when he got down from his horse. He did not look in Standing Doe's direction.

She had heard that he had been taken to the white man's jail. The leaders of New Echota were angered, and two days ago the drums had sounded and the Cherokees had danced war dances as of old. She herself had stood in the circle of women who danced around the warriors, invoking the names of the spirits who had helped them free Red Hawk and the others. And now he had returned.

Standing Doe's pulse quickened in her throat. She would speak to him tonight. He was too distracted with working for his people to notice her now. She could not wait for him to decide it was time to find a wife. She had her own plan. The moon was in its first quarter. The time would be right.

That evening Standing Doe met Red Hawk as he returned from his private ablutions by the river. She waited until he approached a turn in the path and then noiselessly stepped out in front of him.

Deep in thought, Red Hawk brought his chin up abruptly at the sight of Standing Doe dressed in a deerskin jacket and wrap-around skirt with beaded fringe.

He paused and waited until she spoke. Standing Doe moved slowly nearer to him, then raised her face to his.

"Red Hawk you are so consumed with the cares of our people that you do not notice those who watch you and care for you."

He took a moment before he spoke.

"It is true. I have had weighty, unpleasant matters on my mind of late."

Tilting her head and flashing her eyes at him, Standing Doe said boldly, "Have you forgotten the time we used to spend together? We used to walk in these woods and talk. You used to tell me then of your concerns. It can be so again."

254

Red Hawk leveled his eyes at her. He spoke with kindness. "My life has changed since then. I sought companionship then. I do not seek it now."

"Why not?"

Red Hawk considered. It would be better to be truthful. If Standing Doe, or any other woman, still considered him marriageable, he must let her know that this was not so. Although he had not brought the woman he desired among his people yet, he sensed that that day was not far away. They should be prepared.

"I have found a woman," he said bluntly.

Standing Doe's brow creased slightly. She had not noticed him spending time with any other woman in New Echota. Of course, he could be seeking the hand of a maiden from one of the other villages, but rumor would have spread. Those things were always known.

"Who?" she said.

"She is a white woman."

Standing Doe took a step back, surprised. Intermarriage between Cherokees and whites was common, but she had never thought that Red Hawk would mix his pure blood with that of the enemy. For the Cherokees had again begun to think of white men as enemies rather than the friends they had hoped them to be.

"Why?" she said.

Red Hawk met her perplexed gaze. "It is meant to be."

Standing Doe moved nearer Red Hawk again, her fingers reaching out to touch his dark skin.

"You have been poisoned by this white woman's evil

charms," said Standing Doe. "Let me remind you of what an Indian woman can offer a brave like you."

Though his body reacted to her touch, he held his chin firm, disciplining his mind. "It is useless, Standing Doe. I do not care for you in the same way. We can be friends only."

She gave a low laugh. "You have been bewitched, my brave warrior. You have betrayed your Indian heart."

She stood next to him now, her breath feathering his shoulder as her hands strayed to his waist, caressing his skin.

He reached for her offending hands to remove them, holding them tight in his grip.

"Enough of this Standing Doe. It is you who have been bewitched. It is true I once thought of you. We shared joy together riding through the woods, bathing in the streams, and catching the fish. But that time is past. I have other concerns now. I do not allow myself such distractions."

Fire blazed in her eyes as her tone mocked him. "I am not fooled," she said. Then her voice turned to honey once again. "You are not so perfect as you believe yourself to be. Your skin still quivers to my touch. Do not deny it."

He gave an exasperated grunt and pushed her hands away. He admired her dark beauty, the more enticing in her rage. But it was his body only that responded to such a ploy. His heart was not his to give. How would he make her see that?

Standing Doe lost not a moment. As he stood glaring at her, she quickly untied the lacings on the deerskin jacket she wore, letting it fall from her shoulders. Naked to the waist, she posed before him, displaying her perfect, round breasts with their dark, erect nipples. Red Hawk tried to remove his gaze from them but could not.

A sly smile curved Standing Doe's lips as she moved her torso and shook her head, making her breasts sway, her black hair falling over one shoulder. She raised her hands to him, her chin lifted, her lips half-parted.

"Come to me," she said in a husky voice.

Somewhere near an owl hooted as Red Hawk's blood raced. He was drawn toward the vision of dark beauty standing before him in the moonlight. But a voice in his mind reminded him that she was a temptress, no more.

"No," he said, his voice guttural as he forced himself to take a step away. Body and mind split in two, the one fought to control the other. "Go from me," he said.

But she did not. Instead, she lowered her gaze, her dark eyes penetrating his.

"You do not mean it," she said. "You want me Red Hawk. You want a woman who knows the ways of love. I am not fooled by the words of a white woman. White women know nothing. For them the act of love is to bear children only. What do they know of giving pleasure?"

Then she reached to the fastening of her skirt and it too dropped away. She stepped out of it, a lithe figure with the grace of the doe for which she was named. Playing on Red Hawk's indecision, she placed her hand on the part of him that was ready beneath his clothing, filled with desire.

With a mighty effort, Red Hawk grasped her shoulders. Her victory was held in the balance as she felt him waver. Then with an angry sound, he pushed her backward so that she lost her balance and went tumbling into the leaves. When she looked up, he was striding through the forest.

"Wait," she cried after him, her confidence of a moment before turned to desperation and then tears. "Wait."

Rage seized her and she roused herself, running after him. He had a head start, but she caught up to him before he had reached the clearing, and she threw herself at him, tears and hysteria blinding her.

"Red Hawk, don't do this. Stay with me."

He turned and lifted her up by the shoulders.

"Listen to me, my little one. Do not soil your honor by throwing yourself at a man who does not want you. Offer your body to the man who loves you instead. It is beneath you to behave this way. Where is your Cherokee pride?"

Her face was a mask of pain and anger, and she tore herself from his grip, wiping her cheeks with the back of her hand.

"Go then," she shouted at him. "Go on. See to your own bad fortune. You'll regret this Red Hawk. I promise you."

Then she crumpled into a heap, angrily sobbing. She knew much black magic that she could wreak on him and on his despicable lover.

He stared at her, pity mingling with the other emotions tugging at the edges of his heart. Then he turned away.

When Wytheridge came into view Kit brought herself up in surprise. Though they were still some distance away, there was no mistaking the authoritative figure astride the dapple-gray mare that was her father's favorite riding horse. Jonathan Newcomb addressed his black foreman who nodded and gestured broadly in reply.

Kit's eyes strained toward the stables where she saw Brutus leading horses still harnessed to the carriage in the direction of the carriage house. As the wagon rumbled along the drive, Jonathan broke off his conversation and turned to see his daughter being driven up. They were too far apart to speak, but he lifted his chin in reply to Kit's wave.

Ossie Lee held the front door open as Oscar carried in what must have been the last of the trunks. The family had arrived earlier than expected.

Kit bit her lip as Amos reined in the horses so that she could get down. How would she possibly explain her appearance?

"Thank you, Amos. If you hadn't picked me up, I surely would have had to walk all the way."

"Lucky I came by in time, then. I'll tell Master Jared I been busy savin' the damsel in distress."

She got down and waved again to her father, then turned to face the surprised Ossie Lee who stepped out on the porch to meet her. Shep ran down from the steps and licked her hands.

"Well, my sakes, girl," said Ossie Lee. "We was afraid you was dead or worse, and from those clothes it looks like it too. What happened to you?"

Kit ran a hand over her rumpled clothing. "There was a fire in town. I was waiting to see the governor. I'm afraid the horse I took to escape the conflagration ran away with me. He threw me in the woods. I must have been stunned. Amos found me on the road and brought me home."

"Umm-hmm. Well, leastwise you're not dead. Come on in the house and we'll have a good look at you."

"I'm all right, Ossie Lee. Truly I am."

"Just the same, if you had a bump on your head it might need tendin'. Get yourself up to your room and I'll send up Samantha. She's getting Miz Merilee settled in now."

Kit nodded to Ossie Lee and hurried through the door, heading for the stairs. Shep followed her in, his toenails clattering across the wood floor. Kit hoped to avoid seeing anyone else until she had cleaned herself up and changed.

But she heard her name shouted and the running of feet upstairs. Then Merilee flew downward, holding her skirt, her curls bouncing on her shoulders.

"Oh, Kit, we were so worried. I saw that man bring you up the drive. Good heavens, were you caught in the fire? The town is totally destroyed. We saw it when the stage dropped us."

She grasped Kit by the shoulders and looked her up and down.

Embarrassment filled Kit, but she tried to explain

as she had to Ossie Lee.

"I hate having you see me like this. I was going to have dinner with the governor, you see, and I was dressing when the fire started. Luckily I got away."

"Well, I'll say it is." Fletch's voice came from behind her.

Kit turned and looked apologetically at her brother. "A fine welcome I've made for you all. I had hoped to have the house ready. But I didn't expect anyone for another two weeks."

Fletch did not seem to notice his sister's disheveled appearance.

"Father was needed here. When President Jackson realized that Father was so well acquainted with the problems our state is having just now due to this gold rush, he asked him to return at once and send back reports of what is really going on. President Jackson wants to know how many federal troops are needed to keep order. He hesitates to send too many, feeling that this problem with the Cherokees ought to be resolved at the state level. And so, here we are."

"It is a terrible problem," said Kit.

She bit her lip, unsure how much to say. "I was supposed to meet with the governor last night before the fire."

"You?" asked Fletch, surprised. "What have you to do with this?"

Kit tossed her head. "I was at Sander's Bend, where the Indians were trying to dig. The miners threatened them. They were ready to drive the Indians from their lands. That's when the troops came. But all they did was arrest some of the Indian leaders."

261

She broke off her speech at noting the shocked glances of Merilee and Fletch. Her brother glowered at her.

"You were there?"

She swallowed. "Yes. I'd heard there was going to be trouble, so I went to see. . . ."

She did not have time to speculate on how much Fletch would put together after what had happened in Washington, for the front door opened and Jonathan stepped into the hallway.

"Go on," he said, his eyebrow raised at his daughter's appearance. "You say you were at the gold field. What, pray tell, were you doing there?"

Her cheeks flamed, but she resented his tone of voice. Evidently his concern about the local problems outweighed his happiness at seeing his daughter again. When she didn't answer, he glanced with disapproval at her disheveled garb.

"I am not sure I want to ask how you came to be in such a state," he said in a cutting tone of voice.

But Kit rose to the challenge. "I was just explaining to Merilee and Fletch that I was caught in the fire."

"As I heard from the porch. Apparently you were going to dine with the governor. I applaud the high level of social acquaintances you seem to have cultivated in my absence, but may I ask what brought on this sudden interest in a married politician twice your age."

Again her cheeks colored. "It was not like that. I wanted to talk to him about the Indians."

Jonathan raised a hand. "I fear this conversation has gotten out of hand. Go to your room child and

262

change your dress. This house is in an uproar. I trust that between now and the evening meal we can all put ourselves in proper order. I will see you in my study an hour before we dine.

"And, my dear daughter, now that we have a full household, I do hope you will take time away from your country adventures to instruct Ossie Lee and our cook properly. A fine welcome we make Miss Fitzsimmons. Before her wedding vows are taken, I would not be surprised if she changes her mind. I had hoped to be able to impress my son's wife-to-be with the efficiency with which we have always run this plantation."

Seeing that his meaning was clear, Kit said no more but turned and whisked up the stairs and to her room. Of course, it was embarrassing to have Merilee, Fletch, and her father descend on the house with no warning. She feared that Merilee would harshly judge her abilities as mistress of a home. This wasn't at all the way Kit had planned to greet her sister-in-law-to-be. The manner in which the plantation was run had always been a matter of pride to Kit, since she had had to fill her mother's shoes at a young age.

The urgency of the Cherokees' situation warred with the necessity to put her own house in order. And the threat of her father's certain disapproval of what she had been doing was like a leaden weight. Her head began to throb with the confusion her life had become.

In her room she quickly bathed herself in front of the wash stand. Samantha laid out a fresh gown, and then Kit sat in front of the dresser so that the maid could brush the leaves and tangles out of her hair. Her curly tresses flared about her face like a red whirlwind until Samantha gradually tamed them into soft curls, gathering them at the base of her neck in a loose snood.

Kit forced her mind from the events of the last twenty-four hours and sent for Ossie Lee. As she was dressing, she assessed the state of the household with the housekeeper's help. Luckily that capable woman had already taken most matters into her own hands.

"When I saw that carriage pull up, I sent Samantha to make up the rose room for Miz Fitzsimmons. She can finish it while the family's at dinner."

"Very good, Ossie Lee. Whatever would we do without you?"

It was a relief that Ossie Lee was not the sort of housekeeper who simply threw up her hands when no one was about to give her orders. As Ossie Lee named possibilities for a menu, Kit hastily approved her suggestions."

"Those turkeys we bought from that Tennessean are fat enough. Would you be wantin' Brutus to kill one for tomorrow?"

"Yes, please. And the pork for tonight. I'll begin showing Merilee everything tomorrow." Then she turned on the dresser seat and looked worriedly at Ossie Lee. "Do you think the servants will take to her, Ossie Lee? She being a stranger and all."

"Well now, if she be the young master's wife they'll have to take to her. Long as she rules with a fair hand, there won't be no trouble."

"Good."

With her mind splintered with worry and confusion

264

over all the new emotions she felt, Kit decided that having Merilee with her would be a blessing in disguise. She couldn't foist all the work of the household on her at once, but if Merilee had heeded any of Kit's warnings, she must not expect to be treated like a guest for too long. Kit prayed that her friend would fit into the household routine immediately.

"That will do, Samantha," said Kit when her hair was in place. She dismissed the girl.

Samantha hesitated. "If you don't mind my sayin' so, miss. Your pearl ear bobs would go nicely with that dress."

"Yes, yes, thank you, Samantha. I will put them on before dinner."

Still feeling no calmer in spite of her improved appearance, Kit went downstairs to make sure things were proceeding according to plan in the dining room. Going out onto the porch, she saw that Fletch was giving Merilee a tour of the outbuildings on foot. They leaned on the fence near a young colt nursing at its mother's teat in the horse corral. At least Kit did not have to worry about Merilee for a while.

The time passed so quickly, it wasn't until the clock on the mantel in the parlor struck six that Kit remembered her father wanted to see her in his study an hour before dinner. She finished her instructions to Samantha, who was helping her roll up the material they had been cutting, then left the parlor, crossed the entry hall, and knocked on her father's study door.

"Come in."

She entered the paneled room to find her father turning the pages of the ledger they used to record agricultural transactions. While Kit had seen to it that receipts were tucked into one of the cubbyholes in the mahogany pedestal desk, she had not recorded any of the transactions she had overseen since she had been back.

"I'm sorry the accounts are not up to date," she said. "I meant to see to them before you returned."

He flipped the book shut. "No matter. There will be time to see to that."

He leaned back in the wooden swivel chair and looked at his daughter. Then he motioned to the chair in front of the desk.

"I am more concerned about what else you have been doing with your time since you've been here."

She could not stop the flush she felt creeping up her neck. With the urgency of the governor's arrival, she had forgotten all about helping Lucius get the planting underway. But of course he would have followed her orders and begun without her.

"Why I've seen that the planting is being done and the weeding in the garden. I'm nearly finished cutting out cloth for summer work clothes for the servants."

He raised a hand to stop her. "That isn't what I mean."

She swallowed. "Then what do you mean?"

"You know very well what I mean. Gallivanting off into the middle of a fray is hardly an occupation I would consider proper for a young lady of your breeding."

"Father, don't you believe that some things are more important than standing on etiquette? What's happening to the Cherokees isn't fair."

266

He narrowed his gaze and examined her carefully. "How can you be so sure it isn't? What do you know of this matter?"

She lifted her chin. "I knew about the Indian delegation in Washington. You yourself told me you were present when President Jackson interviewed Chief John Ross. I fail to understand how you can believe that allowing itinerate miners to invade Cherokee lands to take away gold that doesn't even belong to them can be fair."

Jonathan brought his fist down on the desk. "The Cherokees will be paid for their lands once they agree to a treaty."

Kit rose, unable to suppress her irritation. "But they don't want a treaty."

Jonathan sprang to his feet and came around the desk. "Some of them do."

"But not all of them."

Father and daughter glared angrily at each other for a moment, and then Jonathan frowned and paced beside the windows. When he spoke again, it was with a lowered but firm voice.

"And since when has my daughter given any mind to such matters?"

Kit remained firm. "Perhaps taking me to Washington City opened my eyes to things I was not aware of before. I also met the wife of a missionary who lives and works among the Cherokees at New Echota. We were on the same coach."

He turned his head. That was unfortunate, he thought. His daughter was at a vulnerable age, and without a mother to look after her properly, she might easily have been exposed to elements in the nation's capital that he had not intended her to meet. He exasperatedly ran a hand across the back of his neck. It was partly his own fault. But leaving her here with the nearby counties in such a state of unrest was no solution either.

"We have a wedding to get through," he said. "Then, after I have assessed the situation here, on which you consider yourself so well informed, I must return to Washington. Perhaps I will take you with me so that I can keep an eye on your activities. I have been remiss in not seeing that you were provided with an adequate social life. It is a father's duty to make sure his daughter is properly introduced to matters of the world. I cannot expect you to understand politics and the like without guidance."

"I would gladly go to Washington with you," answered Kit, the fire still in her eyes. "At least there I could speak to those with influence and tell them what I know—that the Cherokees are fighting for their rights. And there will be bloodshed unless President Jackson listens."

"How dare you defend those red barbarians? Before our kind came to this country the Indian tribes shed just as much blood killing each other. The Christian white man's law and order is exactly what they need."

"They are Christians in case you didn't know, and if they have been driven to barbarism, it's only because of white hypocrisy.

Jonathan's temper flared, and in an instant his hand was in the air and he stepped forward to slap her. But as she stood her ground defiantly, she suddenly resembled her mother very much. Jonathan's late wife, Margaret, used to place her hands on her hips in just such a way. Her eyes would flash with the same commitment to a cause that he saw in Kit's. Mother and daughter mingled in the image that stood before him, and his hand slowly lowered. He grasped the rounded back of the walnut chair he stood beside.

"Go to your room and stay there until this nonsense is driven from your mind."

Kit thought her heart would burst in her chest. How could she remain here, shackled to her plantation petticoats, unable to communicate her concerns to her father. When he turned from her, she reached out a hand toward him, but he did not see it. Grief threatened. She wanted so badly to talk to this man she had revered all her life. But she knew him well enough to realize when he had his mind made up on an issue. Once he'd done that, she had never known him to change his opinion, no matter how strong the opposition.

Swallowing a sob, she grasped her skirt and fled from the room. She passed Samantha in the upstairs hall—the maid was carrying fresh towels to Merilee's room—but did not speak. The house could very well just run itself without her.

She slammed her door behind her and flung herself onto the fourposter bed in the center of the room. Her sobs were quick and deep. But a slow-burning anger soon replaced her grief. She turned over and lay staring upward. What was happening to her? Instead of the happy days of life well run on this plantation where she had grown up, she had come back to unrest and confusion. That which happened within her seemed to reflect the outward turbulence taking place only a few miles from here. Would life never again be the placid existence she had once thought it?

Some time later there was a soft knock on Kit's door. From the settee on which she was doing some needlework, Kit looked up.

She did not care about this domestic project that demanded her attention, but concentrating on the tiny stitches helped order her mind.

"Come in," she called.

Merilee stepped into the room.

Kit tried to smile. "Hello. I hope Fletch has been entertaining you. I meant to see if you had everything you needed, but I . . . I didn't feel too well."

"When Ossie Lee told me you had taken a tray in your room at dinner, I was concerned. Are you ill?"

Kit pressed her lips together and set her work aside. She badly wanted to unburden herself to her friend, but she was unsure how much she could say. She smoothed her skirt and spoke carefully.

"I'm afraid things in Georgia are not as they used to be."

Merilee settled herself on the hassock near Kit, her skirt spread around her.

"Fletcher told me about the gold rush. Is that what you mean?"

Kit nodded.

"But that is on Indian lands, is it not?"

"Yes. But I'm troubled about . . . all the intruders.

The land isn't even theirs, and yet they're taking gold out of the ground."

Merilee frowned. "Fletcher and your father spoke of it at dinner. Is it very dangerous, then? Might there be fighting?"

Kit winced. "Yes."

Her friend tilted her head curiously. "Your father thought the Indians would be brought quickly under control. Surely he told you President Jackson sent him here to report on the need for federal troops."

Kit clenched a fist and brought it down on her lap. "That's not fair."

She rose and paced across the room, lowering her head to her hands. She sensed Merilee watching her back, and when she had regained control of herself she turned, tears still at the corners of her eyes.

"Oh, Merilee. I don't understand it all myself. But you remember the man I met in Washington City."

Merilee nodded slowly.

"He's here. He was with the Cherokees. They . . . they took him to jail."

Merilee's eyes widened and she got up to come take Kit's hands and lead her back to the settee on which they both sat.

"Have you spoken to him?"

Kit nodded. She could not tell Merilee everything, but she needed to pour out her emotions to someone. She trusted Merilee to be discreet, and besides, her friend had a woman's heart. Who else would understand if not another woman?

"I went to the jail to speak to him," Kit said, trembling as she recalled the scene. "It was awful. He

271

hated me because I hadn't told him who I was—that is, that I hadn't told him it was my own father who advised President Jackson to try to get the Cherokees out of Georgia."

Merilee shook her head. "This really means a lot to you, doesn't it, Kit?"

Kit closed her eyes. "I know it sounds impossible, but I . . . I came to care about him . . . about what happens to his people." She shrugged and gave a disheartened little laugh. "I guess I began to see things as an Indian."

Merilee did not say anything for some minutes as she sat holding Kit's hand. But when she got Kit to look at her, she asked the question with her eyes.

"Kit. This man, the one you called Red Hawk. He is more to you than just an Indian, isn't he?"

Kit's ears rang, and the blood rushed through her. She nodded, not looking at Merilee.

"Then you are in love with him."

The hand that seemed to clench Kit's heart clamped shut. Her pain was visible in her eyes, and she exhaled deeply.

"What do I know of love?" The question was barely a whisper.

Merilee shook her head. Then she put an arm around Kit and pulled her head onto her shoulder.

"I'll tell you what love is to me," she began, gently rocking Kit back and forth. "Love is when your beloved is in your every thought. Love is when you cannot tear yourself from his side."

She brushed Kit's hair back from her forehead and allowed her to sit up. "Love is the sensation of his

272

touch on your skin, his lips on yours," she continued.

Then she grasped Kit's shoulders and turned her squarely to face her. "Tell me, have you experienced these last two?"

Kit's face was tinged with a hot blush. She met Merilee's dark eyes and knew she could not lie. She nodded.

Chapter Fifteen

Merilee's hands slid slowly back to her own lap. The two women sat in silence. Outside the curfew bell called the servants to their quarters. A door slammed downstairs. As the wind rose, the rafters creaked above them.

"Then you are bound to experience difficulties that I never will," said Merilee.

She rose and paced a little in front of Kit, hugging herself. "For me, love is the comfort of being drawn into a home with the approval of generations that have preceded me on both sides. It is being with people of my own kind, speaking the same language, someday giving birth to the heir of the plantation."

She sat down again beside Kit. "But, Kit, my dearest friend, what can this infatuation with an Indian you hardly know bring? Can you not forget him? There are other marriageable men."

"Don't you think I've tried to forget him?" Kit said testily. "As to the other marriageable men, if you mean Breckenridge Grover, I wouldn't place my life in his care if he were the last man on earth." She wrinkled her nose at Merilee. "And I am all too familiar with some of the other landowners hereabouts. I don't want a drunk for a husband, nor do I want to watch my husband's mulatto children growing up in the servants' quarters behind the house. No, thank you."

"Oh, Kit. Don't be absurd. Nobody wants you to marry someone you dislike." She sighed. "Daniel Webster asked after you before we left. I think he was quite taken with you. And he is a very eligible widower."

Kit nodded. Thinking of Daniel Webster brought comfort to her. He was a very warm person, and she felt she could talk to him. To Merilee she said, "I'm glad to count Senator Webster among my dear friends. I hope to see him again. But I don't think of him in the way you mean."

Merilee sighed, and for a moment both women sat in silence. Then Kit spoke softly, gazing out the window at the night.

"How do you know if a man loves you?" she asked her friend.

"You will know," said Merilee, smiling gently and taking Kit's hand. "You will know."

Red Hawk was filled with bitter pride as he walked through New Echota. The town had thrived since its founding. Here the great Sequoyah invented his alphabet so that their people could write down their language. Directly ahead stood the courthouse where cases were tried by the young Cherokee lawyers educated in the white man's Eastern schools. From across the square, Red Hawk heard the heavy rhythmic thud of the printing press turning out the pages of the *Cherokee Phoenix,* their newspaper, which was printed in both Cherokee and English.

But with all their progress, the Cherokees kept their old traditions alive as well. And now it is all threatened, thought Red Hawk bitterly. Not only by the greedy white miners, but by the traitors within the tribe who urged removal to the Western lands.

As Red Hawk approached the seven-sided council house to take part in the debate, his fists clenched. He stood just inside the door, his eyes adjusting to the dim light. Already John Ridge was speaking to those gathered to listen to his venomous words.

Red Hawk folded his arms and observed the men and women sitting on the benches, listening. He was gratified to see the cold reception they were giving the man who stood before them. Though it broke his heart that there would be bloodshed before this matter was settled, he was proud that there would be people who would not give up any more of their lands.

Chief John Ross rose and spoke. Red Hawk listened with respect to his words. The venerable chief had not given up on negotiations. Their leaders were well trained in the law. They were prepared to take the issue to the United States Supreme Court. Red Hawk relaxed slightly. Chief John Ross appealed to the people's reason.

Red Hawk's eyes slid to where John Ridge had taken a seat with his father, Major Ridge. He did not like the sly, covert look in the younger Ridge's eyes. Red Hawk narrowed his own gaze, and cold fear slithered up his spine. Evil was afoot, and Red Hawk was not sure he would be able to prevent it.

Outside, Standing Doe watched the council house as she coiled strips of clay to fashion a pot. When Red Hawk emerged, her fingers dug into the clay, ruining the design she had formed. He had humiliated her, and he would pay.

She narrowed her gaze and watched him cross the square toward the log building that housed the tavern. A group of children laughed and shouted as they skipped past Standing Doe, but she did not see their merry faces. Instead she closed her eyes and her lips moved.

> *"You, Red Hawk, are a lonely man.*
> *Pass on toward Nightland!*
> *Your two souls are not to behold each other again.*
> *Now quickly another man must come to strike in the very middle of your soul!*
> *Ha, then! The Seven Thunderers glitter all about me!"*

She repeated the chant four times, adding the required lines to each repetition. When she opened her eyes Red Hawk was no longer in the town square. But she knew that because of her spell he would suffer.

She molded the clay once again to refashion her pot.

Kit was forced to set aside her thoughts as the wedding drew near. Merilee's family arrived, and the tasks in the kitchen doubled. Beds were turned and rugs beaten. Furniture was polished, and pigs were slaughtered. And when Merilee tried on her wedding gown for Kit, it was with pain that Kit watched her friend turn to display the bows and the pearls sewn into the lace and silk trim. The veil that would cover Merilee's face on the day she took her vows made her a vision of purity.

In the evenings Kit sat with Merilee and Mrs. Fitzsimmons in the parlor, making small talk and bending over her needlework. Mrs. Fitzsimmons was city-bred, but she was charmed by the Georgia mountains.

"Merilee tells me you met several eligible men in Washington City, my dear," said Mrs. Fitzsimmons one evening.

Kit shrugged. No longer could she rely on the excuse that her father needed her at Wytheridge. For Merilee would be mistress now. It was time she married and found a home of her own. But she glared stubbornly at her needle and thread.

"I am not in a hurry to marry."

"Oh," Merilee's mother replied.

The finality of Kit's statement seemed to put an end to the conversation.

On another occasion Merilee read aloud from Dickens as Fletch stretched his legs out on the hassock in front of him, sipping his port and gazing at his fiancée. When Merilee raised her eyes to glance at him, her cheeks colored, and Kit quickly looked down at her work, afraid that the couple would catch her staring at them. At such times her own heart twisted with yearning.

The grand day finally arrived, and the families of bride and groom gathered with the wedding guests outside on the lawn. Reverend Shepherd read the service and the couple exchanged vows. Then the entire party was invited inside for a spread of smoked venison, roast turkey, chestnuts, tomatoes, cucumbers, wedding cake, and strawberries and cream topped off with champagne.

Then there was dancing. The furniture had been moved out of the dining room, and black musicians got out their fiddles, flutes, and banjos. The party danced until dawn. Kit wore herself out by dancing with every man there at least three times. At sunrise, breakfast was served, and then the tired guests climbed into buggies drawn by horses that luckily knew their own way home.

Kit was thankful for the physical exertion, and while Ossie Lee and the household staff began to put the house back in order, she climbed the stairs and slipped in between the sheets. Her drapes were drawn to keep out the morning sunlight, and as soon as her head hit the pillow she slept.

The following day was oddly quiet. Fletch and Merilee climbed into a carriage drawn by a pair of grays that was a gift from Jonathan, and the household waved them away as they left for the coast on their honeymoon. It would be a short one, since Fletch was needed on the plantation as soon as Jonathan left again for Washington City. Still, Jonathan had promised the newlyweds he would send them to Europe on an extended trip next winter to make up

279

for that.

Merilee's parents left, on the stage, and that evening Kit wandered about the house after dining with her father. Their conversation had been strained, and she felt restless. The wedding preparations had at least distracted her, but now loneliness hung heavy on her. When she went into her father's study to tell him she was going to retire early, he closed the book he held on his knee and she bent to kiss him on the cheek.

"Good night, Father."

"Good night, Kit."

They retained the formalities, but there had been no warmth in their relationship since the night they had argued.

Shep, who had been lying with his head on his paws, got up and followed her to the door. Jonathan's voice stopped her.

"Kit."

"Yes, Father."

He rose and stood in the center of the room, his hands folded behind him.

"I feel the wedding went off successfully. I thank you for your part in it."

"Well, of course, Father. After all, Fletch is my brother."

Jonathan strode toward the brick fireplace. He paused and gazed at a miniature that had been painted of Kit's mother.

"I like to think of my children's marriages as bringing life to this plantation rather than thinking of them as taking either of you away. I'm glad Fletch has decided to follow in my footsteps here. I was afraid city life would be too tempting for him."

She reached down to scratch Shep's ears as the dog panted companionably. "Has he decided to do that then? I did not know."

"He has agreed to stay on here and raise his family now that his education at Chapel Hill is finished."

She straightened and waited. Her father seemed thoughtful, and she wondered if he was going to say more. She felt guilty that she did not enjoy passing the time with him when he waxed eloquent as he so often did. If only he would listen to her as well. She pressed her lips together and wrung her hands.

Jonathan turned toward her. "I don't suppose you've given any more thought to the subject."

"What?"

"Marriage, my girl. Now that Fletcher is married off, I consider it my responsibility to get you settled."

Her lip trembled. "I . . . I hadn't thought of it. I've met no one who has made an offer."

Breckenridge Grover's offer doesn't count, she decided. No need to mention it to her father.

"Hmmm. Well, in time then. You are, of course, welcome to live here. It is only your happiness I am thinking of. A good marriage . . ." His words trailed off as he picked up the miniature again and gazed at it.

He was lost in the past, and Kit quietly moved toward the door, Shep noiselessly following her as if he, too, understood that Jonathan ought to be left with his thoughts.

* * *

The night was warm and Kit slept with her windows open. As she fell asleep she could hear the darkies' singing coming from the servants' quarters.

She did not know the hour when she awoke. But she came wide awake, feeling as if Red Hawk were calling to her. She threw the covers aside and slipped out onto the rug. Shep whined as she walked to the window and looked out. The hunter's full moon had come up through the tall trunks of the old pines to the east and now touched the landscape with unearthly light. She felt drawn to the arbor surrounding the gazebo. She half expected Red Hawk to be standing under one of the spreading oaks, waiting for her.

But she shook her head and knelt to wrap her arms around Shep's warm body.

"It must have been a dream, old boy."

He whined and licked her face.

She petted the dog and sighed. The room was too hot and still for sleep. Wide awake now, she put on the wrapper that lay across her dressing-table bench.

"How about a walk down to the stream, Shep?" she whispered to the dog. "We mustn't wake anyone."

Shep danced in a circle and wagged his tail. She held a finger to her lips and grasped his jaws, holding them shut to communicate that he mustn't bark.

She didn't bother with bedroom slippers. They weren't going far, and if the dew had risen on the grass, it would feel good to walk on the soft ground.

They made their way out of the house. Shep bounded ahead as Kit followed, inhaling the fresh, misty night air. Her lungs expanded with the scent of pine, and the fragrance of Russian olive trees and of the roses that bloomed all around the house.

She passed the gazebo and held up her night clothes as she knelt by a little pool that had formed at the edge of the stream. Dipping her hands into the cool water, she lifted them to bathe her face, then froze. As the ripples of the water settled, a face stared back at her.

She spread her hands, releasing the water she had cupped in them. It had to be a figment of her imagination. Nevertheless, she gazed at Red Hawk's face in the dark water and reached down to touch the reflection.

Then she heard the crunch of twigs behind her, felt a firm grasp on her shoulder. She gasped and turned, but his hand went over her mouth. Her arms clutched his shoulders as Red Hawk lifted her to stand beside him.

For a moment all she could do was stare with widened eyes. Her heart pounded in her chest, and her breathing became shallow. When he saw she was over her surprise, he released her mouth, but he held a finger to his lips.

Behind her, Shep started to growl, and Kit turned quickly.

"It's all right Shep. Quiet."

Red Hawk knelt and held out his hand for the dog to sniff. He spoke something softly in Cherokee. Shep came closer, sniffed Red Hawk's fingers, rolled his brown eyes upward to look at the Indian's face, and then began to lick him and wag his tail.

Red Hawk smiled and petted the dog, scratching

his ears.

Kit was still speechless, but knelt beside them both. When the dog had lain down in the grass at their feet, Red Hawk turned to look at her again. His lips curved in pleasure, and he raised a hand to lift her loose hair off her shoulders.

"Red Hawk," she said breathlessly. "Why are you here?"

"You did not feel my call?"

"I did feel it. Often," she said.

But she could think of no more words, for he slid one hand behind her head and the other went to her back. Her hands drifted to his deerskin-clad chest, and her eyes locked with dark ones in which she saw the flames of desire.

He bent his head to her, and her arms snaked around his neck. He held her against his chest, the lengths of their thighs meeting. Their kiss was urgent. Kit filled herself up with this man who would not let her thoughts rest. Though others might call her mad, she knew she was lost to him. She no longer fought her deep need for him, and his very presence spoke of his need for her. On the soft Georgia night under a full moon Kit surrendered to a moment of pure ecstasy.

When his lips left her mouth to drift down her neck and shoulders, she dug her fingers into his back.

"I've missed you," she breathed out.

"And I you," he returned, his mouth on her ear.

Then he pulled her down on soft pine needles under a protective tree. His hands awoke within her fires that had smoldered since their last union, and

284

she hungrily returned his caresses. When he lifted her nightgown to reveal the soft white flesh he remembered, he covered her with his limbs as she held him close and opened herself to his burning desire.

Their passion mounted quickly, finding fulfillment in taking each other's bodies as their souls mingled. The longed-for release came at last, accompanied by short gasps of ecstasy. Then they held each other tightly as the last thrilling pulses faded away. Red Hawk lay with his head against hers, his long black hair splayed over her breasts.

After some moments he rose to his knees and pulled her into a sitting position, brushing leaves from her hair as she pulled her nightdress about her. Then he replaced his clothing and pulled her up, holding her for a moment against him as his heart beat loudly against his chest. Silently he led her to the chestnut gelding tethered to a tree. He led the horse to a tree stump and helped Kit mount. Then he leapt onto the horse behind her.

Kit noticed that Shep was no longer with them, but perhaps the dog had returned to the house. Suddenly she heard a rustle of leaves. The horse jerked its head, and Red Hawk uttered a Cherokee oath.

Kit froze as moonlight glinted off a double-barreled shotgun. Blue-black as the night surrounding them, Brutus moved forward, the weapon wavering slightly in his hands. Then white men in blue uniforms moved out from cover, their flintlock rifles pointed at Kit and Red Hawk. They were surrounded by Georgia militia, men who hated the Cherokees. Kit gasped as she saw the man who had leered at her from his post at the hotel in which Governor Gilmer had made his headquarters.

Then she saw her father riding toward them, his pistol drawn, his face red with rage. He uttered an oath she had never before heard on his lips.

Red Hawk cursed under his breath. He should have known men were near. Passion had made him careless, and he had let down his guard.

"Release my daughter," Jonathan shouted, pointing the pistol at Red Hawk's head.

Red Hawk held his hands loosely on his thighs. "She is free to go."

Kit stiffened her back against Red Hawk's chest.

"Get down at once, Kathryn Margaret Newcomb. I don't know what you are doing with a man dressed like this in the middle of the night. Words cannot express the shame I feel. If you don't get off that horse now, I will swear to the world before God that I have no daughter."

Red Hawk did not move, but sat very still on the horse. It was Kit who confronted the man threatening them.

"I tried to talk to you about the Cherokees," she said angrily, tossing her red hair over her shoulder. "I would gladly have told you about Red Hawk, had you had ears to listen."

Jonathan's lips curled in an ugly expression of disdain. "You have shamed me. I am only glad that your poor mother is not alive to see this." The hatred that flooded Jonathan Newcomb flared in his bloodshot eyes.

But Kit's own heightened emotions would not allow

her to do what her father ordered. Her knees gripped the horse tighter. Her fingers entwined in its mane.

Red Hawk carefully eyed the black-powder rifles and shotguns trained on them. He sensed Kit's resistance to her father. Suddenly he realized that the men would kill him as soon as Kit got off the horse. He must prepare for a quick flight, and even then he knew that ball and shot would travel faster than his swift horse. He concentrated on the scene around them.

There was a small opening between Kit's father and the soldier who had dismounted to his right.

Kit's father again ordered his daughter off the horse. But still she tensed, knees gripping the beast beneath her. She was alert for flight.

The horse beside Kit's father sidestepped, and Red Hawk waited no longer. He pressed his heels into their mount and the horse sprang forward. As they passed the soldier on foot, Red Hawk brought his hand down and knocked the rifle out of the man's hands. A shotgun blasted over their heads, then Kit's father shouted.

"Hold your fire," he ordered. "You might hit my girl."

"After them," shouted the captain.

The chestnut gelding flew through the forest, and Kit hung on, trusting Red Hawk's sense of direction as the soldiers came on behind. She hunched over the horse's neck as Red Hawk pressed forward. The gelding took flight and galloped over rough land and underbrush that slowed the mounts behind.

Kit knew when they left Wytheridge lands, and she

recognized their path as they wound upward and then downward, leaving well-beaten trails behind.

She glanced backward once, to see a soldier's horse slide along the side of a hill that the red gelding had picked his way up. Red Hawk and Kit were far enough ahead to prevent the soldiers from achieving accurate aim. Her heart pounded and thought fled as she became one with Red Hawk in this flight from the brutal soldiers and the prejudice of her father.

They circled a meadow, keeping to the cover of the woods, for the bright moonlight would make them a ready target. And in the open it was possible that some of the soldiers' plains-bred horses could gain on them. In the hilly country the sure-footed Indian pony had the advantage.

Red Hawk lost the soldiers, but only gradually slowed his horse when he was sure they were safe. Still he guided the mount along trails used mostly by the Indians. Kit finally tired and leaned back against his chest. Red Hawk's chin rested against her hair, and he supported her easily as they rode.

At dawn he stopped near the top of a ridge well covered with trees. A stream ran there, between oddly shaped boulders. From this vantage, they could see the surrounding tree-covered rolling hills while remaining protected by a pocket of black birch and blooming dogwood.

Finally Red Hawk dismounted and then lifted Kit down. She stood sleepily, blinking at the wilderness around them.

"We will wait here until sunset," he said. "We are not many miles from my village. But the white soldiers do not stop at the border to Indian lands. We have evaded them in the night, but it will be less easy to lose them if there are a number of them during the day."

Kit nodded. She had no idea whether the soldiers were still following. Perhaps they had given up. Her mind was too fuzzy to think about it. And the reality of what she had done was too new to face. The look on her father's face had made it clear that she could not go back home. But hadn't she known that for a long time now?

Her feelings were still torn, but as she gazed at Red Hawk's caring face and felt his fingers caress her cheeks, she stilled such thoughts. She felt safe with him. After she had rested, she would have to think about her situation and decide what to do. For now she would entrust herself to Red Hawk's care. This was his domain, and he would know how to keep them safe.

He led the horse to the water and removed the blankets, saddle, and bridle. Then he hobbled the gelding among the trees, within easy reach of grasses and leaves. From a pouch he brought forth dried beef and handed some to Kit. She sat on a broad flat rock and ate. Then Red Hawk spread the blanket under the cover of spreading branches.

"Come and rest," he said, when they had consumed the food. "We will search for more to eat after we sleep."

Kit stretched out beside him, and he pulled her against his hard-muscled body. He leaned an elbow and pulled his fingers through her tangled hair, then caressed her cheek.

How odd, she thought as she shut her eyes to the sun warming her face. She lay on an Indian blanket in Cherokee land. Her father had disowned her. The thought that she would not be welcome at home brought a knot of grief into her chest.

Would she ever see Fletch or Merilee again? But Red Hawk stroked her shoulder and arm, soothing her troubled thoughts. Her heart sang when he pulled her closer. The strength of his limbs gave her comfort.

"Sleep, my dove," he murmured.

And soon, she matched her heartbeat to his.

Chapter Sixteen

A rough tongue woke Kit, and she sat up in confusion. It took her a moment to remember where she was, but Shep's friendly whines and anxious licks brought everything rushing back.

"Shep, for heaven's sake," she said as the dog climbed all over her. "How did you find us?"

Then she saw Red Hawk squatting nearby, watching girl and dog. Shep bounded aside, and Red Hawk reached out to pet him. Shep gave his hand a lick and then lay down next to Kit.

"He must have followed us," she said.

In a moment she understood Red Hawk's look of concern. "Do you think they used him to track us?" she asked.

Red Hawk stood up. "When I saw the dog I scouted the area. There is no one else."

She sank back against the tree trunk in relief. "Thank goodness." She smiled at the dog who gazed at her with love.

291

"Shep, good dog. Did you sneak away from the house? Did the soldiers muzzle you so you couldn't warn us?"

Shep flopped his tail and Kit buried her face in his fur. "Thank heavens they didn't hurt him."

Red Hawk grunted. "They might have tried to use the dog. He may have slipped through their grasp. I will watch."

And he disappeared into the woods again to keep a lookout.

They feasted that day on chokecherries and plums that grew wild. They did not hunt for meat because they could not risk a fire. Though Kit was tense and watchful, she enjoyed being in the wilderness with Red Hawk.

He pointed out roots that were good to eat if cooked, and she told him of garden vegetables she had raised at home. They bathed in the stream, and Kit walked to the middle and lay back, her hair floating in the clear, cold water, while Shep splashed about nearby. Red Hawk rubbed Kit's scalp with his fingers and watched her hair eddy with the current. He held her tresses to his lips and let them drift through his fingers.

After drying off with the blanket, they made love again and stretched out in the sun. In the afternoon Kit slept while Red Hawk scouted the surrounding area to make sure they were not being tracked.

At last night fell, and they broke up their little camp. Kit mounted the red gelding, and Red Hawk took the reins to lead the horse.

Shep walked at Red Hawk's heels, and Kit wondered if the dog had adopted a new master. But every so often Shep stopped and turned to look up at Kit to make sure she was still there. Tonight they were not running, but would make their way carefully over the mountains and into the valley where the town of New Echota stood at the confluence of the Conasauga and the Coosawattee rivers.

As they rode toward the Cherokee capital, Kit's blood flowed with a new energy. Her love for Red Hawk gave her courage, also a sense of adventure, for she was about to embark on a new life. How right it must be, then, that she had sought this new experience. She had tried to broaden her horizons in Washington City, but there she had felt stifled by the formalities of fashion and etiquette. Had it been fate that had thrown her into the company of Harriet Worcester as she had left one capital behind before heading for another? She wondered if Harriet would be surprised to see her again so soon. Something Harriet had said to her as they had parted made Kit suspect that she might not be, that she had somehow sensed that Kit's path would lead her to the Cherokees.

Beyond that Kit could not fathom what her new life would be like. But surely Red Hawk's love and the friendship of Harriet and the Reverend Samuel Worcester would sustain her as she became accustomed to this new way of living. As to how long she would remain in New Echota she dared not speculate. Red Hawk had said nothing of marriage, but she knew from what Harriet had said that the Cherokees took Christian wives.

Coming down from the hills, Red Hawk led the horse carrying Kit across flat grasslands. In the moonlight, buttercups looked like snowflakes dancing on a grassy meadow.

Several hours later the moon had passed over the night sky, and dawn appeared as they traveled by cultivated fields. Black-haired Cherokees straightened from their plows to watch the white woman with red hair springing off her shoulders, but they relaxed at Red Hawk's gesture of greeting and raised their own hands in return. This deep in the Cherokee Nation Red Hawk no longer feared to travel by day.

He struck a path along the bank of the Coosawattee. The rhythmic gait of the horse and the warmth of the spring day put Kit to sleep, and she dozed as she rode.

When a branch brushed her face, she awoke as the horse stopped. They stood on a riverbank, but as she blinked her eyes she came fully awake.

"Here the Coosawattee and the Conasauga form the Oostanaula," said Red Hawk pointing at the place where the two rivers joined. "This is the center of our nation."

On the other side of the river a town appeared. Hewn-log buildings were spaced comfortably from each other, and residents moved about industriously. Their bright colored, woven clothing and copper skin identified them as Cherokee. But even though Kit had heard how highly civilized these people were, she was unprepared for the impressive sight of this town.

"New Echota," said Red Hawk proudly.

He led the horse to a footbridge that had been constructed across the river, and Kit looked about curiously as they crossed it and then stepped onto a path that led to the town.

A squarely built man with wide jaw and broad fore-head, dressed in fringed shirt and trousers tucked into high deerskin boots, opened the door of his cabin and came down the steps. When they were within a short distance of him, he held out his arms to them. Red Hawk met his embrace, and the two men grasped each other's shoulders.

"A safe return," said the man, who looked with open friendliness at Kit.

Red Hawk turned and helped Kit down; then he led her to where the other man stood. Shep sat on his haunches as if waiting to be introduced.

"This is the woman, then?" said the man. His face lit with cheerfulness, and he looked Kit over with open curiosity.

Kit felt self-conscious, but Red Hawk nudged her forward.

"Her name is Kathryn," said Red Hawk. "She is my bride-to-be."

"Kathryn with flaming hair," said Red Hawk's friend. He grinned in pleasure.

Red Hawk turned to Kit. "This is my friend, Waiting Bear. He helped me find you."

Kit felt shy and did not know if she should offer her hand. She had heard Red Hawk say she was his bride-to-be when he had not even informed her of that fact. And this happy-looking friend had helped Red Hawk find her?

She wrinkled a brow. "I don't understand," she said.

"Waiting Bear is a medicine man," explained Red Hawk.

Kit blinked. She had heard of Indian magic, but the thought it had been used on her was surprising. She had no more time to speculate on the powers of the medicine man however, for a familiar woman in blue print prairie dress and a straw bonnet crossed the grass toward them.

Kit left the two men and ran toward Harriet who held out her arms.

"Kit, my dear," said Harriet as she hugged her, then held her away. "I had heard rumors, but I did not know we would see you so soon."

Kit blushed, but she could not hold back her joy at seeing a friend. Here at least was someone she felt she could lean on in these confusing times. When she glanced back at Red Hawk, he was walking off with Waiting Bear. Other men, who had been conversing on the porch of a two-story log building, came down the steps to join them. She could see that Red Hawk was speaking and the others were listening. Perhaps he was telling them of their flight from the soldiers. She pressed her lips together and turned back to Harriet.

"I'm glad to see you, Harriet. I don't know what to say now that I am here. My father . . ." She paused to swallow. "My father saw me with Red Hawk. He threatened to disown me. I tried to talk to him, but he wouldn't listen."

She shook her head, the old emotions churning. Harriet put an arm around her shoulders and led her in the opposite direction from the men.

"Why don't you come to my house and tell me about it?"

Kit nodded. Then she glanced back at Red Hawk, who was not looking her way.

"Don't worry," said Harriet. "He'll know where to find you."

Kit took a deep breath and exhaled. "I suppose what I've done is wrong. My father disowned me. And I fear I've only given the soldiers more reason to seek out the Cherokees and punish them."

Harriet squeezed her shoulders. "If you came of your own free will, they cannot punish anyone for that. I believe Red Hawk loves you. He has informed my husband that he wishes to make you his wife."

Kit gave a nervous laugh. "It seems he has told everyone but me."

They followed the street, passed several cabins and places of business. People looked curiously at the new woman and her dog. Kit stared in amazement at the scene. The people worked at tasks that might occupy any rural villagers. The women were dressed much as Harriet, in printed cotton dresses or yoked blouses and long skirts. Their hair was braided or fell straight down their backs. Several women carried on their backs babies wrapped in cloth.

Men stood about in groups, some with breech-loading rifles under their arms. On the porch of the merchandise store were two men dressed in black frock coats much like those the delegation had worn in Washington. She recognized Chief John Ross. The other man had olive skin and light-colored eyes.

Seeing Kit's look of curiosity, Harriet said, "That's Joseph Vann with Chief John Ross," she said. "The Indians call him 'Rich Joe Van.' He's descended from a Scottish trader and is a very good businessman himself."

"Does he live here?" asked Kit.

"No. He has a large brick house a few miles from

here."

The house Harriet led Kit to was a white frame dwelling with an outside stairway to the second story. Pillared porch and balcony extended across the front, and Harriet explained that they used the rooms on the second floor for church and school. Samuel was teaching there now. The house was set among shady maple trees, and the site looked restful.

"Come and freshen up," said Harriet. "Then we'll have some tea."

Kit looked at her sheepishly. "I'm afraid I've nothing to wear. It was a sudden leave-taking."

Harriet smiled in understanding. "Don't worry. I'll find something for you."

Kit told Shep to wait on the porch; then she followed Harriet into the house, where Harriet showed her a small room furnished with bed, dresser, and wash stand. Kit stripped off her ruined clothing and put on the wrapper Harriet handed her. Then she poured water from the ewer and bathed her face and limbs, using soap and a fresh cloth.

She sat on a stool and gazed out a curtained window at some Indians working in the corn fields not too far away, while Harriet brushed her hair then gathered it into a single braid down the back of her neck. Strands of red hair drifted about her face in a loose fashion that Kit liked when Harriet handed her a mirror.

"I've never worn it braided," Kit admitted.

"I think Red Hawk will like it," said Harriet, a teasing look in her eye.

Kit blushed and put the mirror down.

She put on a brown and yellow calico dress that

298

fitted her well enough, then Harriet loaned her some moccasins.

"We'll have to get some that fit you, but for now these will do," her benefactor declared.

When Kit stood up, she found herself smiling. The sedate Indian village and the comfortable house in the shade were so pleasing she'd been able to banish unrestful thoughts. She impulsively hugged Harriet.

"Do you think I should marry Red Hawk?" she asked.

Harriet held her away and looked into her eyes. "Do you love him?"

"Yes, I do." Kit sighed. "I know now there is no one else for me."

From her cabin, Standing Doe had watched Red Hawk bring the woman into the village. She had seen Waiting Bear greet her and had watched her go with the missionary's wife. Standing Doe's heart filled with hatred. Red Hawk had not looked at her since the night she had offered herself to him in the woods. She had been humiliated, and she would not go without revenge. The evil spell had not worked yet, but she chanted it the required four times every day. And there were other ways.

She looked out the window of her cabin and saw William Longbow leave the group of men he had been standing with in town and begin to walk in the direction of her cabin. She frowned in impatience. William Longbow wanted to marry her. She had refused him, having no eyes for anyone but Red Hawk. But he still came to see her. Now he brought something wrapped in cloth.

She opened the door and waited on the porch as he approached.

"Greetings, Standing Doe," said William.

He was a well-proportioned half-breed, and his light-footedness and swiftness had made him an excellent hunter. He climbed the steps and stood with her on the porch of her cabin.

"Greetings, William," she said. She did not indicate that he could sit down.

He smiled patiently at the fierce look in her eyes. He was used to her ill temper, but he believed the fire in her could be tamed with the right touch of gentleness.

"I've brought you something. Don't you want to see what it is."

She shrugged.

He handed her the gift, and she unwrapped the cloth to find a side of smoked pork.

"Thank you," she said.

Standing Doe raised all her own grains and vegetables, but she sold her animals and traded for meat. Since her father had died in the last year, she had lived in the cabin alone with only herself to feed, and it was too big a job to butcher animals for one person. The pork would go to good use. She would take it to the root cellar after William left.

"You have been watching Red Hawk and his bride-to-be," said William. He was not unaware of where Standing Doe's heart lay. But he knew Red Hawk did not have eyes for her, and was not a rival.

She glared at William and then sat down on a bench made from a split log. He sat down beside her.

"You are foolish to hold out hopes for him, Standing Doe. He has told everyone he will marry this white woman. He has brought her here for that purpose."

"The white woman will bring evil down upon us," she said angrily.

William looked out over the village and said nothing. It was pointless to argue. Time would make her see. He had done all he could until Standing Doe changed her mind. He made one last appeal.

"With your father gone, you will need a husband to chop wood and to cut ice for you from the river in the winter."

"It is near summer now," was all she said.

After some time William left. Standing Doe picked up her hoe and went to her small corn patch. She attacked the weeds angrily. When darkness fell, she went to the stream to wash and to repeat the chants to separate Red Hawk from his woman. But as she dipped her hands into the cool water, her heart was heavy. She had seen the determination in Red Hawk's eyes. It could be that he would not be affected by her magic.

Kit sat in the modest parlor with Samuel Worcester as Harriet prepared the evening meal. Harriet insisted that Kit relax and talk with her husband. The meal would be a simple one and did not need both women to prepare it.

Samuel Worcester was an intelligent, kind man with a fervent dedication to his work among the Cherokees. He had short dark hair, and there was a fire in his eyes as he spoke in a sure, melodious voice.

"I have a writ from the governor of this state, telling me to stop my work among the Cherokees."

Kit frowned, regretting that she never got to see the governor the evening of the fire at the hotel.

"And will you?"

Samuel waved a hand. "Of course not. I take orders from a higher source."

He smiled gently as Harriet came into the room. Behind them, on a table covered with a white cloth, she had laid out a hearty meal.

"Come and eat," she said. "Kit must be starving. She's had nothing but a bit of tea and bread today."

Kit sat in a cane-seated chair and bowed her head for the blessing Samuel offered. Then, finding she was ravenous, she filled her plate with roast pork, hot beans, cornbread, and wild greens. In between mouthfuls she told them everything that had happened since she had first seen Red Hawk at the President's House in Washington, filling in details she had omitted when she had first spoken with Harriet on their journey together.

Samuel was deeply concerned when she spoke of the Indians being arrested in Dahlonega. He had been told of the incident and was inflamed at their treatment.

"The United States government is putting pressure not only on the Cherokees," said Samuel, "but on the Chocktaws, Chickasaws, Creeks, and Seminoles as well. I fear the other tribes will sign treaties for removal very soon. If that happens, the Cherokees will be like a solitary tree standing when the rest of the forest has been uprooted by a storm."

Kit shook her head. "I don't know what to do. I thought I could make someone listen. Perhaps I still can."

She glanced hopefully from Samuel to Harriet. "If I left now, returned home, perhaps there would be a way . . ."

Her words drifted off as she saw their compassionate expressions. Harriet reached over and patted her hand.

"You have a noble heart. These are dark times for the Cherokees. You have done what you could."

Kit lowered her eyes. "But that is so little."

They finished their meal in somber conversation, and Harriet promised to teach Kit what she would need to know in order to survive in New Echota.

"There may be some who will be suspicious of you. Hatred for the white race runs high right now. You will have to prove to them that you have chosen this way of life over the hypocritical lifestyle of the Georgians who want to displace them."

"I will try," said Kit.

After they had cleared the table, Harriet told Kit that Red Hawk waited outside for her. Kit could not hide the joy she felt, and yet timidity was also present as she left the Worcesters sitting and reading by lamplight.

She stepped out onto the porch. At first she didn't see him in the shadows, for no lamps lit the outside of the house. But she heard a movement at the side of the porch and then saw him silhouetted against the moonlight. Her heart trebled its beat.

Red Hawk gazed at her pale face lit by the moon behind him, and then his eyes took in the modest curves covered by the dress given her by the missionary's wife. No longer was her hair flying wildly behind her, but it was plaited in a tight braid that hung down her back. The sight of her so demurely attired only made him want her more.

He held out his hands, and she came to him and gazed up at his face, moonlight reflected in her blue eyes. He rested his hands on her waist.

"And so," he said, curving his lips upward, "these people have made you welcome."

She nodded. Though she had only been separated from him for a matter of hours, his presence filled her with happiness. The strong limbs touching her soft flesh thrilled her. She raised a hand to touch his face, and he parted his lips to taste of her fingers. Desire grew as he pulled her closer against him and bent to kiss her forehead, her temples. Finally he took her mouth in his, and she swooned against him.

He held her, his embrace tightening. But finally he lifted his head and pressed her cheek against his shoulder.

"You must stay here, my little one until we are married. I have already made you mine, but it will please the white missionary if we wait until you are my wife. Then I will take you to my cabin."

She heard the reasoning in his words, but her greed for him was stronger. She turned her head to look into his eyes.

"Must I?" she asked.

His loins throbbed and blood coursed through his veins. He gave a guttural laugh.

"You tempt me too much. But I am a warrior, am I not? I am used to depriving myself when there is a purpose. You will be Red Hawk's wife, and then you will have the respect of all the people."

He jerked his chin upward, and she thought she saw a flicker of doubt pass over his eyes. At the same instant his grasp on her eased. She backed out of his embrace, her hands still lingering on his shoulders.

"If that is what you wish."

Then he looked back into her eyes and cupped her face in his hands. "It is not what I wish, but it is for the best."

She nodded. "All right."

He straightened and assumed a formal tone. "You must prepare yourself for the ceremony two days hence. The women will instruct you."

She blinked. She did not know what women he meant, but she would take him at his word. Then a shadow of doubt crept into her mind.

"Will it . . . ?" She swallowed. "Will it be a Christian marriage."

He lifted a corner of his mouth in amusement. "It will be a Christian marriage, but our old ways will also be observed."

She smiled in understanding. Both peoples would be satisfied. Surely then her father would accept the fact. If Samuel Worcester performed a Christian ceremony, she would be married in the eyes of her own society as well.

Married. Her heart sang, and yet she was filled with nervousness at the same time. Was she truly ready for this step? She could not continue living with Red Hawk the way she had been. Her life would be ruined if she did. And since she knew now that she could not tear herself away from him, she must marry him.

There was really no other choice.

He slid his hand along the back of her neck and took her mouth with his. The warmth she felt in her heart answered her question for her. Then he released her, strode across the porch and down the steps. She watched him walk toward the village in the moonlight. A coyote sang on some distant hill. She raised a hand to support herself on the smooth white pillar next to the railing. She had to blink twice to tell herself that what was happening was real. She was going to be a Cherokee bride.

Chapter Seventeen

The women of the village presented Kit with a white deerskin gown with long fringe. Kit was overwhelmed by its beauty. Only one woman stayed away from the merry crowd that gathered in the yard of Harriet's house. When Kit asked who the attractive young woman who did not join in the merriment was, a matronly squaw named Hannah Morningstar told her that Standing Doe bore much bitterness in her heart. Kit did not ask why.

The women gave her a white beaded band that would be worn around her forehead with a single eagle feather turned downward at the back of her head. Kit had a hollow feeling in her heart when she realized that Fletch and Merilee would not witness her wedding, but she did not know if they would understand. Still, Merilee knew how much Kit loved Red Hawk, and on that thought Kit pinned her hopes that she would one day be reconciled with her family.

On the morning of the wedding Kit stood on the porch of the Worcester home as a procession wound its way toward her. Her heart swelled with pride when she saw Red Hawk dressed in magnificent new buckskins beaded with vibrant designs. The people gathered around the porch, and Red Hawk presented Kit with a ham of venison, symbolic of his intention to keep his household supplied with game from the hunt.

Kit, in turn, gave him an ear of corn, signifying her willingness to be a good wife. Waiting Bear chanted a song, and then Kit and Red Hawk led the others up the stairs into the room that served as church on the second floor of the house. Samuel Worcester in his stiff collar and dark suit blessed the union, and Kit and Red Hawk exchanged vows.

Kit smiled radiantly at her husband, and then the drums began outside, signifying the dancing and the feast that would last all through the day and into the night.

Red Hawk led her through the village to his own hewn-log cabin, and as she stepped into their two-room home, her heart caught in her throat. It was a simple dwelling, but one she cherished because Red Hawk had built it. The scent of cedar was strong, and the floor was swept clean. The sturdy tables and chairs and the shelves for dishes would serve them well. A door opened into a small bedroom, and Kit gasped in wonder at the beautiful multicolored handwoven blankets covering the large bed and hanging on the walls.

After she had examined everything she approached Red Hawk who stood pensively at the window, watching the feast get underway. His somber look worried Kit, and with a sudden awful panic, she wondered if he now regretted taking her as his wife.

She bit her lip, trying to prevent tears. But when he saw her, he placed an arm about her shoulders and drew her against him.

"What is it?" she asked tentatively, her head against his cheek.

"I am troubled."

"About the marriage."

He shook his head. "No. Your father is my enemy, but it troubles me that I have caused a breach between father and daughter. You will miss your family in time. You will miss your people, even though I have bound you to me with powerful medicine."

"Powerful medicine?" She looked up at him.

He smiled and released her. "There are Cherokee ways."

Kit remembered Waiting Bear and the satisfied looks he gave her. Had they really used some sort of love incantations? Her eyes widened.

"You don't mean love chants or some such thing."

Red Hawk looked grave. "I should not speak of them. It might weaken the medicine."

She couldn't help the amusement that rippled within her. "Oh, Red Hawk, you don't believe that, do you? Your people are civilized. I love you, that is why I am here. Not because of some sort of magic."

He grasped her arms, but his look was one of teasing rather than anger. "Do not discount the power of Cherokee medicine."

She tried to suppress her laughter. "I'm sorry. I'm just not used to such things. In any case, according to my religion, a wife is supposed to leave her father and mother and cleave to her husband."

309

She reached up to stroke his forehead. "It says so in the Bible. You can ask Reverend Worcester."

Red Hawk held her against him again, and they rocked to the rhythmic sound of the drums outside.

"Red Hawk," she said, after a time. "There is a woman here who does not seem to like me. Her name is Standing Doe. Who is she?"

She heard the exasperated grunt he gave as he expelled a breath.

"Standing Doe is troubled. Her father died last winter. Her brothers have all died."

"She is alone, then? Why doesn't she marry?"

She saw Red Hawk's jaw tighten, and she immediately understood.

"Oh, I'm sorry." She couldn't stifle a pang of jealousy. "She loves you?"

He shook his head. "We grew up together. She needs a husband. But she will be better off marrying William Longbow. He is courting her, but she has refused him."

Kit could understand how the woman would prefer Red Hawk to any other man. But she can't have him, she thought possessively. She slipped her arms around his waist, laying her head against his shoulder. He lifted his hand to let his fingers drift through her hair.

"Do not worry, my little dove. I am wary of Standing Doe's wily ways. She may use evil medicine to try to drive us apart. But she will not succeed."

The seed of anxiety stuck in Kit's heart. "More chanting?"

Red Hawk squeezed her. "Today I have declared to

the world that I have taken a wife. I need no other woman."

Surely Red Hawk is a man of honor, Kit thought as she allowed his kisses on her ears to soothe her. If he was as principled in his marriage as he was about matters of his tribe she would have nothing to worry about, she decided. Still, she would be careful of the evil woman, and would pray that something might happen to change Standing Doe's heart's desire.

Kit kissed Red Hawk fiercely as if to express the determination with which she meant to keep him by her side. Red Hawk responded eagerly. But before their passion could consume them, he set her away from him.

"We must join in the feasting," he said. "There will be many more blessings and many gifts. Tonight, my love, we will renew our union in this house."

She smiled at him and pushed her hair back over her shoulders. She was ready to join the people and let them see how happy she was. Red Hawk led her to the square near the council house, where green branches were tied to high poles to provide shade for the dancing area.

The celebration lasted all day. Gifts were presented, and Kit watched with fascination as the Cherokees, dressed in tribal costumes, executed skillful, rhythmic dances to the rattle of turtle shells and gourds, the beat of the drums, and the haunting sounds of flutes. Some of the warriors had painted their faces and chests and wore feathers on their arms. As the bride, Kit was brought into the circle of dancers and followed the steps she was shown. But she felt more comfortable sitting on the side with Harriet and some of the other women, watching.

She saw Standing Doe, who kept well away from her, but she could not tell how the young woman felt. Red Hawk never once looked at her, and Kit noticed another handsome young man who seemed to stay near her when he wasn't dancing with the other men. But being the center of attention as bride, Kit had little time to think of the other woman.

Waiting Bear came to stand by Kit and they walked a little away from the drums. She felt at ease with the medicine man, as if he were someone she had known before, though that was not so. Perhaps it was his gentle understanding of human nature that made him a good medicine man and made her comfortable. She decided she was glad he was Red Hawk's friend.

"You will make him a good wife," said Waiting Bear.

They stood near the edge of the square, and Kit looked over the buildings of New Echota. She wished suddenly that her father and brother and Merilee could see this place through her eyes. But she shut those thoughts away.

"I will try, Waiting Bear," she said modestly.

"These are troubled times," he said.

She glanced at the lines of concern creasing in his forehead and at his dark eyes shaded with sadness.

"I know," she said, "though one might not know it, for this is such a peaceful setting."

"We wish it to always remain so," he said.

"And you do not think it will?" she asked.

He shook his head. The shells that hung from the

feathers in his headband rattled. "Our ways served us for centuries. But when the white man came two hundred years ago we learned from them. Now I see fearful things in my heart. I see my people leaving this land for the lands in the West. Many hearts will be broken. Many people will die."

His words rang ominously, and Kit could say nothing. She herself had seen the greed in the men who had chased the Cherokees away from their fields near Dahlonega. New Echota felt safe from such intrusion, here in the heart of the Cherokee Nation, but she knew that unless the Cherokees had powerful friends on a government level, the rape of their lands would not cease.

Her mind drifted back to the governor who was a friend of her father. A pang went through her when she thought of her father. Would he even talk to her now? And she thought of Andrew Jackson, that tall, determined popular hero. Could he not see that the Cherokees needed his aid now?

They were interrupted by Red Hawk who came to lead his bride back to where a bonfire was being lit. The drums and chanting had intensified as evening stole over the hills.

The feast was not yet ended when Red Hawk rose and took Kit by the hand. The look he gave her told her that they were leaving. Her heart filled with love as he stood in front of her and lifted a hand to touch her chin. Then he turned in the direction of their cabin.

Kit glanced over her shoulder and caught Harriet's eye. The woman nodded encouragingly. Then Kit glimpsed Standing Doe, who stood near the fire watching them. The tears on her cheeks seemed to reflect the firelight. Then she turned and fled toward William Longbow who cast his arms about her shoulders.

Kit swallowed and turned to follow Red Hawk home. She hoped she would be forgiven for taking the man Standing Doe loved. She did not want any enemies in the Cherokee camp.

In the weeks that followed Kit learned many things. Game was not as plentiful as it once had been, so the Cherokees were farmers now. Kit cultivated the garden Red Hawk had planted behind his house. From the other women she learned to smoke venison, tan hides, weave on a loom, and make bread on a hearthstone. Having always worked with her hands, she found using the methods and tools of the Cherokees manageable.

But her real joy came when Red Hawk took her into the forest and taught her something about tracking. She began to understand more of the Indians' reverence for the land the Georgians threatened to take away.

From Waiting Bear she learned about the old religion and the white men's misunderstanding of it. And she learned the wisdom of the greatest teacher, Mother Earth. The Indians sought harmony of man with the universe in the way of the rainbow, the waterfall, and the sunrise in which ugliness was impossible.

She became a part of Red Hawk in ways she would

not have thought possible. Their love was no less spiritual than physical. From him she gained the strength she knew she would need, for she was aware that the day was not far off when she must go back into the white man's world and contact her family.

Late one evening Harriet sat with Kit in Red Hawk's cabin. Kit had made curtains, and a new woven rug covered the floor near where the two women sat on a settee that had been made here in the village. Oil lamps cast a cozy glow over the freshly cleaned cabin. Shep lay curled up at their feet.

"Married life seems to agree with you," said Harriet.

"Yes," sighed Kit. "But I miss my family."

"I can understand that."

Kit got up and walked to the wooden desk next to the wall. She opened the top and brought a folded piece of paper back to where Harriet sat.

"I've written my sister-in-law a letter," she said. "Do you think that's wise?"

Harriet smiled. "Of course. You will want to hear from your family."

Kit's look of anguish made Harriet lean forward and pat her arm sympathetically. "Someone must open the door. Your father may be angry now, but in time he might come to understand. He must have loved you very much to be so angry."

Kit shook her head. "I don't know. I suppose I am afraid to write to them for fear they won't write back. Then I'll know for sure I am no longer a member of the family."

"It is a chance you must take," said Harriet gently.

Jonathan Newcomb stood before Governor Gilmer, his fists clenched and his face flushed.

"I tell you, George, you've got to send the militia in. They've abducted my daughter. I tried to warn her against their savage ways, but she's a stubborn girl.

"I remember Kit," said the governor, leaning back in his swivel chair. He took a cigar from a box on his desk and offered Jonathan one, which was refused.

Jonathan resented the fact that the governor was behaving so casually.

"I was to have dinner with your daughter in Dahlonega the night the fire broke out," said Governor Gilmer. "In the confusion, of course, she must have fled the burning town. I regretted not seeing her."

He shook his head and stroked his salt and pepper beard. "These are trying times." He brought his gaze back to Jonathan.

"Now you say they've abducted her. Do you know where they've taken her? If I'm to send in troops I must have some justification for doing so. It's still Cherokee country. We must tread carefully or else the federal government will stay my hand. President Jackson is pressing the Cherokees to move westward, but I cannot act without provocation."

Jonathan lost patience. "I tell you I was with the President when he refused Chief John Ross's request.

He will not interfere."

Governor Gilmer rocked back and forth in his chair. "I would hope so. But tell me more about your girl. That will make a case."

The company of Georgia militia tore through Cherokee country, led by the captain who had been with the governor at Dahlonega. At last he had his orders. Capture the escaped prisoners and bring them back. Make them release the white woman they held hostage.

Cherokee scouts saw the invading troops and sent word to New Echota. Chief John Ross was absent, going from village to village to talk to the people. In his place Major Ridge, John Ridge, Red Hawk, Waiting Bear, and other leaders spoke to the people. The faces of the men that sat around the council house were tense.

Snake Hawk, the tribe's war chief spoke. "You have heard the scouts. The soldiers are coming. We must lose no time. We must paint our faces and do the war dance. It is time to fight, my friends."

Major Ridge stood at the front of the council house and raised a hand. "My people, listen to reason. If we fight, more blood will be shed. The white man's army outnumbers us. Do you want a useless slaughter?"

Negative murmurs came from the listening men and women.

"Then hold up the white flag," Major Ridge continued. "Negotiate with the generous president of the white man's government. Accept their offers of pay-

317

ment for the land they covet. It is useless to fight any-more."

"We don't know what they want," said William Longbow from his seat on the hewn-log bench. "What do these soldiers come for?"

"Let us listen to them when they come," said Major Ridge. "We will speak to them and find out what they want."

Red Hawk strode forward, and the assemblage looked at him eagerly. Proud warrior, strong brave, he had moved among the white man. What would his advice be?

Red Hawk let his gaze of disdain fall on Major Ridge and his son John, a man who thought too highly of himself. Then Red Hawk turned to the war chief, whose courageous heart beat to the drums of war. Finally he addressed the silent people.

"Enough of this talk," said Red Hawk. "The white government no longer respects the Cherokee. Those who will go with Snake Hawk will show their spirits. The white man has spit on us. Cherokee have never been a people to lower their heads to an insult. We will repulse these white intruders. They will be made an example to those who would follow."

He nodded to Snake Hawk who raised an arm and emitted a piercing war cry. Several of the braves stood and did likewise. Red Hawk and the war chief slipped out of the council house and moved among the young warriors waiting outside. The word was passed, and the braves hurried to their homes to don war paint and to fetch their horses. They would ride at once.

Red Hawk strode toward his cabin. When he

opened the door, Kit looked up from her work. She saw the fierce, determined look on his face and knew at once what was about to happen. She had heard the rumors accompanying the hasty assembly of the council.

"Red Hawk," she cried, dropping her work and going to him.

He grasped her arms and held her as she laid her head against him, tightening his grasp for a moment and then firmly setting her aside.

"We are going," he said, and he moved about the cabin gathering his implements of war.

She bit her lip. "The soldiers are coming?" she asked, her voice shaking. She knew she could never ask Red Hawk not to go. Facing danger was a part of him. But that didn't make it any easier for her. She clasped her hands together in order to keep from reaching for him again.

Then she took a deep breath and helped him gather blanket, rifle, spear, knife, and buffalo-hide shield. She watched him smear the war paint on his face and shrank back in fear of his fierce demeanor. Her feelings were mixed. Her dread of war stood at odds with the knowledge that the inept soldiers she had seen at Dahlonega would not have a chance against these primed warriors defending their own land, except that the Georgia militia had more firepower than the Cherokees.

A cold hand seemed to grip her heart and she stood, looking in the direction of the hills. She knew suddenly that these were not ordinary militia.

She raised a hand to touch Red Hawk's arm.

"I know why they have come," she said in a faraway voice.

He paused in his preparations to look at her, and she turned to him. "I must go with you," she said. "They have come for me."

He narrowed his gaze at her luminous eyes. "Your place is here. You will stay here," he said.

She swallowed, knowing she could not argue with him. Already she heard the drums of war. The Cherokees were going to fight. And she knew with certainty that she was the cause of it. Her father would not stand by and let her run off with the Cherokees. He had sent the militia to retrieve her.

The thought filled her with anger. Was she never to be mistress of her own fate? Had her life been determined for her the day she had been born on a Georgia plantation?

No, she thought resolutely as she watched Red Hawk leave the house and call his chestnut gelding to him. She would not let a troop of soldiers come to tell her how to lead her life.

Chapter Eighteen

The warriors following Snake Hawk had a head start on Kit by the time she saddled a pinto pony and went after them. But since they were making no effort to cover their tracks, she had no difficulty following them. She pressed the pony, not to try to catch up with the war party but in order to be able to arrive before there was a serious confrontation. Somehow she knew that the soldiers were coming after her, and she reasoned that if she showed herself to them and spoke to them, telling them she was here of her own free will, they would leave the Indians alone.

For the rest of the day, the trail followed that which Red Hawk had brought Kit over when she'd first arrived in New Echota. Toward evening she saw where the party had left this trail and climbed higher into the hills. She had not felt any apprehension riding through Cherokee country alone, but as the shadows began to lengthen, Kit felt her first tremor of anxiety.

She should have known that high above her on the ridge Red Hawk sat with William Longbow, watching her progress.

"I saw that we were being followed on the last rise," said William. "I did not see that it was your woman 'til now."

Red Hawk stifled his displeasure. A woman was a hindrance to a war party.

"You did well," he told William. "Ride on with the others. I will wait for her. We cannot leave her now. Night is coming on, and she will not be safe. She does not know the way home well enough for me to send her. I will speak with her."

The brave nodded and turned his horse up the trail to catch up with the others. When he was over the ridge, Red Hawk urged his horse downward.

Kit heard the scrabble of hooves on the hill above her, and sat up straighter. She was not aware that there was anyone between the war party and herself, and the idea of running into a stranger frightened her. Cherokees outside New Echota would not know who she was. She berated herself for not bringing any sort of weapon. She had left in haste, so as not to be too far behind Red Hawk, but that haste might now be her undoing.

Then the branches in front of her parted and she saw Red Hawk on the chestnut gelding.

She breathed out in relief, but a moment later she stiffened. His face, rigid with displeasure, was made more frightening by the war paint across the bridge of his nose and his cheeks. She reined in her pony and waited. He stopped when he had ridden up beside her.

"Why have you come?" he asked gruffly. "A woman is not welcome on a war party. It is not safe."

322

She leaned a little toward him and used a persuasive tone. "It's because of me the soldiers are coming. Don't ask me how I know. I just know it in my heart."

She held a hand to her breast, hoping he would be convinced. Indians were more sensitive to intuition and second sight than her own people. Perhaps Red Hawk would believe her.

"After you left, I knew I should come," she continued. "It's me they want. If I speak to them and tell them I am here of my own free will, perhaps they will leave your people alone. Don't you see?"

He still glared at her, but he said nothing. She trembled, fearing that he would remain angry, or worse, that he would send her back. She squared her shoulders, determined to prevent that.

"These men are from my people. Perhaps my father sent them. I must talk to them. Don't you see, Red Hawk, I may be able to prevent bloodshed."

The gelding sidestepped, and Red Hawk pulled its head around so that he and Kit were facing in the same direction. He gave no indication as to whether or not he approved of her plan, but he nodded his head in the direction of the trail.

"You cannot stay out here alone," he said. "We ride hard, but you must keep up."

He gave her a look that she interpreted to mean, since she had made the choice, she was stuck with it. But she leaned forward and pressed her heels into the pony's sides. She would keep up. She would not be able to face Red Hawk's anger if she caused him embarrassment. Nor did she want to be a burden.

Fortunately her horse was surefooted and easily followed Red Hawk's mount. Darkness overtook them, and they were forced to stop until the moon rose. It was not until she had ridden up beside Red Hawk and felt his restraining hand on her pony's bridle that she realized they were not alone. She heard rather than saw the rest of the party and realized that they were in a protected clearing. She heard the snap of twigs and then saw William Longbow approach Red Hawk.

"Snake Hawk says we wait here. The top of this hill provides a good lookout. We can see the enemy approach."

"Good," said Red Hawk.

He turned to help Kit down from her pony; then they led their horses to water. With the other Indians near, Kit felt self-conscious. A Cherokee woman would know what to do to help make camp, but she was inexperienced and wished to shrink out of sight among the trees.

Red Hawk's movements were quick, and in little time he had spread blankets for them to sleep on. He handed her some beef jerky, then he went to squat down with the other men. They spoke in low voices so that Kit didn't hear. She wrapped the blanket around her and leaned against a firm tree trunk.

When the talk was over, Red Hawk returned to join her. He slid in between the blankets and lay back.

"We must sleep," he said. "Tomorrow we meet the enemy."

He did not touch her, and Kit's heart sank. He was angry that she had come. Tears stung her eyelids. What if she was wrong? What if these soldiers had nothing to do with her and she merely proved to be in the way? She felt humiliated and slid down in the blankets, keeping as far to her own side as she could so that she would not touch Red Hawk.

She felt more miserable than she had since she'd left Wytheridge. What was she doing in this hopeless situation? Why had she ever thought she could understand these Indians?

Tears ran down her cheeks and onto the rough horse blanket. Maybe when they met the soldiers she should go with the troops back to Wytheridge.

The Indians had broken camp before Kit was barely awake. She hurriedly bathed her face in the stream, then harnessed her pony, mounted, and rode out of camp behind Red Hawk.

They rode silently through forests of tall birch and cedar, and as the sun rose higher, sunlight dappled the red dirt through which the horses trod. Once a scout appeared from the opposite direction and conferred with the war chief. Then they set off again. The day turned hot, and Kit sweltered in the saddle. She tied a kerchief around her forehead to keep the sweat out of her eyes, but she didn't dare ask to stop.

Then she saw the riders ahead dismount and cautiously approach the top of the next ridge. Guided by the scout, they began to take positions behind cover with a view of what lay on the other side.

Kit's spine tingled. They must have sighted the white soldiers. She urged her horse forward, but just before she neared the rest of the party Red Hawk turned to her.

"Get down," he said.

Instead of obeying, she rode up next to him, watching the warriors pull weapons from scabbards and check ammunition.

"What's happened?" she said.

Red Hawk glared at her, and seeing that he wasn't going to answer, she dismounted and scrambled up behind a boulder to look at the meadow below them. A small company of soldiers rode in the open, the flag of the Georgia Guard fluttering in the breeze from the standard borne by the lead rider. The soldiers looked about them, but not above them.

Kit heard one of the warriors next to her ram a ball home in the black powder, and she gave a start. The danger of the situation hit her full force, and she bit her lip, peering down at the soldiers once more. Then she gave a gasp and stood up, not caring who saw her. Fletch rode at the rear of the soldiers.

The explosion of the rifle beside her scared her into action.

"No, don't shoot," she cried, running toward the warrior who had fired the first shot.

Return fire skimmed over their heads, and she glimpsed the soldiers fleeing for cover. Some aimed rifles at the ridge as they ran.

"No, no," she cried, scrambling back to her horse.

The Indians were all firing now, but Kit grasped the pony's reins and threw herself onto its back. Heedless of the flying shot, she yelled as she thrust her pony's head between the shooting warriors.

"Stop shooting," she shouted at the top of her lungs.

Her horse's hooves sent dirt flying as she flew past the Indians, who looked startled. She had the sense to bend over the pony's neck. But she kept on crying out as she crossed the ridge and rode down into the meadow, hoping the soldiers would see her.

"Fletch," she called out, though she had not seen where he had taken cover. "Fletch," she called again, her pony's hooves thundering over the soft ground. "Stop shooting."

There was a pause in the firing, and in her breathless state, Kit realized it was because the men who had been firing didn't want to hit her. She turned the pony's head and circled the meadow, coming close to the ring of trees. The soldiers evidently didn't show themselves because they thought the Indians might fire. She galloped her pony around in a circle, then a swath of red off to her right caught her eye and she looked up to see Red Hawk on his chestnut gelding flying down the slope.

"No," she said, but it was more to herself than anyone nearby, for her voice didn't carry.

She wheeled her horse again and shouted, "Don't shoot." Then she galloped to meet Red Hawk.

They drew up next to each other, and he pulled back on his reins so quickly, his horse reared. Kit's pony shied, but she got it under control and then slid off. Red Hawk dismounted, and she turned to confront him.

His face was rigid and angry as he glared at her. "Why do you ride into the crossfire?" he asked. "You are foolish."

In two strides he had crossed to her and gripped

her shoulders. But she held onto his arms with her hands.

"Don't you see?" she said. "They stopped firing because of me. "My brother is here. I must speak to him."

Red Hawk glared. "Your brother?"

She nodded quickly, but set her chin in determination, meeting his angry gaze with her own stubborn one. In a fleeting thought, she realized that they were no more than a husband and wife having a marital squabble, except that two opposing factions watched them. If lives were not at stake, she would find the situation humorous.

"Your brother is not fond of Cherokees," Red Hawk said.

She remembered Fletch's angry confrontation with Red Hawk in Georgetown. But it would be different now. She was married to a Cherokee.

She waited until Red Hawk released her, then turned toward the rifles poking out over boulders and from around trees. And she saw her brother come out from behind cover.

As he walked through the high grass, she turned to face him directly. His approach was rapid, and by the expression on his face, she began to wonder if she was wrong. He might treat her no better for marrying a Cherokee than for consorting with one.

Fletch's eyes raked her up and down; then he came to a standstill before her.

"Hello, Fletch," she said.

For a moment Kit thought he must be so angry he could not speak. His fair complexion was red with exertion and rage, and his blue eyes snapped. Fletch saw Red Hawk standing with his hands on his hips behind Kit and stepped nearer, indicating that his words were meant only for her.

"You will come home with us at once," he said. "I don't know how all this came to pass, but these heathens cannot hold you prisoner."

"I am not a prisoner," Kit said, aghast at the fury she saw on her brother's face.

It hit her that Fletch's reaction was exactly the same as her father's had been. The fact that father and son were cut of the same cloth might not have been so surprising if it had not come at such a bad time.

"I live among the Cherokees," Kit said. "I came of my own free will."

She grasped Fletch's elbow, hoping that the physical contact would soften him.

"I wanted Father to understand. I wanted to help the Cherokees, but he wouldn't listen. They're not what you think they are."

Fletch glared over her shoulder at the war paint on Red Hawk's face.

"You don't call that savage?" he said to Kit, nodding in Red Hawk's direction.

She instinctively moved in front of Red Hawk.

"No, they're not. They're just prepared to fight because their rights have not been respected. They are brave people and will not give up what is theirs any longer."

The passion of her argument spurred her on. Were all her own people as prejudiced as her own family? The thought appalled her.

Fletch took her hand. "We can talk about this at home. But you must come with us."

She jerked her hand back. "No, I'm not going."

"I don't understand what's gotten into your head, sister. Father will not mention your name in our house. He says you are lost to the Indians. But I persuaded him he was wrong, that this man standing behind you abducted you. I volunteered to bring you back. What does your captor want, ransom money?"

"No," Kit said, standing straighter and tossing her head. "He is my husband."

Fletch took a step in her direction, and again his expression frightened her. He lowered his voice.

"I will not hear such sordid talk. If you mean this man has molested you, then the company of soldiers who have accompanied me will arrest him and hang him."

"That is not what I mean. We were formally married. Harriet Worcester stood up beside me."

"If you mean that the Indian made it look acceptable to bed you by enacting some heathen ceremony, then you are surely lost, sister."

"It was a Christian ceremony. Reverend Worcester married us."

Fletch stared at her as if her words did not reach him. She tried again.

"Please, Fletch. Come with me to New Echota. Come see my home. I don't want to be cast out from Wytheridge. That is my home, too. Why must I choose? Why can't I have both?"

Fletch sent a contemptuous look in the direction of Red Hawk and saw the muzzles pointed in his direction from the top of the ridge.

"I'm afraid I would not be welcome," he told his sister.

They stared at each other, both aware of the barrier between them. Fletch tried one more time. He bent his head so that Red Hawk would not hear his words.

"If it will save face, my men can abduct you. I am sure they would not mind shedding a little blood to rescue a woman from the Cherokees' clutches."

"I already told you I wish to remain here." She glanced back over her shoulder. "Red Hawk is my husband."

She saw the emotions that played over Fletch's face, but he gave her a final nod.

"If that is what you wish. I cannot guarantee your safety. You realize that this disagreement will come to war if the Cherokees do not agree to the terms offered them for their land."

A tingle of fear rippled down Kit's spine, but she knew her choice was already made.

"I will stay here."

Warring emotions showed in Fletch's face. "In that case, I may not see you again."

Her lip trembled. She had hoped it would not come to this. Surely, even though the situation seemed hopeless, there would be a way.

"Don't say that, Fletch. I can't bear to be parted from everything I knew. You are my family."

He glanced again at Red Hawk. "But your desire not to be parted from this man you call a husband is stronger."

She did not answer but turned and walked back to

where Red Hawk was standing with the horses. When she took the reins of her pony from him, she spoke.

"The soldiers will leave. I told my brother I was here of my own free will. They will not fight you."

Red Hawk turned and gestured to the war chief who stood at the top of the ridge.

Kit and Red Hawk waited in the meadow for Fletch to return to the company of soldiers holding their fire. Fletch spoke to the captain who threw a look of disdain in Kit's direction. Nevertheless he gave the command for the soldiers to mount up. A confrontation had been averted for the moment.

Chapter Nineteen

In June the corn was green and the village prepared for the Green Corn Festival. Dressed in ancient tribal costumes, the Cherokees danced all night to the rhythm of the drums in the torch-lit square next to the Town House. For the occasion Kit wore a hand-woven skirt edged at the hem with down plucked from the breast of a white swan.

As yet there had been no more trouble from the white soldiers, but the Cherokee Nation was quietly preparing itself for war. Kit saw it as warriors readied their weapons, sharpening knives, oiling rifles, strengthening their spears, and fashioning breast plates.

On this night, as the drums beat, every heart in the village seemed to beat with them. Even Kit's blood pulsed through her veins in a building rhythm that sought an outlet. Voices were raised in ancient chants that expressed the emotions of the singers and of the people. Yet Kit was spellbound by the ancient rituals.

She stood with the other women to watch the male dancers weaving in and out of a circle. Then the dancers formed a cross and moved together in a wind-mill turn. The drummer changed the beat, and the dancers broke rank, jumping, stamping, some standing on their hands and kicking the air.

Red Hawk's bare skin and rippling muscles glistened in the flickering firelight. His fluid movements and sudden turns moved her as they must have moved the others watching. She caught a glimpse of Standing Doe, who was following the sensual movements of Red Hawk's dance. Kit saw the yearning in the other woman's eyes and could not hold back the surge of jealousy she felt. But she also felt pity. Standing Doe wanted what she could not have. Perhaps her own magic had turned against her.

Suddenly the drumbeats stopped, and Standing Doe found Kit's eyes as if she knew she was being watched. Kit saw the tears at the corners of her black eyes, and as Standing Doe's chest rose and fell, Kit thought the maiden's lips trembled.

Then William Longbow stepped beside Standing Doe, his breathing hard from the dance. He touched her shoulder, and Standing Doe melted into his arms. Kit could not hear what he said, but his lips moved as he squeezed Standing Doe's shoulders and led her away.

Kit followed them with her eyes, standing near some boughs that protected her from revealing that she was watching. She saw William turn Standing Doe to face him. He lifted her chin with his fingers. Her drooping black eyelashes fluttered, and then she looked into his eyes for a long moment. He spoke to her gently.

Finally she laid her cheek on his shoulder as he caressed her. He lowered his mouth to hers gently. Standing Doe responded, and for a moment they stood with their arms around each other. Kit moved farther backward, embarrassed at witnessing the personal scene. But compassion poured forth from her, for she truly wished that Standing Doe could find happiness with William Longbow. He seemed like a good and patient man.

Slowly, William Longbow raised his head, and with one arm around Standing Doe's shoulders, he led her toward the darkness in the direction of her cabin.

Kit returned to the circle of the dance, but before she reached the women, Red Hawk appeared. Sweat still glistened on his arms and chest, and he was breathing heavily from the dance. The drums beat on incessantly. When Kit met Red Hawk's gaze she saw the primitive impulse in his eyes. She herself was affected by the wildness, the savage instincts being invoked this night.

Her breasts tingled at his glance, and when he touched her, her skin burned. He pulled her back among the boughs, out of the firelight, and they stood close together, their bodies throbbing. Red Hawk's hand drifted up her side, touching her waist, her breast, finally lifting her chin. He opened his lips and took hers, his tongue probing deeply.

Suddenly she wanted him. She wanted to consummate the act that acknowledged he was hers. Brought up the proper daughter of a Georgia farmer, she had never expected to display such open desire. But she had never known desire like this. Red Hawk made her feel like a child of nature; he brought out her deepest yearnings.

She molded her body against his as he pressed himself against her. Red Hawk did not seem to want to wait until they were back in the privacy of the cabin. Here, where the drums thundered in their ears, where the chants floated upward with the sparks from the fire, where they were one with an ancient ritual — here was where he must take her.

They moved into the darkness, and he led her to a bed of pine needles beneath spreading trees. There they lay on the ground, and Red Hawk cradled her in his arms, his mouth taking hers again as his strong thighs pressed against her.

She opened her limbs willingly, as his strong hands molded her calves, her thighs. They quickly joined together, and Kit closed her eyes, giving herself up to the night, the celebration of life, of the green corn that promised harvest, of the love between Red Hawk and herself that she realized would one day also bear fruit, for she felt the life growing in her.

Red Hawk moved against her urgently until sensation overtook them both and their spirits flew upward to the stars. Kit felt as if she traveled among the planets gazing at an endless sky, feeling one with eternity. It was only because she felt Red Hawk calling her back that she returned earthward and settled again into her own body as the pulsing gradually slowed, as her muscles relaxed, and ecstasy gave way to a deep calm and the certainty of one man's love.

Tears of joy formed at the corners of her eyes as she held him tight against her breast. Nothing . . . nothing, she decided with fierce determination, would ever strip him from her. She would do what she must, but she would hold on to Red Hawk. He was hers forever.

The days that followed were filled with routine chores. Kit went with the Indians into the fields to cultivate the crops. She was working in a corn field when she saw Harriet Worcester coming down the row toward her, she straightened and leaned on her hoe.

As soon as Harriet reached her, she said. "A friend has come to see you."

Kit wrinkled her brow. "Who?"

But rather than answer, Harriet beckoned for Kit to follow. Curious, Kit picked up the hoe and trod along the row to the edge of the field. From there they could see Harriet's house, where a lady stood in the shade of the verandah. At once Kit recognized the dark curls.

"Merilee," she gasped.

She unconsciously put a hand to the kerchief tied over her head and behind her neck to keep her hair off her face. She knew she looked a sight and felt embarrassed that Merilee should see her before she'd made herself presentable. But the urge to be with her friend overcame such self-consciousness and Kit dropped the hoe and, lifting her skirts, began to run toward the house.

At that moment Merilee saw her and flew down from the porch calling her name. The two girls embraced, laughing and crying at once as they stood on the grassy slope in front of Harriet's house.

"How ever did you find me?" said Kit when they finally released each other.

Merilee shook her head. "It wasn't easy, but I prodded Fletch until he finally told me where you were. I said I wanted to write to you. He doesn't know I've come."

Kit's heart filled, and tears moistened the corners of her eyes. "It was dangerous for you to come here."

Merilee lifted one shoulder in a coquettish gesture as if to say that she was used to getting what she wanted if she wanted it badly enough. By this time Harriet had joined them.

"You've met Harriet Worcester, then?" Kit asked.

"Yes," said Merilee. "The Indians on the farm where I stayed last night directed me here."

"I can hardly believe it," Kit said again. "What does Fletch think?"

"He and your father think I went shopping in Atlanta."

Harriet interrupted them. "Why don't you both come to the house and have some fresh lemonade. It will be more comfortable there."

Arm in arm, Kit and Merilee climbed the slope and sat in wicker chairs on the verandah while Harriet went to the spring house to fetch the jar of lemonade she had just made that morning from newly picked lemons. Kit plied Merilee for all the news.

After relaying the status of life at Wytheridge, her friend turned to the more serious matters.

"The miners are trying to hold on to their claims on Indian lands. In Washington it is said that President Jackson is pressing his Indian Removal Bill. And from what Fletch and your father say, if that is passed the Cherokees will be forced out of Georgia."

Kit stiffened. "How can they think that will happen? There are treaties."

Merilee waved an impatient hand. "Don't you see, Kit? No one thinks the treaties are binding. That is, they seem to think new treaties can be negotiated."

Kit felt sick and lowered her head. There had to be a way to stop this insanity.

Merilee leaned forward and took her hand. "That is why I came. If the Indians are sent away, you must come back to us."

Kit looked up, her eyes widening. "And leave my husband?"

Their eyes locked, and gradually Merilee seemed to understand that Kit was truly committed to the life she had chosen. She released her hand and leaned back again.

"Very well," she said. "In that case, we might never see you again."

Kit swallowed. "Oh, Merilee, please don't say that. I know that Father is angry with me. But surely in time . . . Does he ever speak of me?"

Merilee would not meet her gaze. "He says your name is never to be mentioned in his house."

Kit looked helplessly about her. Then she took a sip of lemonade to ease the dryness in her throat. "There must be something I can do. Tell me more about the news from Washington. How soon will this bill be voted on?"

Merilee shrugged. "Who can say? There are many who oppose it, including your friend Daniel Webster."

"Daniel!" Kit exclaimed. She had not thought of him in some time. "Do others oppose it?"

Merilee nodded slowly. "Yes, some ministers who try to point out that the civilized tribes have been Christianized. Some politicians agree with them, but most side with the state of Georgia in the name of progress. At least that is what the few newspapers I have laid eyes on say."

She pressed her lips together as if there was more she wished to say, but she hesitated.

"Go on," Kit said.

"Your Father is leaving next week for the capital."

Kit rose out of her seat and stared out over the verandah railing as if looking into the distance. "He is going?"

"To influence President Jackson to sign the removal bill if it passes in Congress." There was a hard edge to Merilee's voice as she said it.

Kit turned and stared at Merilee. After a lengthy silence, she gave an hysterical laugh.

"My own father is so interested in being rid of me that he wishes the President to send the Cherokees across the Mississippi River, knowing I will go with them and he will never have to set eyes on me again."

Merilee rose and came to Kit. "Oh, please don't put it like that. You have to understand, he is very hurt. He feels you have betrayed him."

Pain stabbed at Kit's heart, but she fought off the accompanying grief. "How could I tell him what had happened to me? How could I explain my love?"

She bit her lips to prevent them from trembling. Merilee moved to the end of the verandah and

340

watched the people of the town going about their business for a few moments.

"It's not unlike many rural towns," she commented. "Except they are Cherokees. Harriet told me a few things. She showed me the *Cherokee Phoenix*. And I saw some of the Indians dressed in frock coats at those buildings over there." She pointed to the merchandise store and the law office.

"Yes," Kit said absently. "Many have been educated in the East and act as lawyers for the tribe. They, too, want progress." She said it bitterly, as if all the delegates efforts had come too late, which was indeed the way she felt.

She could not think of anything else to say. Merilee tried to make conversation about the servants and their children. She spoke of a letter from Ruby in Washington City.

Something fluttered at the edge of Kit's thoughts, and she turned to stare at Merilee. "Washington," she said.

"What?"

The idea began to take shape. "I could go to Washington City."

Merilee tilted her head in curiosity. "You would go to Washington?"

"Yes," said Kit, warming to the idea. "I could speak to Daniel Webster and the other politicians. Perhaps even to President Jackson himself." She grasped Merilee's arm.

"Don't you see? They haven't been here. They don't know what it's like. But I do. I could tell them. I could be a witness to the fact that the Indians' rights

341

are not being upheld. Oh, Merilee, I think this is what I must do. I must go."

Merilee frowned at the fervor that had seized her sister-in-law. "It might be difficult for you. You might be . . ." She hesitated, not wanting to offend Kit. "Shunned," she forced herself to say. Better to warn Kit than to let her run off wildly and be confronted with insults when she got to her destination.

"You are a Cherokee's wife. There are people who would think ill of you."

A sense of purpose began to replace the feeling of desperation that had plagued Kit for the many weeks she'd seen the Cherokees' lands slipping away from their grasp. Going to Washington City and seeking action on behalf of the Cherokees seemed like something she could do. Hadn't she wanted to influence the progress of the government when she had first shared her father's interest in politics? Wasn't this the way to do it? Wasn't this exactly what she was suited for?

Her eyes filled with excitement. "I shall go," she said, no longer seeing Merilee or even the verandah on which they stood. "I shall fulfill this purpose."

Merilee could not dissuade her, so they did not discuss it further. Harriet invited Merilee to spend the night, and the women spent the late afternoon preparing a meal. Samuel joined them, and after dinner, Merilee asked Samuel a number of questions while Harriet and Kit applied themselves to needlework. As the night drew on, Kit rose to leave. She kissed Merilee warmly.

"I shall not be able to come again," said Merilee.

342

"But I will try to send messages. The people who helped me come here will surely relay them. As long as they are there," she finished doubtfully.

"Yes, of course," said Kit. "Please give my love to Fletch. I know he is angry with me."

"He loves you," said Merilee. "Even if he does not understand your choice."

Walking to her cabin later, Kit went over in her mind what she would tell Red Hawk. She would have to inform him of her desire to go to Washington City and try to influence the debates over Indian removal. Surely he would understand that for one who stood in both the white man's world and that of the Cherokee, it was a sensible thing to do. Surely he would approve.

He did not.

"You will not go," he said stubbornly as they sat by lantern light on their modest handmade furniture, with Shep curled up on the braided rug on the wooden floor. "You will not debase yourself in such a way."

"What do you mean debase myself? I am known in Washington. My father is on intimate terms with President Jackson. I, myself, have met him."

Red Hawk spat in disgust in the direction of the fireplace. "He will not listen."

Kit tried again. "My husband, I understand your feelings, but I feel I must do something. I cannot bear to sit here in New Echota, this wonderful place, and simply wait until the day the soldiers come and force your people, who are now my people, to leave. I know many men in government. I can talk to them."

343

Her face took on a defiant expression. "I must go if only to tell them my father is wrong."

Red Hawk observed his wife. He had never known a woman to speak against her father the way she had. His heart would have been troubled that he had torn her from her own parent, but when he thought about what her father was, he felt no guilt. Even so, in this matter Red Hawk had made up his mind.

He rose to stand before her and reached out a finger to touch her cheek. "My heart is warmed that you care for my people. But I will not allow a woman to do as you ask. You have made your choice. The white man sees that. Your silence on the matter is more eloquent than argument where ours has failed.

"If you return to Washington City there may be much to attract you. You could even be swayed to stay there and forget the Indians."

"That would never happen, my husband."

He grunted. "I do not know. But I do know that I wish to keep you by my side now and forever."

She grasped his hand and kissed his fingers, imploring him with her eyes. "I do not wish to leave you, but I must do this. Your place is here with your people. You must keep up their hope."

He moved his head imperceptibly from right to left. "No, you will not go. I forbid it."

Kit stared up at the finely chiseled face, at the intense dark eyes. He was wrong, but she could think of no more arguments. She knew that Cherokee women's views were respected in the tribal council house, but it was the men who did the final negotiations. Red Hawk's stubborn pride would not allow him to see the rightness of her motives.

But she slid her arms up his until she stood pressed against him. He moved his chin against her hair, his arms wrapped around her. Instinct led her to hide her disagreement in lovemaking. Her lips parted and sought his. Soon their bodies yearned for each other, and Red Hawk led her to their bed.

Putting aside their clothing, they lay down on the soft robes. Kit thought no more about her decision, but found release in Red Hawk's arms. Later, when the night closed over them, her dreams were torn.

The next day when Kit returned to the chores of house and field, her disquieting thoughts would not leave her. Several times she found herself looking toward Harriet's verandah as if to see Merilee standing there. She thought over what her friend had told her about events outside the Cherokee Nation, and she became obsessed with finding a way to act. She felt helpless in an Indian nation that was dying. Perhaps what Merilee said about the white civilization's progress was true, but it did not satisfy Kit's desire to do something to prevent that progress from ignoring the well-being of the white men's red brothers.

She could not bear to incur her husband's anger, and she feared losing his love, but a greater commitment began to torment her. The Cherokees' cause was vital. How could she sit docilely by her husband's side as he wished her to do when there were people in Washington City who would listen to her?

From that point forward, Kit cleaned Red Hawk's

house, made his meals, sewed his clothing. But she also visited Harriet Worcester and worked on a dress that would be fitting for her to return to society. She told Harriet merely that she wished to make it in case she had an opportunity to wear it, not mentioning where she meant to go in it.

At night as she lay by Red Hawk's side, Kit's heart ached with the knowledge that if she left the village on her mission, she was cutting herself off, not only from the man she loved but from the only home she had left.

On a warm spring day when Red Hawk joined several hunters to replenish their supply of meat, Kit wrapped the dress she had made together with the other personal articles she would need. She caught the pinto pony and tied the bundles onto the saddle. For her husband, she left a note written on a piece of white paper set in the middle of the table on which they took their meals. She tried to explain that the greater cause had won over her own grief and fear that Red Hawk would abandon her. But she declared that her love for him would never end. And added that if he would have her, she would look forward to the day she could return to his arms.

She told Harriet that she wished to visit her family at Wytheridge to try to reconcile her father to her marriage, a motive Harriet did not question. Nevertheless, tears formed at the corners of Kit's eyes as she hugged her friend goodbye.

"Your husband will miss you," said Harriet, not knowing the cause of Kit's torment.

"Tell him," said Kit as she stepped back from Harriet's embrace, "that it is my greatest wish to return to him, and that I will keep his face before me in my heart."

She mounted the pony and turned into the woods, wishing to avoid the main road out of New Echota on which those she met might ask her questions. She urged the pony upward through the trees joining the main byway where it twisted and turned into the hills. Tears streamed down her face, and her heart fluttered with fear. But resolve kept her face turned eastward. She must carry out the task she was determined to accomplish.

Chapter Twenty

Stopping at Dahlonega, Kit found the town much as it had been before. The population was swelled with miners of all description. New pine boards had been thrown up to repair the burned buildings, and merchandise stores did a brisk business, goods being paid for with gold dust and nuggets as well as currency.

She took a room at the hotel and sat down to compose a note to Merilee. She couldn't risk going to Wytheridge, but Merilee could supply her with money for a ticket to Washington City.

She did not have long to wait. The next morning Merilee appeared at the hotel just after Kit had taken breakfast downstairs.

Kit opened her door and her sister-in-law swept in, reaching out for a hug.

"Oh, Kit, how good to see you. What is this about your going to Washington City?"

Seeing Merilee helped bolster Kit's spirits, which were still plagued with doubts about defying Red Hawk. She ushered Merilee into the room and over to the settee.

"I must go and speak out about the plight of the Cherokees."

Merilee shook her head. "My brave sister, you risk so much."

Kit looked grave as she relayed the fact that she was defying her husband in going. Merilee's dark eyes grew even wider.

"What will your father do when you make it known publicly that you oppose him?"

Kit lifted her chin, her expression hardening. "He has already disowned me as a daughter. What more can he do?"

Merilee impulsively hugged Kit again. Then the two separated, their hearts full with the knowledge of what life had brought them.

"I have the money you wanted," said Merilee, reaching for a beaded bag. "But I brought more. You will need clothes if you are to appear in society. I managed to pack a trunk and had Brutus load it on the wagon I drove here."

"You didn't tell anyone—"

Merilee's quick shake of the head cut her off. "The servants think I have brought some of my old clothes to give to a poor family. Neither Samantha nor Ossie Lee have occasion to look in your clothes press. The secret will be kept."

Kit looked at Merilee gratefully. "In that case, I thank you. I have this dress to wear, and that is all. I had not thought so far ahead."

"You have had so much to worry about it would be impossible to consider all the details. Here is the

349

money. Shall I purchase the ticket for you?"

"No, thank you. I can do that. There are so many people coming and going in Dahlonega, I'll be scarcely noticed." She paused. "Did anyone discover your visit to New Echota?"

Merilee's curls flew around her face as she shook her head. "No. They still believe I went to Atlanta."

Kit felt relieved, and for a few moments they sat in satisfied silence. Finally Kit rose and embraced Merilee.

"I thank you for all you have done. A sister could be no dearer to me."

There were tears in Merilee's eyes as she bid Kit goodbye. She said she would have the trunk unloaded at the tavern where Kit would take the next coach for Washington City. As Kit watched her friend leave, she smiled to herself. Truly Merilee Fitzsimmons Newcomb had turned into the clever, able wife Kit had predicted she would be.

Kit had no trouble purchasing a seat on the next stage. After her trunk was loaded she took a seat in the crowded coach which carried a family with two children, a circuit judge, two young men returning to college in North Carolina, and an elderly spinster who told Kit she had been invited to live with her niece in Baltimore.

As they proceeded over the rolling hills and across the now familiar swamplands, with stops at inns that varied from the austere and filthy to the clean and comfortable, Kit's mind was numb to her surroundings. She did not allow herself to think of what she had left. Nor did she want to consider what she was about to do or what her reception in Washington City would be like. Nevertheless, a thousand times she considered turning back. But every time the coachman yelled for the passengers to board, Kit placed her feet on the steps and took her place in the coach. Georgia was finally left behind.

Kit paid the hansom cab driver and stood in front of her aunt's house, gazing at the brick homes, the seedpods that had drifted down from the protective trees to lie in the cracks of the bricked sidewalk. Carriages rumbled past and pedestrians strolled in the dappled lane. The domestic scene was so tranquil it almost made her forget that Georgia was simmering with trouble.

She directed the cab driver to take her trunk around to the back; then she climbed the front stoop.

A surprised Bella answered the door. "My lands, child, where did you come from? No one was expectin' you. Or if they was they forgot to tell the likes of me. Come in, come in."

Kit smiled warmly. Bella had many qualities that reminded her of Ossie Lee, except that Bella was more subservient to her employers whereas Ossie Lee ruled Wytheridge with an iron hand.

"Your aunt will want to see you," said Bella waddling before Kit toward the stairs.

"Is my father here?" Kit asked anxiously.

"He's at the Capitol."

Kit sighed in relief. She wasn't yet prepared to

face him. As Bella led the way to Ruby's sitting room, Kit touched the chignon she had hastily managed to arrange before dawn at the inn where she'd passed the night. Surely she wasn't presentable enough to see her aunt, but it would be rude not to put in an appearance before freshening up.

Bella knocked on the door, and at Ruby's invitation to come in, she pushed it open and grinned broadly at her employer.

"Miss Kit is here to see you, madam."

Kit shyly entered the room as Ruby replaced her sewing in the work box in front of her and rose. Her face wore a startled expression. But she managed a smile and held out her hands.

"My dear, this is a surprise. I had no idea."

"Oh, Aunt." Kit ran to her and took her hands. Then Ruby bent and kissed Kit on the cheek.

"I wasn't sure . . ." Kit stammered, uncertain what to say.

Ruby nodded and dismissed Bella. Then she patted the sofa next to where she had resumed her seat.

"I know what you're thinking. Jonathan has told me everything, at least everything he could. But now that you're here I can hear it from your very own lips."

Kit's hand trembled as she squeezed Ruby's, relief sweeping through her at knowing that Ruby was not going to banish her from the house without hearing her case.

"Oh, Aunt, it's been so awful, I mean about my father and the Indians." Then her eyes widened and she looked into Ruby's face. "I mean I am married, and I love my husband. We would be happy except that there is a terrible situation. The Cherokees are fighting for their lands in Georgia, and no one will help them."

Ruby looked at her, a gentle expression in her eyes. "Perhaps you had better begin at the beginning and tell me everything so that I may grasp the significance of these incidents in proper perspective."

Kit relaxed. "You are right, only there is so much to say, and I haven't spoken to anyone about it since I left. Only Merilee knows I have come."

"I see." Ruby pulled the velvet rope, and when Bella reappeared, she asked for tea. Then she turned back to Kit.

"Now take your time, my dear. Your father left after the midday meal. He has a meeting this evening in Georgetown. He will not return until very late tonight. We have all afternoon."

Ruby's patient attitude helped Kit order her thoughts. After soothing her throat with tea and quieting her hungry stomach with sandwiches, she began to speak.

She told Ruby how she had met Red Hawk and what she had learned about the Cherokee delegation. She told her how she had seen Red Hawk again, leaving out, of course, the intimate details. But she explained that she knew such a course would bring ruin upon her and that when she had left for Georgia it was with the intention of returning home to a familiar life. She did not expect to see him again.

353

When she described the scene she had witnessed in the gold fields near Dahlonega and the fire afterward, her passion mounted and even Ruby was held spellbound. Then she told of how her father had scolded her, how he would not listen to her pleas to do something to help the Cherokees.

"Then Red Hawk came for me," Kit said, again seeing his face in the pool. She faltered. "I had to decide. I don't know how to explain. It seemed the decision was made for me. I know it sounds awful of me." She looked imploringly at her aunt who nodded soberly.

"You had fallen in love," Ruby said simply.

Kit nodded quickly. "Yes, of course. But Father will never understand."

Ruby's lips twitched. "No, I am afraid you are right there. He will not ever understand. But he might forgive you. Tell me, my dear, why have you come? To see your father?"

Kit lowered her eyes and clasped her hands in her lap. "I want to see him, of course, if he will speak to me. But I want to see others in government as well. I have hopes yet of averting this Indian Removal Bill."

"I see." The acknowledgment was heavy with incredulity.

Kit could think of nothing more to say. "Perhaps I'd best freshen up and change out of these clothes."

Her remarks jolted Ruby out of her reverie. "Of course. How rude of me to keep you here when you are tired from traveling." She seemed to hesitate.

"I will freshen up and change then," said Kit. "And

thank you for welcoming me."

"It is not me you need to worry about," said Ruby speculatively. Then she seemed to make up her mind about something.

"I was planning to attend a small party at Mrs. Mortimer's tonight. Perhaps you would like to come."

"Oh," said Kit, uncertain.

"If you intend to speak to members of government, perhaps the best way is to seek them socially. Daniel Webster will be at Mrs. Mortimer's. He has inquired about you. Your father told him, of course, that you were married but not to whom."

At the thought of carrying out her plan, Kit's heart fluttered, but her aunt was right. She had come all the way to Washington with a mission. She could not simply sit at home until the President agreed to see her. Daniel Webster was a friend. Surely he would help.

"Very well. What time shall I be ready?"

Though dressed in one of the elegant gowns Merilee had been thoughtful enough to pack for her, Kit felt shy about going out in society. For the last few months her life had been simplified, first by the hardworking routine on the plantation and then by living even closer to nature as a Cherokee bride. To ride in a carriage and pass through a door held back by a servant, to gaze at the sea of faces in Mrs. Mortimer's drawing room made her feel dizzy.

Ruby spoke to a few acquaintances, and then Kit spied Daniel Webster's dark head and broad shoulders. He turned his head and caught sight of them, broke off his conversation, and came toward them, extending his hands to Ruby.

"My dear Ruby, how lovely you look."

He kissed her hand and then his black, penetrating eyes examined Kit. "And Kit. I did not expect to see you here. May I congratulate you on your marriage. I cannot get your father to speak of it, but you shall satisfy my curiosity."

Kit lifted her chin, glad to see him and suddenly afraid of what he might think. But she had no wish to prolong the anxiety.

"I married a Cherokee. His is name is Red Hawk."

Webster blinked and remained staring at her for a second. Then his refined manners took over. He leaned forward slightly and said, "In that case, you have much to tell. May I fetch you ladies some refreshment?"

Ruby made excuses and dove into the crowd to speak to another friend. Webster took Kit's elbow and said in a low voice, "Let us seek a quiet corner."

Her agitation lessened as he took control of the situation, and she forced a pleasant smile onto her face, nodding to those they passed until Webster took two goblets of wine from a passing tray and handed her one. Then they took seats in matching satin upholstered chairs in a corner. Guests filled the room, but everyone seemed too engrossed in his or her conversation to do more than barely notice Kit and the senator in their quiet tête-à-tête.

Webster's dark eyes stirred with curiosity. Kit

thought she might have imagined it, but hidden in those turbulent depths she thought she also perceived disappointment, and indeed his manner toward her was, while still friendly, more reserved than when they had last met.

"Please tell me about your husband," said Webster. He sipped some wine.

"He was with the Cherokee delegation here in Washington," Kit began. "That was how I met him."

"Ah, yes. A friend of the notable and brilliant Chief John Ross."

His words heartened her. "Then you know Chief Ross."

Daniel bowed his head. "I've had the pleasure."

"Then perhaps you understand how desperate the situation is," said Kit, leaning forward. "Federal troops were sent to protect the Cherokees, but all they did was arrest some of them. It is grossly unfair."

She leaned back and tried to regain her composure, for she knew that reason would do more good than an emotional outburst.

"I have come to Washington to explain to those with influence how wrong it would be to try to force the Cherokees off their lands."

Webster studied her and nodded gravely. "And these Indians are acting within their legal rights."

"Very much so," said Kit. "It is the white men who are intruding."

Webster rubbed his chin. "I see the problem. Technically it is a problem for the state of Georgia. But

357

the state wants their lands and so will not send in militia to keep the intruders out."

"Exactly," said Kit. "That's why the Cherokees have sought the President's help."

Webster gave her a gentle, sympathetic look. "But the delegation went to see President Jackson. What do you hope to accomplish that they can't?"

"I can speak about what the Cherokee nation is like. As one from both worlds, it is my hope to be able to say something that will convince him to send in more troops to protect the Cherokees. If he does not, there will be more bloodshed. Both Indians and Georgians will be killed. Surely no one wants that."

Webster raised a dark bushy brow. "No one ever asks for bloodshed, but that has never stopped our government from making decisions for other reasons." Then in a softer voice he added, "You may have raised your hopes too high, my dear. Your cause is noble, but in the end you must surely lose. These are not words you want to hear, but I am afraid the growth and power of our new nation will be delayed for the good of the less fortunate people whose ancestors were conquered long ago. It is the way of history."

Her eyes snapped as she met his gaze. "I must try."

Webster was distracted by some movement across the room, and he glanced up. "I did not know your father would be here tonight," he said. "I must speak to him."

Kit gasped and jumped up from her seat. "My father! Where?"

Webster rose more slowly, surprised by her reaction. "Why there, beside Ruby."

A couple moved aside, and Kit indeed saw her father, his head bent, his face drawn in an expression of concentration as Ruby said something to him. Kit's heart skipped a beat, and her palms felt damp. She had not expected to see him here and could scarcely imagine what her reception would be. She unconsciously took a step forward and moistened her lips.

At that moment Jonathan turned his head and saw his daughter. He straightened beside Ruby, not answering his sister. Father and daughter stared at one another. The emotions that passed over Jonathan's face were unreadable. Then he slowly began to make his way toward her.

When he was within two feet of her, he stopped and stood stiffly, his hands clasped behind his back.

"Hello, Father," she managed to get out.

He nodded his head slightly. "I am surprised to see you here," said Jonathan. His cheeks were tinged with color, his eyes had a hard edge to them, but in his voice was a question, as if he still held a ray of hope.

"And I am surprised to see you." Kit cleared her throat and struggled to smile. "I wanted to speak to you, but Ruby said you were out when I arrived."

He gave a jerky nod. "I did not expect to be free until later this evening." Then with a little less formality, "I thought you planned to live among the Indians. Or have you had a sensible change of heart?"

Her chin quivered, but she looked him straight in

the eye. "I have not had a change of heart if you mean to ask if I have decided to leave my Cherokee husband. In fact, it is on behalf of the Cherokees that I have come here."

The guests around them had one by one stopped talking until that part of the room was nearly silent. Jonathan failed to notice this, but continued to engage his daughter in conversation.

"I am sorry," he said, his brows drawing down. "For a moment I had thought you had come to your senses and had returned to seek a reconciliation."

Kit, too, ignored those around them who were surreptitiously watching the confrontation. "I want nothing more than to be reconciled to you, Father. If you will let me explain myself, we would be so much better off." Her lips trembled and she approached him, reaching out to touch his arm.

But the angry cloud that hung over his face only darkened. "I do not understand this. You want to be reconciled to our family, yet you still claim to be married to this Cherokee. Why do you persist in this foolishness?"

The grief and exasperation mingling in Kit forced her to speak more sharply than she might have. "I came to Washington to defend the Cherokees, not to betray them."

A murmur escaped the ladies and gentlemen standing near them, and Kit became aware that her conversation with her father was not private. But there was no turning back; anger drove her on.

"I risked a great deal to come here," Kit said. "My

husband forbade me to do it. He does not believe there are any men in the government of our country who will listen. But I disobeyed him because I cannot believe there are no just men left in government."

"Just as you disobeyed me," returned Jonathan in an angry tone. "I see you have learned nothing."

He was perspiring, and he raised his arm in an angry gesture. Then, suddenly, his face turned into a mask of pain. His hand flew to his chest, and he bent forward in pain.

"Father?" Kit rushed toward him, but even as she grasped his arms, she could not support him, and he crumpled to the floor.

Ladies gasped and several gentlemen hurried to Kit's side to ease Jonathan to the floor. His face was white, and his eyes bulged.

"What is it, Father?" Kit said, her own heart pounding.

"Is there a doctor?" someone called.

More people rushed over, and someone began to loosen Jonathan's cravat and to undo the buttons on his waistcoat. His eyes were open, but he did not answer. From his expression, it was apparent that he was in a great deal of pain.

"Let me through, let me through, please," said a gentleman who knelt beside Jonathan. From the babble of talk around her Kit discerned that this man was a doctor, and his quick movements demonstrated that he indeed knew what he was doing.

He rolled back Jonathan's cuff and felt for his pulse. Jonathan's face was still ghastly white tinged with blue, but he seemed to begin to breathe easier and the doctor instructed that he be carried upstairs and placed on a bed.

The room swam around Kit as she followed the doctor and the men carrying her father. As they settled him on a bed and the doctor continued his examination, Kit pulled a chair over near her father.

"What is it, Doctor?" she asked.

The physician flicked his eyes in her direction. "His heart, miss."

Kit felt as if she might faint, but held onto the bedpost. "His heart. Will he be all right?"

"The fit didn't kill him, but you can't tell about these things. We must keep him quiet for the next twenty-four hours. He mustn't be upset or disturbed for any reason."

Upset! She had upset him by what she had done. She swayed on the chair, but held on. This had been her fault.

Remorse swept over her, and she stared at the prone figure of her father. His eyes were closed now, and she dared not speak but watched the doctor minister to him. The hostess of the house came in and asked the doctor what else he needed. Kit barely heard their exchange, but she remained seated by the bed until she was sure she would not faint.

Still guilt and fear plagued her. She finally found words to ask the doctor what she could do to help.

"He'll have to rest, for his heart is very weak," the physician replied. "But I'll bring around some medication and show you how to give it to him. Keep the room quiet."

Kit nodded, ready to do anything, realizing that she might have killed her father. For surely distress over her betrayal had been too much for his heart.

A short time later Ruby arrived, her own face nearly as pale as Jonathan's had been. She saw that she could do nothing more for him than had already been done, so she sat by Kit for a while.

How the next hours passed, Kit was only dimly aware. She remained by her father and watched his breathing, praying it would remain even. She must have dozed off in the chair, for at dawn Mrs. Mortimer sent her to bed, promising to sit by Jonathan and wake Kit if there was any change. Ruby had gone home but would return later.

It was late morning when Kit awoke in the strange bedroom. Then it all flooded back to her, and she rose and threw on a dressing gown to go down the hall to her father's room. She saw that he was awake, and she stood just inside the door, unsure of her welcome.

"Ah, there's Kit now," said Mrs. Mortimer, getting up from the chair she had occupied while reading aloud to her sick guest.

Jonathan turned his head just enough to see Kit, and she stepped farther into the room. His color had returned to normal.

"Hello, Father," she said, her voice sounding hoarse. "How are you feeling?"

His voice was weak, but he responded. "Better."

Kit nodded her thanks to Mrs. Mortimer, who

squeezed her hands and left them. She sat down near the bed, looking at her father worriedly.

He had straightened his head and closed his eyes. Kit did not know whether to make conversation or sit back and simply stare at him. From the flutter of his eyelids she could tell he was not sleeping. The best course, she knew, was light, trivial conversation. She reached for the book Mrs. Mortimer had been reading and saw that it was poetry. Of course, something to soothe.

"I see you've been listening to Keats," she said and read a few lines out loud.

She looked up at her father and saw that his lids had raised and he was looking out at nothing in particular. Taking this for a good sign, she continued reading, glancing up when she reached the end of the page to see that his lids had dropped and that he was truly asleep. She gently put the book down and tiptoed out of the room.

Kit dressed then and went dawn to breakfast. Mrs. Mortimer insisted that Jonathan not be moved until he was entirely fit. With her household staff to care for him, he would be in the best of hands, and Kit, too, was welcome to stay on to look after him as long as she liked.

Kit declined the latter invitation, but said she would spend the days at Mrs. Mortimer's. No sooner had they risen from breakfast than Ruby returned to look in on Jonathan. For the rest of the day Kit alternated with Ruby in sitting with him. For her part, Kit read to him, breaking off to comment on such trivialities as the weather, the people she had seen at Mrs. Mortimer's party, what he had eaten, and other such insignificant subjects. Gradually Jonathan began to respond.

"That medicine tastes like poison," he said, running his hand across his mouth after Kit had fed him a spoonful. "Probably got poison in it."

"Now, Father," she admonished. "You must follow the doctor's orders. You'll soon be on your feet, but only if you do what he says."

Jonathan grumbled. However, he asked her to help him sit up, so she raised the pillows and then helped him into a sitting position, making sure he did not strain himself.

In her heart was the tenderness of a daughter for an ailing parent, and while she was in her father's room she banished all thoughts of politics or of the Cherokees' predicament. But as Jonathan grew stronger Kit began to think about her own plans. She knew she was still going to pursue her course.

One evening a maid came to inform her that Daniel Webster was downstairs and had asked to see her. She checked her appearance. The gray muslin was modest but suitable. Her hair was coiled neatly.

Webster was in the drawing room, talking to Mrs. Mortimer when Kit entered. He broke off and extended his hands to take hers.

"Ah, my dear Kit. How is your father?"

"Much better thank you. He will be pleased you asked about him."

Mrs. Mortimer excused herself and shut the double doors behind her as she left.

"Please sit down," Kit said, taking a seat on a red plush sofa while Webster seated himself on a matching upholstered chair.

"I'm glad to hear that he's better," said the senator. "I was concerned that you had shouldered quite a burden in looking after him."

She could see genuine concern in his dark eyes. "My aunt shares the duties. It is no trouble, I assure you."

His eyes became quizzical. "And have you given any more thought to speaking to the President on this matter you mentioned?"

"Yes, I have. I am determined to do what I can for the Cherokees' cause."

"Even if it might kill your father? I understand he is not to be upset by controversial issues just now."

Kit thought for a long moment before she spoke. And when she did her eyes had a faraway look in them.

"Surely one man's life is not as important as those of the thousands who will die if the government removes the Cherokees from Georgia."

Chapter Twenty-one

Kit walked with straight back up the curving steps of the President's House. She held up the skirt of her gown in order to negotiate them. The liveried servant held the door for her, and when she handed him her card, she was directed along the spacious hall past the Ionic columns to the center door, which opened into the oval room.

How well she remembered the first time she had come here along with the throngs of people wanting to see the President. Now a weight seemed to lodge in her chest. If she had not come to Washington City then, she would not be here now, for she never would have seen Red Hawk. But in that case, she would not have known his love, the beauty of his spirit, the tenderness of his caresses. Thinking of Red Hawk only brought pain to her heart, and she blinked the tears away, concentrating instead on the approaching interview.

Another servant held the door for her, and she stepped into the large salon with its crimson flocked wall paper. Now she could better see the marble chimney, the crimson silk draperies and the famous carpet woven with the coat of arms of the United States in the center.

A young man in morning coat and stiff white cravat came through a side door and bowed. "The President will be with you directly. If you will please wait here . . ."

"Thank you," she said.

She walked to the window to look out on the gardens and at the new buildings, the blossoming of a new country. She remembered Ruby's comment that the greatest talent of the nation was gathered here when Congress was in session. How, with so many great minds, could such injustice still reign? Kit wondered.

She heard the door open and turned her head. President Jackson stood just inside the room. His white hair was combed neatly away from his forehead, and spectacles were tucked into the pocket of his dark blue coat.

She turned fully to face him and took a few steps forward.

"My dear Miss Newcomb," he said. "A pleasure to see you. I am most concerned about your father. How does he fare?"

"Well, thank you," she said, approaching and giving the President her hand. "He is receiving the best of care and will soon be on his feet again, I am sure."

The President's already lined brow wrinkled further in concern. "That is good. I cannot afford to lose such good men as your father."

"Thank you," said Kit. "I will give him your regards."

Jackson nodded and then waited. Kit knew that he did not have time for frivolities, and that suited her. She had not come here to make small talk, so she plunged into what she had determined to say.

"I wanted to speak to you, sir, on a matter of great import."

"Oh?"

He glanced around the room, and she realized that he must want to sit down rather than remain standing. He gestured to two oval-backed, upholstered chairs near a large window. She led the way and took a seat.

When she had his attention again she went on, her back stiff, her words carefully articulated.

"I don't know if you have heard that I have spent time in the Cherokee Nation."

A cloud descended on the President's hitherto pleasant expression. His blue eyes hardened.

"I did not know," was all he said. He leaned back in his chair and seemed to observe her more critically. But she would not be put off by the haughty expression accentuated by his hawklike nose.

"I am much concerned by the Indian Removal Bill now being debated in Congress." She leaned forward an inch. "Surely you cannot consider removing from Georgia an entire nation of civilized people whose only wish is to live in peace beside their white brothers. But perhaps you have not heard of their progress. I myself come directly from the Reverend

369

Samuel Worcester who has done much good work, educating the Indians and teaching them Christianity. They are an advanced people, Mr. President. They have already given up much. If left on their lands in Georgia, they will make great contributions to the nation."

He gave a thin smile. "I have already heard these arguments from the Cherokee delegation. I am afraid I am being pressed to enforce the Georgia Compact in order to keep an agreement already made with the state of Georgia."

"And break an agreement made with the Cherokees." Kit shut her mouth. She struggled to keep her temper.

"New agreements will be made," said the President smoothly. "Many Cherokee leaders favor removal to the Western lands. Their people will be paid for the lands in Georgia."

"Many of the people consider those who favor removal as traitors. The Cherokees say they will fight rather than give up the lands they now inhabit."

President Jackson waved a hand and glanced out the window. His eyes were impatient as if to let his visitor know that she was wasting his precious time and tiring him. But Kit was not ready to admit defeat.

"Surely you remember how the Cherokees helped you against the angry Creeks you fought in Tennessee so long ago."

He gave a slight nod. "That debt has been paid."

She felt herself being dismissed. She was powerless

against this man who had so coldly made up his mind.

"But surely until such treaties are signed you will send federal troops to protect the Indians from the white intruders who are now invading their lands."

He turned cold eyes back toward her. His gaunt face did indeed look fatigued. "That is a state problem. The Georgia militia should be called in to settle any dispute."

Kit rose suddenly, unable to contain her irritation. "The Georgia militia take orders from the state, which, as you have already stated, has a vested interest in seeing the Indians removed."

She was trembling now. President Jackson had been her last hope. She could not stop the flow of words as she raised her head and spoke defiantly.

"President Jackson, the boldness of your reputation does you justice. You have a decisiveness the Cherokees would appreciate. It will forever remain one of the greatest tragedies in history that President Andrew Jackson was the Cherokees' enemy and not their friend."

And she turned her back to him and hurried toward the door, her skirts rustling as she walked. The servant barely got the door open in time for her to sweep through. She looked neither right nor left as she swept through the hall and down the steps. Her tears blinded her to everything around her.

Outside, she looked for Caleb. Not waiting for him to maneuver the carriage through the busy drive to the steps, she wove through the pedestrians coming and going from the entrance.

"Take me home, Caleb," she said, wiping away tears.

She climbed into the carriage, and Caleb shut the door after her. Her heart was heavy with failure. Suddenly she longed to be out of Washington. The tight stays and clumsy skirts she had to wear here no longer appealed to her. Her heart was in Georgia, if there was anything left there for her. But there was one thing she must do before she took leave of Washington City.

She changed clothes at Ruby's house and asked Bella to help her pack her belongings. Then she set out for Mrs. Mortimer's. The distance was not great, so she walked.

On the street she passed ladies of society out making calls, merchants hurrying to business, servants doing chores for their masters. She even passed a group of Indians in robes, feathers in their hair. Their faces were rigid masks as if they felt no emotion. Pity welled up in her. If there was going to be no mercy for the Cherokees, what fate indeed awaited the more colorful tribes that these Indians represented, those who clung to the ancestral ways and performed their rituals at exhibitions, where they were little more than a curiosity.

Mrs. Mortimer assured Kit that her father was doing well, but she climbed the stairs with mixed feelings. She knocked softly and heard his subdued "Come in."

She let herself into the room and approached the bed.

"How are you, Father?"

"Better than the doctor believes. He was here this morning and insists I remain in bed. Hmmph! As if I have nothing better to do."

"You must obey his orders."

Jonathan glowered. Then seeing that his daughter was dressed for calling, he inquired as to where she had been.

She swallowed. "I went to see the President this morning. He sends his best wishes for a speedy recovery."

Jonathan's eyebrows worked in agitation. "You called on the President?" He eyed her suspiciously. "Surely you did not need to go in person to inform him of my health."

She moved her head imperceptibly to the right and then the left. "No. I called on another matter."

"And what matter was that?"

Kit hesitated. She was not to upset her father. But other forces clawed at her. How long could she remain here at his bedside when she realized her life was no longer in this city.

"I went to speak to him about the Cherokees."

Jonathan's eyes widened and then he stared at her for a moment. Finally, he turned his face away from her, frowning.

Kit seated herself. It was time she let him know as gently as possible that she must leave. Not daring to touch him, she ran a hand along the quilted coverlet.

"Now that you are better, I must make preparations to return home."

He was silent for a moment; then he said, "To Wytheridge?" But by the irony in his voice she knew what he implied.

"No," she said softly. "To my husband in New Echota."

Her heart pounded as she waited for him to reply. But Jonathan did not speak. Instead, he slowly turned on his side facing the wall, his back to Kit.

Blood pulsed in her temples and a dagger thrust into her heart. This, then, was his answer. She rose slowly, hardly trusting her legs to carry her, but knowing that she was not wanted in this room.

Her desolation complete, she walked to the door, but turned to, one last time, see the figure of her father, the sheets drawn under his arms. The floor seemed to swim under her. Coming to Washington had been a terrible mistake. She had not only risked her husband's love, she had lost her father.

On that day, the Cherokees in the council house of New Echota adopted a firm resolution that "Inclination to remove from this land has no abiding place in our hearts, and when we move we shall move by the course of nature to sleep under this ground which the Great Spirit gave to our ancestors and which now covers them in their undisturbed repose."

Red Hawk stepped forward to sign his name on the piece of paper that contained the words. He watched the others file forward and use the quill pen to scrawl their names by his. He stared hard at Major Ridge as the members of the council waited.

The white-headed Indian dressed in black suit and snowy white shirt shook his head.

"My friends," he said to those assembled, "your noble words will be to no avail. You will see. A time will come when you will want to accept the offer our white father in Washington has made us. The future of our tribe lies not here but in the West."

Snake Hawk, the war chief, stepped forward. "No," he said. "I will be buried here before I shall take a step westward." He pointed in defiance at the red soil beneath his feet.

Major Ridge stared at him in condescension. "I have no doubt Snake Hawk, that you speak the truth." And he turned on his heel and left the council house.

Kit returned to Wytheridge in a daze. During the ten days journey she scarcely spoke to her fellow passengers. Arriving at last in Dahloncga, she braced herself for the noise and hustle of the booming town. Hiring a trap to drive her to Wytheridge, she rounded every curve, gazed at every familiar landmark with renewed pain. She was no more welcome at Wytheridge than she was at New Echota.

But when the trap came around the last bend and the Wytheridge fields came into sight, her heart filled. Servants began to look up from their work. And then she saw Lucius straighten his back and stare for a long time as the trap made progress toward the house.

Finally he raised a hand and came toward the fence. As Kit passed where he stood, she waved back in greeting, her red hair flying out behind her bonnet.

"Miss Kit," he called, his ebony face beaming.

Then the other servants recognized her and began to wave. Kit's heart filled and tears moistened her eyes as she waved back to them. Had she betrayed these loyal workers too—the very backbone of Wytheridge? It seemed to her in that moment that she had done nothing right at all.

She wiped her eyes and climbed down when the trap stopped. The door opened and Merilee appeared. Her face lit in greeting, she bounded down the steps and embraced Kit.

"Oh," she said. "I'm so glad to see you."

"Well, if it ain't Miss Kathryn." Ossie Lee's loud voice came from where she stood on the verandah, her hands on her wide hips.

"Hello, Ossie Lee," said Kit, climbing the steps. She felt shy, certain of the housekeeper's disapproval.

Instead, she saw a tear in the black woman's eyes, and then Ossie Lee grasped her in a bear hug. Kit clung happily to the big woman, finding no words to express the feelings that were wrung from her.

"Come in, come in," said Merilee, and the three of them entered the house.

A light breeze cooled the drawing room, which was shaded from the hot June sun. Merilee drew Kit to a sofa and begged to hear everything. While Ossie Lee went to fetch cool lemonade, Kit told Merilee all that had happened in Washington City, ending with the heartbreaking scene with her father.

"So," Kit finished. "I truly have no home."

"That's not true," said Merilee, tightening her lips. "As long as I live here, this will be your home. I will insist."

Kit smiled gratefully. "That is kind of you, my dear friend. But you have your husband to think of, if not my father."

"I have spoken to Fletch," Merilee said. "I think he is ready to listen."

A ray of hope penetrated the blackness in Kit's heart. "What has he said?"

"Not a lot, but he has been forced to listen to me."

Kit's heart swelled in amusement at thinking of Merilee bending Fletch's ear on a subject which must have caused him much displeasure.

"Where is Fletch now?"

"Surveying the crops. He'll return for the midday meal. You can see him then."

"All right," Kits said tiredly. "I'll freshen up and change."

She climbed the stairs, every creak in the floorboards causing her a pang of nostalgia, and found the housekeeper hurriedly putting fresh sheets on her bed.

"Oh, thank you, Ossie Lee. I did not mean to cause you extra work. I know this is a busy time of the year with so many field hands to feed."

"No trouble, child. It's worth more than a change

of sheets to see your face in this house again."

Kit did not want to spoil Ossie Lee's generosity by speaking of Jonathan's insult or the fact that she did not feel completely welcome here.

At noon, Kit descended the stairs cautiously. She heard the murmur of voices in the drawing room and, taking a deep breath for courage, she put her hand to the half-open door.

Fletch and Merilee broke off their conversation, and her brother turned to stare at her. She smiled uneasily. How like their father he looked, his trousers tucked into high black boots, his riding crop still in hand.

"Hello, Fletch," she said.

Emotions worked in his face and finally he said, "Hello, Kit. Merilee was just telling me you've returned from Washington City."

Kit glided into the room, but kept her distance. "Yes. Father had an attack. But he is better now. He did not need me any longer."

"And what are your plans now?" His tone was guarded.

"I . . . I am not sure." She sank onto an ottoman, then shook her head. "My husband forbade me to go to Washington City, but I went anyway, thinking I could influence the President. I was wrong. My father does not want to see me again. Truly, I have no home."

Fletch took several steps until he stood before her. He shifted the riding crop from one hand to the

378

other, turning it nervously in his hands.

"I do not like to see you this way, sister," he began. Though his speech sounded stilted, she could hear the emotion in it. "I tried to intervene when I felt you were going down a path to ruin. But as usual your stubbornness prevented you from listening to me."

She glanced up at him. His expression, while revealing exasperation, was tinged with concern. She felt his defenses weakening, and her heart was renewed by hope.

"I meant to do nothing that would hurt you or father. But I could not have my marriage insulted. I love my husband." Her lips trembled. "Whether or not he will accept me again," she finished.

Fletch laid the riding crop on a small round table and bent down to raise Kit to her feet. He sighed and shook his head, but he forced her to meet his gaze.

"I cannot accept your choice, nor shall I attempt to understand it. But I will not banish you from this family. You may not know it, but our anger is caused by the love we have for you."

Tears threatened, and she reached for him. He took her in a brotherly embrace and held her tightly.

"I will always love you, Fletch," she said. "You're the only brother I have."

"And I love you, Sis. I will not allow bitterness to stand between you and those who care for you."

He held her away and brushed tears from her cheeks with a handkerchief. She thought she detected moisture at the corners of his blue eyes as well.

He cleared his throat. "I must admit that when Merilee told me she had been to New Echota I was angry with her. But she forced me to listen. What she told me about the Cherokees was not what I expected to hear. My opinions had been colored by our father's prejudice. I was wrong."

Kit touched his arm. "Thank you, Fletch. I know what it must cost you to say that."

Suddenly Merilee was hugging them both, and they all laughed and cried at the same time. Finally Fletch took a deep breath.

"We'd better go to the dining room," he said. "Ossie Lee will throw us all out of the house for the ungrateful wretches we are if her food gets cold."

Kit's stomach was in such turmoil she did not know if she could eat a mouthful. But she was full of sustaining nourishment of another kind.

That night Kit sat at her writing desk for a long time, a candle burning beside the piece of paper at which she stared. She finally began the letter to her father.

The Cherokees' battle would be lost, she could see. Now that Cherokee removal was inevitable she wished to be at her husband's side, if he would have her. She hoped that her father would one day forgive her.

At dawn she rose, certain of her decision. She packed her Eastern gowns away in the clothes press and donned the homespun gown she had worn in

New Echota. She placed soft leather boots on her feet, and plaited her hair into a single braid hanging down her back.

Walking softly, she left the house. She had made her goodbyes last night and didn't want to renew the pain of separation. She found Stormy in the stable and saddled her. Then she set her face westward, the singing of the slaves in the fields reaching her ears as she paused on the hill behind Wytheridge. She took in the scene, imprinting it on her memory for all time. Then she dug her heels into Stormy's sides, urging the horse forward before she could change her mind.

Chapter Twenty-two

Kit passed the first night on a farm at the edge of the Cherokee Nation. On the road to New Echota she stopped often to speak with Cherokees working in their fields. By sundown the road turned upward to the hills again. She stopped at a creek to drink and to water her horse. Then she mounted again.

Glancing upward at the western ridges her heart stopped. Silhouetted against a pink sky, the proud figure of horse and rider stood on the top of the ridge, still as a statue. Her heart swelled at the sight of black hair gleaming in the last rays of sunset. She shut her eyes and opened them again. Perhaps it was only a figment of her imagination.

But when she opened her eyes again, he was still there, only now he urged his horse forward, down the trail that would bring him to her. Frozen, watching his approach, Kit waited, much as she had the night he had carried her away from the fire. She did not know if Red Hawk had come to punish or forgive her.

She wanted to face him on foot, so she dismounted, wrapping her horse's reins around a nearby branch. Then, forcing herself to be patient, she sat on a large flat rock near the gurgling stream.

Darkness had fallen by the time she heard the horse's hooves. Then the branches parted and Red Hawk appeared, his chestnut gelding slowly walking toward her. She rose to meet him.

He drew rein and sat erect on the horse's back for a moment, looking at her. Her heart raced as she gazed at his handsome, bronze face, the rippling muscles under his buckskin leggings.

Then, without a word, he rode to where her horse was tied and unwound the reins. Leading her mount, he guided his horse to a tree stump and with a gesture indicated that she should mount behind him.

Tears of joy blinding her, Kit walked to the stump and took the hand he extended to her. She just stood looking up at him for a long moment, holding his hand. His chiseled face betrayed nothing, but in his eyes was a depth of desire and devotion.

She mounted up behind him and slipped her arms around his firm waist. He clucked softly to the two horses and turned them back toward the ridge.

Kit buried her face in her husband's back, his long hair mingling with hers in the night breeze. His silence was more eloquent than any words could be, for she knew he had forgiven her for defying his wishes and that he admired her strength and determination.

They would go many miles together as they led their people to the Western lands, and they would have the strength of knowing that they faced the future together. She would never leave him again. But they would never forget these dear Georgia mountains where their people once walked and where their spirits would remain forever.